THE HUNTED ONE
A FALCON FALLS SECURITY NOVEL

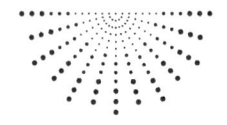

BRITTNEY SAHIN

EMKO MEDIA

The Hunted One

By: Brittney Sahin

Published by: EmKo Media, LLC

Copyright © 2021 EmKo Media, LLC

This book is an original publication of Brittney Sahin.

In accordance with the U.S. Copyright Act of 1976, the scanning, uploading, and electronic sharing of any part of this book without permission of the publisher constitute unlawful piracy and theft of the author's intellectual property. If you would like to use material from the book (other than for review purposes), prior written permission must be obtained by contacting brittneysahin@emkomedia.net Thank you for your support of the author's rights.

This book is a work of fiction. Names, characters, places, and incidents either are products of the author's imagination or are used fictitiously. Any resemblance to actual persons, living or dead, business establishments, events, or locales is entirely coincidental. The author acknowledges the trademarked status and trademark owners of various products, brands, and/or restaurants referenced in this work of fiction, which have been used without permission. The publication/use of these trademarks is not authorized, associated with, or sponsored by the trademark owners.

Chief Editor: Deb Markanton

Editor: Arielle Brubaker

Proofreader: Judy Zweifel, Judy's Proofreading

Cover Design: LJ, Mayhem Cover Creations

Image/Model: Beto Malfacini

Ebook ISBN: 978-1-947717-32-9

Paperback ISBN: 9798492511777

Created with Vellum

For Joey Bowden

Thank you for reading my stories, for bringing such joy to this world, and for serving our country. You're amazing!

CHAPTER ONE

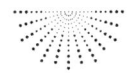

BIRMINGHAM, ALABAMA

"You're getting my display window dirty with that big hand of yours. *Also*, Ella's bound to leave soon, and she'll catch you spying." Savanna *tsk*ed and set her palms on the Brazilian cherry countertop inside her café.

Jesse quickly removed his hand from the glass and pivoted around to face her, an adorable hand-caught-in-the-cookie-jar look on his handsome face. Which was fitting, not merely because he was obviously spying on her friend, but also because he was clutching one of the cookies she'd baked this morning and arranged in the front window, all frosted in orange, black, or Casper-white in honor of Halloween next week.

She not only sold her signature baked goods created from recipes passed down by her grandmother, but mouthwatering artisan coffee drinks brewed with the best imported espresso beans she could afford.

"I am *not* spying. I was just doing a perimeter sweep. Making sure no one tries to rob you as you close up shop."

He bit off the black hat of the witch cookie. "The butcher had a break-in last week. Didn't you hear?"

"The butcher, the baker . . . any news on the candlestick maker?" She shot him a cheeky smirk.

Cheeky? Oh. Right. I just read a book by a British author. Hell, she'd even begun thinking with the accent the other day too. British accents were hot—who could blame her?

"Hilarious," he grunted, polishing off the cookie and wiping the remnants of the finger-licking-good frosting onto the sides of his jeans.

Savanna winked and snatched one of her pink-and-white hand towels, which matched the striped sign hanging outside the brick storefront. She'd chosen her own name for the café. Her parents had wed in Savannah, Georgia, and it was her mother's favorite Southern city. But her mom had dropped the H from her name on the birth certificate. And owning a place like this had always been her mother and grandmother's dream, so she'd recently decided to take the plunge in their honor.

The café had been a bakery before she'd purchased the building, so it already had the bones for what she needed. And it was conveniently located near Rhodes Park, which happened to be within walking distance of her townhouse. She could barely afford her rent after sinking every last dime and nickel she had into the café, though.

She was already a month past due paying her landlord. And she didn't want to borrow money from the business to pay her bills, but she was running out of options.

Well, there was a *last resort* option, but it was *strictly* a last resort. She couldn't touch that money . . . could she?

Was the café doing well? Yes. Well enough to survive? Barely. But that was the nature of it, wasn't it? She didn't know anyone who'd gotten into this sort of business expecting to be rolling in dough. No pun intended.

Annnnd focus. What were we discussing? Not my bills.

"So, what happens next? Does Ella call or text you to let you know if she's met Mister Right?" Jesse unhooked the Ray-Bans that clung to the front of his gray V-neck shirt, fiddled with them, then latched them back in place.

Well, hell. The man was a nervous wreck.

Savanna lifted her chin, her attention lingering on the wall of espresso beans off to her left—Central American beans with caramel undertones were her favorite—before looking out the window to view the restaurant on the other side of Highland Avenue.

The building opposite hers remained frozen in time. The large white mansion harkened back to the days of *Gone With The Wind*, its Greek pillars gracefully guarding the wide porch and the quintessential Southern rocking chairs on which to sit and enjoy a cocktail or two before or after dinner.

"Ella always picks the Italian place across the street to meet her online dates since she knows I'm here. If it goes well, she texts me. If it doesn't, she'll fake an emergency and jet over here."

Jesse's light blue eyes studied Savanna as he tapped a fist against his lips for a moment before dropping his gaze to the floor. He was wearing black boots, which were a change from the brown beat-up cowboy ones he normally donned. The boots also matched the leather jacket he wore, giving him a hot "bad boy" look. Not that he probably gave a damn about fashion, which was the opposite of Ella, who designed clothes and shoes as a hobby. "And how often does Ella text?" he muttered, his brows coming together in a frown.

"So far? No texts. All extraction plans via fake calls."

He looked up at Savanna, the faint creases at the corners

of his expressive eyes crinkling deeper as he smiled with obvious satisfaction. Typical Jesse. Brooding one minute, smirking the next.

"So, why are you spying on her tonight? Why not the other nights when she's had dates?" *Why am I poking a bear? Mentioning the other dates?*

He cursed under his breath, then ruffled up his already-tousled semi-short blond strands. "I was in town. I'm checking on you. Saying hi. *Not* spying on my . . ."

Savanna arched a dark brow, which no longer matched her hair since she'd gone mostly caramel blonde last week at the salon. She'd needed a change. "Not spying on your *what*?"

According to Ella last night, she was *Done, done, done with Jesse*. She'd texted Savanna some TikTok video lamenting that all men with J names were heartbreakers and then followed it up with her "done, done, done" text. *No more waiting on that man. I'll date every man from Birmingham to Boston before I think about Jesse again,* she'd added a split second later.

"Let's talk about Shep instead and how you slept with him the night of—" Jesse's deep voice jolted Savanna back to the present.

"The night of what was supposed to be Ella's wedding to Brian," Savanna finished for him. "The wedding that didn't happen because you told her not to marry him at the dress rehearsal dinner the night before. That night, right?" Savanna crossed her arms over her chest and scowled at her friend. She was close to both Jesse and Ella, but if push came to shove, she'd have to side with Ella. "And why are you bringing *that* up?"

Savanna vaguely remembered babbling about that oops-moment to Jesse when they'd had too much tequila a few weeks ago, commiserating over their mutual singleness.

Shep was a firefighter in a small town outside the city, and he was one of Ella's four overprotective brothers. And then there was Jesse. Definitely not a brother, but according to Ella, the most frustratingly overprotective guy in her life.

Savanna didn't think Brian was the right man for Ella anyway, and she'd been quietly thrilled when Ella had canceled the ceremony. Ella went ahead with the reception, though, insisting the party was paid for, so why not?

The guests had let loose in classic Southern style—drinking, dancing, and singing until late into the night of Ella's would-be wedding reception. Savanna and Shep had been drunk that night when they had sex, and upon waking the next morning, had both quickly agreed it was a never-should-have-happened, one-time-only mistake. Savanna was pretty certain Shep was also worried that A.J. would knock his teeth out if he found out his brother had slept with Savanna. In addition to being another one of Ella's brothers, A.J. had also been Marcus's best friend.

Marcus . . .

Savanna closed her eyes as the memories of her late husband gathered in her mind, still vivid after all these years.

Their wedding had been small and quaint, held in the middle of an open field surrounded by friends and family. Well, *almost* all of their family.

Savanna's dad had walked her down the makeshift aisle—a freshly mowed strip of fragrant grass strewn with wildflowers—to the man she thought she'd spend the rest of her life with, but then Marcus died in 2015.

"You danced with Ella that night. Too bad it wasn't you two who'd had a drunken moment together. Yours wouldn't have been a mistake, at least," Savanna said a moment later after pushing through the pain of her loss.

She drew in a deep breath and was instantly comforted by the lingering fragrance of her favorite Halloween-scented candles, the zesty orange, pumpkin spice, and dark plum mingling with the rich aromas of espresso beans and sweet cookies.

She double-checked all the candles had been blown out as Jesse headed toward the bookshelf he'd handmade for her café.

While working on a concept for the café last year, she'd butted heads with her designer, Ella's mother. Deb had proposed about thirty shades of pink along with colors Savanna had never heard of before, but Savanna had declared that the color pink was to be limited to the hand towels, the sign outside, and the frosting on cakes and cookies.

She'd opted to go darker instead, wanting the shop to have a more intimate, almost romantic vibe—a place where you'd expect to see Hemingway tucked away at a corner table with his typewriter. Jesse had helped with construction to cut the costs too, and his furniture and cabinetry skills were a major plus.

He'd agreed with Savanna and helped her match the woodwork to the color of the full-bodied Italian-blend espresso beans, as well as tie in the slightly lighter hues of the beans she imported from Nicaragua into her furniture selection.

Then there was her favorite part, a small nook that seated up to eight guests and could be closed off with a sliding barn-like door Jesse had refurbished in whitewashed wood with brown accents.

"Does anyone other than you actually read these?" Jesse's

big paw of a hand abruptly snatched a novel from the bookshelf as if it'd somehow offended him.

The bottom three shelves were reserved for games. Who didn't love to play *Scrabble* or a good old-fashioned game of *Clue* while sipping on coffee and munching on sugar cookies? But her favorite shelves were those designated for the book exchange. Romance novels lined the top three.

"They do, actually. And damn, Jesse. Dirty handprints on my windows—that's one thing. Manhandle my romance novels and you're looking for a fight." She didn't bother to hide her teasing grin when he peered at her, holding up a book whose cover featured a dashingly handsome man wearing a well-tailored suit. Billionaire bad boy. *Alphahole*. Office romance. All the sexy things.

He flipped it over and began reading the blurb as if he'd ever in a million years read the book. "The guy sounds like a real winner," Jesse casually tossed out as if *that* was what he really wanted to talk about, then placed her book back on the shelf.

"Oh, he's an asshole, actually. A dumbass who didn't see a good thing right in front of him. And honestly, I wanted to smack him in the back of the head on more than one occasion." The parallels between Jesse and the book's hero had her smiling. "Like someone else I know."

"So, you didn't like the book?" he asked, ignoring the jab as well as the hint that he should quit dancing around his attraction to Ella and do something about it.

"Loved it. The woman brings him to his knees. Don't worry."

Jesse's chin dipped ever so slightly as if he were about to launch into yet another denial of his feelings for Ella and remind Savanna not to hold her breath waiting for a romance book happily-ever-after because "it ain't gonna happen." Instead, he said, "I don't understand women."

"Clearly," she couldn't help but remark, eyes traveling back out the window, wondering if tonight would be the night that Ella's date went well. And if so, would Jesse's head explode? "She's done waiting, by the way." Savanna swallowed, feeling a bit bad, but she was angry on Ella's behalf. "Probably."

"Good. I don't want her to wait for me. She needs to get on with her life. No idea how people got it into their heads we're supposed to be together." Jesse brought his knuckles to the side of his head and knocked as if everyone else was insane. Nope, that'd just be him for not making a move on Ella.

Savanna slapped a palm to her chest. "I swear, when it comes to that woman, you have no sense. I could swap you two nickels for a dime, and you'd think you're rich. What is wrong with you?"

"Didn't know it'd be comedy hour tonight. You charging for the show?" he returned with the same snark she'd delivered. "And also, I didn't come for a lecture."

"No, just to S-P-Y." Did she really need to spell it out for him?

"I am here for *you*."

"Mm-hm. And I'll fall in love again one . . ." Her words trailed off, because well, they hurt. A little too much.

November was around the corner, the month her husband was executed by terrorists years ago. Marcus, along with Ella's brother, A.J., had worked for an off-the-books team that ran special operations for the President of the United States. A team of ten Navy SEALs that the world didn't know existed. Jesse probably had no clue his sister's husband worked clandestine ops for Uncle Sam instead of handling security gigs for a private company, which was the story they told everyone.

"Savanna," Jesse said on a soft exhale. "Marcus would be proud of you and this place." His tone remained gentle, a sharp contrast to the overall ruggedness of a man who was once an Army Ranger and now worked with his hands designing beautiful pieces of furniture and cabinetry. "I only wish he was here to see it."

And what if she lost this place? This was all she had left. That and Marcus's red Ford Mustang, which he'd loved second to her, parked in the garage of her townhouse.

No way would she ever sell that car, either, even if it'd keep the shop open and a roof over her head. Nor would she touch the money hidden under her bed.

Savanna went back behind the counter to make sure everything was put away before she left for the night.

Tomorrow promised to be a long day. There were a few early Halloween activities happening, like the big candy-eating competition, which had been such a bad idea last year that Savanna was shocked the town council planned a repeat. Little Shawn Franklin won the contest by eating the most candy within five minutes, and then he immediately puked it back up, missing his empty candy bucket. To this day, Savanna still gagged at the sight of a Kit Kat bar or a piece of candy corn.

So she wasn't exactly looking forward to it, especially since she was providing all of the cookies for the frost-a-cookie contest, which turned into the eat-as-many-of-those-cookies-as-you-can (another dumb idea) competition afterward. But the winner won a thousand dollars and . . .

Hell, maybe I should enter? I could use the cash.

She pressed the heel of her hand against her forehead

when money frustrations crept back up. It was going to be another sleepless night worrying, wasn't it?

Might as well read. Maybe a good fantasy romance? Paranormal? Hm.

"Your café closed five minutes ago," Jesse said while checking his watch. "Does she always stay this long?"

"No, but she's fixin' to catch you here."

A second later, Ella pushed open the door but caught it mid-swing with her palm and stopped in her tracks because she'd set her sights on the one and only Jesse McAdams standing but a few feet away from her.

I swear if I am only ever a side character within their epic love story . . . She wasn't ready to give up on the idea of a "them" and assumed one day Jesse would remove his head from his ass, and Ella would forgive him for taking so long to make a move. But would she herself ever be able to feel anything for another man again?

There'd been no spark between her and Shep, and she was almost disappointed by that, which was a shame because she loved the feel of a man's body against hers. The smell of cologne wafting in the air. Even doing laundry after a guy's sweaty post-lift workout. She just couldn't seem to actually *feel* anything in her heart for another man since Marcus died.

She knew Marcus would want her to move on. But she felt his presence everywhere. It was as if he were always watching over her. And she loved that, but she also felt as though she'd be cheating if she were to develop feelings for another man. So, fictional boyfriends were where it was at for now.

Savanna focused back on what seemed like a showdown between her two friends.

Jesse's back was to her, but from his rigid stance, she knew his eyes were thinned and focused on the woman he loved standing before him in her skinny jeans and brown boots, paired with a fitted white top beneath a leather jacket, very similar to the one he wore.

"Not go well?" Savanna spoke up, hoping to break the awkward silence.

Ella finally stepped all the way inside and let the door swing shut, but she kept herself near the exit.

Done, done, done my ass.

The way she was looking at Jesse wasn't a look of adoration. No, Ella's eyes burned with anger.

And how would a romance author describe what was currently happening between them?

Palpable tension? The air crackled? Or something like that.

She wasn't a writer, just a fan of the written word. And she was fairly certain their story was no longer going to be a friends-to-lovers romance but more like enemies-to-lovers at the rate they were going.

After all, the man did ruin her wedding and then basically ghosted her, breaking her heart just like the TikTok video had warned.

"Not go well?" Jesse repeated Savanna's question when Ella's lips remained glued shut.

His arms hung like dead weights at his sides, but his hands were tightly clenched like he wanted to go hit Ella's mystery date.

Ella ignored his question and turned her attention to Savanna. "Same time tomorrow, okay?"

"*What?*" Jesse gasped, his strangled tone clearly conveying his shock. "You dating everyone with a pulse in town? How many dates has it been this week?"

Oh, oh, oh. I need some popcorn for this. Yup, I'm a side character.

Ella stepped closer to Jesse, menace in her eyes, and set her manicured forefinger to his chest and jabbed. "None. Of. Your. Damn. Business." There was a hell of a lot more bite to her tone than even Savanna had expected.

"I'm walking you to your car. Make sure you get home safe," he relented without adding more fuel to the fire, which was almost surprising. "I'll be right back to walk you home, Savanna."

"You don't need to. I'm fine," she returned.

Ella shook her head. "No, he's right. There was that break-in the other day."

How come she hadn't heard about this break-in? *Ignorance is bliss, sometimes.*

Jesse brushed past Ella, then took a step back to hold the door open. If Savanna had a dime for every time that man pissed off Ella in the last two years, she'd be able to pay off her business loan twice over.

Ella was almost out the door when she turned and cut a hand through the air. "Oh shit, I almost forgot I promised to help you with the baking competition tomorrow. Want me to cancel my date?"

"No, it should wrap up by five. You can use my place to shower and get ready for your date afterward." Savanna caught Jesse's murderous glare as he stood behind Ella, a total contradiction to his bullshit claim that he wanted Ella to move on . . . but move on from what? They'd never even kissed. But hell, everyone knew they belonged to each other.

"Thanks, babe. See you tomorrow." Ella's smile dissolved as if in preparation to face Jesse.

Once she and Jesse were gone, Savanna went to the framed photo she kept tucked away on one of the shelves behind the counter of baked goods and held it. The picture was of Marcus in his dress whites when he'd been with his platoon before joining Ella's brother to work the top-secret ops that ultimately led to his death.

Her hand shook as she stared down at the photo and let out a soft sigh, but a sudden noise in the kitchen area startled her into nearly dropping it. It sounded like someone had opened the back door. *But there's no one else in the café . . . is there?*

She hurried to the window and searched the street for Jesse, but no one was out there.

Maybe she was hearing things, or damn, maybe someone was going to rob her?

After carefully setting down the frame, she decided not to be some dumb girl in a horror film that calls out hello and seeks out the noise.

She snatched her iPhone from the counter and slowly walked backward, keeping her eyes on the closed door to the hallway, which led to the kitchen where she'd swear the noise had come from.

Savanna's eyes grew wide as she watched the handle slowly shift down and the door open an inch. The voice inside her head was yelling, *Run.* But before she had a chance to escape, the door opened all the way, and her shoulders fell with relief.

"Jesse Freakin' McAdams, you're going to be the death of me!"

"Why in the Sam Hill was your back door unlocked? Didn't I just tell you about the recent burglaries?"

She huffed out a breath. "And why were you creeping up on me?"

"Ella's car was on the street behind your place, and I thought I'd just double-check since I was back there. I didn't think you'd be careless enough to leave that damn door open."

"You're grouchy. Wonder why? First name, Ella. Last name, Hawkins." Now that her heart rate had returned to a normal rhythm, she walked over and playfully swatted him on the chest with the back of her hand. Then she grabbed her purse and keys to lock up the front so he could be his overbearing, protective self and walk her home.

"You should consider finding a better place to live," Jesse said a few minutes later as they passed Rhodes Park, speaking up for the first time since they'd left the café. "Not that this is a bad location. But your townhouse is a bit more Motel 6 than Marriott. And at the very least, I think we'd all feel better if you had a security system." He hip-checked her as they neared her townhouse, which had *maybe* seen better days. Like in the '70s.

"Oh sure, I'll go lease one of those fancy condos on Arlington. I'll get right on that tomorrow after a bunch of kids puke up candy and cookies right outside my bakery."

She slowed in front of the short path leading to the two-story brownstone townhome with a small fenced-in side yard and a one-car garage.

Her shoulders slumped as she stared at the place, wondering how in the hell she was going to avoid the property owner another month without paying her rent.

The suitcase of cash beneath her bed in the master bedroom was beginning to call her name louder and louder each day.

But her principles and morals quickly shut that voice up.

"Don't tell me you left this door unlocked too?" Jesse fully faced her with a humorous scowl, which looked a little scary in the nearby streetlight that blinked as if on the verge of dying.

"You're the comedian now, I see." She brushed past him, drawing up the to-do list in her head for tonight. A hot shower. Some sulking about her lack of money. Then she'd drown her sorrows by reading. Hot alpha or beta?

Who am I kidding? Alpha. Always.

"Stop," Jesse hissed urgently, his voice pitched so low she almost missed it as she inserted the key in the lock.

Savanna looked back to see him sprinting up the three brick steps to get to her. "I think someone is inside."

She smiled. *More joking, huh?* Ignoring his antics, she turned the key and opened the door.

Within seconds, Savanna was grabbed, hauled through the doorway, and thrown against the staircase wall. She cursed when her cheek smashed against the plaster just before rough hands spun her around in one fast movement and hoisted her up, her feet dangling in the air.

"What the—" A gloved hand covered her mouth, and without a second thought, Savanna brought her knee up and shoved it into the asshole's groin.

He let loose a painful grunt and released her, but only long enough to turn her around and lock his big arms around her chest, holding her still as she watched in horror while Jesse fought *two* other men she'd had no idea were there.

"Jesse," she called out before the hand slapped over her mouth again, and the beast of a man held her squirming body tight in his arms, keeping her back to his chest so she couldn't plant another wicked blow.

It took a second for her eyes to adjust in the dim lighting to realize Jesse was . . . a really freaking good fighter. It was like watching a scene from *The Matrix* or *John Wick* playing out before her with Jesse in the role of Keanu Reeves.

She continued to try and escape her captor as Jesse dodged the blade of a knife wielded by one assailant, then deftly took him down.

No guns? That was good, right? Or maybe they didn't

want to be heard by her neighbors, and Jesse could use that to his advantage.

The man loosened his hold of Savanna as if realizing his partners needed an assist before it was game over for them.

Jesse was barely breathing hard as he maneuvered left and right, dodging blows while connecting his fists with the men, almost like a choreographed dance.

The man freed her, then darted for Jesse.

"Look out!" she warned, but Jesse didn't miss a beat.

He'd already stabbed one man with the guy's own knife and drew the flat of the blade across the front of his shirt, wiping the blood free as an intimidation tactic to scare off the next enemy he was about to confront.

Savanna kept herself flattened against the wall, trying to stay away from the action while keeping her sights on Jesse. The blunt sounds of fists connecting to flesh and boots scuffling against the hardwood floor weren't loud or dramatic like fights in the movies, though.

The intruder, who she'd kneed in the balls, was on his back in seconds, and Jesse knelt over him, holding the blade to his throat.

"Who sent you?" Jesse hissed, drawing his face close to the man.

With a growl, the guy wrapped his legs around Jesse's back like some grappling UFC move she'd seen on TV, and he swapped positions with Jesse.

But only for a second.

They were back at the fight again, and the two other men . . . were gone. *Shit.*

The way Jesse moved, though . . . did they even teach that stuff in the Army?

Savanna slowly crouched to try and grab her purse when the big guy hit the ground with a hard thud by her feet. His eyes clocked her, but before he could make a move, Jesse dragged him away by the ankles, scraping his body across the floor.

She quickly seized the chance to snatch her phone just as the room grew dead silent—as in literally dead.

"Oh my God, Jesse. What'd you do?"

Jesse stood over the motionless body, his chest heaving with deep breaths. "Where are the others?" he growled out, obviously still charged from the fight and momentarily forgetting she was on his side.

"I think they ran away when they realized they couldn't beat you. Must not have been carrying guns," she said in a shaky voice, trying to piece together what happened. But it was messy and fragmented in her mind with a lifeless body by her booted feet.

Jesse knelt down next to the man, lifted his ski mask, then set his fingers to his neck, feeling for a pulse. "Are you okay?" he asked upon standing as if shaking away the anger that'd wound him up to the point he'd ended someone's life. "I wanted to question him, but he was relentless." Jesse slid his hand under his shirt, and Savanna flicked on the lights.

A pool of red blood spilled onto the hardwoods from beneath the body, but it was the blood on Jesse's hand when he pulled it out from under his shirt that had her worried. "Oh my God." She removed his jacket and lifted his tee. "He cut you."

"Superficial. As long as you're okay, I'm good." His brows pinched as he offered her an easy nod.

"You told me not to come inside. How'd you know? And where'd you learn to fight like that?" She was dizzy. Her thoughts were spiraling. "That was more Denzel in *The Equalizer* than Army Ranger. I-I don't understand."

"Did they hurt you, did you hit your head?" Jesse reached

for her chin with his non-bloody hand and angled her head side to side as if checking for damage. "No way are you making jokes after three guys broke into your place to do God knows what to you."

"I'm not joking," she said when he released her. "Who in the hell are you, Jesse McAdams?"

CHAPTER TWO

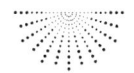

Savanna lay flat on the ground, a bed of red and gold leaves cushioning her body, and she stared up at a cloudless blue sky. She folded her arms over her chest and smiled when a crisp fall breeze kicked up, fanning across her face and sending leaves swirling in the air.

"How'd you know I was here?" she asked upon hearing the crunch of dried foliage as someone approached.

"Where else would you be? This is where you and Marcus got married. His casket is empty, so I know you don't go to the cemetery when you want to be near him." The husky voice belonged to Ella's brother, A.J., which was a surprise because last she'd heard, he was in D.C.

Savanna turned her head to the side to find A.J. parking himself on the ground next to her.

"I hate that they never found his body," she whispered. *And that I witnessed my husband being beheaded on national TV by terrorists.* She grimaced at the painful memory from November of 2015, a memory she'd never be able to scrub from her mind for as long as she lived. "You know," she began softly, needing to change the direction of the conversation before her already upset stomach worsened, "Marcus and I were going to travel the world together. He promised he'd find time to take me on adventures, but we just never got a chance."

A.J. reached for her hand and squeezed it between where they lay. "You'll get a chance to see the world, though."

With who? With what money? But she kept those thoughts to herself because she didn't want to burden A.J. with her problems. Clearly, he'd been apprised of all that went down last night. *That* being a guy ending up dead on the floor of her townhouse. Whether A.J. was aware of all the details, like Jesse breaking out some serious *Equalizer* moves, Savanna had no idea.

"You think Marcus had some sense of foreboding, and his spirit guided Jesse to me? I don't know, can people who've passed on have premonitions?" she whispered, knowing A.J. would be the last person to think she was crazy. The man was convinced Marcus's ghost visited him on occasion. A.J. said he preferred to believe that rather than think he was having hallucinations, so . . .

"I'm just glad Jesse was there with you. I can't begin to imagine the alternative. Refuse to, in fact," A.J. drawled. "But yeah, I think Marcus had a hand in that. You know he's always watching over us. Probably literally."

"Yeah, and it does make it hard to move on," she confessed, immediately feeling guilty for complaining.

"He would want you to, Savanna. Marcus would hate for you to remain single forever." A.J. cleared his throat, and when he spoke again, his voice was somber. "Just not with Shep."

"Shit. You know?" She yanked her hand free from his grasp and brought it up to cover her face, thoroughly embarrassed he'd found out about her and Shep's drunken mistake.

"Uh yeah, Shep felt all kinds of guilty and told Beckett, and Beckett told Caleb, and well—"

"Caleb told you," she interrupted because, of course, Caleb spilled the beans. The Hawkins brothers told each other everything. "I'm surprised your feathers don't show with how much you boys cluck like hens. So did you punch Shep?" She turned her head back toward him, willing her face not to betray how embarrassed she was. Although if the heat radiating from her cheeks was anything to go by, her skin was probably bright scarlet.

"Haven't seen him since I've been home. But you know, it's a possibility later." He lightly laughed as if trying to diffuse any awkward tension.

"So why exactly are you here, A.J.? Did you hear about my ninja-like moves and come to see for yourself? Learn from the master and all that?" It was her turn to lighten the mood, but based on the *you've got to be kidding me* look he was giving her, she might have missed the mark.

A.J. dropped his shades back in place and directed his attention toward the denim-blue sky. "I'm pretty sure I was the second call Jesse made after Beckett, who doesn't think the home invasion was random, by the way. He believes those men were after you."

That's insane. Savanna propped herself up on an elbow and stared at A.J. "Why did Jesse call Beckett anyway? Your brother doesn't have jurisdiction in the city. And how did that whole mess not make the news? Three thugs broke into my house, and one of them ended up dead. Why didn't we call the local police department to tell them what happened and provide a statement? Where's the dead body?" She took a deep breath after rambling off her questions, then squeezed her eyes closed.

Everything that happened last night felt more like a dream, well, a nightmare, than reality. She had no idea when the denial stage would end, but did she even want it to?

"At least I'm free from the candy and cookie contests today," she joked when A.J. had yet to respond, and after another beat of silence, her mind wandered back to the aftermath of the incident.

Jesse had convinced Beckett, the infamously growly sheriff of a small town outside of Birmingham, as well as Savanna, not to call the local PD. And for some insane reason, they'd both agreed. As for where the dead body was now, she couldn't even fathom a guess. Savanna had stayed at Jesse's house last night, choosing not to tell Ella, at least not yet, what had happened so as not to put her in danger. Beckett had suggested she stay with him, but he had a young daughter, so that was also out of the question.

Because what if Jesse was right and someone was after her? She'd never forgive herself if anyone innocent were to get caught in the crossfires of her problem.

But *what* problem? Yet another question she didn't have an answer for, and the more she thought on it, the less sense it made.

"The man Jesse killed had no ID, nor did he have a gun or phone on him," A.J. finally answered. "We have a photo of his face, though, and my team ran it through our facial recognition software program earlier. We got a match on one of the airport security cameras the day before the attack. International terminal. Still working on an ID and his original location."

"I take it this is why you hopped on a plane from D.C. Because someone from another country was inside my house?" She sat upright and hugged her knees to her chest to try and comfort herself.

"I'm here to check on you, Savanna, of course. But yeah, anyone attacking you makes my blood boil. But someone coming from overseas to go after you, well, that has me more on edge."

She let go of a deep, sobering breath. "Is that why they didn't have guns? They'd flown here commercially from wherever?"

"Most likely." This was probably business-as-usual for A.J., but it wasn't for her. Not at all. But not a day went by that she didn't still worry about Marcus's former teammates. She couldn't lose any of them. *The idea of something happening to me, though, I never considered that.*

"What could those men possibly want from me?" she asked, somewhat incredulously, when the news that three men hopped an international flight to come for her had finally sunk in.

"I don't know, darlin'. At least not yet, and this is outside of Beckett's wheelhouse."

"It's right in line with yours, though." She collapsed back onto the bed of leaves she'd made and closed her eyes, trying to stave off full-blown panic mode for a bit longer.

"The problem is that POTUS called at zero nine hundred hours and ordered both Bravo and Echo to spin up tomorrow. There's some dicey shit going down overseas, and we're needed. I'm so sorry. I hate leaving you after what happened, but it's wheels up for me tonight."

"The President needs you. I would never ask you to stay."

A.J. was sitting upright now, and he reached for her arm, urging her to sit and face him. "You know I'm not about to abandon you." He pushed his sunglasses into his hair. "But I do have the next best thing to me. Remember Wyatt's wife's brother, Gray? He now co-runs a security company with a former Delta guy."

Wyatt and A.J. were part of Echo Team, whereas Marcus had been on Bravo. It still amazed her that these guys were putting their lives on the line every day to handle operations the world would never know about.

"I'm going to call in a favor. Hopefully, I can get them here by the end of the day."

No, that wouldn't work. "Thank you, A.J., but I can't afford to pay some guys to protect me."

"First of all, you're not paying anyone anything. And secondly, if I'm going to be overseas doing shit that technically I can't talk about, I need to leave you in good hands. Not that I don't trust Jesse and my brother, but this isn't—"

"In their wheelhouse." But based on what she'd seen of Jesse last night, maybe it was?

"And also, I'm not just asking them to protect you. I need them to isolate the threat and handle it."

"Kill more people, then, huh?" The memory of the dead guy would be haunting her dreams for quite some time. She shivered despite the warmer-than-average day.

"Jesse did what any of us would have done. He had to protect you," he said in a firm voice, backing his childhood best friend's decision to end a life.

"Where did Jesse learn to do what he did? I don't think even Marcus was capable of those moves, and Jesse has been retired from the Army for years now."

A.J. looked off toward the forest in the distance. What was he hiding? "You sure you have no clue, no matter how small, as to why those men were in your place?"

"No, and you know I've never even left the U.S."

He frowned. "Well, you have my word we'll figure this all out and keep you safe."

Her eyelids fell closed, and she hugged her knees again. "Marcus gave me his word too. I made him promise I'd die before him."

A.J. wrapped his arm around her back and brought her to his side. "And that's one vow no man in love would ever want to keep."

CHAPTER THREE

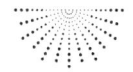

OFF-THE-GRID LOCATION IN PENNSYLVANIA

Griffin stripped free of his rucksack and gear, and hissed under his breath, frustrated and annoyed with his aching body for having the audacity to be such a whiny baby. He was only thirty-nine, but after the grueling morning, he felt as old as Methuselah. He grabbed two Motrin from one of the desk drawers nearby and dry-swallowed them. Back in the Army, he used to pop them like candy. But today, hell, the last two weeks, he'd been feeling more like a new recruit, and it sucked.

Griffin peered over at his boss, Carter Dominick, curious as to what thoughts were running through his head. He was leaning against the ATV they used to travel through the tunnels when in a hurry to escape what Griffin liked to joke was Batman's lair.

Their new base of operations was hidden inside the Pocono Mountains near Bushkill Falls. The bunker was constructed during the Cold War as a nuclear fallout site by some tycoon back in the day.

Griffin lifted his gaze, wondering if there had ever been stalactites above him before the bunker had stamped out nature altogether, and there were only clean lines and hard man-made surfaces from wall to wall. Well, until you reached the exit tunnels, and then it felt more like they were inside a network of caves.

He didn't bother to ask his boss how he could afford this place or who he'd acquired the bunker from, especially at the last minute. Carter kept everything close to the vest and on a need-to-know basis, and he never talked about himself. He also refused to acknowledge the rumors that he had piles of cash tucked away in about every pocket of the earth as if he were saving up for a Noah's ark-sized rainy day.

Since Carter's life had been splashed all over the news years ago, he was somewhat of an open book in that regard. That is, if the media stories were to be believed, which Griffin wasn't so sure. So, he opted not to bring up the man's painful past. It wasn't like Griffin wanted to talk about his own life or the ghosts that haunted him.

"Are we done making sure these boys can hang with us?" Griffin asked Carter, hoping for an affirmative.

Carter stroked his dark beard, eyes carefully tracking the other three men inside the bunker. "They weren't required to undergo and survive the navigation phase of selection like we were. I have to make sure they can hack it."

The navigation phase, designated the "stress test" of selection into the Army's most elite unit, meant carrying a too-damn-heavy rucksack through the Appalachian Mountains using an old-school map and compass to complete a forty-mile mission. The test required you to make it to the rendezvous point by a specified time. One minute late and you were out. It was a hell of a lot harder than it sounded, and ninety percent of the guys quit before moving on to the psychological evaluations, where more would drop like flies. Landing a position with the Unit, commonly known to the public as Delta Force, was considered next to impossible.

"And you had to drag me along for the ride, huh? I was twelve years younger than I am now when you and I qualified back then." Griffin turned his attention to the other three team members Carter had somehow acquired at a Navy SEAL's wedding of all places.

"Well, I need a massage. Or maybe an ice bath. Or both," Oliver said around a yawn. Oliver Lucas was basically the reason why Carter began working with the two other men, Gray Chandler and Jack London.

Oliver had had some shit luck this year while working a bodyguard gig in Dubai, and Griffin and Carter had assisted a group of SEALs in what amounted to a rescue mission to ensure Oliver didn't wind up executed by the Saudis for a crime he didn't commit. Being a good ol' Army boy and in need of a job, Carter had offered him one. But Gray Chandler, who ran a security firm out west, also wanted Oliver on his team.

From what Carter told Griffin, they'd argued over Oliver in the midst of the wedding reception, and in a bizarre turn of events, the men had decided, then and there, to join forces.

And although Gray was going to co-run the new team with Carter, Carter liked to be a serious pain in the ass to new recruits.

He'd been one hell of a hard-ass to Griffin last year when he'd recruited him despite the fact they'd gone through selection together twelve years ago. Carter hadn't had an official company per se when he'd offered Griffin a job, but apparently, during the years since Carter had left the CIA, he'd been handling missions of his own choosing with men from all over the globe.

And now the plan was for his people to work alongside Gray's, but based on the last two weeks of training, Griffin wasn't so sure that would pan out.

Gray and Jack were more old-school Army, and Griffin assumed the rest of their men back in California were of the same garden variety. Whereas Carter was the definition of a wild card, which was what had drawn Griffin to working with him. That and the six-figure income.

"Now that we proved we can, uh, hang with you fuckers," Jack began, winking at Griffin just to be an ass, "when do we spin up on our first job? My trigger finger is itchy."

For some reason, he and Jack had been butting heads since the moment they began training together two weeks ago. He couldn't imagine working alongside Jack out in the field, considering he'd wanted to kill him more than a few times while running practice missions and field training with the man.

Gray wasn't so bad. And damn, for a guy who'd lost part of his leg in a helo crash while serving, he kept up with everyone. Passed a few of them on the trails too.

"We'll be back at this again tomorrow," was all Carter said as he pushed away from the vehicle and twirled a finger in the air, signaling for them all to get the hell out.

"So, that's a no on being done with training, then?" Jack asked with a touch of humor to his tone.

Carter took a knee when Dallas, his Alaskan Malamute, headed toward him after jumping off the leather couch at the center of the place that was loaded with enough artillery to weaponize Philly.

"I don't think we're meshing all that well based on what I've seen in the field," Carter explained, which was an understatement. They weren't jiving together at all. "We can't operate until we can learn to trust each other."

Oliver unstrapped his vest full of mags as he said, "Well, I don't have any trust issues. But I think these two boys do." He stored the vest in its place and waved a finger between Jack and Griffin.

"We should probably divide into teams. East and West Coast. We'll head back to Cali and stick with our other team members out there," Jack suggested, ignoring Oliver's comment or maybe speaking up because of it. "You guys stay here in your Batman bunker." Jack shot Griffin a lopsided smile. "How about we divide into the Spartans and Trojans?"

Griffin lifted his palms in the air and stepped closer to the comedian. "I'm not a condom company, and based on that smart mouth of yours, you probably don't have any use for them. Doubt you're getting laid." Even if the ass did look like Ryan Reynolds, the actor everyone seemed to love. *Well, not me. Not anymore.*

Jack barked out a laugh and locked eyes with Griffin, then said, "Projecting much, Griff?" Yeah, there was something simmering behind his eyes. Griffin had hit a nerve, hadn't he?

But Carter wanted them to work together, so he'd back off out of respect for his boss.

"Military call signs, then?" Oliver proposed, and now they were all standing around Carter and Dallas.

"Nah, twenty years in the Army, bro, and I'm done with all the acronyms." Griffin was a bit more polite this time since he was speaking to Oliver, and there was no tension between them. Not that he knew what Jack's beef with him was, but it was there-there-fucking-there. *Maybe I should ask?* He thought about it for a hot second. *Nah.*

Jack snapped his fingers and nodded. "I think Oliver's right."

"Okay, how about three teams. And you can be a one-man show." Griffin returned his attention to Jack. "Let's go with whiskey, tango, foxtrot. Because what the fuck, man." Griffin shook his head, remembering how many times he'd repeated those words over comms during his years in service. Back then, there was a constant stream of WTF moments, especially when the brass ordered the Unit to do some dumbass shit they often disagreed with.

"We're not dividing into teams," Carter spoke up, taking command of the room while rising to his feet, and Dallas hurried back over to the couch. "Gray and I agreed we'd stick together as one unit. I have plenty of other men positioned around the globe if we need backup, but the five of us should—"

"Get our heads out of our asses and start acting like we'll take a bullet for each other if need be," Gray finished for him in a serious tone.

Jack peered at Griffin from where he stood next to Oliver a few feet away, giving him the stink-eye as if he were about to pop off a smartass answer instead of *Roger that*. "If I survived years of marriage to my ex, I guess I can survive this new, uh, situation." He turned and went to one of the desks set up in the space, and a second later, music began to play from the computer speaker.

"We still need a company name, too, right?" Oliver asked as he strode over to the couch, sat next to Dallas, and began scratching him on the head. "Not splitting into teams works for me. Call signs are probably going to be needed. But what is the company name? We sticking with Chandler Security?"

This had Carter flashing a smile, which came across as slightly menacing, considering the man rarely smiled. "No. Gray and I are still negotiating the whole fifty-fifty thing, and since I'm funding this team, I'll be damned if we call our organization Chandler Security."

Gray's eyes fell to the ground. He was resisting getting

into an argument with Carter, wasn't he? "We'll figure it out." He turned in Oliver's direction. "What'd you go by when you were in the 82nd?"

Oliver had been Airborne, which meant Griffin and Oliver most likely crossed paths at some point at Ft. Bragg in the past, but it was a big damn base, so he didn't remember him.

"Kodak." Oliver held his palms to the sky as if it were self-explanatory how he'd earned the nickname. "I have a photographic memory. Well, as close to one as possible."

Gray motioned to the comedian. "Jack was Ace."

"Play poker?" Oliver asked him. "I'm down for a game whenever."

"Nah, it's because I always have an ace up my sleeve." Jack's eyes remained steady on Griffin, though.

What the hell is that look about? "Midas," Griffin offered. "Got the golden touch. Always get my guy." He smiled. "Or woman." And damn, speaking of women, he needed to get laid. It was only two p.m., so maybe he'd drive into Philly, which was a little over an hour and a half away and hit up the bars. Try and get lucky before his balls turned blue, and he developed a new nickname. "What about you?"

Gray scratched his head as if he didn't want to share, his eyes flitting around the room before he reluctantly said, "Romeo."

"Ah, mm-hm. Enough said." Griffin clapped his hands together, ready to get on the road. Well, maybe a shower first. He'd have a better shot at meeting a woman if he didn't smell like roadkill.

"What about Carter?" Oliver asked as he stood and went to the desk.

"The Devil," Griffin answered for Carter, knowing the man had scored that name for becoming a legend in Iraq, a man their enemies feared even before his boots stepped off a bird.

"I'm not using that. I'll think of something else," Carter replied in a clipped tone, eyes lifting for a brief moment to the ceiling as if his prior legend status weighed on him instead. "And what the hell are we listening to?"

"Bieber. The TikTok version of the song," Jack said before Oliver could answer.

"You've got Bieber on your playlist?" Griffin lifted his brows in surprise. "Well, you just get better and better by the second."

"What's TikTok?" Oliver asked, and had he been living in a cave? Pretty much everyone knew of the app that Griffin abstained from using, worried about the safety of his personal information and privacy.

Jack strode up to Dallas and sat on the other side of him. "It's an app that offers some decent advice, actually. Lots of people that are divorced and now single use it and—"

"And you want me to take a bullet for this man?" Griffin asked Carter, and Jack flipped him the bird.

The Unit leaders liked to say they didn't always pick the best guy for the job, but they picked the right one, and Griffin sure as hell hoped Carter was right about Jack.

"You'll need to delete that app," was all Carter had to say on that matter just as Gray's cell phone began ringing.

"It's A.J.," Gray announced.

Griffin remembered the SEAL from their op together on the Sudanese and Egyptian border that summer when they took down a terrorist who'd decided he wanted to make the world rain with drugs in order to "infect" Western society. A.J. wasn't active duty from what Griffin had gathered, but according to Carter, his team ran off-the-books ops for the President. Not so retired, then.

From the sounds of this new team Griffin and the guys were currently forming, would their missions be all that different? They just wouldn't be taking orders from the Commander in Chief. In actuality, they wouldn't be answering to anyone and had zero red tape to cut through. And that was the beauty of it, which was how Carter had won Griffin over and convinced him to leave the Army after twenty years serving.

"Wait, what? You're serious," Gray said into his phone, and now he had Griffin's attention. "Yeah, of course. I'll talk to the guys." He lifted his wrist and checked his watch.

And shit, I'm not going to get lucky, am I?

"Yeah, I think we can get in tonight. See you soon." Gray ended the call and looked around the room, setting his attention on Carter last. "A.J. needs us for a job. His team works with my sister, Natasha. I can't say no."

Gray's sister was also CIA, and he hoped they'd be able to rely on her from time to time for intel if needed for a job. His father was an admiral . . . and also the Secretary of Defense. A good man to have in your corner if push came to shove and shit ever hit the fan overseas on an unsanctioned op.

"Where are we going?" Carter asked, no hesitation in his voice.

"Birmingham, Alabama," Gray said, already on the move.

"Well," Jack said while smiling, "looks like training is over, boys."

CHAPTER FOUR

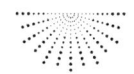

WALKINS GLEN, ALABAMA

"Five more minutes, right?" Savanna asked from where she stood at the kitchen sink, silently congratulating herself for sounding calm when she felt anything but. She looked over at A.J., who'd stationed himself by the two French doors that led to Jesse's back patio, thumbs hooked in the front pockets of his jeans and a cowboy hat perched on his head.

Jesse lived in Walkins Glen, a thirty-minute drive from her place in Birmingham. In her mind, Walkins Glen was a storybook town. The kind of place you'd see on the show *Hart of Dixie* or in a cute Hallmark Christmas movie. Everyone knew each other, and there were only two bars in town, the most popular one being the Drunk Gator.

"Yeah. Five guys on the team will be arriving," A.J. answered, squaring his shoulders back.

At one time, Savanna had considered relocating to Walkins Glen, but she was concerned the small town wouldn't be able to support her business. And she didn't want to compete with Liz's place, the only bakery and coffee shop already there, so she'd stuck to Birmingham.

"Five is a bit much, don't you think? We have your three brothers and this wonder boy over here." The memory of Jesse in action last night flashed to mind, and she swung her gaze to where he sat on a barstool at his kitchen island with his head in his palms. A heavy heart for killing that man? Or was something else bothering him?

"I'm not a wonderful anything," Jesse commented grumpily without looking up. Savanna was tempted to joke that the "grump" status in this town was already taken by the sheriff, Beckett Hawkins, but decided she'd best not. Jesse had killed a man to save her from, well, she wasn't exactly sure what, and now wasn't the time for wisecracking.

Jesse lifted his head and began wordlessly drumming his fingers on the handmade red oak top in an almost soothing rhythm.

Savanna stepped over to the island, opposite Jesse, and returned her focus to the ingredients she had assembled for baking cookies, an activity she always found therapeutic. Jesse didn't have a stand mixer, but she'd made do with the old-fashioned method for the first couple batches, chocolate chip and then oatmeal. Her arm muscles were definitely feeling the workout, but it was a nice distraction. Now she was ready to make her signature butter cookies. There was no time to let the dough rest overnight in the fridge for a better bake, but oh well. Butter-anything in the South was a sure bet.

"No sifter. No mixer. No rolling pin."

"I don't bake," Jesse cut her off while lifting his head, his light blue eyes fixing on hers. "You seem to be doing just fine without all the equipment." He winked, and his foul mood was temporarily gone. She'd take that as a win.

If anyone should be in a bad mood, shouldn't it be her? Last night, there'd been three men waiting *inside her home* for her. If Jesse hadn't been there . . .

And now, blood had ruined the floor of the townhouse she was about to get evicted from, and—

"You sure you're okay?" A.J. sat next to Jesse, and now she was under scrutiny from both of them. She'd rather be back in Hilton Head with her grandmother, learning how to bake cookies for the first time when she was seven, than think about blood and bad guys.

Her grandmother had lost her husband at an early age, and sadly, becoming a widow was something Savanna could relate to.

She closed her eyes for a second, remembering her grandmother's lessons.

The secret to making delicious cookies is to put a little of your heart into them, she'd instructed earnestly, a hand over her heart. Then she'd smiled and dusted Savanna's little nose with a flour-covered fingertip. Abuela had a beautiful smile and lovely hazel eyes, and Savanna felt lucky to have inherited both of those features.

"I'm doing much better than the both of you. You're the ones acting as nervous as a cat in a room full of rocking chairs." She added sugar to the softened butter in the silver mixing bowl and began the process of creaming them together with a wooden spoon, an arduous task that would have been much easier with a mixer. But again, anything to take her mind off the current mess she seemed to be in.

She needed to act like everything was business as usual, play this whole thing off like last night was some kind of mix-up, that she hadn't been the target because what was the alternative? Living in fear? Going down a rabbit hole of *what-ifs*?

She'd fallen down that rabbit hole when Marcus was killed. *What if he'd never joined the teams? What if they hadn't gotten called on that op? What if he'd killed the terrorists first?*

But the two *what-ifs* that plagued her to this day, because his body had never been recovered, were *What if that hadn't been Marcus I saw on TV? What if he isn't really dead and one day he'll walk through my door?*

A sharp stabbing pain hit her ribs at that last thought, one she couldn't deny crossed her mind on a regular basis.

When she glanced at A.J., he was adjusting his hat for what seemed like the tenth time in as many minutes, as if his head had somehow grown since she'd started on her butter cookies. It was probably nerves. And a nervous SEAL didn't sit well with her.

She didn't need a handbook to understand a Hawkins man. She knew all four of them through and through. And well, hell, she was familiar with Shep a bit better than the others. *And that was a mistake.*

"Let me guess, you're disappointed you missed out on the candy-and-cookie-eating competition today." Deflection attempt number two, but could she even lighten the mood when it felt like a dark cloud was hovering over their heads with no blue skies in sight?

She looked around the quaint kitchen, always impressed by Deb's handiwork. A.J.'s mom pretty much had a hand in decorating everyone's place in town, now that Savanna thought about it.

Jesse's 2,000-square-foot one-story gray brick house would make the perfect place for him and Ella too. Savanna could totally see them having two little girls with blonde pigtails running around in their fenced-in backyard, as well as a son pulling their sisters' pigtails, because why not? Boys. Enough said.

"I don't like leaving you," A.J. admitted. "Even with five capable guys, and my brothers and Jesse here to watch out for you. But moving you to another location worries me as well. Doesn't usually go as planned whenever we've, uh, tried that with people in the past."

Hm. She honestly had no clue how much Jesse really knew about what A.J. did for a living. But he wasn't a fool. Surely, he had his suspicions. Savanna had signed an NDA—non-disclosure agreement—a requirement by the President when Marcus joined the clandestine unit in 2013. It was her promise never to reveal the secret, and she was forever tied to that document too.

"I'll be fine. And don't you dare lose your focus while overseas and make Ana a . . ." *Widow.* Her stomach dropped.

A.J. stood abruptly, and Jesse did the same. But they both remained quiet as if unsure what in the hell to do. She didn't really know what to say, either, so she turned away from the island and set her sights out the window over the sink that looked out at the backyard. The sun would be setting soon, and A.J. needed to get on the road to the airport within thirty minutes.

And of all songs to come on the radio from the other room—*damn*. If she hadn't already known Jesse had turned his sound system on in the living room, she'd swear Marcus was there and sending her a message.

Savanna set her palms on the counter and bowed her head as Thomas Rhett's "Die a Happy Man" played. Had Marcus been happy before he died? She liked to think so.

Tears fell down her cheeks as she listened to the song, and then a pair of large hands braced the sides of her arms from behind.

But she was already lost in her memories.

Page by page.

Starting with the first chapter when she'd met Marcus in Tampa while he'd been attending a meeting with some admirals at SOCOM—the United States Special Operations Command center, headquartered there.

At the time, Savanna had been attending The University of Tampa and waiting tables part-time. One afternoon at the bar, Marcus passed her a note asking her on a date.

He had to leave the next day, so they'd had their first sort-of date over the phone and spoke every day after that through email or by phone until he returned a month later.

She'd fallen in love with him through his words like she was a character in a Nicholas Sparks novel, which her romantic heart had loved. He was sweet and caring. Strong, with the heart of a lion, as well. The most amazing and decent man she'd ever met.

And although they'd only spent maybe five days together in person over the course of their year of courting, such as it was, she accepted his proposal, and a year later, they married in Alabama in 2011. But in 2015, his life was taken, leaving hers ripped apart.

The epilogue of their story really was one for Sparks's tragic books, wasn't it? Often, there was no guarantee of a happily-ever-after with that author, and before she'd met Marcus, that hadn't bothered her. But ever since Marcus was stolen from her, she refused to read any story that didn't end with a happily-ever-after.

"Savanna?" A.J.'s voice was in her ear. "They're here."

Savanna sniffled and swiped the backs of her hands beneath her eyes, wiping away a few tears, then pulled herself together like she'd learned to do over the years and looked up to see five guys heading toward the French doors.

One of them seemed to notice her watching, and he paused for a second, freezing like a buck that realized someone had a scope on him.

Their eyes remained locked for a moment longer, but at the sound of the doors opening, she flinched and turned away from the window to check out her new crew of protectors.

But what exactly are you here to protect me from?

She recognized two of them, but just barely. Grayson Chandler, Wyatt's brother-in-law, had come in first, followed by Jack London, whom she'd met once or twice at gatherings after Wyatt and Gray's sister, Natasha, had married.

The other three, especially the guy she'd noticed outside, were question marks.

"Gray. Jack," A.J. greeted. "You remember Jesse and Savanna."

"Something burning?" Gray asked as he sniffed the air.

"Oh, shit." Savanna ran over to the double ovens, and Jesse was on her heels helping to pull out the burning cookies. Thank God, because the last thing she needed today was to have to call A.J.'s firefighter brother, Shep. She'd prefer A.J. leave town before seeing Shep, too, just in case A.J. really did want to punch him for their oops-moment.

After tossing the ruined cookies in the garbage and the baking sheet in the sink, she rested her palms on the edge of the sink and took a deep breath—*could she be any more embarrassed right now?*—then she slowly turned to face the room, only to come nose to chest with someone. Her hands flew up and went flat against that chest, which was amazingly hard and muscular, and felt really, really good. It was as if her fingers were on autopilot when they slowly climbed up the planes of his chest and to his shoulders, leaving a faint trail of sugary powder in their wake.

She looked up to find a pair of dark brown eyes staring down at her.

"Griffin," he said, his lips twitching in amusement.

The "buck" had a name. A *sexy* name. And a deep, sensual voice to go along with that firm, muscular frame and killer eyes she could lose herself in.

His granite jawline (*that's what authors would call it, right?*), masculine nose, and great overall bone structure were . . . well, *hot damn.* No full beard at the moment, but he was rocking a few days' worth of facial hair.

His dark brown hair was artfully styled at the top and faded a bit at the sides. Savanna figured him to be about an inch or two over six feet tall.

She swallowed, but it was more like a loud gulp. "Hi," she squeaked. And then, to her horror, she giggled. She didn't usually act like a tongue-tied teenager, so what the hell was going on?

"You have a little something on your face." The pad of Griffin's thumb swiped over her cheek, then he leaned back a little and licked his thumb. "Mm. Sugar."

Why am I still clinging to this man?

"Ahem. Savanna, want to let go of him?" That was A.J. adding fuel to the fire, blowing this moment up into something even more awkward.

Thanks, sailor. I'll remember that.

"Take your time, Sugar." Griffin flashed her a cheeky grin, tipping his head to the side a little.

Cheeky again? Woman, focus.

Savanna lifted her hands and backed up, bumping into the counter behind her, catching Jesse's eyes in the process as he stared at her with curiosity.

She was a bit curious too. When was the last time a man

had stirred such an intense reaction outside the pages of her favorite novels?

Before she had a chance to even try to decipher her feelings, she spotted Shep and Ella heading toward the back doors. Shit, incoming. "Shep and Ella are here."

"Jesse McAdams," Ella said the second she burst inside, her hands going to her hips with dramatic emphasis.

"What?" Jesse eyed Griffin on his way to intercept Ella while Shep hung back by the door.

"Why'd you bring Ella here?" A.J. asked. "She doesn't need to be caught up in this. What if someone were to show up?"

"You try telling our sister not to do something she sets her mind to do," Shep quickly returned before scanning the five strangers in the kitchen, appearing to quickly size up the other men.

Shep was tall, well-built, and had muscles for days. From the looks of the five guys there to assist Savanna, they did too. And she'd already *felt* the ridges of muscle beneath Griffin's shirt to verify that fact in regard to him.

"Why'd you say my name like I did something offensive?" Jesse spun his black ball cap around on his head like he was preparing to go argue with a ref during a football game.

"You killed a man." Ella unglued her palm from her hip to swish it through the air as if she were going after an irritating fly. In this case, a fly named Jesse.

"So?" he casually remarked. "Not the first time."

Ella's lips parted, but she remained quietly staring at him.

"Give us a minute." He reached for her elbow and guided her outside, shutting the door behind him.

"Girlfriend troubles?" one of the men, whose name she didn't know, asked.

"Oh, they're not together," Shep replied, which drew A.J.'s attention. He made a beeline for his brother, fists locked and loaded at his sides.

Shep tipped his head and caught Savanna's eyes. "He knows?" he mouthed. She grimaced and nodded, then watched in surprise as Shep stuck out his chin and *let* A.J. punch him in the jaw.

"This is not how I was expecting y'all to roll out the welcome mat for us," Griffin said, obviously trying hard to suppress a laugh, which distracted even A.J. to look away from Shep and over to Griffin.

A.J. shook out his hand and winced. "He had it coming. Trust me."

Somehow, she could have sworn Griffin knew why, too, because those brown eyes ping-ponged back and forth between her and Shep. But then, he was probably an operator, good at reading a room and people.

Savanna went to the freezer and grabbed two bags of frozen peas—these boys worked hard and played harder, so ice packs of some sort were a staple in everyone's freezer, including Jesse's—and handed one off to A.J.

When she offered the other to Shep, their hands brushed for a quick moment, and he flinched. "Thanks," he said softly. "Sorry about that."

Her gaze journeyed up to his face, finding Shep's eyes narrowed. *Maybe I'm losing my mind?*

"I'm Oliver, by the way. Didn't have a chance to say hello," one of the strangers piped up, another attempt to reset the tone of the room.

"Carter," said the guy with hair the color of midnight and eyes like bittersweet chocolate. Everything about him screamed villain rather than hero.

"Nice to see you again, Savanna," Jack said, and she couldn't help but return his captivating smile.

And wow, what is wrong with me? These guys were there to help her, and for some insane reason, she was cataloging every detail about them as if she were the Bachelorette with her very own season and suitors. But damn, these men were smoking hot. And if they were all single—

She usually thought it was a load of BS that so many of the men in romance novels just happened to be insanely handsome. And that every hero who was in the military was a hot badass with, at *minimum,* a six-pack. Looked like she needed to reconsider that opinion because hello to the men in the room. *Fiction meets reality?*

"Well, thank you all for coming." She felt the need to kick things off since they were there for her, and she had a few things she needed to get off her chest. "But I have no idea what happened last night. Or why those men were in my place. I also can't afford to pay you. And I can't afford to close my café for another day. I don't have any employees. It's just me. So, please don't ask."

"I told you not to worry about money." A.J. tossed the bag of peas on the kitchen island, shot his brother an irritated look, then focused back on Savanna. "But you can't operate the café until we're certain all threats have been extinguished. Whoever may be after you might target the café next."

Her shoulders fell at the bad news A.J. laid out for her. If she closed *Savanna's,* even for a few days, she might lose her townhouse. On the other hand, she would never put anyone in harm's way.

I'm not touching that money under my bed, either. No, no, no.

"You don't need to worry about paying us. I can cover any loss of profits while you're closed as well," Carter said.

Savanna shook her head, but it was Griffin her eyes fixed on. And her romance-novel-addicted self promptly jumped headfirst into a fantasy of the many repayment options a heroine in a book might offer the hero. And why did she have the desire to pay this man back in naughty, naughty ways? *Oh. My. God. Savanna, stop.*

Sex. I need it. It's been . . . well, since . . . She shot Shep a quick glance and hid her face in her palm for a moment, worried it was beet red and everyone would instantly become aware of her dirty thoughts.

But did it end there? Nope. Her lustful thoughts hijacked her vocal cords, and she blurted, "Well, don't expect me to trade orgasms for protection."

She was sure Shep and A.J. were having mild heart attacks right about then.

But it was Griffin she was unable to rip her gaze away from when she looked up. He had his palm flat on the kitchen island off to his side as he observed her with an amused and slightly cocky expression on his face. Like he was picturing just such a repayment plan playing out in his head.

Now her cheeks were really on fire.

"Savanna," Jesse barked out like a dad chastising his daughter.

"She was kidding," Ella softly said, prompting Savanna to tear her eyes from Griffin and turn toward the French doors. It seemed her best friend had finished lecturing Jesse outside.

"I don't like not paying for your time and help," Savanna explained, hoping her faux pas would quickly be forgotten. "There might be a way I can pay you back." Although, if she wouldn't use that money to pay her bills, why would she use it to pay these guys?

"I've got you covered, and that's all you need to know." Carter's voice was firm and deep, and she found herself not wanting to argue with the man. There was a slightly dangerous gleam to his eyes.

Well, glad you're on my side.

"We took my private plane, so I brought everything we might need," Carter added, diving back into the business of why they were there.

"What types of things might you need?" Savanna asked.

Ella planted herself alongside Savanna and crossed her arms as they stared at the eight men crowding the kitchen.

Jeez. Eight? Four short of a sexy calendar. "What is it that you aren't telling me?"

"We're still working on identifying who may have sent those men," A.J. began, his tone low and deep, and she recognized the look in his eyes. He'd flipped that operator-mode switch in his brain and was "Just the facts, ma'am" like Marcus used to do whenever he engaged in work talk. "These types of guys usually operate under someone else's orders, which means their boss, whoever he or she may be, wants you. Or something you might have."

"Might have?" *What in the hell would I have? Who would want me?* It made no freaking sense.

"My sister sent a secure email transmission on everything she found, but Natasha will be going off-the-grid for a bit, so I hate to say that's the extent of the help she can offer," Gray spoke up.

"What'd Natasha find?" Savanna turned her gaze to A.J., wondering why he hadn't shared Natasha's info earlier while she was baking up a storm. Surely he knew what Natasha had provided to Gray.

Her attention moved back to Gray as he folded his arms over his black tee and focused on her. "Natasha ran the dead intruder's photo through the CIA's facial recognition software," Gray began, "and she tracked him to the airport in

Birmingham. He was using an alias. Fake passport. After a little more digging, she identified the man as Greek. He took a flight from Athens. We're under the assumption the other two men with him were Greek as well."

"Natasha was also able to determine the hotel he stayed at using her software, but the men stayed off local CCTV footage in and around the city," Jack added. "Well-trained to know how to avoid almost all cams."

"Beckett and I went to that hotel earlier," A.J. dropped the news on her.

What the hell? She hated being in the dark. But they were only trying to protect her, she supposed.

"From what we can tell, the men didn't return to the hotel after what went down at your townhouse. They most likely emptied the room before they ever went to your house," A.J. told her, which set her heart pounding against her rib cage.

"Also, as far as we know, the men were only in Birmingham for one night before they came after you, so they didn't spend much time stalking you to learn your patterns," Gray pointed out.

Stalking? This was becoming too much. "They wouldn't have needed to do any stalking. I work and sleep. Pretty simple to figure out."

"We're monitoring all airports, and they'll get flagged if they try to leave the country," Jack said. "Our next step is to figure out who the hell they really are, who they work for, and why they might have come after you."

Yeah, a pretty important next step. "But you don't think they plan to give up? They still want me." A million thoughts swirled through her mind as she turned away from the men. She wanted to burst into angry tears, but when Ella set a comforting hand on her shoulder, she calmed down. Thank God for her friends.

Savanna's eyes focused on the flour-and-sugar-covered island, then to the floor when a pair of black boots appeared in her peripheral vision. She shifted to the side and slowly pulled her gaze up. Dark denim, black button-down shirt open to reveal a black tee and then on up to Griffin's tan throat before settling on his piercing brown eyes.

"We're fairly confident they're going to connect the dots to your friendship with Jesse, and they'll come here looking for you too. It's not a matter of if," Griffin said in a low voice, "it's a matter of when."

"You trying to scare her?" Jesse bit out, the brother she never had, but she'd always wanted. Now she had more than she could handle. She'd basically been adopted by A.J.'s teammates as well as the entire Hawkins family.

"Savanna needs to understand the danger she's in. And that if she stays here much longer, she's basically offering herself up as bait," Griffin said, turning his attention away from her and to Jesse on approach.

She faced both of them, and Ella lowered her hand from her shoulder.

"I'll stay here and wait for them," Jesse offered. "I'd like a second chance at those bastards."

"No way." Ella's worry for the man she claimed she was *done, done, done* with surely wasn't done.

"You know I'd never put Savanna in harm's way." A.J. strode closer, and some of the other guys fell back and out of Savanna's line of sight as if sensing this was a family matter.

And yet, Griffin remained firm. He didn't appear to be going anywhere.

Why was there a little jump in her pulse when her eyes met his again?

"If the remaining two guys from last night are as good as

you say they are, you sure you can protect Savanna?" Ella tossed out, and Griffin's brows lifted in insult.

"Jesse singlehandedly wiped the floor with them. But I don't think that was because those men lacked skills. It's just that Jesse's are, well, superior," Griffin responded, his gaze cutting to Jesse for a moment, then back to Savanna's best friend.

"Would you rather her stay at some hotel an hour away with just one guy? Or here with us?" Carter joined the conversation.

"Savanna's not going to be bait," Shep intervened.

Ugh. Too many men in here. Too many guys gearing up to butt heads. It was her life. Shouldn't she have a say?

"Over my dead body," Shep added, and ouch, those words hurt. The idea of losing him, or anyone because of her, was too much to handle.

"I'd still like to know why anyone from Greece is after you," A.J. addressed one of the main issues at hand.

"That makes two of us," Savanna said softly, and then a lightbulb went off in her head, and she squeezed her eyes shut. There was one possibility. A weird one, but still a possibility.

When she opened her eyes again, she found a room full of onlookers staring at her with curiosity as if they sensed she'd had an ah-ha moment.

"What is it, Savanna?" Griffin spoke first, and for some reason hearing him say her name had goose bumps scattering across her arms.

"We need to go to my place. There's something I want to show you," she confessed, hating that she'd kept this secret from everyone, and she was worried how A.J., in particular, would handle the news.

But didn't he have a flight to catch?

"Fine," Carter said. "We wait for sunset. Jack and Oliver will clear your house, then keep an eye on the front and back streets to ensure it's safe to arrive. Griffin and I will escort you." He pointed to Jesse. "Shep and Jesse, you stay here. Keep an eye out in case we get visitors sooner than we expect."

"I still have one more question," Savanna said, her brows tightening. "Whatever happened to the dead body, and are we telling the police?"

CHAPTER FIVE

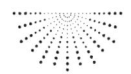

"So, Griffin. Is that with a Y or an I? I'm Savanna without the H, so I was just curious."

Before answering, Griffin glanced over at Jesse from where he sat shotgun. The man was driving his gray Dodge Ram on I-65 into the city, checking the rearview and side mirrors every few seconds. With A.J. leaving, Jesse had demanded to stay by Savanna's side, even for a short trip to her townhouse. Considering how he'd handled the three intruders last night, Carter and Gray had given in to his demand.

Griffin turned to address Savanna in the back seat. "I didn't know there were any Griffins with a Y." He gave her a slow smile. "But my first name is actually James. Not that I want you calling me that."

"James?" she repeated as if the word were foreign to her, and she needed to roll his name around in her mouth a little.

"Yup, James Griffin Andrews."

Her tongue peeked out between her lips, and heaven help him, why'd that have his dick waking up?

Was she gorgeous? Absolutely. He'd studied her dossier during the flight to Alabama, so he was already aware that she was a beautiful woman even before meeting her. He just hadn't been prepared for the up close and personal version.

But she was their team's new client. And then there was the fact that her husband, a Teamguy buddy of A.J.'s, had been brutally murdered by terrorist bastards who'd broadcast it on live television for the world to see. So yeah, there was that. A big, huge THAT.

He sure as hell didn't need any below-the-belt reaction to her. But he'd be lying if he said he hadn't gotten a semi when she'd had her hands on his chest in Jesse's kitchen. Or when he'd swiped the pad of his thumb across her smooth cheek and imagined running his tongue along the same path.

She looked casually sexy in her dark skinny jeans and short brown ankle boots, with a loose-fitting white tee tucked in just at the front. When she'd removed her Roll Tide apron, he'd spied a few thin gold necklaces dangling around her neck instead of her late husband's dog tags, which he half expected.

"So, Griffin with an I, why do you go by that instead of James?" Was she nervous and trying to make small talk?

"Well, Savanna without an H, my mom always preferred my middle name to my father's, which is James. So, she called me Griffin." He caught Jesse side-eyeing him with a disapproving scowl on his face. Shit, he was acting borderline flirtatious, wasn't he?

"Oh, I see." Savanna scooched back a little as if feeling the need to add distance between them.

Even though the sun had set, there was still enough ambient light from outside to see that she was assessing him like a sudoku puzzle she couldn't quite figure out. Good luck with that.

He honestly had no clue why he'd divulged that bit of personal information. He never told anyone his first name was James, especially not a gorgeous woman.

She tucked her wavy, shoulder-length hair behind her ears, revealing two small gold studs he hadn't noticed earlier. Probably because he was distracted by the glimpse of cleavage he'd gotten when he'd dipped his chin to look down at her while she'd walked her fingers up his chest.

Being a sniper, as well as a red-blooded man, he was always grateful for a clear view and a perfect angle. And her scooped-neck top had provided just that. Was he an ass? Affirmative. So, that was another reason he ought to behave himself. He had a feeling A.J. wouldn't hesitate to punch him in the jaw if he found out Griffin had so much as looked at Savanna sideways. He hadn't held back on socking his own brother, so Griffin wasn't eager to find out what A.J. would do to him.

And what was the story with her and Shep? There was a story, right?

Am I on one of Mom's soap operas? Shiiiit.

"I heard you were in the Army." Griffin faced forward while redirecting the conversation to Jesse. He wasn't sure how much longer he'd be able to tolerate Savanna staring at him with those gorgeous hazel eyes, and if she licked that pouty bottom lip again, he might launch himself into the back seat.

"Ranger." Jesse's answer still didn't quite square up with what Griffin had heard happened last night and how he'd handled three trained men. Most likely, hitmen or mercenaries. Sure, they may not have had guns, but three to one while Jesse also had to keep Savanna safe wasn't an easy task.

Griffin briefly contemplated whether or not he ought to

mention he'd met Jesse's sister, Rory, last year on an op. Jesse most likely had no idea what all went down off the coast of Puerto Rico last October. Or that Carter's team had locked his sister up in Carter's house on the island. Technically, it was to keep her safe, but Jesse may not see it that way.

He'd most likely have come at Carter or me swinging tonight if he knew.

"I was also with the 75th Ranger Regiment before . . ." Was it still a secret? Cat was out of the bag that the Unit existed, and he had no plans to write an autobiography. He'd leave that to the SEALs. So, he supposed he could share. *But I'll keep a lid on the Rory thing.*

"Delta," Jesse finished for him. "I heard Carter was Delta, and you two worked together before joining Gray. Figured you were part of the Unit too."

"Delta Force. That's similar to DEVGRU, right?" Savanna softly asked. "SEAL Team 6?"

He twisted in his seat to observe her again and nodded.

"How long have you been retired and in the private sector?" she followed up with another question, so he kept his attention riveted on her and that nervous lip tucked between her teeth.

"About a year ago, Carter pulled me over to the dark side," he replied with a wink. *Turn off the charm, man.* But it was second nature at this point.

"And—" Savanna prompted him to continue.

"Sugar," he cut her off and faced forward. "I'm not an open book." *Hell no.* "How about you go ahead and tell us now why you think you might be in danger?"

"I'd rather wait," she softly answered.

Griffin twisted around again to find Savanna's head

down, focused on her hands now clasped in her lap. Was that guilt? What was she hiding?

"Well, maybe while I'm down here in Bama, I'll get my first CONUS kill." He was trying to lighten the mood with some humor. Dark humor, sure. But that's how he rolled. How he and the guys back in the day had to roll to keep their sanity. "Looks like you got yours." Attention back ahead, he shifted his eyes and looked at Jesse. "Unless you've already popped your Stateside-kill cherry?"

"First Stateside kill? That's horrible," Savanna spoke up, and at least he'd distracted her.

"It was a joke," he said with a sigh. *Mostly.*

Jesse tightly gripped the steering wheel with both hands, and Griffin couldn't help but wonder if Jesse, like many veterans, was fighting an internal battle right about now. Killing that man last night had most likely triggered some bad memories for him.

"She was lucky to have you with her last night," Griffin felt the need to remind Jesse in case he *was*, in fact, fighting some demons about what he'd done.

"He morphed into John Wick last night," Savanna commented, and Griffin smiled at the fact she sounded impressed and not disgusted by that.

Maybe Rory hadn't told Jesse all of the details of the danger she'd been in last year because her brother would have gone into John Wick revenge-over-his-dog rage mode?

"Huh. Well, who doesn't love John?" Griffin smiled, not that she could see it since he had his eyes on the truck's side mirror off to his right, checking that there were no suspicious vehicles following them. "You're strapped tonight, though, right?"

"I have a piece in a lockbox under the seat." Jesse

unglued a hand from the wheel and jerked a thumb behind him. "You have an extra for her?"

Griffin almost laughed. The baker girl with flour and sugar on her cheeks knew how to shoot? Before he could respond, Savanna spoke up.

"I hit the range frequently. My husb . . . Marcus made sure I was an excellent shot." There was a painful pause mid-sentence, but she pushed through it.

Reaching behind his back for the 9mm holstered beneath his button-up shirt, Griffin turned to offer it to her. "I'm going to hope you don't need this, but here."

Savanna hesitated but accepted the gun, then stared down at it, a nervous-puppy look on her face. Not ideal for someone holding a loaded firearm. Practicing at the range was worlds different than aiming or firing at a live target.

He cocked a brow, one she probably couldn't see as the evening darkness began to seep in and overwhelm the cab of the truck. "You sure you want that?"

"Actually, no." She shook her head and offered it back to him. "I don't want a, um, CONUS kill, or a foreign one. Or any for that matter." She was trembling hard enough that he was able to clock the shakiness despite the darkness.

He stowed the weapon, feeling better with his piece where it belonged, and a few minutes later, once they were in the city, Jesse parked down the street from Savanna's townhouse as planned by Carter and turned off the engine.

Griffin promptly exited the vehicle and went around to open the door for her.

"How chivalrous of you. And unexpected."

Griffin knew she meant it as an insult, but the sass in her voice and the way her gaze slid up and down his body had his blood heating when he needed to focus.

"Stay by my side." He issued the command in a clipped

tone of voice, irritated that a woman had so quickly and easily derailed his attention while on a mission.

Jesse maneuvered to Savanna's left, and they kept her close between them as they made their way to the rear of the townhouse. Heads on a swivel.

Carter was waiting at the back door, and with Jesse now at Savanna's six, Griffin led the way into her dark kitchen.

Beckett, one of A.J.'s brothers, and also the sheriff in Walkins Glen, had the body hidden as a John Doe at the local morgue for now. But he must have sent some men he trusted to her townhouse to wipe away all evidence there'd ever been an invasion or a death. The place smelled of bleach rather than stale blood, thank God. Savanna didn't need to walk into that. And until they knew what and who they were dealing with, they didn't want the local PD or FBI taking over the case. Not that they didn't trust either, but as far as Griffin was concerned, he and his team were better suited to handle a situation that might involve breaking a few laws.

"Okay, now that we're here, what's the story?" Carter came out of the shadows alongside Gray.

"It's in my bedroom." Savanna reached for Jesse's arm and looped hers with his as if needing an assist to walk.

The story is in your room?

Griffin and the others followed Savanna and Jesse upstairs and made their way down a short hallway to her master bedroom.

Carter held a flashlight low to the ground to follow her movements and offer them a slight view of what this mysterious woman was doing.

Savanna released Jesse's arm and knelt by her bed, then reached for something underneath. She pulled out a suitcase and lifted her eyes toward the light.

"This is the only thing I can possibly think of," she said in a soft voice before leaning over and unzipping the bag.

Carter aimed the flashlight inside the bag to reveal banded stacks of hundreds. An entire suitcase of cash.

"Who are you? A bank robber?" Griffin spoke up, unable to hide his shock.

Savanna shook her head as Jesse dropped down by her side and reached for a stack of bills, clearly taken aback by what he was seeing.

"No, but I'm pretty sure it's a criminal who has been sending me this money on a regular basis," she confessed. "A lunch box containing ten thousand dollars packed inside a much larger box is sent every month. No return address, but I assume it was sent domestically."

"Did you save any of the original packages? We might be able to still track a location," Carter said.

"No, I'm sorry," she apologized. "I never knew what to do with the money, either. Still don't, so I've been storing the money under my bed. I can't spend dirty money."

"Why would a criminal send you money? When did this start?" Jesse's voice was tense as he dropped the bills back into the case, which appeared to contain enough dough to buy a nice vacation villa in the Caribbean.

Savanna slowly rose and sat on her bed, her attention remaining on the suitcase. "It started a month after Marcus died."

Griffin's eyesight began to adjust to the lack of lighting, aside from the flashlight, and he watched as Jesse stood and drew his hands to his hips.

"Marcus's brother?" Jesse's low-pitched and concerned tone was a red flag.

Savanna nodded and remained quiet. Was she ashamed?

"Right. Your file mentioned your husband's brother

wasn't exactly an upstanding citizen," Griffin said at the memory of what he'd read on the plane, but her brother-in-law didn't seem to be in her life, so they hadn't thought he'd have any connection to the threat. *Maybe we were wrong.*

"No, he's definitely not." Savanna shook her head. "Nick's a thief," she added what they all already knew. "A safecracker, and one of the best in the world from what I've heard."

CHAPTER SIX

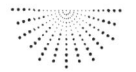

An hour after her confession, Savanna silently sat on the couch in Jesse's living room. He hadn't spoken a word to her during that hour either, which had her stomach in knots. And she knew when A.J. found out that she'd been keeping that money a secret from everyone, he'd be more than a little hurt. But she hadn't wanted to cause them any worry. It was also just a theory. A damn good one, though, because who else, aside from Nick Vasquez, would suddenly begin sending her lunch boxes full of cash? Criminal or not, she assumed Nick was trying to take care of her after Marcus died. It was the only theory that made sense.

"They should be done soon," Griffin announced, taking a seat in the leather recliner off to her left. Griffin also hadn't said anything about her big reveal.

After they'd exited her townhouse, Carter had demanded they set up security points around the perimeter of Jesse's place ASAP, in case anyone decided to pay them a visit, particularly while she was still in the house.

"If anyone tries to come within five hundred feet of the house, we'll know about it. Plus, we'll work in shifts. At least two of us will stay awake tonight," Griffin explained, and she noticed his attention moving toward the kitchen where Jesse had just called out he was going to get some fresh air.

That meant she was alone with a man whose presence mysteriously produced a warm, tingly sensation throughout her body. He was a good-looking guy, so she assumed that was all there was to it. But Shep was hot too, and she didn't experience the same sensation in her stomach, like a kaleidoscope of nervous butterflies taking flight, when she was around him.

It was possible the butterflies were a product of Griffin's proximity. Butterflies aside, it was nowhere near what she called "The Marcus Effect." Because how could any man compete with her late husband and what she'd had with him?

No one made her cheeks hurt from smiling like Marcus had.

Or had the ability to use the power of words to melt her heart the way Marcus had won her over in their first weeks getting to know each other.

And sadly, the list went on and on.

She'd be forever alone, which she knew was the last thing Marcus would ever want for her. But she wasn't sure she could stop herself from comparing every man that tried to come into her life to Marcus.

Savanna's eyes wandered over to the three boxes in the corner of the room the guys had brought back from her townhouse tonight. Marcus's belongings. Some of them, at least. It'd taken her two years to box up his stuff, but these three boxes Marcus had packed himself when they first moved in together.

It was his handwriting in black marker on the boxes too.

My Pre-Savanna Stuff written on one.

My Before I Met the Woman of my Dreams Stuff in a combo of print and script on another.

And last, the one that made her laugh when she'd first seen the label: *My When I Did Stupid Shit Stuff.*

She hadn't opened those boxes until one day while he was on a five-month deployment in Afghanistan. She'd been bored, and he'd never said they were off-limits, so she decided, why not? There were a lot of photos of him and his brother in the "When I Did Stupid Shit Stuff" box, as well as letters Marcus had written to his brother while Nick was serving time. Letters Marcus had placed in envelopes, addressed, and stamped . . . but never sent.

She hadn't violated Marcus's privacy then, and she still refused to read them, to be the one to unseal them, unable to violate her husband's privacy even after his death. But that's how she learned Marcus had lost contact with his brother, the man he and his parents rarely discussed. Like a son they'd already lost. A brother Marcus had buried.

She'd waited until he was Stateside to ask him about the letters, and it'd also been the first and only real fight of their marriage.

"Maybe you should reach out to him?" she remembered pressing, which had set Marcus off and had him pacing their small living room. *"What if he needs you? You could be a positive influence in his life, and since he's no longer in prison, you could help him change."*

Marcus had spun around and lifted both hands to the ceiling as if praying to the heavens for Savanna to understand the insanity of her proposal. *"That man disrespected our family. All my parents ever wanted was to give us the kind of life they never had. And Nick became everything that's wrong in this world."*

The tears that filled his eyes when he'd finally looked at

her told a different story, though, and had her slowly approaching him. Trying to plead with a hurt man. *"Is that what you told him in your letters, then?"*

He'd set his hands on her arms and gently squeezed while looking into her eyes. *"No,"* he said, his voice cracking. *"I told him I forgave him. In every stupid letter, I told him I would help him when he got out."*

"But you never sent the letters," she whispered, and he nodded, tears starting to fall from the eyes of her stubborn husband.

"No, because I wrote them when I was weak."

"Forgiveness is not weakness," Savanna repeated what her grandmother had always said when she was growing up, and even now, the sound of her grandmother's voice warmed her chilled body as she battled with her emotions when reliving the memory.

"It is to me." He let go of her, and for the first time in their marriage, he turned his back on her, unable to look her in the eyes.

"Then why'd you keep the letters?" she softly asked, setting her hand on the middle of his taut back.

He slowly faced her and said, *"They're a reminder of the stupid shit I've done."* He pointed to the box. *"The fact that even in a moment of weakness, I could ever forgive him for the hell and shame he put my parents through is crazy."*

And with that, he'd left the house and gone to the local bar to drink with some of his buddies, preferring to escape her and her line of questions.

She'd tried to bring up reconciliation over the years, but he'd always shot her down. And then, eventually, it was too late.

"I'm sorry. What were you saying?" Savanna blinked a

few times, time-traveling back to the present. To the fact maybe Marcus had been right, and his brother was trouble.

But why'd he send me the money if he didn't care at all?

"I was saying that if anyone tries to get to you tonight, we'll handle it, but we've decided it's not safe to keep you here for more than one night." Griffin's husky voice filled her ears, and when he began to roll up the sleeves of his black button-up shirt, her eyes immediately fell to the movement, tracking his corded forearms.

And boom. Hello, nervous butterflies. There you are.

What was that all about?

Oh, right, I know.

This man was a bad boy, wasn't he? One of those guys she'd have fallen for before Marcus. She could tell by the way he looked at her like he was God's gift to women, as well as the self-assured way he carried himself. Those cocky, devilish smiles he'd sent her earlier? Red flag. The way he'd called her Sugar? Another red flag. Oh, and his first name began with J, so yeah—red flags all over the place.

Yes, there'd been a time when she'd have tripped all over herself for a man like him. The kind of guy that made a game out of sending mixed signals. Acted like he didn't give a shit one minute, then was into her the next. Why she'd wanted that kind of man rather than a good guy who was totally responsive and caring . . . she had no clue. But she'd promised herself she'd marry a good man. A man who didn't play games.

And Marcus had been that man. Aside from keeping his brother's past a secret, he'd always been an open book.

The opposite of Griffin from what she'd gathered in the short time they'd spent together.

Why am I thinking about Griffin? A stranger. Like at all? A distraction from those three boxes? From reality? From the fact that at any minute, Jesse's home may be stormed by men searching for her?

"You're tense." Griffin rose from the chair and retrieved his phone. "You need to loosen up a bit before the boys come back in."

"Baking usually helps. You know, with the nerves." She stood as well and couldn't help but check out his ass in those well-worn jeans while he'd gone for his phone.

"Based on what I saw when we arrived, I think you made enough cookies to last at least one night with a bunch of men in the house." He smiled. There it was. The smile he'd meant to pass off as friendly and innocent, but the way those perfect lips curved and teased at the edges was pure seduction. Did he even know he was doing it?

Bad boy.

Through and freaking through.

And who was she kidding, Shep was the same. One other reason she'd done her best to avoid anything other than friendship with him before and after their oops-moment.

If she were ever capable of falling for someone again, she needed another good man. Not the kind of heartbreakers she'd dated before her one true love had passed her that note in the bar in Tampa over a decade ago.

"What are you doing?" she asked when an unfamiliar song began playing loudly from his phone.

"This should help. It's called 'Arise.' Pumps me up when I need to go—"

"Fight?" Her wide eyes met his brown ones. "Shoot someone?" Because yeah, the chaotic-sounding music even had her wanting to throw down with someone. At least throw a few punches at the air.

Griffin edged closer. Close enough that if he looked down, he'd likely get an eyeful of her cleavage. He dipped his chin but kept his eyes focused on hers. Savanna's heart began to race as she waited for his answer. Was he going to say yes? Yes, this song made him want to fight? To kill?

But before he could speak, she said, "This won't calm me down. Quite the opposite, in fact." And wasn't that the truth? She'd meant for him to believe the music was disturbing to her senses, but maybe the pounding rhythm also had her wanting . . .

"Oh, so you want something that'll get your hips moving?" he asked seductively, leaning in closer. "Maybe Shakira?"

Savanna ordered her heart to slow down and her voice to remain steady, then said, "You have Shakira on your playlist?" *No way.*

His brows pulled together as he kept his eyes locked with hers. Griffin took the staring contest to the next level. "You don't?" he asked, appearing truly shocked. And then the jerk winked.

Oh, this man was trouble.

"You're a sniper, aren't you?" She inched back a step and tried to remember how to do that breathing thing. "Snipers always wink."

"Got a lot of men winking at ya, huh?" Did he just turn the tables on her? Boy, he was good.

She tore her focus to the pine floors, then squeezed her eyes shut. "I don't need music to relax." *What I need is for this problem to disappear.*

After a couple of deep breaths, she opened her eyes and looked up to see he'd stepped back a bit, but he hadn't dropped that devilish grin. He was thinking about sex, wasn't he?

"You're right, sex is relaxing too," she replied as if he'd actually voiced what she'd assumed he'd say.

Griffin lowered his phone to his side, the song ending and another one she didn't recognize coming on next. "Oh really?" His free hand settled on that hard chest of his. "Did my mouth move and I spoke without realizing it?"

Before she could defend her insanity, she heard the doors in the kitchen open. *Thank God.*

Griffin surprised her by leaning in behind her, placed a palm to the small of her back, and set his mouth to her ear. "Relaxing isn't the word I would use to describe sex."

She stood still for a moment and watched Griffin walk away, shell-shocked and trying to process what he'd said. The man had the nerve to saunter into the kitchen and join the others like he hadn't just whispered words into her ear that had her blood heating and pulse racing. The insinuation buried in those words.

And that only made her wonder what kind of sex he preferred. Hard and rough? Hot and intense? All of the above?

Within a matter of seconds, she'd drawn up a list of her favorite book boyfriends to see if Griffin matched any, but from where she stood now, admiring his backside in those jeans as he talked to Carter, he was an original.

Original bad boy, she reminded herself. *I already made a mess with Shep.* This man was there to protect her, and reality was a far cry from fiction. She'd clearly need to keep reminding herself of that, which was nuts since she should be more concerned about the three men who had attacked her last night. *It's a coping mechanism,* she decided. Deflect and distract herself with sexy thoughts to ignore the fact she was in danger and that it might be connected to her late husband's brother.

"We're all set for tonight." Carter came into the room, but she didn't see Jack or Oliver. They were most likely positioned outside. "You ready to share what you know? We received the bullet point version about Nick on our flight to Alabama, but we were under the assumption he was never part of your life. The money under your bed changes things."

Her attention journeyed to Jesse, seeking comfort in the clear blue eyes of one of her best friends. He returned her gaze with a conflicted look on his face, which had her chest tightening. He'd been off since last night, though, and with Nick Vasquez added to the mix, he was most likely shook.

Savanna walked over to the boxes, not prepared to dig through them and relive that fight she'd had with Marcus. "Nick is a few years older than Marcus. He and Marcus were really close until Nick committed his first crime at seventeen. He was tried as a juvenile for an attempted bank robbery with three other guys who were older than him," she slowly revealed the story, hearing Marcus's voice in her head as if he were speaking for her.

Goose bumps gathered on her skin beneath her clothes, and she pinned her arms over her chest, worried her lace bra would showcase her nipples through the thin fabric of her shirt when she turned to face the room.

"Nick didn't learn his lesson, and once on the outside, he was arrested again, not even two years later." Savanna pivoted back around to see the three men observing her like a suspicious group of operators might if she were the subject of an interrogation herself.

Well, not Jesse. But the look Jesse was now directing Savanna's way was disappointment, maybe even betrayal for keeping the money a secret. Both she and Jesse also knew Marcus would never forgive her for keeping that money, and she couldn't imagine how he'd feel if she'd ever spent a dime of it.

"Marcus said if Nick screwed up again, that'd be the third

strike, and he'd be out of the family. At least, he'd disown him as his brother." She swallowed. "And while he was deployed, Marcus learned Nick was back at it again, and he was working with even more dangerous criminals. Not Stateside, either. He was never arrested again that I know of, but Marcus had said he was done with him. He wanted nothing to do with a criminal."

"I assume Nick got into safecracking, and as one of the best in the business, because of his father?" Carter spoke up.

"Right. Their dad worked for a company that built and installed safes and bank vaults for large corporations and government facilities. Lots of government contracts, most of them top secret. Like the one back in the 1950s when they provided the twenty-five-ton vault door at Project Greek Island. You know, the nuclear fallout shelter designed to house top government officials at the Greenbrier Hotel in West Virginia during the Cold War. Marcus's dad taught both his sons the ins and outs of safes and vaults. He'd hoped they might follow in his footsteps," she explained, trying to keep her voice steady. Also, sort of wishing Griffin had left the music on in the background so it didn't feel so absolutely quiet in the room.

"I guess Nick did just that, only he used the skills to steal," Jesse mumbled under his breath.

"You ever meet Nick? We have no record of you ever together in our file," Griffin asked, and she turned her attention to him.

Had her life really been collected as bullet points in some file?

But she thought back to when she'd met Nick, a time when her husband had been alive. A year or so after she'd discovered the letters. "Only once. Marcus kicked him out within five minutes, and I barely spoke to him." Her tongue pinned to the inside of her cheek for a moment as she did her best to keep her emotions in check. "I tried to get ahold of Nick after Marcus died to ask him to come to the funeral. Their mom did too. We couldn't reach him."

"Then the money started to come after that?" Jesse asked, and she nodded.

"Their mom passed away a few years ago from what I remember." Carter moved farther into the room and closer to her as she nodded. "I'm not convinced the money has anything to do with why those men showed up last night, but we'll check into him and see what we can find out."

"So, you're Nick's only family?" Griffin asked.

Savanna lifted her gaze back to Griffin, finding his brown eyes leveling her with a soft look, one that reminded her to "try and relax." She swore he was even nodding ever so slightly as if music still played as another reminder to her to let go, to trust them and share what she knew.

And it worked.

Some of the tension started to drift free from her limbs as she called up Shakira, of all singers, in her head.

When she spied a smirk on Griffin's lips, she looked down to discover her hips swaying.

Yeah, I'm fifty shades of red for sure. "Unless he's married, yes," she finally answered. "Nick didn't even show up for Marcus's funeral, so it's shocking he was sending me money, but who else would it be?"

"Those men last night weren't there for the money. Doubt they even knew you had it," Jesse noted. "Three guys like that don't travel across the globe for a bag of cash. They were hired to make a hit. They had to be after you."

"Agreed," Carter said in a firm tone. "We'll dig deeper into Nick's background and inmate history since we didn't beforehand. See who he's been hanging out with since his convictions. It's also possible he made contacts while in jail to help set him up with work once on the outside. It shouldn't be too hard to pin down his whereabouts the last few years or so." He looked back at Griffin. "We'll have you roll out of here before the sun is up tomorrow. And we'll switch to the plan we discussed on the plane."

"What plan?" Jesse strode around to confront Carter.

"Taking Savanna to a property in Northern Alabama near the Tennessee border. Not too far from here. But far enough," Griffin said, and wait, what?

"Not without me," Jesse interjected, hands raised as if prepared to fight.

Jesse, always the fighter. He'd been like that since he was a kid from what Ella had told her, but she'd said he'd calmed down some after the Army.

"You're not going," Griffin returned in a deep voice, one he hadn't used with Savanna yet. He'd stuck to a sexy, playful one so far with her. "Oliver will come for backup, but trust me, the place we're going to is as secure as they come. Anyone who tries to infiltrate the property will regret it." He lifted a hand to Jesse's shoulder, but Jesse took a step back from his reach. "No. She doesn't leave my sight."

Savanna raised her hand. "Hey, hello. I do get a say, right?"

"No," Carter and Griffin responded without missing a beat, and what the hell?

"We'll talk about this later," Carter said, but she knew that was the same as a mother telling a kid, "we'll see." Nope, that meant no.

Before she could open her mouth to rebut, Carter lifted his wrist and peered at a red flashing light on his watch. "We've got incoming. More than two guys from the looks of it." His voice was so calm and steady, that . . . *what?* He answered his phone a moment later before the first ring finished. "How much time do we have?"

Noise outside that sounded like fireworks had Griffin reaching for Savanna and flinging her behind him like he was a human shield. From the corner of her eye, she spied Jesse reaching for a weapon hidden beneath his shirt.

"They're here for you," Carter announced, and in a low voice, said to Griffin, "We're going with plan B. Just you and her," he hissed. "Go."

CHAPTER SEVEN

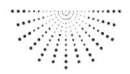

"I'm still trying to comprehend what just happened and why we're in a minivan with a Baby On Board sticker on the back window," Savanna said in a rush, her hand clutching her chest as if she'd just run a mile over rough terrain and witnessed another murder.

Griffin returned his eyes to the road. And yeah, that last part *had* happened, so he didn't blame her for being shaken up.

He also didn't need to peer her way again to know her hazel eyes were fixed on his profile. He felt her curious stare travel over him as he sat unaffected by what had gone down.

Maybe not totally unaffected. He was damn exhausted. He'd spent all morning in Pennsylvania—*was that really just this morning?*—running tests meant for much younger operators, immediately followed by jumping on a flight to Alabama, during which he got no rack time as the guys went over the mission details. Add to that this intriguing woman with her sexy voice and her breathy sighs that only served to call his attention to her tits, and he was worn out. It took a hell of a lot of work to keep himself from scoping her out every few minutes.

"You're safe. That's all you need to wrap your head around," he finally replied, which probably wasn't the answer she'd hoped for.

The minivan's tires crunched over the gravel along the unpaved road clearly meant for an ATV or other off-road vehicle, but it'd been their only option to safely flee without notice. The heavily wooded area butted up to Jesse's property, and fortunately, all but one man had stormed the property from the north and south sides, which were the more vulnerable entry points.

"I don't think we have a tail, but I'll feel better when we're a klick or two farther from Jesse's."

"We're only two klicks away now. Still too close," she said after another one of her breathy exhales, but at least he wasn't looking at her this time.

Savanna's use of the word "klicks" was yet another reminder she wasn't just a civilian in danger. She was a civilian that'd been married to an elite operator, a Teamguy once upon a time ago.

"When exactly did y'all park this van out in the woods?" she asked, bumping against his forearm resting against the console as she twisted around to get a better look at their ride.

"We decided to have a backup vehicle in a secure location ready for an exfil in the event anyone made a surprise visit." He paused for a second when she bumped into him again while facing forward, then shifted his gaze to see her wriggling in her seat and adjusting the seat belt as if fumbling with a reserve chute she was worried she might need to deploy.

The belt caught the scooped neck of her shirt, pulling it

down enough to reveal the top edge of her bra. It was too dark in the van to make out the material or color, but his imagination skipped ahead and decided on nude and lace. A thin material that'd have her nipples poking through if—

And his dick twitched.

Not *all* of him was exhausted.

"So, are you going to answer me, or continue to stare at my breasts instead of the road?"

Welp, as his uncle from the Midwest would say, slapping his legs and standing from his chair as a signal for visitors to leave his house . . .

She. Just. Went. There.

"Is it really that hard?" *Okay, now she was just fucking with him.*

"That a trick question?" Because yes, his dick was getting to that point despite the fatigue.

"Is it really that hard to answer my question," she clarified, enunciating each syllable as if he were hard of hearing too.

"Yes, it's very hard." Griffin shot her a grin, the one his friends called his "cocky asshole" grin, but immediately regretted it. *Rein it in and get your mind out of the gutter, Griff.* "My team made arrangements while on the flight here for an inconspicuous vehicle to be accessible if needed. Since A.J. and Jesse know the lay of the land, they chose the location for it. Good thing we had that foresight too, or else we would have been hiking to the nearest highway." He congratulated himself for dodging her blunt accusation that he'd been staring at her breasts.

"I assume you didn't anticipate having to shoot that man on our little jaunt through the woods to the escape van? Speaking of which, whoever decided that an abandoned minivan with a Baby on Board sticker and no car seats in sight qualified as 'inconspicuous,' needs to be fired."

He wasn't sure which surprised him more, her sass in using air quotes or that she made it through her little speech seemingly in one breath.

"It was you, wasn't it," she mused, and he could see her fully facing him now from the corner of his eye. "You were the one who thought a deserted murder van was a good idea."

He cast her a quick look, doing his best not to be a dick and check out her cleavage again as he verified her shirt was back in place. "I was prepared for any possibility," he finally answered since she'd only lifted a brow in response, notable even in the dim lighting. "This is plan B. And plan B involves taking you to a secure location about an hour and a half north of here until we can regroup and reassess what happened."

"And what if someone gets hurt back there? We haven't heard from Jesse, or the others, yet." Her sass was suddenly stamped out by fear. She couldn't lose anyone else in her life, and he could relate to that on many levels.

"Not their first rodeo," he calmly said, knowing Carter could hold down the fort singlehandedly from what he'd seen in the past, so he wasn't concerned.

The guys had all worked as a cohesive unit tonight, which he'd had his reservations about even after two weeks of training, especially in regard to Jack, so maybe there was hope for them yet.

"Your confidence is comforting, I suppose," she returned, sounding skeptical.

"Plus, your boyfriend or friend, whoever he is to you, is John Wick, remember?"

Why did I say that?

"Jesse's my best friend," she quickly answered. "I don't have a boyfriend."

He chuckled. "There's no such thing as men and women being best friends. Single men don't chill with gorgeous, single women without hoping for more."

"You think I'm gorgeous, huh?"

He turned onto a main road, feeling a bit better now that they were out of the woods. Figuratively as well, he hoped. "Yes, ma'am, I do." And from what he'd witnessed so far, Savanna was much more than gorgeous. She was smart and sassy and able to hold her own in a room full of testosterone-fueled men. She also kept a level head during a crisis. Not many people would have been able to handle what she'd been through in the past twenty-four hours. So no, it wasn't just her beauty that made it difficult for him to collect his thoughts every time she stood close to him or stared into his eyes as if trying to read him like a novel.

He opted to keep his gaze forward, worried that if he were to look at her, she'd see right through him yet again. She'd know that there was no way in hell he could ever be friends with a woman like her. Because he would constantly be angling to take her to bed. Sex was all he could offer any woman right now, and although he didn't know Savanna, he knew she deserved more than that from a man. A hell of a lot more.

"Jesse has the hots for A.J.'s sister, Ella. Remember their little showdown in the kitchen tonight?"

Ah, right. He'd almost forgotten about that, what with so much having happened since then.

"And we *really* are only friends. Not all men need to bang every woman they know. Sounds like a *you* problem."

He lightly laughed. "Mm-hm, sure."

"Besides, pretty much everyone in the state of Alabama has labeled me as off-limits because of, well, you know."

"Pretty much means not everyone. Who's the exception?"

The words rolled off his tongue a bit too easily, and it had him wondering why he was having this conversation because it was clearly none of his business. "Shep, huh?" he asked, a moment later, even though he'd tried to stop himself from speaking his thoughts, but it was like trying to stop a bullet from traveling down the barrel of a rifle after squeezing the trigger. Not gonna fucking happen. "I reckon A.J. isn't in the habit of punching his brother for no good reason." Griffin had slipped deeper into his Southern accent that time. After twenty-plus years spinning up on countless ops and over five deployments overseas, his accent had a tendency to come and go depending on his mood or level of fatigue.

"Anyways," Savanna dragged out, elongating the syllables in a way that his tired brain found suggestive. Like *anyways*, let's pull over and practice making that baby that's supposed to be on board.

Sex on the brain after shooting a man in the head seven minutes ago. Sounds about right.

"Did you have to shoot the man in the head? You couldn't have gone for a shoulder?" Had she read his mind?

She massaged her right hand, the one he'd been gripping on to for dear life to keep her running at his pace when they'd torn across the property.

"It was us or him. Rules of engagement, in this case, should help you sleep at night. I'm not some stone-cold killer." And why did it bother him so much that she might think that?

"I'm not questioning why you shot him. He did have a gun aimed at us. And," she continued, a touch of surrender in her tone, "if you'd only wounded him, he may have had a chance to kill Jesse or the others. I, um, guess I get it," she whispered as though getting it, but not liking that fact. "I've now seen three people killed before my eyes."

Three?

Fuck.

Her husband. She *had* witnessed that moment.

"You got your Stateside kill," she added lightly, back to relying on humor to deflect and distract from reality, just like him.

He turned onto another road, allowing the GPS on his phone mounted to the dash to guide them, then he peeked at her. "Is it working?"

"Is *what* working?"

"The humor? Is it helping you?"

Her shoulders fell. "I don't know what I'm doing, to be honest. I just need to know everyone is okay back there."

"They're fine."

"Yeah, and I overheard Carter before we left." She looked away from him, so he reset his attention on the road, where it should be. "Eight men stormed Jesse's property. *Eight* freaking men were sent to get me. This time, with weapons. It doesn't make sense. Who am I to these people?"

"If this is connected to Nick, I'm gonna assume he stepped into some deep shit, and you're somehow getting pulled into the fray," Griffin answered as honestly as he could. It was also the only thing that made sense.

He was about to toss around a few more theories, but the incoming call from Carter stopped him.

He grabbed the phone and brought it to his ear instead of answering on speakerphone. "Go ahead," he said straight away.

"The house is secure. None of our people were hurt," Carter shared the good news. "Six tangos, including the one you shot, are down. A bloodbath that I don't think the sheriff will be able to cover up this time."

"Everyone is okay," he mouthed to Savanna, watching as she closed her eyes and brought both hands over her heart.

"We've got two survivors we kept alive for questioning," Carter went on. "We need to move to a new location before the local PD, FBI, or whoever the hell else decides to make an appearance shows up."

"Where are you taking them?" Griffin asked.

"Too risky to bring them to where you're headed, so we're working on securing a site now. You think you can handle her on your own for a night or two while we figure out what the fuck is going on in this small town?"

Griffin stole a look at the woman he'd have to "handle," knowing keeping her safe wouldn't be a problem. But the strange gut-punch reaction to her whenever she looked into his eyes or even when her arm innocently touched him was a curveball he hadn't prepared for, and he did his best to prepare for everything.

"Yeah, I'm good. I'll let you know when we arrive."

"I'm calling in some of our other guys to put together a five-man team for additional protective detail for the town. We don't need more tangos showing up and attacking one of Savanna's friends to try and draw her out. Between the five of them, the sheriff, and the rest of A.J.'s family, we should have everyone covered."

Contingencies for their contingencies. Better to be prepared. "Roger that." Griffin ended the call and placed the phone back on the mount, explained what Carter had said, then added, "We won't be able to keep this mess from the police. And that many bodies will draw out the Feds. They're leaving Jesse's soon with the two guys they kept alive to question."

"A.J.'s wife is FBI. Well, she teaches at Quantico now,

but maybe she can help cover our tracks?" She paused for a moment. "Do we turn back or keep going?"

His body went stiff at the feel of her hand on his forearm, and he slowed the vehicle a bit to take a second to peer at her. "For now, we stick to the plan," he said before swallowing. "It's just you and me."

* * *

"I wish I could at least talk to Ella or Jesse. I hate not being in contact with them." Savanna drummed her fingers on her thighs as they neared their final destination for the evening. She hadn't spoken much during the remainder of the trip, which suited him just fine. "And it feels weird being without my phone."

"We couldn't take the risk that someone might use it to track you. Also, someone may be listening in on your friends' calls. So, that's out for now too," he calmly explained.

"Where's this place you're taking me?"

"My dad owns a large piece of property he uses for hunting near the Tennessee River. Muscle Shoals is only about fifteen minutes away if we need to go into town, which I'd prefer not to do, but I should probably feed you." He smiled without looking over at her. "Don't worry, the place is heavily fortified and secure."

"Your dad won't be there, I take it?"

Griffin shook his head.

"Why does your dad have a heavily fortified hunting property? What's he afraid of, someone poaching deer on his land before he can get to them?"

"Something like that." He glanced at Savanna to find her eyes focused on the side window, watching the trees blur by in the dark of night.

"My dad was with the 101st Airborne Division," he found himself admitting as if that'd explain why his father had such a secure property. "I was born at Fort Campbell. My mom's water broke at the PX."

Before he looked away, she pivoted to find his eyes as if shocked he'd just shared a page from that closed book he'd claimed to be. "That's the Army base on the Tennessee and Kentucky border, right?"

He nodded, then set both hands on the wheel as he fixed his focus on the road. They were getting close to his old man's place, and he didn't want to miss the turn that wouldn't show up on his GPS.

"So, you joined because of him?" Before he had a chance to consider if he was going to answer, she said, "Never mind. You're not an open book. Forgot."

His shoulders damn near collapsed at the sound of hurt echoing in her tone. "Yeah, I joined because of him. The Army has been my life since I was born, I suppose." He couldn't bring himself to look at her because he was still surprised he'd opened up even the slightest bit.

"I assume he taught you how to shoot?"

"Mm-hm," was all he'd surrender.

The few minutes of silence that followed made him uncomfortable for some reason, and when she piped up with her next question, he realized why. She was going to ask him something he wasn't sure he was prepared to answer. "Killing someone so quickly like you did earlier, and how Jesse did . . . I guess I just don't understand—"

"How we do it and stay sane?" he finished for her, his stomach knotting. "Not all of us do, by the way." *Why did my voice just break?* "A lot of guys survive on a combination of Ambien, alcohol, Prozac, Red Bull, and dark humor to deal with deployment. To cope with the horrors of war."

"And did you? Is that how you survived?"

Damn it, it was too late in the day for this conversation, and also, not one he ever wanted to have. "I have my own ways of dealing."

"It's okay," she said, her voice now soft, almost tender. "I shouldn't have even asked. Marcus never wanted to talk about any of this, either. Jesse's the same. A.J. too."

That knot in his stomach loosened a bit with relief that she seemed to be wrapping up the topic. So why he opted to remark, "Dehumanize the enemy," was beyond him. "The guy I killed tonight wasn't a father. A brother. A son. He wasn't human. That's how I do it. That's the only way I can take a life." He turned left onto the back road that'd lead them to his father's land. "Yes, it's a them-or-me, or a them-or-my-friend kind of thing first and foremost. But you also have to train your mind to believe that they're evil. Not human. It will fuck with your head and your emotions if you don't."

"I'm sorry you had to do that for me tonight. And thank you for sharing. That's not easy, I know."

Griffin's chest grew tight when she gently placed a hand on his thigh, the warmth of her touch passing through his jeans.

And she did know because she'd been married to a SEAL and had witnessed him render the ultimate sacrifice—his life. Savanna knew more than she should ever know about such things.

"It's okay," Griffin lied, then reset his focus on the road ahead. He didn't want to trigger one of the security measures his overly paranoid father had installed. Though tonight he was grateful for his father's paranoia because they'd have a safe haven. "We're here," he announced a minute later when he stopped outside the gated entrance. "Stay in the van."

He hopped out quickly and strode over to the security

panel off to the side of the main gate, but at the sound of the passenger door opening, he quickly spun around.

"Stay in the car." He lifted a hand in the air, redirecting her to get back.

"Why?"

"This fence," he said, pointing to what amounted to an eight-foot-tall border wall topped with barbed wire, "will shock the fuck out of you if you touch it. Not to mention all the other shit my dad has booby-trapped out here to catch anyone trying to breach his property."

"Wow, so he really took security to the next level, huh?"

You have no idea. He twirled a finger for her to get back in the vehicle, then opened the small panel and set his palm on the scanner. Next came the eight-digit passcode. And lastly, a key.

Overprotective or crazy? Maybe both.

"I guess we will be safe here," she said once he was back inside the van and the electronic gate parted for them.

"Hopefully," was the best answer he could provide because, at this point in time, they didn't know exactly what they were up against or who was hunting her down.

"Wow," she said as they neared the two-story lodge that sat at the highest point on the four and a half acres of property. The log home with a green roof also had a matching guesthouse out back that could be used as a temporary command center in case the rest of the team decided to show up to work from there. "I mean no disrespect, but how does someone in the Army afford all of this?"

"My mom's money," was all he'd said on that matter, and then he parked inside the attached three-car garage between a black Jeep and black GMC Sierra truck.

He went around to the back of the van once the garage door closed and opened the trunk.

"Well, lucky you, you have stuff," Savanna said with a smirk as he grabbed the duffel bag.

Griffin smiled and motioned for her to head inside. "Your stuff is in here too, Sugar." He resisted a wink, remembering her comment earlier about snipers.

He *was* a sniper, but he didn't need to play into any stereotypes.

"When did you have a chance to get clothes for me?" She didn't move as directed and planted her hands on her hips.

It was late. They'd been through a lot. And yet, this woman with the most beautiful hazel eyes he'd ever seen hadn't lost the fire in her belly.

"When we were at your townhouse tonight, I grabbed some stuff from your room in case we had to implement plan B. Jesse put the bag in the van when we got back to his place afterward," he explained as if it were no big deal, and why would it be?

Her plump lips parted as her eyes fell to the bag he had clutched in one hand. "Underwear too?"

"Um, well, yeah. I assumed you'd want clean drawers."

"My drawers," she said, exaggerating her Southern accent so that it sounded more like "draws," "are not for you to be touching." And damn it, just like the last time she employed that technique, his dick, who he'd just gotten down for a nap, woke up yet again.

"Fine. I can toss them," he teased, then started to turn, but she snatched his forearm, igniting a rush of heat that traveled up to his shoulder.

When they both looked down to where she was touching him, Savanna gasped softly and yanked her hand away like she'd been burned. "Just give me the bag."

"So you can touch *my* drawers?"

Her lips twitched as she narrowed her eyes, and Griffin

knew she was biting back a quip. But she turned and climbed the three steps that led to the door, and he brushed past her to unlock it.

"Plenty of bedrooms, I assume?" She wandered through the large living room once he'd turned on the lights and started for the big fireplace that was the focal point of the open space. "Just glad this isn't a one-bed trope."

"What's a one-bed trope?" he asked after locking up and turning the security system back on.

A touch of red traveled up her cheeks as he set down their bag and approached her.

"Forget what I said," she whispered shyly.

But how could he, especially when it caused her to blush? He folded his arms across his chest and raised his eyebrows in expectation.

"Fine." She licked her lips, and he couldn't stop the low groan that escaped his throat. "I love to read romance novels, and in a lot of the books, well . . ." Her cute stammer and the way she'd wet her lips were distracting as hell. "The hero and heroine in the books often end up having to share a bed, and you know . . ."

He did know, but he found himself wanting her to spell it out for him. Such a bad idea. "No, I, uhm don't." He feigned ignorance, but his husky tone may have given him away as he stalked closer, fighting the urge to wrap a hand behind her back and draw her tight to his body.

"The dance with no pants," she stage-whispered, eyes wide as if willing him to understand without having to actually say it. When he didn't respond, her cheeks flushed again. "You know, to 'share body heat,'" she said while using air quotes. He cocked his head to the side as if he still didn't understand, though if she kept on with the double entendres, he probably wouldn't be able to keep a straight face for much longer. "Sex," Savanna finally blurted, lifting a hand up and under her hair and clasping the back of her neck. "They usually have sex."

He dipped his chin to take in the sight of this woman who'd kept him on his toes from the moment they'd met.

Savanna's straight eyebrows were darker than her hair, which meant she was most likely not a natural blonde, but it suited her. The honey-colored waves framed her oval face, with its prominent cheekbones, delicate nose, and full lips enhanced by slight laugh lines, even when she wasn't smiling. And right now, those high cheekbones were stained pink with embarrassment. She was absolutely stunning.

"Do you think romance novels set unrealistic expectations?" Griffin asked, seemingly out of the blue, and hoped he didn't insult her with the question, but he had his reasons.

She sucked in a shaky breath before replying, "You don't approve of them?"

"I didn't say that. But the idea of a happily-ever-after is what I find unrealistic. When in life do we get that guarantee?" His chest squeezed as he stared into the eyes of the woman he knew understood that reality far too well.

"You know a thing or two about romance novels," she commented. "But that happily-ever-after is one reason why I read them. Because you're right, life doesn't offer many guarantees, and I need that escape. I need to know that the guy she falls in love with won't . . . die."

He leaned into her, unable to stop himself despite the mess of awful that had gone down tonight—beginning with her confession about the money and ending with them hightailing it up to his dad's place. And he couldn't forget her seeing him shoot a man in the face. He desperately wanted to hold on to her. To take away her pain, which wasn't in his job description.

She faltered, nearly losing her balance, but he quickly caught her by the hips to keep her from careening into the fireplace. "But I am, um, a sucker for a good one-bed scene."

"Not in real life, though?"

Savanna's efforts to distract herself were working on him as well. His responsibilities were a million miles away while her gaze was set on his mouth, and his hands were on her body.

She answered with a shake of her head, but when she looked up, her hooded eyes said otherwise. "No, I-I don't want that."

He brought his mouth dangerously close to her full, pink lips and whispered, "So we're both relieved that there's more than one bed here?" With every word he spoke, Griffin's body grew tenser, which was ridiculous. But his hands were still on her body, and she didn't seem to be going anywhere.

"Right. Very relieved." Her eyes fell closed for a second, and his attention skated down to her breasts lifting and falling with shallow, choppy breaths.

The bra was nude. And lacy. His imagination had been accurate earlier.

He was also an asshole for checking her out. But this tempting woman was practically right against his body, and she was beautiful. And smelled like a mix of cookies and pumpkin spice. He wanted to eat her right the fuck up, starting between her thighs.

Let. Her. Go. He swore he heard another man's voice in his head. It definitely wasn't his own. Marcus? He quickly released her and backed up, a reminder that the author of this woman's story had stolen the man she'd loved, and Griffin wasn't sure if anyone would ever be able to replace him.

When she opened her eyes and shot him a haunted, mystified look, as if she'd heard that voice, too, he forced out in a throaty voice, "I'll show you to your room."

CHAPTER EIGHT

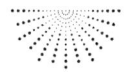

Savanna stared at the pile of clean clothes stacked on the leather armchair by the bed. She was in the second-floor guest room where Griffin had deposited her last night. Or, more accurately, today, since it had been one in the morning. She'd immediately taken advantage of the en suite bathroom and stood under the waterfall of a hot shower until she'd almost fallen asleep standing up. Yesterday had been one of the longest days of her life, and she'd not only needed to decompress, but she'd also wanted to wash away the dried sweat and dirt clinging to her skin from literally running for her life, as well as the stench of death in her nose.

Just the thought of Griffin rifling through her bedroom, picking out those clothes, including her underwear and bras, was enough to make her blush all over again. And why was she always blushing around the man? She reached for the plain white cotton panties and matching bra and tossed them onto the bed beside the jeans and white V-neck she'd already picked out.

For some reason, he'd opted to pack only her boring

undergarments, bypassing all of the lace and frilly stuff sitting right alongside it in her top drawer back at home.

The clock on the nightstand indicated it was only seven in the morning, so she wasn't sure if Griffin was awake yet, but she'd barely slept and was hoping Jesse or Griffin's teammates would have some news soon. How long would she have to stay in this romantic custom log house with the sexy man?

She peeled off the oversized tee she'd slept in, the one that Marcus had bought her on one of their trips to Myrtle Beach years ago, her thoughts slipping back to last night and the moment she and Griffin shared by the fireplace. And it was definitely a "moment." The way his firm hands had grasped her hips while he'd stared deep into her eyes had stirred something she hadn't felt in years. But then he released her like he'd been burned, and the "moment" shattered.

Probably for the best. He reminded her too much of Marcus. The dark hair with a hint of a wave. The golden skin and deep, soul-piercing brown eyes.

However, unlike Marcus, Griffin gave off a "wicked" and "dangerous" vibe. That, along with his rugged looks, shockingly hard jawline, and amazing body, was proof positive that the heroes in romance novels did exist in real life. But he was dangerous, and Savanna felt that in her bones. Not a danger to her physically, unless you considered a broken heart a physical injury. No, he would protect her with his own life, of that she was sure. Her heart though . . .? They'd been together for less than twenty-four hours, and the magnetic pull he had on her already, even if it was purely sexual, was scary.

"Forget it," she mumbled under her breath while stepping

into her jeans. *Forget the way he looked at me. How it felt to have a man touch me.*

She went through the motions of getting dressed, still in somewhat of a daze, then slipped into her ankle boots, the ones she'd worn as she tore through the yard at Jesse's last night, fearing for her life.

The smell of coffee was the first thing to hit her once in the hall. Much better than the stench of death, that was for sure.

Each step Savanna took in her boots announced her descent on the stairs like a hammer hitting wood, so she wasn't surprised to see Griffin waiting for her.

Gripping the railing for support, she stopped three steps from the bottom, her mission to seek out coffee forgotten as she took in every inch of the man standing before her.

The first thing she noticed was that he was shirtless. That alone almost did her in. The next thing she noticed was that he was glistening with sweat, causing his dark brown hair to appear almost black, the messy strands going every which way. Black running shoes and loose-fitting black gym shorts hanging on his hips completed the look.

The biggest gulp of her life followed as she tracked the ridges of muscles on his core. The hard, deep cut of his abdominal wall was most definitely romance-novel-worthy. And the partial sleeve of black ink from his left shoulder to elbow had her knees going weak like she was Belle the moment she witnessed the Beast become a man for the first time.

Savanna didn't even like tattoos, despite Marcus having had them, *but wow, oh wow, oh wow*. Why did the ink on Griffin's body make him even more attractive to her now? God, the man looked lethal.

Yup. Dangerous, she reminded herself, eyeing the black

tattoo of the large bird feathers, or maybe angel wings, at the top of his shoulder.

He was holding a dark green mug in one hand, and the lip of the cup hovered near his mouth as he studied her before taking a sip. And, of course, his bicep bulged in the process, the ink-free one.

"You just finish working out?"

He lowered the mug and advanced across the living room, skirting the brown leather couch to get to where she remained glued to the step. "If you want to call it that, sure. I did a perimeter sweep of the property and checked to ensure all security measures were in working order."

He smiled, flashing her his pearly whites. Yeah, they were always pearly and white in books, right? *You're losing it, Savanna,* her inner voice chided.

"Over four acres, so despite the cool morning, I got hot."

Not to point out the obvious, but you were already hot. Savanna lifted the hand not clutching the banister and feathered her fingers across her collarbone as she took in all that hotness.

"I didn't expect you to be up so early." He glanced at the thick black watch on his wrist she hadn't noticed until then. "There's coffee. Folgers. Not exactly the fancy stuff you're probably used to. No food, though."

She needed to say something soon. How long could she gawk at this beautiful man? No, beautiful wasn't the right word. Beautiful wouldn't call forth the achy, needy tingles going on down south, between her thighs. It was the chiseled body and handsome face and those intense brown eyes that made everything inside her come alive. *Just a body. Just a face. I can do this.*

Griffin stilled at the bottom of the staircase, dark eyes

steady on hers as he held the mug away from his mouth. "You okay?"

"I just, um . . ." She trailed off, not knowing what in the world to say. He had actually made her speechless.

This man needs to quit screwing with my head and get down to the business of screwing my . . . Oh my God, what in the hell was going on with her? *Just a body. Just a face. I can do this,* she replayed what might need to be her new mantra if he came near her shirtless ever again.

"Savanna?" His dark brows tightened with worry.

"Fine. I'm fine," she answered, relieved she'd managed to finally speak. "Just hungry. Didn't sleep much."

"Yeah, I was thinking we could grab some food at the store and cook here. I'd rather not take you into town, but I don't want to leave you alone either."

"Any word from the guys?" There. She'd said something important. Whoop, she felt like she just earned herself a triple word score playing Scrabble.

"Yeah, Carter is still working on getting the two men to talk, and Oliver is going through your, um, husband's boxes to see if he can find anything about Nick." Griffin's eyes briefly lifted to the rustic beams overhead as if searching for Marcus there. "Is it okay if Oliver reads the letters Marcus wrote to Nick?"

The letters.

She'd never read them, but . . .

"If Oliver thinks it'll help, then yes." What choice did they have? People were potentially at risk because of her.

"Gray and Jack are focused on digging into Nick's whereabouts over the past few years, and if anyone he met in prison might connect to him now. Or to what's happening to you," he added when returning his focus to her face.

"Have the Feds arrived at Jesse's? How's Jesse handling all of this?"

"Jesse had Beckett make some calls last night, just to be proactive about it. Beckett didn't mention what happened at your townhouse or that you were ever at Jesse's home. We'd prefer to keep your name out of this."

Her body relaxed a bit. "Makes sense, I suppose."

He nodded, his mouth drawing into a tight line as his gaze briefly took a detour to the V of her shirt. "I'd rather go to the store now while it's still early. Less chance of anyone seeing us." His eyes found hers again. "I'll just take a quick shower." He cocked his head, a request to navigate around her on the step.

"Right. Sorry." She turned sideways instead of doing the rational thing and just going down the last three steps, so in order to pass her, Griffin had to step sideways as well.

His sweaty, towering frame now faced her, his sculpted chest right at eye-level. She got caught up in the slight dusting of dark hair on his chest and glanced down to the waistband of his shorts, wondering if that hair continued on down to . . .

But to her credit, as much as she wanted to reach out and touch him as he maneuvered around her, she refrained. *Good girl.*

"Be down soon."

Last night he'd told her that the master was downstairs, but he preferred not to sleep in his dad's bed. She hadn't exactly wanted to, either, which was for the best considering she'd had a few naughty runaway thoughts about Griffin while she'd tossed and turned last night.

Once he was out of sight, she decided to check out the rest of the downstairs. She preferred to grab different coffee when they went shopping, so she'd hold off on the cup of java for now. She was a bit of a snob when it came to espresso.

The blinds covering the big windows in the living room were slanted to let in some natural light, enough for her to get a good look at the room—the furnishings were stylish but looked comfortable, and the home was spacious. It was either relatively new or recently renovated. She took a left down the second hall, remembering Griffin had said the first hall off to the left of the kitchen only led to the master bedroom.

Ella had always said Savanna was nosy, but she considered herself merely curious. Upon opening the first door in the hallway, she discovered a cozy office, and the blinds were open to reveal a beautiful view of the foothills off in the distance.

She was about to pull the door closed when a bookshelf on one wall caught her attention. The chance she'd find something to read was a long shot, but why not try?

Military history books and autobiographies lined the first few shelves, and she smoothed her hands over the spines. It was somehow comforting to know his dad enjoyed reading, even if his choice of reading material would be more useful to her as a sleep aid.

But then, jackpot. Was she hallucinating?

Savanna crouched for a better look at the bottom shelf of familiar-looking paperback novels. Closer inspection revealed they were all written by her favorite historical romance author. She carefully extracted the first book on the shelf and stood. Ironically, this particular one had popped her historical romance cherry, and she'd loved them ever since. After she'd devoured every book in the author's backlist, she'd binged a dozen other authors who wrote in the same genre. At the time, Marcus had been deployed, and it was their first year of marriage. These books kept her sane. They transported her to another time, another part of the world. The characters became real when she was immersed in their story, and their lives kept her from worrying about her own every second of every hour of each day.

Maybe she could distract herself with a book or two later? Better than being constantly tempted by Griffin and all his sexiness.

"What are you doing?" Griffin's voice had a rough edge to it that she'd yet to hear since they'd met. And damn, the man showered quickly.

Griffin brushed past her and took the book from her hand as though it was a rare first edition, and she was about to dog-ear a page. What was that all about?

He knelt and returned the novel back to its place. "Did you open it?" he asked while rising.

"I'm sorry, what?" She planted her hands on her hips and stared at him in confusion.

His hair was still wet from the shower, and had he even dried his body before pulling on that white polo with his black jeans? The fabric clung to his chest, outlining his muscles like a delicious tease, and it had her forgetting his accusing question and weird behavior for about two seconds.

"Are these books special to your dad? I'm sorry." She turned to the bookshelf, realizing that it appeared his dad owned every single book by that author. Twenty-four, to be exact. Savanna followed her on Instagram and remembered she'd announced last month that she was writing book number twenty-five. "He must be a fan. Or are they your mom's books?" She faced him again, confused once more to see him breathing heavily. "You keep referring to this place as your dad's, so I assumed your mom didn't come here, that she didn't like hunting or something." *But he said it was his mom's money. Hm.*

"They're . . . his," Griffin said hesitantly. "She doesn't come here." His eyes went to the window over the desk. "Not anymore." Tilting his head toward the door, he said, "Can we go?"

Her shoulders collapsed. She hated feeling as though they were having a fight, but that was the vibe she was getting.

"Are you mad at me?"

Griffin raked his fingers through his thick locks a few times before meeting her gaze. "Why on earth would I be mad at you?"

"Because you're Mister Moody now."

The grumpiness slipped away in a second, and one of his handsome smiles replaced the downturned lips. "Mister Moody, huh?"

"Would you prefer I call you Sugar?" she teased, walking toward him, feeling a bit more confident in her ability to behave herself now that he had his shirt on.

"I'd like to see you try," he said darkly.

Her stomach flipped at the provocative way his eyes were eating her up, just daring her to call him Sugar, so he could shut her up by covering her mouth with his. Or put her over his knee. Or something equally naughty.

Maybe she couldn't behave even with his shirt on after all?

"Mm-hm." She smiled. "Roger that." She'd hoped to come across as sassy, but her body was mush with his sexy eyes and smile pointed her way, and so she'd pretty much only whispered the answer.

"Savanna, Savanna, Savanna." Griffin strode over and surprised her by brushing her hair over her left shoulder while staring down at her. "What ever am I going to do with you, Sugar?"

CHAPTER NINE

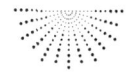

Griffin unpacked the groceries in the kitchen alongside Savanna, his mind replaying their exchange in his father's office an hour ago. So help him, he'd almost pinned her to the wall and kissed that sassy mouth when she'd whispered, *Roger that*.

"You really like this coffee, huh? Bought three bags as if we'll be here for a lot longer than I anticipated."

He gave her a sidelong glance as she held up a black bag of Freedom Fuel dark roast made by Black Rifle Coffee Company, an American flag on the front overlaid with the silhouette of a rifle. "It's strong the way I like my coffee, and it's also a veteran-owned-and-operated company, and I try to support vets whenever possible."

"Oh, I love that." She busied herself with setting out the ingredients she'd insisted on buying during their somewhat rushed shopping trip. "I hope you love my biscuits."

Why did that sound dirty?

He spied her hand hovering over the bag of flour she'd just opened and wondered if she'd had the same thought.

"You don't need to cook for me." He set his palms on the expansive kitchen island and looked over his shoulder at her.

"It's therapeutic and distracting," she reiterated her reason for filling their shopping cart almost to the brim.

For someone whose last two days had been pretty much hell, she in no way appeared as if the weight of the world sat on her shoulders. Griffin figured she'd had less than five hours of sleep, yet her hazel eyes were clear and bright, and her olive skin looked freshly kissed by the sun. And she'd waltzed through the grocery store happily chattering away about baking and ingredients. Savanna seemed surprisingly unphased. Well, for the most part. When he'd unexpectedly greeted her that morning bare-chested, she'd grown quiet and awkward.

He sure as hell hoped she wasn't attracted to him because that would just make his efforts to behave himself a hell of a lot more difficult. But the way she looked at him, touched him . . .

Her eyes were fixed on his hands, so he lowered his focus to see why she was staring. "What?"

"Veiny. Your arms. Hands. Just, um, lots of veins."

He smiled and lifted his eyes to hers. "I feel like veins are vital to life. Am I missing something?"

The adorable smile playing across her lips created an unexpected response inside him. His chest tightened, and he nearly drew a hand there in disbelief.

"Nurses must love you is all I meant."

Are we really talking about nurses and my veins? "I do my best to avoid getting jabbed with needles when possible."

What was she really thinking about?

Maybe he didn't want to know.

The awkward moment disappeared when she began

opening cabinets in search of whatever she needed to bake her biscuits. Once upon a time ago, his mom cooked and baked in this kitchen, so he knew everything she'd need would be there. But where? Hell if he knew. And he was enjoying the view of her bending over and searching. A little too much.

The sight of her heart-shaped ass in those skinny jeans had him turning away and adjusting his crotch.

"You're going to help me, so wash your hands," Savanna announced from behind him.

Crap, had she seen him readjusting his dick in his pants? He quickly turned and smacked right into her, knocking the silver bowl in her hand to the ground. They both froze and watched it do a little spin on the pine floor before simultaneously crouching and reaching for it. Then, in a seemingly choreographed move, they each grabbed on to one side of the bowl as if they both desperately needed the damn thing.

Like a surprised little rabbit, Savanna's eyes grew wide. And when her pink tongue slipped out to wet her lips right before catching the bottom one between her teeth, all he could do was stare.

"Sorry," she mouthed and released the bowl, surrendering to him.

What am I doing? He blinked away the lust-filled haze and stood, setting the bowl on the counter, then he followed her command to wash his hands. He also needed a moment to figure out why his chest hurt again and how this woman managed to constantly throw his focus.

"When was the last time you had homemade biscuits?" She was trying to chase away the awkwardness, and he was grateful.

He dried his hands and swapped places with her at the sink so she could wash up next.

"It's been a long time since I've had homemade anything," he admitted.

"Ah, that's not true." She tossed the towel over one shoulder. "I saw you eat one of my cookies last night."

Fuck, I want to eat a lot more than one of your cookies. And he almost sputtered the dirty thought aloud as his focus dipped to her jeans.

"Um, so, anyways." She was doing it again—dragging out the word in that suggestive way of hers.

When he forced his eyes back up, he saw she was blushing. Had she read his thoughts?

"A few key things when making biscuits. Keep the butter as cold as possible by not overworking the dough, and um." More ums. More pauses. She was getting as worked up as him, wasn't she? "If you touch the dough too much," she said as her eyes fell to his hands, "you'll wind up warming the butter. You know?"

He stepped closer, her breathy tone making him itch to set his palm on her cheek and ask if his hand was too warm. "No, I'm afraid I don't know." Doing his best to behave, he lifted his calloused palms in the air. "I know bullets. Not biscuits."

When her mouth fell open with a gorgeous laugh, his heart thwacked hard in his chest. *So, it's not a heart attack.* It was *her* eliciting the strange sensation he wasn't used to experiencing unless running with a rucksack in the heat under enemy fire.

"Okay, well, I'll teach you how to do it." More color appeared on her cheeks, and her eyebrows rose as her gaze slipped down to the crotch of his jeans. Griffin almost laughed when she slapped a hand over her heart. And, of course, his dick woke up at the sight of *her* checking it out. But was he noticeably hard yet? "Well, you already know how to do *that*. You don't need teaching there. I'm sure."

He frowned, worried he wasn't going to last another hour with this woman without pulling her into his arms. "Maybe I should just let you do it without me?"

"I've been doing it alone for a long time," she said, sounding wistful. But as though realizing what she'd just said, Savanna looked to the floor and turned away. Was she embarrassed she'd steered the conversation from biscuits to sex? And that was the case, right?

Griffin couldn't help himself now. Approaching from behind, he gently gripped the sides of her arms but held back his desire to rest his chin on top of her head and pull her against his chest. "Show me, then," he whispered in her ear. "The biscuits. How to make them. Teach me."

When she twisted around, he dropped his hands from her arms. She was mere inches away, but her head remained down, so he tipped up her chin with his knuckles. Yeah, she was embarrassed, but what he hadn't expected was to find her eyes glossy with tears.

"Okay," she said softly and took one deep pull of air in through her nose before focusing on the counter where she'd laid out everything.

Yeah, they were going to do this. Make biscuits, huh?

But as she spoke, explaining the basics of baking, all he could imagine was how badly he wanted to offer her some relief in another way. Sex was far more therapeutic than baking. Not that he could compare since he didn't bake, but he was confident in his assumption that an orgasm was more beneficial than rolling dough.

"Ready?" She peeked at him with an arched brow.

He hadn't heard a thing she'd said, but he smiled and nodded.

A few minutes later, and with his hands in the dough, doing his best not to heat up the butter, he asked, "Why'd you open the café? You worked for an advertising company for years before that. Was that a childhood dream of yours?"

She took a moment to consider his question, her hands still as her mind worked. "My grandmother and mom loved to bake. It was their dream to have such a place, and although my grandmother is no longer alive, and my mom is busy with her job, I thought it'd be something I could do to honor them, I guess."

"But you love it?"

Savanna fixed her focus back on the task at hand. "I do. And I feel like my grandmother is there with me for every batch of cookies I bake." She smiled as though remembering a special moment with her grandmother. "She was born in Cuba but married an American, and when they tried to flee Cuba in the sixties, he was killed. She became a single mother and raised my mom in America." She paused. "Sorry, not sure why I'm telling you this. You know my story. You had a report on me."

He did know it all, but hearing her share was a lot more impactful than words on a paper. And it crushed him to know she must have also felt the bond with her grandmother over the fact they'd both lost their husbands much too soon.

That was also the blow to the head he needed to remind himself she was off-limits. The woman didn't need any more pain in her life. He'd never allowed himself to get close enough to any women in his past to actually break their hearts, but Savanna was . . . different.

"What's the rest of your ancestral background?" He

needed to fill the uncomfortable space that filled the air, even if it was with small talk.

"My mom said I am a little of this, and a splish-splash of that, and a sprinkle of Irish."

He smiled. "She say what the 'this' or the 'that' was?"

"No, and for some reason, I never asked." She reached for his forearm and set her palm there. "I think it's ready." When she cleared her throat and pulled her hand away, her lashes fluttering quickly, she asked, "What about you?"

He removed his hands from the bowl and washed up. He still couldn't believe he was making biscuits. What would the guys from the Unit say about that? They'd laugh their asses off and pop off a dozen sexual jokes.

"Greek, Brazilian, and also a sprinkle of Irish."

"Ah. So, that's why you maintain such a golden tan year-round like me."

"Checking out my tan, are you?" he teased, then faced her while drying his hands.

Her eyes were level at his chest as if she were thinking back to when he'd been shirtless earlier. Or damn, maybe now she was thinking about the Greek men who tried to come after her. *Hm.* "You okay?"

"Do you have family in Greece?"

Yup, door number two.

He'd rather go back to their sexually charged biscuit conversation, even if that were dangerous, than have her nervous or afraid. He wouldn't let anything happen to her, and he hoped she knew that.

His shoulders dropped. *Why would she? She doesn't actually know me.*

"No, I don't," he finally answered. "Two cousins in Brazil, though."

She returned her attention to the biscuits. "Do you speak Portuguese?"

"Not well." He strode back up next to her and set his clean hands on the counter. "How's your Spanish?"

"I'm fluent." A subtle throat clear from her before she added, "Marcus's parents were Mexican, which I guess you know, but I had always liked the idea we'd be able to raise our kids bilingual. I felt like if they knew Spanish, it'd somehow keep my grandmother's memory alive."

He swallowed the lump down his throat, then resisted the ridiculous impulse to begin speaking Spanish to this woman, one of the four languages he was fluent in.

"I think we're done." She pivoted to the side, nearly bumping into him. The look in her eyes had his chest aching.

Memories of her late husband and her grandmother were competing for her attention, and he could see the pain prominent in the draw of her brows and lines cutting across her forehead.

"So, how'd it feel for your first time?"

He faced her and dragged a hand over his jaw—the weeks' worth of facial hair was in that annoying itchy phase. "I don't think I can answer that until I have a taste." He hadn't meant for his tone to drift back to sexual, but yup, it did.

She visibly swallowed, but before she had a chance to say anything, his phone began ringing. And the sexual tension that had risen between them faded away when he saw it was Carter calling.

"Yeah?" Griffin answered a beat later while leaving the kitchen. "Anything new? Did they talk?"

"Still working on it. They're loyal to their boss, whoever it may be." Carter paused. "But I need you to ask Savanna something. I need you to get the truth from her. I think she's holding back."

Griffin slowly turned to look at the woman who, in his mind, didn't have a dishonest bone in her body. "Why?"

She was drying her hands with a towel when she came into the living room.

"Nick Vasquez was at her house four days ago," Carter dropped the news on him. "And I'd like to know why she didn't tell us and what the hell he was really doing there."

CHAPTER TEN

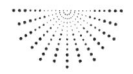

Savanna folded her arms over her chest as Griffin dropped onto the leather couch in front of the fireplace, a scowl on his face. His mood had abruptly changed after the phone call with Carter. A call where Griffin listened while Carter spoke, so Savanna hadn't been privy to even a few hints.

"What is it?" She advanced closer, but he avoided looking her in the eyes and slowly tapped his phone on his knee. What was it he didn't want to tell her?

"Nick Vasquez was at your house four days ago," Griffin finally said, directing his words toward the fireplace.

She faltered a step at not only the revelation but the accusatory tone in his voice. She knew he was implying she'd lied and withheld that bit of information, but she was still hung up on the news that Marcus's brother had been at her house. It had to be a mistake.

"How do you know? Are you sure?" Her arms fell limply to her sides as he turned his attention on her and set his phone on the couch.

"So, you didn't talk to him? See him?"

And there it was. She didn't blame him, she supposed. They were strangers, so why wouldn't he question her? But that didn't make it hurt any less. "No, I would have led with that last night when I showed you the money."

He stood but didn't approach.

"You don't believe me?" She tipped her head and studied him while he quietly observed her, feeling as though she were on the other side of a scope. Was he going to take the shot and trust her?

"I believe you," he said softly, not making her wait long, thank God.

She sidestepped the coffee table but left some space between them. "But Carter thinks I lied."

"He doesn't trust anyone."

She arched a brow and moved within arm's reach. "And do his trust issues extend to you?" When he didn't reply, she tossed out, "I didn't think so." Her gaze slowly moved to his phone. "How do you know Nick was at my place? I don't have security cameras."

"No, but the people across the street from you have a Ring doorbell camera, and our guys hacked into their security footage. Four days ago, at twenty-one hundred hours, a car was rear-ended in front of their house. Nick happened to be at your door and looked back when the incident happened, and his face was captured on camera. Fortunately, your porch light was on. Carter sent me an encrypted shot of him." Griffin grabbed his phone from the couch, and she did her best to process the information while he opened it.

"At nine o'clock, I would have been closing the café."

"Well, he went inside your place. As for how long he was inside, we don't know. The clip of the accident was all we could pull." He handed her the phone, and she stared at the screen while his app worked on whatever decryption thing it was doing. When the photo went from completely pixelated to showcasing a man who looked just like Marcus, she squeezed her eyes closed. Looking at Nick was like looking at Marcus. They were practically twins aside from a few years' difference in age.

"That's him. I mean, I only met him once, but based on the picture, it's definitely Nick." She handed him back the phone and dropped down onto the couch.

"I assume he picked the lock, but I have no clue why he'd break into my house," she shared her thoughts aloud. Her heart was thumping furiously in her chest as she tried to come up with a reason that'd make sense.

"Gray's checking CCTV footage in and around Birmingham to try and pick up where else he may have gone. No record of him on any flights. Pretty sure if he traveled, he used an alias. But if we can pull his photo from an airport security camera the way Gray's sister did for the man Jesse killed, we will," Griffin calmly explained. The tense tone in his voice was gone, which had her believing he really did believe she was telling the truth.

Now she needed him to convince Carter. Surely Jesse would step up to bat for her as well. Unless, of course, he no longer trusted her in light of the fact she'd kept the suitcase of cash a secret for years.

"If someone is looking for Nick, it's possible they managed to track him down to Alabama, and—"

"And to my house. Someone is definitely after him, not me." She popped back up to her feet, unsure if this was good or bad news. A little bit of both?

"My guess is they want to question you to see if you

know where he is. Given the number of men they pulled together and so fast that were sent to Jesse's yesterday, someone wants him pretty damn bad too. Any idea what Nick might have wanted from your house?"

"No," she quickly answered because there was literally nothing he could possibly want from her. Unless it was the money, in which case, how'd he know she hadn't spent it or put it in the bank? Or that it was hidden under her bed?

"Okay, well, if something comes to you, let me know."

Her eyes fell closed as an uncomfortable knot formed in her stomach.

At the feel of his hand beneath her chin, guiding her to look up, she opened her eyes. Griffin's deep brown eyes pulled her in and momentarily calmed her nerves. "We'll figure it out. We'll find out who's after him and why," he reassured her. "It's what we do."

Savanna clenched her hands as worry flowed through her like a tidal wave. "I know Nick is a criminal, and Marcus wanted nothing to do with him, but can you . . . save him too?"

"I'm not sure if he needs saving, but I'll do my best." Griffin let go of her and backed up a step before offering her his phone again. "Why don't you call Jesse. I'm sure you'd like to talk to him as much as he wants to talk to you. He's got a burner right now, and I saved the number in my phone under his name."

She wrapped her hand around the phone and nodded her thanks. "What will you be doing?"

"I'll be out in the garage. When we roll out again, we'll take the truck instead of the minivan. Probably needs an oil change." He peered at her for a moment, brows drawn together in a frown that he quickly replaced with a small smile. "It's my form of therapy, a distraction while we wait for news."

Ah, well, she could understand that. And, oh shoot, they hadn't eaten yet. She needed to put the biscuits in the oven.

"I'll let you know when breakfast is ready."

Griffin nodded and started for the garage.

"Hey, Griffin?" Savanna called out, and he peeked back at her. "Should you tell Carter about our conversation?"

"I have another phone," he answered. "I'll call in the garage." She just hoped Carter believed her innocence in all this and that she was telling the truth.

"Okay, don't get too dirty before you eat." *Oh my God, Savanna, he's not a five-year-old going outside to play.*

This time when he turned to face her, one corner of his mouth turned up in an amused smile. "Kind of hard not to get dirty when changing oil, but for you, I'll do my best."

Once he walked away, she rolled her eyes and palmed her face. Apparently, she was determined to make the man think she was nutty. She sighed and headed into the kitchen, turned on the oven, and then dialed Jesse.

"Savanna." He answered on the third ring, so he must have been expecting her call and from Griffin's number. "I've been worried. Are you okay?"

"I'm safe, but I'm freaking out that Nick was in my house. It's crazy, right?"

"I told Carter you didn't know about that," he quickly said. From the sounds of it, he'd never doubted her, and for that, she was grateful.

"Is he treating you okay?" she heard Shep call out in the background.

"Tell him I'm totally fine, and Griffin is . . ." A gentleman? That didn't sound like the right word to describe the man. She couldn't go with sexy, strong, and a total alpha male, either. Neither Shep nor Jesse needed to know she wanted to jump his bones.

The news about Nick nearly had her forgetting the sexual tension between her and Griffin that could have started a kitchen fire during their baking lesson, but it was front and center in her thoughts now.

Had she really told him, without actually telling him, that she'd been getting herself off because there was no one else to do the job? The words had fallen with such ease from her lips too.

"Hey, you there?" Jesse asked.

Just daydreaming about Griffin pinning me to the counter and screwing my brains out.

She imagined him ordering her to place her palms on the kitchen counter, pressing his hard chest against her back, and whispering "good girl" in her ear before forcefully yanking her jeans down around her ankles. Then he'd run his hand down her spine, pushing her aching breasts against the countertop before . . .

She chewed on her short nail as she considered the multitude of possibilities.

Spank me? Plunge a thick finger inside my pussy to get me ready for his hard cock?

"Savanna?" Jesse. Shit, he was still waiting for her to talk. And now her panties were soaked from her inappropriate fantasy.

Griffin was right. Sex was definitely more therapeutic and a much better distraction than baking. Or changing oil, for that matter. Just *thinking* about sex with Griffin had her momentarily losing all of her worries.

"Sorry. I'm good. He's good. Nice, in fact. We got food this morning. Baked biscuits," she rambled.

"Baked together, huh?" That was a loaded question if

she'd ever heard one. Savanna didn't miss the implication, so she quickly changed the subject.

"How are you holding up? Griffin said no one got hurt last night, or I would have obviously checked in with you sooner. I'm so sorry I ever put you in that position."

"You didn't do this, sweetheart. From the sounds of it, your former brother-in-law is to blame."

In her mind, Marcus would always be her husband, which meant there was nothing "former" about Nick.

Her shoulders fell at that thought. She would never be able to fall in love with another man, would she?

Maybe she could just have meaningless sex. A few one-night stands. That was . . . sad. But what choice did she have?

"I hate that I'm not there with you," Jesse said, followed by Shep repeating the same thing in the background. "We may not know the guy, but before A.J. left, he vouched for Griffin. He said they worked together last summer, and he's a solid sniper."

Sniper? So, she was right. "I'm in good hands, then."

Hands she struggled not to stare at. Hands she wanted to feel touching her . . . everywhere. The roughness of his palms skating over her skin, caressing her breasts, his thick fingers pinching her nipples.

Oh. My. God. And back to horny again. The adrenaline from the last few days must've done something to her libido.

"Are the Feds there?" she whispered around the weird tightness in her throat.

She eyed the mess in the kitchen. She hadn't even prepped the biscuits for the oven, which meant she was out of it for sure.

"They were, but thanks to Gray's government contacts, as well as A.J.'s wife's friends at the Bureau, they didn't give us a hard time. Asked some questions, then bagged the bodies. I think they were instructed not to bother us, but Gray secured photos and fingerprints so we can keep at it."

"'We'? Are you still helping? This isn't your responsibility. I don't want you in any more danger."

"Now that Beckett's daughter and Ella are heavily protected, thanks to Carter's additional reinforcements, I'd like to work the case. Help out."

Work the case? She blinked in confusion. "I know this feels personal for you, but you don't need to do this."

"I want to," he said emphatically. "Don't take this the wrong way, because I'd never want you to be in a mess like this, but I kind of miss doing work that feels, well, important."

Ah, her heart. She understood that feeling, and she also knew it was one reason she was certain Marcus would have served until the day he . . .

He did die, Savanna.

"You're important, regardless of your work. I hope you know that."

"He misses the danger," Shep called out loudly.

"And running into burning buildings is safe, huh?" Jesse countered sarcastically to Shep.

She held the phone to her ear with her shoulder while preparing the biscuits for the oven. "Thank you," she said once the boys were done with their brotherly-like bickering. "Just don't get yourself hurt. I couldn't handle that."

"Roger that. I already got an earful from Rory. She's dying to talk to you, so she's going to buy a disposable phone and call you soon on Griffin's phone."

Jesse's sister, Rory, was another one of her best friends. They'd grown close over the years, despite the fact that, until recently, Rory had been a globe-trotting adventurer. Now she trained military K-9s. "I'd love to talk to her." Maybe Rory could make sense of the insane feelings she found herself having for a man she barely knew.

"We'll call as soon as we know more," Jesse promised.

"Sounds good," she said as she placed the biscuits in the oven and ended the call.

Once she cleaned up the kitchen, Savanna headed for the garage to let Griffin know the food was about ready. She wasn't prepared to see the man standing there shirtless in his black jeans and boots, laces untied, with a streak of oil on his cheek and chest.

Fuck. Me.
No, like literally.
Please.

Her thoughts were blasting on full volume in her head, so loud that she was terrified she'd actually said them.

The sight of him standing there bare chested, tatts on display, all sweat streaked and dirty, clutching a wrench in his veiny hand . . . She was experiencing what the heroines in her historical romance novels referred to as "the vapors." The feeling that at any moment, she might be overcome by the hero's sheer manliness and sexual intensity. Savanna braced herself against the doorframe like a wilting flower, her back holding open the door behind her. How in the world was she expected to do anything with him standing down there looking at her like that?

"You got dirty." Her voice cracked as she forced the words from her dry throat.

He looked down at his chest before his eyes traveled back to meet hers. "From the looks of it, so did you." He tipped his chin toward her shoulder.

"What?" She slanted her attention to where a kitchen towel lay draped over her shoulder, forgotten. She palmed her face with it, assuming there was flour on her cheeks. "Might need another shower." For multiple reasons.

"A shower, huh?" He set down the wrench, or whatever that thing was, and started her way, which had her heart pumping harder in her chest.

He climbed the few steps and braced a palm on the wall alongside where she stood in the doorway like a startled Bambi. Here was her buck.

"Yeah, I, um, feel dirty." Why did every conversation they had somehow go back to a read-between-the-lines sexual one? He made her feel like a good girl turned bad whenever he pointed those dark brown eyes at her. But thoughts of being naughty with this man felt amazing.

"You do, huh?"

She kept the towel clutched tightly in both hands, her back still propping open the door behind her, but at least she was able to stand without support. She may not be a wilting flower anymore, but Griffin's bulging bicep stretched out next to her face wasn't helping matters.

What she wanted to do right now was reenact the fantasy that'd played out in her head earlier and pretend Griffin was one of the characters in her novels, which meant he'd be fictional, and she wouldn't get hurt in the end.

But he is real. That's the problem. Too, too real.
And hard.
Everywhere. So hard.

"You okay, Sugar?" He was testing her limits. Maybe his own too. The way he leaned in close to her ear, his breath floating through the air to send tingling sensations along her neck. "You seem off."

"I should say so, what with everything going on." She tipped her chin and closed her eyes when he skated his mouth so close to her skin she thought he might steal a taste.

"You've held yourself together better than most would in your position." Savanna felt his heat disappear, and when she opened her eyes, he'd pulled away, taking his spine-tingling lips with him.

But oh, he was struggling to restrain himself. His jaw was clenched tight as if he were holding on by a thread right now.

Never in her life had she experienced such raw sexual attraction to someone. It hurt to admit, but this wasn't something she'd even had with Marcus, and if she hung on to that thought for much longer, she'd plunge into a pool of guilt and drown in it.

But right now, she just wanted to be here in the moment with this man. A man that made her feel like he was a book boyfriend come to life. And that happily-ever-afters were possible outside the world of literature.

It hadn't even been twenty-four hours, and she wanted him to remove her clothes with his teeth and make her come. That had to mean something. Was this somehow Newton's Law of Universal Gravitation coming into play? He was a force attracting her to him, and she was growing powerless to stop the pull. After all, how does one fight gravity unless you were designed to soar?

"Savanna?"

"Yes," she breathed out, noticing his bicep flex.

"I'm not romance-novel material, I promise," he murmured darkly as if reading her thoughts and feeling the need to send her a warning—a clear if-you-cross-the-line-with-me-I'll-hurt-you in the tone of his voice. "At best, I could only ever be a side character. Never the lead act."

"Side character?" she whispered, her heart constricting. She could relate to that. "You really think that?" How could this man ever be a side anything, though? And no way would he be the villain. He was a hero, and heroes deserved love.

"It's true." His brows tightened, and he pushed off the wall with his palm and took a step back.

"How do you know?" She stepped away from the door and moved closer to him, so close she had to look up to see him.

His Adam's apple moved as he studied her with a contemplative look in his eyes. "Because it's all I want."

"And what if that's all I want too? To be a side character?" *I'm lying, aren't I?* "Or all that I'm capable of after . . ." For some insane reason, she drew her thumb across the streak of oil on his chest.

He swiftly captured her wrist and lifted her hand between them, and she gulped as she looked up into a pair of dark eyes. "No." He tipped his head to the side and frowned. "You, of all people, deserve a happily-ever-after."

"I thought you didn't believe in those."

His calloused hand was so warm as he gently and carefully held her wrist. "Not for my story, but I sure as hell hope it's true for yours." He released her wrist, turned, and went back down the steps.

"I won't get a second shot at love," she found herself sputtering, and his body went still.

This man had been assigned to keep her safe, and he was still a stranger, but she felt such a deep and unexplainable connection to him.

If this were a movie, Griffin would have received one of Marcus's organs or something in a weird twist of fate after her husband's death, and that would explain her pull to him. But Marcus's body was never found. *So that's not plausible, regardless.* And she really needed to focus on reality.

But still, there had to be an explanation as to why she felt so strongly for a man she hardly knew. Wasn't it worth exploring? Even if it was only between the sheets?

"So, um." She couldn't believe she was going to say this or even had the guts to . . . "If you ever want to try something different for a therapeutic distraction," she rasped around a tight swallow, her stomach aching with the need to be touched by him, "you know where to find me."

CHAPTER ELEVEN

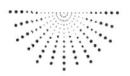

Griffin set his hands on either side of the doorjamb and bowed his head. Then tried to pull himself together and figure out his next steps before he charged into the house and fucked this woman senseless like he was fairly certain she'd invited him to do twenty minutes ago.

Forget the fact that it was highly unprofessional and there were probably rules against it—well, there would be if the company ever became official with an HR department. She was vulnerable. In danger. And a widow. Crossing that line was not only inappropriate, it was also dangerous. He was supposed to be protecting her life, not screwing it up. And despite what she'd said, he knew she wanted to fall in love again. A romance fan who didn't want romance in her own life? He doubted that.

Savanna was most definitely not destined to be a side character. She was the leading lady all the way. It had nothing to do with how gorgeous she was on the outside because he'd seen her heart. She wore it on her sleeve with virtually everything she did. Her concern for her friends, even her shady brother-in-law, was selfless. And it was obvious she put her heart into her baking as well as her café.

But there was also this light around her, and he swore he saw . . .

When he was a Ranger stationed in Iraq, before joining the Unit, an IED killed one of the guys on his team. At the time, Griffin was sure he was hallucinating when a light appeared over his friend's lifeless body like heaven was taking his soul right before Griffin's eyes.

The desert heat. The mourning of his friend. The tragedy of it all. That's how he'd explained what he'd witnessed as merely a hallucination.

But sometimes, when he looked at Savanna, even that first moment when their eyes locked through Jesse's kitchen window, no less, he saw a bright orb of light, or maybe it was called an aura, around her. He didn't always see it, but he knew it was there.

What if it was Marcus surrounding her like a protective shield?

I'm losing my mind again. Too early to drink, and he wouldn't drink on the job, anyway, but he needed to relieve the pressure building in his body before he ignored all the warnings in his head and surrendered to his desires.

Griffin removed his boots and went inside to search her out, to look her in the eyes and tell her flat out that nothing would ever happen between them. Long ago, he'd vowed never to break a woman's heart, and he'd be damned if he reneged on that vow with this particular woman.

He went into the kitchen and found Savanna had set the biscuits on the counter to cool, but she was nowhere in sight. He sure as hell hoped she hadn't gone back to his dad's office for one of the romance books on the shelf. Why'd his father torture himself by keeping those books displayed?

Once upstairs, he walked down the hall to the guest room, prepared to knock on the door, but refrained when he heard a sound inside.

A small cry or whimper had him leaning in and listening. *Holy hell.* He took a deep, bracing breath before raising both hands, now clenched into fists, to gently set them against the door. His entire body was now ramrod straight, including his dick. Savanna was touching herself, wasn't she?

"Griffin," she cried. "Harder." The words were strained as if she were on the brink of an orgasm, but they were quickly followed by a soft "yes" that he barely made out.

She's thinking about me.
Not Marcus.
Me.

He quietly stepped away from the door and ran his hand over the crotch of his jeans as his cock strained against the material.

How was he supposed to look this woman in the eyes and tell her they had to keep their hands off each other after hearing that? How could he face her without giving away the barely controlled desire simmering in his veins with all of the things he wanted to do to her? Harder? Yeah, he could give it to her any way she wanted and then some.

He walked down the hall to his own room, locked the door, and quickly removed his jeans and briefs. Then he went directly to the bathroom, climbed into the shower, and cranked on the water. He didn't even care that the water started out ice cold because if he didn't release this pent-up desire fast, he was going to do something dangerous. Or stupid. Probably both.

He took hold of his cock, imagining it was her hand instead that wrapped around him, brushing her thumb through the precum on his crown, punishing him with slow, gentle strokes before sinking to her knees and taking him between her lush lips. Her warm, wet tongue circling his hard shaft while she looked up at him with those hazel eyes . . . perfection.

Griffin. Harder. Yes. Her words unfolded in his mind once again as he stroked himself, imagining her taking him deep as he thrust into that wicked mouth of hers. As he fucked the sass out of her. But who was he kidding, he loved that sass and would want it back.

He slammed one hand onto the tiled wall inside the small tub where he stood, the water raining down over him, and bit down on his back teeth as he jerked and came hard. The relief of it soothed the ache in his chest—a hell of a lot more therapeutic than baking or changing oil.

But he wanted that relief with her. With the woman he'd just told himself he couldn't have.

He shook his head, angry for reasons he wasn't even sure he understood, but the tension was already building inside of him at the fact he knew the longer they were stuck together, the harder it'd be for him to behave. To not seek her out, as she'd all but requested of him, so she wouldn't have to "go it alone" anymore like she said she'd done for a long time.

Shower finished, Griffin stood at the sink and swiped the steam from the mirror to find his eyes. "No," he ordered himself. "Don't do it." *She's still married in her heart.* He'd have to keep reminding himself of that. Some-fucking-how.

He put on a clean, white button-up shirt and new jeans before starting for the stairs, hoping she was still in her room, so he didn't have to face her quite yet, but her door was open as he passed, and he smelled a fresh brew of coffee.

Savanna clocked him the moment he rounded the corner of the kitchen, and a blush immediately crawled up her golden skin. "You showered." Her attention skated over his body for a moment, and was she remembering how she'd touched herself while thinking of him not too long ago?

Because now he was, damn it.

"I was dirty, remember?" *And needed to get off after I heard you moan my name.*

"Right." She lifted a biscuit from the platter, one of his mother's favorites from what he remembered, and she started toward him. "Here. Taste yourself." She closed her eyes and scrunched her nose. "I mean, taste your work. You did good."

When her stunning hazel eyes focused back on him, he witnessed her shaky exhale as she extended what felt like a peace offering.

Instead of taking it from her, he leaned in and took a bite. Their gazes locked as she brought her other hand beneath his mouth to catch the falling crumbs. The buttery biscuit nearly dissolved in his mouth, and damn, it was good. "Mm." He smiled and pulled away. If he kept staring into her beautiful eyes, he might not be able to control himself.

"Told you." She handed him the rest of the biscuit before heading back into the kitchen.

He turned away from her, needing to, you know, breathe.

The drapes were open now, showing dark clouds had gathered in the sky. "It's going to storm."

"Yeah, that came out of nowhere." She joined him where he now stood by the window.

"I'll go do another security check before the storm hits. Check all of the sensors and cameras out there," he said after polishing off the rest of the biscuit. "We should hear some news soon. When I spoke to Carter in the garage, he believed he was on the verge of getting intel from the men."

"From what I've heard about Carter, I'm surprised it's taking this long." A small smile touched her mouth for a brief moment.

"Blame your friend's brother, Beckett. Both he and Gray, are schoolboys who keep a rein on Carter's interrogation techniques. They keep checking to make sure the two men still have all their fingers and teeth." He was talking about torture and smiling. *What is wrong with me?*

"So are you naughty like Carter or a schoolboy like Gray?" Savanna's brow arched as if this was another challenge.

"I'm trying to be good," he nearly hissed, knowing damn well she'd just tossed him more sexual innuendo. He'd never had such a problem keeping himself in line before. It was . . . strange. "So, I should probably head outside."

Her lips rolled inward as her attention remained on his mouth for a moment. "Jesse's sister is going to call soon. Mind if I hang on to your phone a bit longer?"

"Sure." He smiled. "I have nothing to hide." He cleared his throat and started past her, and she trailed behind him.

"Does Carter believe me?" Savanna asked as he opened the front door to the sound of the sky beginning to rumble. It was eleven hundred hours, but the dark clouds covering an angry sky made it seem like it was early evening.

"He does. But if you can think of anything that might help, he'd appreciate it. We all would."

She edged closer to him, her arms folded over her chest, and he did his best not to lower his focus to her cleavage now on display. "I just had a thought. Instead of looking for something in my townhouse, what if Nick was hiding something?"

Stepping back inside, Griffin let the door close. "If you're his only family, then yeah, maybe. If Nick has people after him, and he had something he didn't want falling into the wrong hands if he were captured . . ." Griffin let his thoughts trail off as he processed the idea. "That's more likely than him searching for something you'd have, I suppose." His jaw tightened. "But he put you at risk by doing so."

"Maybe he had no choice." She took a tentative step closer. Hope in her eyes that Marcus's brother, the only living family her late husband had, might have turned a leaf. Or, in Savanna's case, turned a page. Sadly, seeing as how Nick had been in and out of prison more than once, and his own brother had refused to forgive him for his lifestyle, Griffin doubted that very much.

Nick jeopardized Savanna's safety by showing up at her house, and as far as Griffin was concerned, there was no coming back from that. Marcus would agree.

"Nick's a thief." Her eyes lifted to the ceiling as if working through her thoughts. "What if he stole something that has these men hunting him down for it?"

"It's possible." He reached for her arm and gently squeezed. "But, Savanna, Nick's not your husband. He's not a hero." She would always be married to Marcus, wouldn't she? He let go of her and shifted back a step, feeling as if he'd crossed the line with a married woman, something he'd never do. "In my eyes, Nick's the villain."

CHAPTER TWELVE

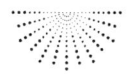

THE SKY OPENED UP AS GRIFFIN WALKED ALONG THE GRAVEL trail leading to the front of the house, but he slowed his pace at the sight of Savanna in one of the two rocking chairs beneath the porch overhang.

He stopped walking altogether and closed his eyes as memories from his teenage years gathered to mind. His mom used to sit in that chair while waiting for his father to return from hunting. She could sit there all day too. A book in one hand, coffee or wine in the other.

Saying his mother loved books was an understatement. And Griffin got the impression that Savanna was much the same.

"Everything okay?"

The gentle timbre of Savanna's voice had him opening his eyes and blinking away the raindrops clinging to his lashes. She was standing at the top of the stairs now, waiting for him.

"While you were on the phone with Rory, one of the sensors was tripped."

"Sensors? What kind of sensor?" She leaned into one of the large columns at her side with folded arms.

"It's basically like a landmine, but instead of exploding when a person or an animal steps on it, it triggers a silent alarm on the security app on my phone," he explained, still standing in the rain for some reason.

It'd only been an hour since he'd shattered her hopes about Nick Vasquez, but he refused to believe there'd be any redemption for that man just because he was her husband's brother.

"Why didn't you tell me?" She pushed away from the column, allowing her arms to fall to her sides.

"Because I checked the cameras on the app, and it was only a deer. I reset the sensor when I made the rounds," he casually said. "That's why I didn't put you in the safe room."

"You mean the panic room?"

"Do I look like someone who panics?" He flashed her a quick smile as he moved to the bottom of the steps. "The room is to keep you safe, it's not for panicking."

"Mm-hm, sure." She closed one eye as if she disagreed on the semantics. "How long are you going to stand there getting wet?"

"Guess I'm getting in my third shower of the day," he tossed out, resisting a playful wink. She didn't need to know why he'd taken that second shower or the fact he'd heard her moan his name.

He worked his fingers down the placket of his soggy shirt, freeing the buttons one by one as he slowly ascended the steps. Once beneath the overhang, he peeled off the shirt and proceeded to wring out the water onto the porch floor.

"Don't forget to do that with your jeans too." There was humor in her tone mingled with . . .

Mingled with? What in the hell, Griff? This woman had him living inside the pages of one of her novels. *Damn, what is she doing to me?*

"I think I'll keep those on," he replied, smiling even though his father's voice had just invaded his head and scolded him to not get his mother's floors dirty.

But they weren't her floors anymore, were they?

He draped the shirt over his shoulder before crouching to unlace his muddy boots and hoped like hell Gray or Carter would call soon and tell them they needed to leave. He wouldn't survive another twenty-four hours with this sweet, sexy dynamo. The sexual tension between them was too strong. It'd been strong from the moment she'd set her hand on his chest in Jesse's kitchen, and it'd only increased since then. He couldn't explain why, but he was drawn to her like no woman he'd ever met.

And that fucking terrified him. Griffin wasn't afraid of much, but this five-foot-six Southern belle with one dimple that popped on her right cheek when she smiled had him on the verge of crossing his self-imposed line.

Married women were off-limits, and Marcus didn't have to be alive for that to hold true. Griffin felt the man's presence as if Savanna shared a heartbeat with him.

Griffin stood and kicked off his boots, noticing Savanna's attention directed skyward as she watched the storm.

"I'd rather you be inside the house. You're at a safe distance from any snipers, but this makes me uneasy." *Everything about you makes me uneasy.* He tossed his shirt on the rocking chair before opening the door for her.

"Okay," she whispered and faced him. "Did Carter or Gray call your other phone while I was talking to Rory?"

"Not yet," he answered once they were inside, and he was grateful his jeans weren't as soaked as his shirt had been so he wouldn't drip water all over the pine floors. The place was renovated about a decade ago, but the property had been a gift to his dad nearly thirty years back.

He closed and locked the door, and when he turned, he found Savanna drumming her fingers at the sides of her jeaned thighs. Her bottom lip planted between her teeth and eyes aimed at the floor.

"What's got you so nervous?" It seemed a bit out of character considering she'd shown the courage and tenacity of a mama bear thus far, so he couldn't help but ask.

"I just want to clear the air."

Crossing his arms over his chest, Griffin watched with amusement as her focus lingered on his damp jeans for a moment, then slid up and stalled on his six-pack. And there was that adorable dimple. He'd bet she was completely unaware of the grin on her face. "What's that, Sugar?"

When her beautiful hazel eyes met his, she softly said, "I wanted to apologize for what I said earlier. It was inappropriate and completely unlike me. I don't know what came over me."

His lips twitched as he resisted a smile. He shouldn't play dumb or prod her to repeat the impetuous invitation she'd offered earlier. He remembered it all too clearly. And it'd be a long damn time, if ever, before he forgot the sound of her crying out his name while she fingered herself to orgasm.

"Can we still be friends? I mean, I know we just met, but I'd like to be friends. You seem nice. And we both have that sprinkle of Irish, so we have that in common. Although based on your name, I'm betting your dad is a bit more than a sprinkle and—"

"Savanna," he cut off her nervous ramble because, for one, it was too cute for him to handle, but more importantly, he needed to crush this friendship idea ASAP.

She swallowed as he relaxed his arms at his sides and took a few steps back.

"I can't be friends with you. I'm sorry."

She frowned, and then her eyes narrowed as if remembering their conversation in the van yesterday. "Because you don't think men and women can be friends without wanting . . ."

"Because one day you'll remarry," he slowly admitted, his pulse picking up. His heart pounding a bit too furiously in his chest like he was betraying the organ that gave him life by turning her down. "And I can't be single and friends with a married woman."

"I'm not going to remarry," she was quick to say before adding, "And do you not trust yourself?"

What could he say to that? "I'd never . . . not with a married woman," was all he managed to work loose from his lips.

"So then, what's the problem?" Her hands landed on her hips, and she stared at him in a way only a Southern woman seemed to know how to do.

He cocked his head and leaned in closer to her, which was most likely a mistake. "Because that wouldn't stop me from wanting to." He needed to add that space back between them before he screwed up.

"Need I remind you, I have male friends, and nothing has happened with them?" She held up her hand and started counting on her fingers. "Jesse. Beckett. A.J.'s other brother, Caleb. Then there's—"

"Shep," Griffin finished for her.

He'd stunned her to silence. Her mouth rounded in surprise, then slammed shut before guilt washed over her face.

He was right. She'd slept with Shep, and why'd that fact infuriate him? An unfamiliar feeling bloomed in his chest. Jealousy?

"Well, I'd like for us to be friends, but I won't push you." Her shoulders fell and she turned.

"Savanna, we just met. You don't know me," Griffin reminded her. "And I don't know you."

"And yet, there's something there. Something I can't put my finger on." She turned only enough to offer her profile. "Maybe it's all in my head. I read too many romance novels." The sadness in her tone was going to gut him.

Because he felt it too. And he was just as clueless as Savanna as to what it was. But it would do neither of them any good if he admitted that.

"I'm confusing my situation with the plot of some romantic suspense novel. You know, where the guy rescues her, and they . . ."

Fall in love? Fuck? He couldn't take this.

"End up having sex," she said. "You know, the one-bed trope. Or the fake couple sharing a hotel room. Or stranded-in-a-romantic-cabin-in-the-woods sort of situation."

"Cabin, huh?" he found himself saying under his breath.

"I'm sorry. I've been living inside the pages of books for a long time." She fully faced him, and the sadness in her voice was now also reflected in her eyes. "I mean, there's nothing wrong with books. They're my escape. Sometimes they're the only things that help me get through the hard days when the real world feels impossibly difficult."

He tipped his head slightly to the side as he observed her and fought the urge to wrap his arms around her, to be the one to help her escape her pain.

"What would happen in the cabin? In the book, I mean. What would happen once they were alone together?" He'd officially lost his damn mind, but he couldn't prevent the questions from tumbling from his mouth.

Savanna looked into his eyes, her brows drawn together,

fists clenched at her sides as if she were channeling restraint the same as him. "Um. They'd argue a few times to heighten the tension. Have some back-and-forth sexually charged banter." A hard swallow followed, and she wet her lips. "Then he'd lose his control. He'd pin her to"—she glanced off to her left to the wall by the door—"that wall, and he'd touch her. Run his hand beneath her shirt and palm her breast. Take her lip into his mouth and gently bite." She was getting breathless as she spoke, and he remained frozen in place and riveted to her every word. "He'd kiss her. Maybe pin her hands over her head. Link her wrists together with one hand as he touched her pu . . ."

She stopped talking as if her throat had become parched, and she'd lost her ability to finish.

"Savanna?" he said quietly.

"Yeah?" she mouthed, her tits lifting and falling with a deep breath.

"Are you wet?" His voice came out in a rasp.

Her eyes widened a little, then she pressed her lips together in a tight line and nodded.

"Good." Griffin erased the space between them and backed her against that exact wall she'd peered at, then captured both her wrists in one swift movement, just as she'd described, and brought them over her head. "But I need proof," he said while holding her steady, his eyes fixed on hers. Intense desire burned heavily between them, and nothing, either in this world or the next, could stop him from doing what he mapped out in his head.

He leaned in, captured her lip, and sucked it as his free hand traveled beneath her tee, tugging down the cup of her bra and palming her perfect breast. She whimpered as he pinched her nipple before he released her lip to slant his mouth over hers.

He was the one groaning now as their breaths mingled and his tongue met hers. He lost hold of her wrists, finding himself coming undone. From just a kiss.

God, I am so fucked.

The feel of her fingernails biting into his back as she gripped him tighter drew out a groan from deep within his chest. Did she have any idea what she was doing to him? Melting at his touch and grinding her needy little pussy against his rock-hard cock? He released her tit, needing to see just how wet she was for him.

He quickly undid the button of her jeans and yanked down the zipper, sliding his hand against the plain cotton panties he'd picked out the night before and gripping her hip in a possessive hold.

"Why'd you choose boring underwear?" she asked between kisses.

"I think you know."

"Even last night, you knew you wanted me?"

He pulled his face back to find her eyes for a moment, breaking their mouths in the process. "Even last night," he admitted before seeking her tongue again. He'd never craved someone so much in his life.

"Touch me," she begged. "Please."

And that was all he needed to hear to comply with the order. He dipped his hand beneath the last layer of fabric and over the smooth V between her thighs, and . . . "You're so wet," he said against her mouth, his cock growing painfully hard at how slick his two fingers were from touching her.

"Griffin," she cried out, and hearing his name was all the ammunition he needed to keep going, to get her off and watch her fall to pieces in his arms as she held on to him like a lifeline.

She rocked herself against his palm, willing him to give

her the pleasure she so desperately craved. Only when her gasps and moans turned into whimpers of frustration did he sink two fingers deep inside her, working them in tandem with the pad of his thumb on her clit.

"Don't stop," she hissed before cupping the nape of his neck and sinking her teeth into his lip as she came for him. And damn, did this woman come, squeezing his fingers like a fucking vise. She released his lip and tipped her head back against the wall as her breathy, freeing moan danced across his skin. "Oh my God," she said when her body relaxed. And then he felt her hand slide down his overly heated skin to the fly of his jeans, and now it was him biting back a moan as she brought her lips to his ear and said, "I—"

But before she could finish her thought, a flash of lightning followed by the crack of thunder made her flinch and let go of her words.

A message from God? Griffin frowned. From Marcus?

Probably both because of how bad I just messed up.

The disposable phone in his pocket began vibrating, causing her to jump yet again.

"They're calling." His voice came out gruff and angry. Angry with himself, not Savanna, and yet he still couldn't take his eyes off her swollen lips. God, he wanted to part them with his tongue and taste her again. *Shit.*

"Maybe they know something." Savanna's words roused him from the daze he'd fallen into. He was on a job. And she was the job, wasn't she?

He stepped back and retrieved his phone, mentally chastising himself yet again as he focused a little too hard on her exposed flesh as she straightened her clothes.

"Yeah?" he said after placing Gray on speakerphone.

"The men refuse to give up the name of their boss, but they confirmed Nick worked on their team before he betrayed them. And they're after something Nick has that he was supposed to turn over. But without crossing the line and torturing them, I don't think we can get them to say more," Gray shared. "Still working on their real identities, but I'm assuming they're also Greek."

And for some reason, Savanna, with her big heart, looked like she'd eaten something sour and winced. She was still having a hard time believing a criminal would associate with . . . well, criminals.

"They did say they believe Savanna is the way to get to Nick," Gray added.

"So, they weren't in her house to see if Nick hid that 'something' there?" Griffin asked.

"They didn't say, but it's doubtful, or they'd have sent more men back to her townhouse to tear the place up, and they came for her at Jesse's instead. But . . ."

Damn, Griffin hated that word. It rarely led to anything good.

"They said they're not the only ones after Nick, which means more people will come for Savanna," Gray finished.

More people after this woman?

Savanna's hand covered her mouth as her chest lifted and fell with nervous breaths. How had they gone from an orgasm just minutes ago to this?

"I'm sure Nick came to my house for a reason, and I'm also sure it wasn't to paint a target on my head."

"And yet, your neighbor's Ring cam clocked him going in the front door," Gray stated as though maybe Nick had purposefully involved Savanna.

"You still haven't found him on any local CCTV footage, right? It's possible he didn't anticipate the camera across the street, nor would he have factored in something as random as the accident that happened at that moment," Griffin suggested. "He may not know he was identified, which means Savanna is right, and he risked a hell of a lot to show up."

Savanna peered at him and mouthed a thank-you as if he were defending Nick, but hell no. He was just stating the facts. Regardless of Nick's motives, he *did* put Savanna in danger. There *was* a target on her head because of him.

"Okay, I'll bite," Gray began. "If Nick used your place to hide something, where might he—"

"The Mustang," Savanna cut him off, shaking her head as if upset that the thought hadn't hit her before. "The one time Nick showed up at our place, he wanted to buy the Mustang from Marcus. It'd been a gift to the both of them as teenagers, but Marcus took it over when Nick went to prison. I overheard Nick saying he wanted a piece of the past back, that he thought maybe somehow the car would help him get back on the right road in life." She squeezed her eyes closed as if reliving the painful memory. "Marcus said a car wouldn't change him and then kicked him out. I never saw Nick again after that." She slowly opened her eyes. "Check the car. It's the only place I can think of where he'd hide anything. Well, *if* he did hide something."

"Will do," Gray responded and issued an order to someone in the room to head to Savanna's place.

"We need to get her out of Alabama," Griffin declared vehemently, just as the lights flickered overhead.

"The storm?" Savanna asked, her eyes wide.

Griffin held up a hand for her to remain silent as he lifted his chin and closed his eyes, listening closely and hoping his mind was only playing tricks on him. That the sound he was hearing was thunder and not what he feared.

"We've got company," he said to both her and Gray when he confirmed the blades of a helo chopping the air over his house.

"I don't understand. I thought this place was secure," she rushed out.

"From the ground, yes. I wasn't expecting anyone to fast-rope onto the property." He grabbed her arm and pointed to the hall leading to the master bedroom. "Move," he instructed.

"I don't know how they found you," Gray said. "But—"

"I won't let anything happen to her. Be in touch." Griffin tucked his phone away and hurried her into the master, then shifted the tall dresser to the side, punched in the code, and the door immediately opened inward to reveal the hidden room.

"Wait, what? I'm hiding in here? Oh my God. You have to stay here with me. You can't go out there." Savanna tugged at his arm.

"I have to handle this. You don't leave this room unless I say so. You understand?" He turned to the wall of weapons behind him in the six-by-six room and grabbed a rifle, a 9mm, then strapped on a plated vest and packed it with mags.

"We don't know how many of them are coming. Please, don't go." Savanna was pleading now.

"I have to." He sidestepped her to access the security cameras and turned on the screens. A moment later, he heard glass shatter and caught sight of at least three armed tangos infiltrating the living room. Faces hidden. Armed to the teeth. And he had to assume more would be coming from the back.

With a calmness he was far from feeling at the moment, Griffin gently gripped her upper arms and looked into her eyes. He wanted to kiss her so damn badly, but she wasn't his to kiss goodbye. So, failing wasn't an option. Failing meant they'd get her.

"I'll let you know when you can come out. If I can't

handle this, there's a panic button to call the police. No one will be able to get in here. You'll be safe."

"Then stay with me. We'll call the police and wait for them to show up. Please," she begged. "We can call them now. Why wait?"

"I need answers. I need to find out what in the hell is going on. I'm sorry." He stared into her terrified eyes for one last moment before shutting the door and cutting off her protests.

He shifted the dresser in its place, then set his back to the closed bedroom door, listening to the sound of boots crunching over broken glass in the living room.

If you're really here, man, he silently implored Marcus while lifting his eyes to the ceiling, preparing himself to go out into battle, *keep your wife safe while I'm out there.*

CHAPTER THIRTEEN

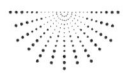

SAVANNA STARED AT THE SCREENS, HER HEART THRASHING IN her chest as she counted three heavily armed men inside the living room and two more on another screen collapsing toward the center of the cabin like well-trained operatives. *Collapsing? Marcus, are you in my head? Because I kind of need you right now.* She was certain he'd been watching over her the other night—otherwise, she'd have walked home alone like normal and . . . she didn't want to even guess what those men would have done to her.

But unlike the men at her townhouse, or the guy Griffin had killed right before her eyes as they made their escape from Jesse's last night, these guys were dressed in all-black combat gear. No night-vision goggles, but their faces were hidden by balaclavas. And that quick flicker of the lights just as they arrived probably meant they'd tried to kill the power, but Griffin's father's security system had overridden that attempt. The real problem was Griffin facing five armed men on his own. And what if there were more waiting outside?

Abuela, if you're up there watching out for me, don't let anything happen to him. Please. Savanna sent the silent prayer to her grandmother, who'd been the most spiritual of anyone in their family. "And, Marcus?" She spoke aloud this time, finding herself wondering if the bolt of lightning that tore her away from Griffin not too long ago had been sent by Mother Nature or her late husband. "We could use some help," she whispered, her eyes shifting to the weapons on the wall, one of which she was particularly familiar with.

A look back to the four screens mounted on the opposite wall had her dragging in deep breaths to calm herself down. Where was the emergency button to summon the police? Once she spotted it, rather than immediately sending the SOS, her hand hovered over the button. Should she wait as he'd requested or go ahead and press it?

She opted to follow his request, then returned her attention to the security panel and discovered that the cameras were equipped with audio, but they were on mute. The moment she flipped on the sound, she spotted Griffin on the second level that overlooked the downstairs. He'd positioned himself flat on his belly, his rifle aimed down into the living room as he looked onto the group of men who'd now all converged there.

She had no clue how he'd managed to get upstairs since the staircase was off the living room, but he now had a strategic advantage, right? What had Marcus called that? *Overwatch?*

"Come out, Griff. I know you're here. Watching us. I don't want to shoot you, so please don't make me." A man broke away from the rest of the group and tilted his face up to view the second floor as if he knew Griffin was there. "We need the girl. Give her up, and we all walk away from this unscathed."

Griff? How the hell did he know Griffin was there with her, even if the place did belong to his dad? Who were these men? Definitely not the Greeks. She didn't think so, at least. These men had fast-roped onto the property like Marcus and A.J. would have done during one of their clandestine ops back in the day.

Griffin remained silent and steady despite the man having just called out his name, and Savanna waited for Griffin to make a move. He'd obviously been spotted, and he was clearly outnumbered. Even if he were to fire, he didn't have enough cover to protect himself.

The man downstairs, most likely the leader, took another careful step and lifted his balaclava. "It's me. You won't shoot me. I know you."

This time, Griffin reacted. She couldn't see his face, but he slowly rose while maintaining hold of his rifle.

"Joe?" Griffin sounded surprised as well as confused. "What the hell are you doing here?"

Joe? Another J name. Freaking perfect. And wow, what is wrong with my brain to think about that right now?

Without waiting for this Joe guy to answer, Griffin approached the top of the stairs. He must have believed Joe wouldn't shoot him. "Tell your men to drop their weapons," Griffin ordered, all signs of confusion and surprise gone as he slowly descended the stairs. That gave her a little hope. "I *will* drop as many of your men as possible if they don't put down their guns, and you know that." His deep voice rang with clear intent. Back to the staircase and head on a swivel, he scanned the room, keeping track of all of his targets.

Joe allowed his sling to catch his own rifle, then signaled for his men to lower theirs. Savanna clutched her chest with relief, but it wasn't over yet.

Despite the melee these men had caused, Griffin and Joe knew each other, so that was promising. It had to be a mistake, right? But the next words from Joe's mouth sent chills down Savanna's spine.

"I don't know why you're harboring an enemy, a threat to national security. But you need to give up the girl," Joe demanded, ice in his tone.

Griffin positioned his attention directly on the man, and while Savanna only had a profile view, his body language couldn't hide his shock and anger.

Criminal? National security threat? What the hell was he talking about?

"You saved my ass in Fallujah, so we'll call this even when I let you live tonight." Joe pulled his mask back in place.

Iraq? This man had been in Iraq with Griffin? Was he military? No, that didn't make sense. Although the way he moved and talked was indicative of a serviceman, so maybe. But why would a team of special operators drop onto the property and storm the cabin? Why'd they think she was a criminal? *What'd you get me involved in, Nick?*

"Well, we're not in Fallujah. You're on private property, and she's not going anywhere. You'll have to go through me to get to her." Griffin kept his rifle level, aimed at Joe's chest.

"I'm not gonna shoot you, Griff. You know I can't do that," Joe said a few seconds later, seeming to be contemplating his options as he looked around at the other men hanging back as though waiting for orders.

"But we'll fight you. And I know you well enough to believe you won't bring a gun to a fistfight." Joe swung his arm out and pointed randomly at his men. "Marines, Army Rangers, SEALs . . . All vets. Are you going to shoot a bunch of veterans?"

Griffin's gaze never veered from Joe. "I won't let you take her. No matter what."

No, no, no. She couldn't let Griffin do this for her. If he killed a fellow serviceman, he'd never be able to live with himself. She didn't need to know him well to be certain that kind of kill would haunt him forever. He wouldn't be able to dehumanize his enemy tonight the way he'd done at Jesse's. "No," she cried out, her hands trembling and her mind racing as she tried to figure out a plan.

"He won't shoot." Joe motioned for two of his men to approach Griffin.

Savanna sucked in a sharp breath when Griffin hesitated. Something he would never have done if they were civilians. Joe had guessed right. Griffin couldn't shoot a brother-in-arms.

He lowered his rifle as the two men approached, fists raised, prepared to fight their way through him to get to her. *Why am I so important?*

"She doesn't know where Nick is," Griffin said while unstrapping the vest of ammo to reveal his bare chest. He wore jeans and nothing else, not even boots for added force when kicking. "If that's why you're here."

Joe didn't respond. He didn't believe him?

"Whatever you think you know about her . . . you're wrong. She's not a criminal," was all Griffin was able to say before the man off to his left came at him swinging.

Griffin struck him in the gut, causing the guy's legs to buckle slightly, but he was still in the game.

As the second man came at Griffin from behind, Griffin pulled his first target into some type of clinch while kicking the guy currently attacking from behind.

Close-quarter grappling. That's a Muay Thai clinch. Griffin's got this. He's in the dominant position. She swore Marcus was once again in her head. Chills coasted down her arms, and she crossed them over her chest.

And as Griffin maneuvered all three of them into what was basically a triangle formation, she knew he'd be able to handle both men. Maybe even a third as Jesse had done at her townhouse.

At that point, Joe ordered the other two men over. "Four to one?" She gasped when the two other guys grabbed hold of each of Griffin's arms.

Griffin tried to resist, and although she didn't exactly have an HD view of the scene, she was sure his veins were popping in his throat and arms as he tried to break free from their hold.

The man who'd attacked Griffin from behind jumped in and helped secure his arms. Three men now held him in place as one man delivered body shot after body shot to Griffin's abdomen, then elbows to his jaw.

She turned her cheek at the sight of blood streaming from his mouth and nose, horrified at what these men were doing to someone who had served and sacrificed for their country just as they had. They should have been on the same side if they were military. She had to do something.

The emergency button. It lit up red when she pressed it, so she assumed it sent out the SOS, but how far away were the police? The cabin was out in the middle of nowhere. The closest town was fifteen miles away.

"When I heard you were the one with our target, I volunteered." Joe's voice had Savanna returning her focus to the screen. He motioned for the man who'd been punching Griffin to step aside. "If it'd been anyone else sent for her, you would have killed at least three before you were finally dropped. I know you, though. You wouldn't pull the trigger on a brother. But hear me when I say this is a fight you can't win."

Griffin lifted his chin, breathing hard as he faced Joe.

Blood rolled down his body like the rain had done earlier during the storm. She was sick to her stomach.

"You're wondering how we found you?" Savanna heard the smug smile in Joe's voice, even though she couldn't see his face now that it was covered by the balaclava again. "Where is she?" he asked instead of answering the question he'd raised. "You, of all people . . . helping a criminal. How the mighty have fallen."

"There's been a misunderstanding," Griffin rasped, his voice barely audible, before turning his head and spitting blood onto the floor. "She's innocent."

"She's hot. I've seen her photo, so I'm guessing she manipulated you into believing she's innocent. That's what it is, right?"

Maybe Joe actually believed he was on Team Good Guy, but where the hell did he get his intelligence? Not from the U.S. government, that was for sure.

She had to do something until the police arrived. Her gaze snapped back to the shotgun. "Twenty gauge, right?" Her fingers skated over the boxes of ammo organized on a table before she hit the jackpot and spotted what she hoped were the right shells.

The men were still talking, but she focused on her memories for a moment, trying to recall how to load the weapon. There was no chair to sit in, which would have made things easier, so she secured the stock under her arm and turned the weapon sideways.

"Insert the shell, and when it clicks, you'll know it passed the mag catch," Marcus had explained. They'd been inside the range that day. *"Load six. And, baby girl, maybe don't aim the gun at me."* He'd smiled and used his finger to redirect the barrel away from himself.

She cursed the tear that fell down her cheek, swiped it

away, and loaded the weapon. Then she unlocked the safe room door and used all of her effort to move the dresser. Gun back in hand, she moved with quick but nervous steps to the closed door of the master.

She tiptoed to the hall, and from the sounds of it, Griffin continued to refuse to give up her location. Joe must have assumed he'd hidden her somewhere other than just a bedroom, or they would have already started searching the place.

"Let him go," she called out in her best "brave" voice as she entered the living room. "I'll shoot." Her bravery waned as she delivered her threat, and she was terrified they all heard it.

Griffin was on his knees, still being held by three men, but when he lifted his gaze and their eyes connected—his energy seemed to recharge, and his jaw tightened with anger at the sight of her, at the fact she was now in the line of fire.

"The police are on their way." Savanna kept the shotgun aimed at her target, which was Joe, but her hands were shaking so damn bad. "If you don't want to be here when they arrive, I suggest you get back on the chopper and exfil."

"Exfil?" Joe peeled his mask up, and his lips twitched as if amused by her word choice. "Well, she's hotter than her photo." He started her way, and Griffin went into beast mode again, finding the fight to try and battle off the men holding him down. "Put that down before you hurt yourself," Joe added in a calm tone, and as he approached, she found herself backing up against the wall by the hallway.

"I can't do that. I don't know what you want with me, but please, don't hurt him anymore. I'm not a criminal."

"Don't you touch her," Griffin yelled as he freed one arm and twisted to clock the guy off to his right, then sent a front kick to the man who'd been punching him. "Do you have any fucking clue who she is?" he rasped as two of the men positioned guns on Griffin as well as Savanna. "That's Marcus Vasquez's wife," Griffin gritted out.

Joe stopped walking as if that news was somehow meaningful to him, then shook his head. "She's Nick Vasquez's sister-in-law. A criminal and—"

"And Nick is Marcus Vasquez's brother. Didn't you do your homework?" Griffin responded, his voice stern with warning despite the battle he'd just waged against four men. "You're really going to kidnap Marcus's wife?"

Griffin's words appeared to level Joe. He took two steps away from Savanna as if she were a flame, and he didn't want to get burned. "I don't understand." He looked toward the windows his people had shattered when they'd entered the home.

"The police will be here soon," Savanna reminded him when Joe focused back on her.

"Who do you work for?" Griffin asked. "Someone's lying to you, Joe. I'm protecting her *from* criminals. She's not one." His tone was a bit calmer now that Joe was backing away from her. "And if you try to take her, *you'll* become the hunted one. I *will* find you and kill every last one of you for so much as touching her," he seethed, and that was a threat she believed. He wouldn't shoot unarmed servicemen, but if they hurt her—game changer.

Joe surprised her by twirling a finger in the air, a signal she'd seen from Marcus. Get to the chopper. Wheels up. "Another team will be sent for her. They won't stop coming." Joe turned and started for the door, motioning for his men to follow, and Griffin moved straight toward Savanna.

She set the shotgun by her feet right before Griffin tucked her against his side, but he kept his eyes positioned on the men as they left the house.

Joe was the last one remaining, and he faced them again. "He won't stop until he gets what he wants, and right now," he said, eyes on Savanna, "that's you."

"Who wants her?" Griffin stumbled forward, nearly losing his balance, almost taking her down with him, but he caught himself before they both went to their knees.

"At this point . . . everyone," Joe said under his breath.

"What?" Griffin went tense at her side. "If you're really on the right side of the law, which is where we are, then give me something. Please." It was the first time she heard his voice crack since the men had arrived.

Joe looked down at the floor for a second before carrying his attention back to them. "All I can give you is Elysium," and then he added while pivoting his gaze to her, "I'm sorry for your loss. Marcus was the best of us." And with that, he left.

Elysium? She turned toward Griffin, scared and confused, but now that they were alone, she hugged him. He held her tight to his chest, setting his chin on top of her head. He was bloody and his breathing shallow and ragged, but he didn't let her go. He held her so tight, and she wanted to cry, but she tried to remain strong.

"The police will be here soon," she said into his chest.

He slowly released her and stepped back. "I don't want to be here when they arrive. We need to go."

"Oh-okay," she stammered.

"I should have shot them." His voice was low and harsh, but his big palms were gentle when he reached up and cupped her face. "I'm sorry I put you in danger."

"No, I understand. I'm glad you didn't kill anyone." And she was. Truly.

"Who was that guy?" she asked as he released her face

and sought out her hand, urging her to move, even though he was struggling to do so.

"He was on Marcus's team back in the Navy," Griffin announced slowly as they started for the master bedroom. "We need to grab weapons before we go, just in case they change their minds and come back."

"Wait, what? He worked with Marcus? Joe's a Teamguy?"

"Yeah, and Joe was also a friend of mine. We worked a few ops together in Iraq."

Friends didn't beat the shit out of each other, though.

"I took a bullet for that man." And in a chilling tone, he added, "But if he ever tries coming for you again, he'll catch a bullet from me."

CHAPTER FOURTEEN

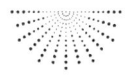

"I CAN DRIVE," GRIFFIN PROTESTED AS SHE HIT ANOTHER pothole on the back road. Savanna glanced over to the passenger seat, where he slowly pulled a tee over his head. He'd only had time to take a wet cloth to his face and body before they rushed from the cabin three minutes ago.

According to the security app on Griffin's phone, the police arrived a few minutes after they made their escape.

"You were just attacked. Still bleeding." She pointed to his lip, and he lifted his shirt and used it to wipe the blood from his mouth. "So yeah, I'm driving." She shook her head and put her eyes back on the road, angry that Nick had put them in this situation. "What about your ribs?" She pressed down on the pedal harder, needing to add some distance between them and the police, but it had resumed storming, and the rain was hammering the windshield, making it hard to see.

"My ribs aren't broken." He cursed under his breath when he shifted on his seat and grabbed his phone from his jeans pocket. "I should never have laid down my weapon. I wasn't thinking."

"And here we go again. You're feeling all guilty. You were blindsided by the fact a Navy SEAL busted into your father's home to kidnap me. *I* don't blame you. *No one* would blame you."

"I don't care if the Pope himself fast-roped into the cabin, you never set down your weapon. Never."

"He was your friend." She had to make him see reason before he drove himself crazy replaying the particulars of the last few hours in his head. She sensed the darkness of guilt and blame crawling its way in to take him over. And that was the last thing she wanted. "It's not so easy to shoot a friend, a man you served with. A man that wore the country's flag on his arm to protect our freedoms." *A man that worked with my husband. A man that ordered four other men to beat you up to get to me.* "Plus, what if he's a good guy, and he's just been misinformed? He thinks I'm bad and that I work with Nick."

Savanna peeked at him as he shook his head while unlocking the phone to call Carter—well, she assumed that was his plan.

"They left without me. That means something, right?"

He turned and caught her eyes, and damn it, she was going to run off the narrow road if she didn't stop swiveling her head his way every few seconds. These back roads were tricky.

"Marcus was watching out for you again, wasn't he? If any other team leader had been sent tonight . . ."

She swallowed at his words, then blinked her focus back to the road.

"Yeah, I could feel him there," she softly confessed.

"Me too," Griffin admitted, his raspy voice carrying a hint of anguish.

Somewhat startled, but really not all that surprised by Griffin's words, Savanna gripped the wheel and told herself to be grateful that Marcus's connection with that Joe guy basically saved them tonight. Unfortunately, she could also feel Griffin pulling away from her because of it. The intimate moment they'd shared at the cabin would most likely be the only one to ever happen between them. Not that she should have been thinking about that right now.

"Hey, it's me. We're okay," Griffin said over speakerphone once the line connected.

"What the hell happened?" It was Gray.

"Joseph Harding, a former SEAL, along with four other vets broke into the cabin tonight. I don't know who they work for, but they're under the impression Savanna is in league with Nick and a threat to national security."

"Are you fucking with us?" A voice she vaguely recognized filled the line. Was that Jack?

"No, he's serious," she spoke up before Griffin had a chance. "But Joe worked with my, um, husband in the Navy."

"Joe seemed as confused as we were that he'd been sent after Marcus's, um, wife." Why were they both using "ums" when referring to Marcus as if they had a secret to hide?

The vibe she was getting from Griffin made her feel like they were guilty of having an affair. Sure, they kissed, and he pinched her nipple, and fingered her, but would he consider that an affair? *But wait, I'm single.*

"Once Joe realized who Savanna was and that the police were on their way, they left. I'm guessing they came in on a modified Black Hawk. How many guys do we know with access to stealth birds like that?" Griffin groaned and clutched his ribs a moment later when she hit another pothole.

Not broken, huh? Well, maybe not. But they'd pummeled him like he was a piñata, so at the very least, he was badly bruised.

And it was her fault. He could have died tonight because of her.

"I'll do a background search on him. See who he's working for," Gray spoke up a moment later.

"He also implied there are several *someones* coming after Savanna, which matches what the guys you're holding told Carter earlier. I'm thinking *several* means more than just those Greeks and Joe's crew," Griffin told him. "I did get him to give me a name. I don't know if it represents a person, a place, or a fucking thing, though," he added angrily. "Elysium."

Silence filled the line for a second. "What the hell is Elysium?" Gray asked, as confused as they all were, from the sounds of it.

"If my memory's right, Elysium's a Greek word. Heaven, I think," Griffin explained.

"And how do you know that?" A touch of humor filled Gray's tone.

"My mom was into Greek mythology. Her mom was Greek," he answered a bit slowly as if he hated the fact she was being hunted by anyone from his grandmother's country. "We need to get more from those guys. Any luck?"

"Not unless we go Gitmo on their asses," Jack said, joining the conversation again. "And with Beckett breathing down our necks, our hands are tied."

The guys did a quick back-and-forth about how to interrogate the two supposed Greeks without crossing a line that'd piss off the sheriff.

"What about the Mustang?" Savanna asked when they'd finished.

"Oliver's tearing the thing apart now. If Nick hid something there, he'll find it." Jack paused. "Sorry, I know the Mustang was Marcus's, but we don't have much of a choice."

She slowed the truck for a moment as she visualized what "tearing the thing apart" might look like and how much that'd gut Marcus. But bottom line, Marcus would want her to be safe no matter what the cost, and that included the Mustang.

"Where are we supposed to go now?" she whispered, afraid her voice would crack, allowing the gamut of emotions she was feeling to spill out.

Despite how shaky she'd been before getting in the truck, an eerie calmness had settled over her once she was behind the wheel. That didn't mean she was taking any of this in stride, though. As a sailor's wife, she'd learned how to push through painfully tough situations and make it to the other side—sometimes feeling more scathed than others.

"The fact they tracked you to Griffin's dad's place, and discovered we're helping you, means our location has also been compromised," Gray announced the shit news. "We're dealing with people who have access to some high-level technology."

"It's possible that whoever Joe works for also has eyes on the Greeks. They may have even seen what went down at Jesse's and followed us to the cabin once they'd assembled a team after figuring out who they'd be going up against," Griffin pointed out. "Guys with Black Hawks will also have drones. Could be how they tracked us undetected." He was pissed off and growling again. No doubt because he'd lowered his rifle, allowing those men to use him as a punching bag.

"I think we need to take Carter's jet and leave Alabama tonight. We'll just have to take these two assholes with us," Gray decided. "Head to the hangar. I'll get a hold of Carter and update him. And hopefully, Oliver finds something by the time you reach us."

"But where will we go?" Savanna asked, clutching the wheel with a white-knuckled death grip again. "You still have no clue where Nick's been lately aside from my place."

"Greece," Griffin muttered as if it were the last place on earth he wanted to go. "We need to track down whoever sent these fuckers in the first place. Figure out what or *who* Elysium is. It's possible we're on the same side as Joe and his men, but we each have different pieces of the puzzle."

"We don't have any fucking pieces at the moment," Jack returned. "Aside from Savanna's thief of a brother-in-law mixing her up in whatever shitstorm he's created."

"Joe said Savanna was a threat to national security, an enemy. Those were his words." Griffin stated. "What if Nick stole something connected to national security?"

"Hang on while I see if I can find out who Joe works for," Gray said. "Give me a second."

The cab of the truck was quiet except for the sounds of Gray typing in the background. Savanna shifted her gaze to Griffin, his body tense at her side in the passenger seat, head leaned back, and eyes focused on the ceiling.

The typing stopped as Gray announced, "He works for the Archer Group."

"Are you serious?" Griffin snapped to attention.

"Remind me who they are," she said, the name sounding familiar.

"The Archer Group is a manufacturing and defense company. They've won multiple contracts overseas for energy and infrastructure development in the Middle East, but they also have another sector, which is responsible for making everything from jet engines to weapons and drones for the U.S. government," Gray told them.

"Well, that explains how Joe and his men rolled up on us in the stealth bird and tracked us in the first place," Griffin bit out. "They have all the tech. But what exactly does Joe do for the company?"

"He's head of one of the security teams," Gray answered. "Looks like he and his men are assigned to safeguard overseas projects from potential threats. Requires top-level security clearance for that gig. Basically, they're PMCs."

"Why would private military contractors be sent after me? I own a little bakery in freaking Birmingham, Alabama." She let her thoughts derail, becoming more and more jarred by the events that had unfolded that stormy afternoon. *What day is it even? Saturday?* "Gray, didn't you take PMC jobs like that in the past for Uncle Sam?" she asked when no one had spoken up with an answer to her question. She'd crossed paths with Gray a few times in the recent past and remembered that detail. "Marcus sort of . . . um . . ." Shit, she couldn't reveal the kind of work he used to do because A.J. and the others still did it. And also, she was bound by contract never to share the fact that Scott & Scott Security was a cover story for the teams who ran ops for POTUS.

She could feel Griffin's eyes on her at the mention of Marcus and the "um" she'd dropped again. But the rain wasn't letting up, so she kept her eyes on the road. Plus, she wasn't so sure she wanted to look at him right now. Oddly, she didn't feel any guilt for what happened between her and Griffin back in the living room, but she knew the next time she looked into his eyes, his gaze would be filled with it.

"My only question . . . why doesn't the government seem to know about this?" Gray asked. "There are enough people that we trust who are aware that Savanna is in danger and that it's connected to Nick. If this Archer Group knows about Nick—"

"That means they didn't notify the Department of Defense," Griffin finished for him.

"Red flag?" Savanna whispered.

"Yeah, I'd say so," Gray hissed. "I'm betting Joe's team was dispatched to handle this situation because the company doesn't want Uncle Sam, or the media and public for that matter, knowing they've been compromised."

"Right," Griffin muttered under his breath.

"I'll do some more digging into Archer and see if I can get any hits on the word Elysium," Gray said.

"You're taking me to Greece, right?" Savanna stole a quick look at the hero off to her right, and he peered her way. "I have a target on my head, and if I'm near anyone in Walkins Glen, they might get hurt because of me."

"As much as I hate taking you with us overseas, we can't leave you behind. Not with an unknown number of threats out there," Gray replied.

Savanna glanced at Griffin to see his hand clench into a fist on his jeaned thigh. He didn't like the idea of her traveling, did he? But he didn't rebut because he was well aware that she couldn't stay behind, either. If those men found her at his cabin, maybe they'd be able to track her anywhere, though?

"Do you have a passport?" Griffin asked her, most likely remembering she'd told him she'd never traveled outside of the country before.

"I do. It's just blank. You know, never been used. Shouldn't be expired yet, though." Marcus had her get it back in 2014, the year before he was killed. They'd had plans to travel, and then . . . "It's in the filing cabinet in my small home office. Third drawer down hidden beneath, um, photo albums." *Beneath more of my memories.*

"Not a fan of Savanna using her real name and passport at customs, but we don't have time to work up an alias," Gray grumbled. "I'll have Oliver grab it while he's there. We'll talk more about everything on the jet. Hopefully, by the time you arrive at the hangar, Oliver will have found something in the Mustang, and I'll have news to share as well." And with that, he ended the call, and Griffin tucked his phone back in his pocket. It dawned on Savanna he'd never changed out of those wet jeans after he'd returned from checking the security sensors just as the storm hit. And that felt like forever and a day ago.

"Are you okay?" she asked after allowing some silence to sit between them. "Do you need me to pull over and do something for you? I don't know, like wrap your ribs? I saw a first aid kit in the back."

Now that they were a safe distance from the cabin, she didn't bother to wait for his answer. She slowed down, carefully pulled over, and parked the truck off to the side of the road. Savanna twisted in the seat to look at the man who'd taken a beating for her.

"I'm fine." He didn't look or sound fine, though. He was currently wiping more blood from his face, this time from beneath his nose. And his words had come out gritty as if her question had aggravated him.

Mr. Moody was back, and after the hell he'd endured today, she didn't blame him for being all kinds of mad. But why'd she feel like he was upset with her?

His next words were a punch to the gut, though. "I should never have crossed that line with you earlier. That's on me. I'm sorry." They were words she'd anticipated, even felt coming, but she hadn't wanted to hear them.

"You didn't cross the line. There are no lines between us." *I don't think so, at least.*

He shifted on his seat, and her eyes were drawn to the honed cut of his ab muscles before he let go of the shirt.

The rain continued to pound the vehicle, and the racket it caused, as well as the limited visibility, seemed to shut out the rest of the world, making it feel like they were surrounded by a protective shroud.

Griffin's brows slanted as he studied her, his lips in a tight line. "There are a lot of reasons I should never have set a hand on you. *A lot* of lines between us." He paused for a beat. "Crossing that line caused me to be distracted. I should have seen those men coming. I should have known."

"How could you know a group of former military guys would fly in during a storm and drop in by rope?" she challenged, knowing damn well they needed to get back on the road and focus on the main problem, but she remained unmoving. Sitting there and staring at a man who made her feel so many things but regret wasn't one of them.

His mouth opened as if he were about to protest, but then his gaze dropped to her chest. "You have blood on you."

She followed his line of sight to the smudges of red on her shirt. "It's yours." She slowly worked her attention back up to find him twisting his torso to reach for their bag he'd hastily grabbed before leaving the cabin. The stubborn man wouldn't ask for help even as he breathed out a hiss of pain.

"The last thing of mine I want to see you wearing is blood," he said while handing her a shirt, which happened to be one of his tees. Her stuff was probably buried at the bottom of their shared bag.

She unbuckled and held his eyes while reaching for the hem of her tee. She expected him to look away. To behave and not cross any more of those lines he was so set on maintaining, but he remained still and focused on her.

They lost eye contact when she pulled her tee over her

head, but she was certain he was watching her every move. Those butterflies made a reappearance in her stomach once she'd removed the tee and saw that, yes, he was watching her. His heated gaze drifted from the shirt in her hands to her breasts, hidden beneath one of the boring bras he'd packed her. She shivered at the memory of him cupping her breast earlier. That rough palm had skated over her skin, and he'd pinched her nipple, rolling it between the pad of his thumb and finger.

She used the shirt to wipe any smudges of blood from her cleavage, then tossed it in the back before finally accepting the shirt he was clutching.

"Savanna." His voice was hoarse, and she doubted it was from pain. It was a plea for her to help him maintain his self-control. The self-control he'd allowed to falter when he'd pinned her to the wall earlier. Despite everything that had gone down today, he still wanted her—she was sure of it.

Even if it was just to screw her senseless, which she thought she wanted too, but . . .

"Maybe one of the other guys should be assigned to keep a close eye on you?" His suggestion had her stomach tightening.

She didn't want anyone else to have her six, as Marcus would have said. Something inside her—her abuela telling her to listen to her heart—insisted it be this man and only this man. The one currently staring at her like he was torn between devouring her and jumping out of the truck and punching something.

"What if I don't want that?" she countered, her voice low and raspy, provocative even. And totally unlike her.

"If I'm near you," he said, twisting to face forward in the seat as if he were incapable of looking at her any longer, "I won't be able to stop myself from crossing those lines again."

"And you don't want to cross them?" It was a dumb question, but she wanted him to spell it out for her. Was he like Marcus, who only saw right and wrong? Black and white? Refused to believe there was any gray area in life, especially when it came to his own brother?

Right now, though, Savanna would swim in a sea of gray if it meant having Griffin touch her again.

When Griffin swung his gaze back her way, he shook his head and leveled her with a hard look. "No." He stroked his jaw, his attention momentarily shifting to her breasts before returning to her face. "Because I'll break your fucking heart before you have a chance to break mine," he murmured darkly. "And hurting you is the last thing I'd ever want to do."

CHAPTER FIFTEEN

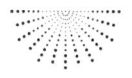

GRIFFIN STOOD INSIDE THE PRIVATE HANGAR AND WATCHED AS Jesse wrapped Savanna in a bear hug, followed by Shep muscling her from Jesse's grasp for his own embrace. And when Shep lifted her off the ground and tightened his hold, Griffin had to back up a step and look away to keep from unleashing his anger on an innocent man.

After the day he'd had, he didn't trust himself. And it wasn't even five o'clock yet.

He was pissed for a multitude of reasons, but stinging jealousy over Shep touching Savanna shouldn't have been on that damn list.

And yet, when he chanced a look back at them, Shep's arms lingering on Savanna's hips as he held her close, jealousy now sat at the top in bold red letters.

Shep had slept with Savanna, and Griffin didn't blame A.J. for punching his brother for that lapse of judgment. Hell, Griffin wanted to connect his fist to the man's jaw as well. How could Shep have even considered sleeping with his friend's wife?

Wife. Would he ever be able to think of her as single and

not married? Probably not. Then again, he'd allowed that detail to slip from his mind earlier when he'd shoved his tongue in her mouth, slipped his fingers in her tight, wet heat, and made her come.

And he was worried that the next time they were alone, and she looked at him with those hazel eyes and begged him to touch her, he wouldn't be able to stop himself from plunging his cock deep inside of her.

He was beginning to think the woman was as crazy as him. Back in the truck, when she was swapping her dirty tee for one of his shirts, she'd wanted him. The way she'd looked at him left no doubt in his mind. And he'd been seconds away from saying screw the pain in his battered body, *and* the fact the police were at his dad's cabin, *and* all the other reasons. He would have crushed his mouth to hers, ripped off that bra and buried his face in those fucking luscious tits, then unzipped his jeans to show her how damn hard she made him.

But a sudden boom of thunder and crack of lightning had materialized close enough to slightly shake the truck. Another warning from Marcus that she was off-limits?

But that was insane.

Marcus died years ago, and surely he wouldn't want her to stay single forever. She was only thirty-four, five years younger than Griffin.

"How are you holding up?" Gray asked on approach while putting on a black ball cap. "Looks like they did a number on you."

Griffin forced his gaze to stay on Gray instead of wandering where he wanted to look. "I'll be fine," he answered, smoothing a hand over his aching jaw.

The storm had let up a few minutes ago, but they were waiting on Oliver, Carter, and Jack to arrive before they could go wheels up. A.J. would most likely lose his shit when he found out they were taking Savanna to Greece, but they were out of options. In addition to a private security team funded by a multibillion-dollar company, there were an unknown number of other threats out there.

And unfortunately, the last Griffin heard, Oliver was coming up empty, and they were losing hope that Nick had hidden anything in the Mustang. A potential dead end when they could really use a break.

"I know you feel like shit for laying down your rifle, but I would have done the same if I was face-to-face with a man I'd taken a bullet for in Iraq. Don't beat yourself up," Gray said, his gruff tone hinting at darker thoughts and memories.

Memories of Gray's own time in war most likely. The helo crash. The partial amputation of his leg. The long road to recovery. The physical and psychological battle the man must have waged with himself, worried he'd never operate again.

And here you are now. A fighter. He had mad respect for him.

"Yeah, I suppose I already took enough of a beating tonight," Griffin half-joked. "But uh, Carter told you how I know Joe?"

Gray nodded. "You think you crossed paths with Marcus in Iraq, then? If Joe and Marcus were part of the same SEAL Team, wouldn't you have met him?"

Griffin squeezed the bridge of his nose, closed his eyes, and tried to draw up those particular memories from so long ago. Tried to remember the other men in Joe's squadron when he himself had only been a young Ranger at the time.

"Joe and his men were pinned down by enemy fire, and my team was in the area, so we were dispatched for an assist," he recalled. "The only reason Joe and I became friends was because he visited me in the hospital after I was shot. After I took a bullet for him. We stayed in touch until he became a civilian."

But Marcus had to have been there that day too.

The possibility they'd served side-by-side in Iraq during that gunfight was a little too much for Griffin to handle right about now.

"There's a chance Marcus helped get me on a chopper and out of the Red Zone to safety. I can't be sure because I was lights out at the time." Griffin opened his eyes and wondered how Savanna would feel about that fact. The connection he had with her husband, one he hadn't considered or even remembered until coming face-to-face with Joe earlier today. "You think you could find out for sure? You have connections. Maybe you can get your eyes on the after-action report."

Gray laid a hand on his shoulder. "I'll see what I can do."

"Thanks." For some reason, he needed to know for sure. He had to know if he and Marcus had truly crossed paths and now . . . well, now this. "Joe told me he requested to be assigned to the op tonight, assuming he could use our past to his advantage, but it backfired on him."

"Lucky for us," Gray said, removing his hand from Griffin's shoulder.

Lucky? Or was it Marcus again?

Griffin lifted his achy arm and dragged a palm over the light growth on his face. "You learn anything new?" He needed to realign his focus to where it belonged.

"I can't get my hands on anything too specific about the Archer Group. Given their military contracts, almost all information that's public is useless to us, and everything else is classified. Too bad my sister isn't available. We need an insider at the Agency."

Griffin nodded. "Carter was with the CIA, and yeah, he

burned his bridges with them, but I assume he has some contacts he can still reach out to that won't try and arrest him for—"

"Going MIA on them?" Gray finished for him. "I'm sure he'll do what he can, and during the flight, I'll try and dig deeper into whatever Elysium is, make sure we're on the right track."

"You tell Jesse about what we learned tonight?" Griffin looked back over at him, relieved Shep was no longer touching Savanna.

"Not yet. Not sure how much to tell him since he's not technically on the team. I'll leave that up to Carter, I suppose."

"He's going to want to come with us to Greece. I don't see him letting that plane take off without him on it," Griffin commented while setting his focus on Shep, who was now rubbing small circles on Savanna's back, just above her ass, with the heel of his hand.

Yeah, he was going to implode. His body grew hot, and as if he hadn't done enough fighting today, his hands became fists by his sides, and he clamped down on his back teeth.

"You good?" Gray moved to stand in front of Griffin, effectively blocking his view of Savanna and Shep.

"Something happen at that cabin?" Gray's brows flew together, suspicion in his tone. "That's not her shirt she's wearing."

His tee looked hot as hell on her even though it swallowed her up. Griffin hissed, "Nothing happened aside from the fact I got my ass handed to me, and she swapped shirts because she had my blood on her." He looked to his left to see a unisex bathroom not far away. "I'm going to clean up." He snatched his duffel bag resting by his feet.

Gray didn't press for an answer, thank God. And Griffin

did his best to avoid looking to where Savanna stood with a man she'd most likely known for a long damn time. *And how long have I known her?* He checked his watch. Twenty-four hours since he'd wiped the sugary flour off her cheek.

So, why the weird possessive feeling he had for her? He wanted to march over and claim the woman as his, which was crazy.

Shoving the bathroom door open with entirely too much force, he let go of the bag, then braced himself against the vanity counter and bowed his head, immediately slammed with the image of Savanna standing in the living room of the cabin, the shotgun shaking in her grip as she faced off with a bunch of armed men. She'd gone against his orders and left the safe room. To rescue *him*. His heartbeat had gone wild as fear like he'd never known, not even in combat, coursed through him.

Griffin hauled in a deep breath, stood upright, and held a hand to his chest. His heart was thumping hard beneath his palm at the idea she'd been willing to sacrifice herself for him, for a stranger.

"Can I come in?" Savanna softly called out, but she'd already opened the door.

He slowly turned to face her, unsure if he could look her in the eyes without revealing his anxiety. Or hell, the jealousy.

"I'd like to assess the damage. May I?" She pointed to his chest as she walked his way. Without waiting for him to agree, her fingers skirted the hem of his shirt.

Her hazel eyes held him prisoner as they locked gazes while she lifted the material. His breath hitched as she looked at him for what felt like years before tipping her head to study his abdomen and chest.

Then, with her bottom lip caught between her teeth,

Savanna ran her fingers across his muscles, easing up on her touch as she skimmed over the bruises blooming on his torso. His entire body tightened at her tender touch, and pain or not, he couldn't handle this. He pushed his shirt down, motioned for her to back up, then gently held on to her arm, a silent plea in his eyes for her to leave. Now she just needed to receive the message.

"I'm so sorry this happened to you because of me." She glanced down at his hand on her arm, but she remained in place. No backing away or a sassy *Roger that* from her.

"This isn't your fault. And I'm fine." He looked up at the sound of the one-person bathroom door opening again to see Shep standing there.

"What's going on?" Shep's growly tone should have had Griffin releasing Savanna like a grenade but remembering that man's hands caressing her hips and stroking her back called up his possessive caveman and *almost* had him reacting.

But he behaved, fighting the beast inside of him, which wanted to yank her behind his back and protect her from all men, even a "friend." Hell, *especially* a friend.

"Savanna?" Shep stepped inside and let the door close behind him.

Savanna turned, which meant Griffin had no choice but to release his hold of her.

"I was checking him out," she said. Then, as if realizing how that sounded, she slapped her palms to her cheeks and shook her head. "I mean, checking for damage. The, um, bruises." Griffin stepped alongside her as she tripped all over her words, unsure what to make of it.

He was clueless as to whether or not she'd read romance books featuring a woman torn between two men, but that was not a place he ever wanted to find himself.

"I'll just . . ." *Leave?* Griffin couldn't get himself to finish his sentence or actually go, though.

"Are you okay?" Shep's stony gaze was pinned on Griffin, but he knew the question was meant for Savanna. Shep wanted to know if Griffin had crossed any lines, and based on the tight draw of his brows, he was ready to throw down with him.

Only friends, huh?

Before anyone had a chance to say or do anything, the door opened again.

Jack was there.

Perfect.

Now it really was too damn crowded in the bathroom.

"Oliver called. He's on his way. He thinks he found something," Jack said before noticing the tension inside the small restroom. "What's wrong?" he asked, his eyes bouncing between Griffin, Savanna, and Shep as he propped the door open with his back.

"Nothing," Savanna quickly answered. "But did Oliver say what he found?" She eased a step forward, but Shep remained firmly in place as if still in the mood to square off with Griffin. But as much as he wanted to punch Shep in the face for having sex with Savanna, which was absolutely nuts . . . they needed to protect her. Not fight over her.

Jack slowly shifted his attention from Savanna to Griffin, his eyes narrowing. "You just can't help yourself when it comes to married women, can you?" And with that, Jack let the door swing shut, sidestepped both Savanna and Shep, and came at Griffin, catching him by surprise and shoving him up against the wall.

"What's your problem?" Griffin hissed, holding his palms up. Fighting Jack was not on his damn to-do list today.

Jack kept his hands on Griffin's chest and hissed, "I'll watch Savanna from now on."

"Like hell you will," Griffin snapped, still unsure what in the actual fuck had set Jack off.

"Would you please back away from him," Savanna pleaded, and Griffin spotted her tugging Jack's arm. "He's taken enough of a beating today, and he doesn't deserve to be hit by his own teammate if that's what you're planning to do."

Griffin's eyes briefly connected with hers, watching this woman fight for him again like she had tried to do in the cabin earlier. She was tough.

Griffin forcefully removed Jack's hands, then shoved him away a good two steps. "You've had a beef with me since day one. Just tell me your deal, damn it."

Jack tore his gaze away from Savanna to find Griffin's eyes. "You fucked my wife. That's my problem."

CHAPTER SIXTEEN

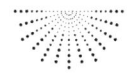

Griffin was trying to make sense of Jack's accusation, which had not only blindsided him but sounded like pure insanity when he caught sight of Savanna quickly releasing Jack's arm, a look of shock on her face.

"You did what?" Shep joined in, his tone a mix of appalled and disgusted. He reached for Savanna, pulled her back against his chest in a protective manner, then skated his hands down the sides of her arms possessively.

Watching Shep take hold of her as if Jack had just alerted the world to the news that Griffin was a serial killer had his blood boiling.

The pain in his ribs and every other thought in his mind faded away at that moment.

Griffin leaned in close to Jack's face. "I. Do. Not. Sleep. With. Married. Women." He slowly enunciated each word so the prick, who was supposed to be a teammate, understood him. "Got it? Yet another man misinformed. It seems to be the theme of the day," he added, thinking back to Joe and his screwup about Savanna.

"What in God's name is going on?" Gray's voice echoed off the walls.

Another guest to the impromptu party. They should pass out drinks and toast to all the insane shit that'd happened in the last twenty-four hours.

"I told you weeks ago not to bring this up. Period," Gray tossed out a moment later, obviously hearing the tail end of the altercation. "That was an order." Gray jerked a thumb toward the hangar from where he stood in the bathroom doorway. "All of you, out now."

Jack slowly backed away, and Griffin sidestepped him, catching Savanna's eyes as he moved past where she remained frozen against Shep. He didn't have a chance to get a read on her, but he hoped she believed him. That he hadn't slept with Jack's ex-wife when they were still married.

"Carter's here," Gray added in a low voice, nodding to where Carter stood outside the hangar talking to Jesse. They were more than a hundred feet away, which explained why Carter hadn't crashed the bathroom party—he hadn't heard the commotion. "Deal with this shit quickly or another damn time," he said before heading toward Carter.

Griffin stopped walking and set his hands on his hips, a hard look in his eyes. "We handle this now, or we won't be able to work together." Addressing Jack, Griffin asked, "Who is your wife? Your ex, I mean?"

"Jill London."

The name didn't register, but he resisted shrugging, assuming that'd only piss Jack off. "Do you have a picture?"

Savanna tugged at the sleeve of Shep's shirt and tilted her head, indicating they should move away to give the two men some privacy.

"No, don't go. You need to hear this. All of you," Griffin

blurted. It would bother the hell out of him if she ever thought, well . . . if anyone ever thought he was like his mom.

His stomach, already in a knot from the beating, clenched even tighter at the memory of his mom laying the news on his father that she'd cheated. Griffin was sixteen when he'd overheard her confession and some of the painful conversation that followed between his parents. Feeling just as betrayed as he imagined his father felt, judging from the hurt in his voice, Griffin had run out to the garage and punched a wall or two, tears falling down his cheeks. Tears he couldn't prevent despite how much he'd tried to stop them.

His mom had been his dad's absolute everything. His reason for living. His reason for doing his best to make it home safely from every deployment. He worshipped the ground she walked on, and she'd betrayed him.

Griffin didn't realize he'd reached out toward Savanna in a plea for her to stay and witness his innocence, but when Jack lifted his phone to show him a photo of Jill, it took him a minute to put the face to a memory. A barely there memory.

"You do know her," Jack said, reading the recognition on Griffin's face. The anger he'd apparently kept bottled inside for the last two weeks at Gray's directive cracked loose, and he came at him swinging.

Griffin raised his palm and blocked the punch in one fluid movement. Clenching his jaw against the pain caused by the effort, Griffin held him off. "If I had slept with your wife, I'd let you hit me ten times over. And tell Shep to hop in and join you. But. I. Didn't." He paused for a moment. "She wanted to, though," he delivered the shit news. "I said no. We were at a bar in Virginia Beach, and I noticed a tan line on her ring finger."

Jack's arm relaxed a little before he slowly pulled back, belief starting to register in his eyes.

"I have no clue if she left with someone else because once I realized she was married, I backed off. I don't know why she gave you my name. My rejection pissed her off, maybe? I don't know," Griffin explained, his tense body starting to relax.

Jack's attention fell to the floor. "She told me this when I asked for a divorce. Gave me your name. So, yeah, maybe she was trying to hurt me." He looked up. "I considered finding you years ago but decided it wasn't worth it."

Griffin dragged in a deep breath and peered at Savanna, whose eyes were set right on him. "I'm sorry, man. But you can believe me when I say I'm not that guy. I'd never be that guy."

And it was also why he couldn't be with Savanna, because in his mind, she was still married to Marcus, and he didn't think he'd ever be able to see beyond that. His own screwed-up past would prevent him from perceiving her situation differently. And he knew that.

With his shoulders collapsing ever so slightly and defeat in his voice, Jack said, "I'm sorry."

That couldn't have been easy for Jack to say, and maybe if Griffin had been in the man's shoes, he'd have reacted the same, though he'd have slugged Jack on day one regardless of Gray's order.

Hell, the mere sight of Shep's hands on Savanna, a woman he'd only known for twenty-four hours, made him nuts. So if he discovered another man had slept with his wife —he'd most likely murder the guy and dump the body— unlike his dad, who'd tried to make it work with his mom, only for it to blow up in his face.

Griffin extended a peace offering by way of a handshake. Jack's shoulders fell, but he accepted his palm.

"You two good now?" Gray called out, coming down the

steps of the jet. "Because Oliver's here, and he needs Savanna's help."

At that news, Savanna started past Griffin, but he couldn't help himself as he reached out and captured her arm. "Can I have one second?"

He waited for Shep and Jack to leave the two of them alone before releasing her arm. She tipped her head up to peer at him with guarded eyes.

"Are you okay?" she asked in a soft voice. "That was intense."

"It needed to happen, I suppose. Clear the air so we can focus on what's important." He tucked his hands in his jeans pockets. "This exchange, though, has me worried that Shep is going to try and come with us on that jet. Jesse too. And I don't think that's a good idea. I don't think either will be able to see clearly when it comes to you, particularly Shep."

She studied him with a frown on her beautiful face.

"Shep has feelings for you," he slowly pointed out. "And if he comes along, I can see that creating some tension," he admitted, "and I might lose my focus."

Her mouth opened, prepared to protest—he wasn't sure about which part—but then she pressed her lips together.

"They're also civilians," he tossed out. A weak excuse, he knew. Even as he tried to convince himself it had nothing to do with the ridiculous jealousy he felt toward Shep's relationship with Savanna and more to do with his concern that Shep would react just as Jack did if he suspected Griffin had crossed a line with Savanna at the cabin.

"You're a civilian, remember?" She arched a brow.

"I may not have the country's flag on my arm anymore, but—"

"You wear it on your heart," she finished for him.

He smiled. "I doubt I'll ever consider myself a civilian again."

She looked back over her shoulder at Oliver, who was carrying one of Marcus's boxes in his hands. "I agree, they shouldn't come." When Savanna turned his way again, she looked as if she'd just gotten the worst news of her life. And he had to believe it was the box in Oliver's hand that'd produced that effect. "Plus, I'd rather them stay here and protect Ella and the others."

Ella, right. Ella was Jesse's girl. *Jesse's girl? That a song?* He removed his hands from his pockets and nearly slapped himself in the back of his head at the distracting thought.

"Savanna," Oliver called out, snagging both Griffin's and Savanna's attention. He jerked his head to the side, motioning for them to join him where he'd set the box down.

When the rest of the team gathered around Oliver, Griffin assumed the two Greeks were bound and gagged inside the jet.

Griffin set his hand on the small of Savanna's back, but that reminded him Shep's hand had been there earlier, so he quickly pulled away. Maybe she wasn't just Marcus's girl? Maybe she belonged to Shep too.

"Tell me this isn't yours, and you didn't do your best to make sure it was never found inside the Mustang," Oliver teased with a smile while holding up what looked like a brass barrel key with some type of intricate design at the top.

Savanna reached out and took the key, turned it this way and that while looking at it closely, but remained quiet.

"Not yours?" Griffin asked as all eyes were on her.

"I've never seen it before," she answered, then looked down at Oliver crouched and searching the box. "What are you doing?"

"I have a pretty good memory, and when I saw the key, the symbol at the top looked familiar. I remembered seeing it when going through these boxes the other day." Oliver stood and handed her a photo.

She swapped the key for the photo, and Griffin looked over her shoulder to view it.

She ran a finger over the face of one of the boys, probably Marcus as a teen. He assumed it was Nick and their father with him in the photo. "I remember this."

"That symbol on the key is engraved on the building behind them. I don't know where the photo was taken, but we can upload the symbol to try and get a match," Oliver explained. "Do you happen to know anything about this photo or why Nick would hide a key with that symbol in the Mustang?"

Savanna glanced up at Griffin for a moment before resetting her hazel eyes on the photo of the man she'd lost. "Marcus was sixteen in this photo. And it was taken in Greece," she dropped the news on them. "I only remember the details because he told me he got to spend that summer with his dad in Santorini. His dad had been hired to design some special security vault, which housed individual safe boxes inside. The place is similar to a bank, but I don't think money's stored there." She blinked a few times, pulling herself out of her memories. "Sorry, I don't remember the specifics. But Marcus also told me about that summer because it's when he lost his virginity to a Greek girl."

"He told you he lost his virginity there?" Oliver followed up as if more shocked by that part of her explanation than the fact some mystery key was connected to Greece.

She nodded and looked straight at Griffin. "He was an open book with me."

An open book? Hell, she had a good memory too. Within

the first hour of meeting her, he'd handed her a snarky comment about not being an open book. Called her Sugar too. God, he was an ass.

Carter folded his arms and steered the conversation where it needed to be. "What else do you remember?"

Savanna peered back at the photo, then closed her eyes as if trying to draw more information to her mind. "Ada-something. Um. Adámas," she said while snapping the fingers of her free hand. "I think that's what Marcus had called it. He'd been pretty proud of his dad."

Griffin opened his phone and looked up the word. "Diamond. Invincible."

"Explains why there's a diamond surrounded by what looks like Greek letters for the symbol," Oliver noted.

"It also means," Griffin added, "unbreakable."

Savanna's eyes opened as if he'd shaken loose another memory with the word. "Yes, that's it. The vault was nicknamed adámas because it was deemed unbreakable. Marcus's dad helped design it to ensure the vault couldn't be breached. That was years ago, so I don't know if it's still impenetrable, but . . ."

"So, I'm just thinking out loud here, but are we assuming, based on this key that matches the one on the building in that photo, that Nick opened an account for a safe-deposit box in the vault his father designed and helped build within that very building in Santorini?" Gray began, his thoughts on point with where Griffin's were at right now. "And the safe-deposit box is where he hid whatever he stole? Obviously, he used an alias. And as an extra insurance policy in case he was captured, he hid the key to the box in Marcus's Mustang so that whoever got to him first would need to keep him alive to track down the key."

"They'd probably need Nick himself to access both the

vault and his safe-deposit box even if they obtained the key. I'm betting that once inside the building, you also need identification along with a fingerprint or retinal scan to access their vault," Griffin added.

"So, are you saying Nick chose that vault in Greece because if he's captured, and um, tortured for the location but refuses to hand over the key, the bad guys can't just force Nick to do what he does best . . . break into the vault to get to the box and recover what he'd stored there?" Savanna added her two cents, and she was spot on in Griffin's opinion.

"Maybe. Because it's probably one of the few places he, himself, can't infiltrate. But most likely, he chose that location because of its significance to him. His memories with Marcus and his father. And he believed it was the safest place to hide whatever he has."

Savanna looked at the photo, then back at Griffin. "Wouldn't they eventually get Nick to give up the key? He has to know they'd kill him if he didn't. But I suppose this all was meant to buy himself time until . . . well, whatever he has planned. And he's hoping he's never captured."

Griffin tensed at what he had to say next. "Or they'd find someone they believed Nick cared about and threaten her. Possibly use *you* to force him out of hiding in the first place." He paused at what that also might mean. "The Archer Group may think you worked with Nick, though, which is why they're also after you."

"*Or* Joe lied about that, and they want Savanna for the same reasons as the others, to bait Nick," Gray said with a grimace because no one wanted a Teamguy to be their enemy.

"I don't think Joe would be okay with using an innocent woman to draw out a criminal," Griffin quickly defended him, despite the fact Joe ordered the beatdown earlier, and his ribs still hurt. "And he genuinely seemed to believe Savanna was dangerous. A threat."

"Multiple possible motives. Multiple people hunting her down. This is messy," Carter bit out.

Savanna lifted the photo and touched Marcus's face again, and it had his stomach squeezing at the pain she must have been feeling right now. "I just don't believe a man I've met one time would give up whatever was important enough for him to risk his life for . . . for me."

"Maybe he won't," Griffin admitted, because Nick was a criminal, after all. "But if you're the only living family he has, it's possible these Greeks, and whoever else may want him, are hoping Nick cares enough to save you if they have you in their possession. But I think we were right to assume no one knew Nick ever hid anything at Savanna's place. They're just after you."

The hangar was quiet for a minute or two, everyone giving Savanna some space to absorb the news. And then Jack said, "Well, I guess it's *safe* to say that *safe* is still unbreakable. Well, the vault containing the safe boxes, at least." He was probably trying to lighten the dark mood settling inside the hangar despite the fact they now had a possible break. A lead.

"So." Carter pointed to the jet. "Lucky for us, I have a new *safe* house in Santorini."

Of course, you do.

Jack cracked a smile. "Yeah, no, you suck at humor. Good try, though." He slapped Carter on the back, and more of that tension fizzled. Thank God for something.

Maybe Griffin would get along with Jack after all.

"Let's go." Carter turned toward Shep and Jesse. "You two are staying."

Jesse stepped forward with palms in the air, preparing his

protest.

"You need to stay with Ella," Savanna spoke up before Jesse could say more. "Please.'"

"Like hell are you getting on that plane without one of us with you." Shep moved to stand in front of her, and the rest of the guys, aside from Griffin and Carter, started for the jet. "A.J. wouldn't approve of you taking her. Period."

"He would if he knew a team of spec ops guys managed to track her down to that cabin against all odds," Carter pointed out.

Shep drew his hands to his hips, and Jesse remained next to him in a guarded stance.

"More reason for us to go with you," Shep interjected, his gaze lingering on Savanna.

Yeah, the man cared about her, but did he want more than friendship? Griffin would bet money on it.

"And what's to stop these guys that were sent to the cabin from following you to Greece? If they found you at the cabin, don't you think they have eyes on us now?" Jesse addressed the elephant in the room, the concern that no one wanted to talk about in front of Savanna. Because yes, they would most likely track them to Greece. And it was why they'd be letting Savanna use her real name and passport for this trip. There was no point in hiding the fact she was leaving the country.

"Yeah, but we'll be in a secure location in Oia, the northern part of the island," Carter began, "so unless these guys try to take us out with a drone strike, they won't be getting onto the property. I have a team prepping the site as we speak."

"Drone strike?" Shep's eyes widened. "That a possibility?"

"If it was, do you think I'd take Savanna there?" Griffin looked straight at Shep. "They want her alive for questioning or as bait to draw out Nick. They won't risk an aerial attack and possibly killing her."

"But we're sitting ducks here," Carter said. "We won't be there. You have my word."

"Who the hell are you?" Shep arched a brow. "For real."

Carter only winked, which was as forced as the humor he'd tried a few minutes ago.

"I still want to go," Jesse insisted.

Savanna handed the photo to Carter, then pulled Jesse's palm between hers. "Ella has to be freaking out. Please stay with her. I'll feel better knowing not just more of Carter's men are here, but that she has you too." She looked to Shep. "And you."

"I can't do this. I can't watch you get on that plane." Shep wanted to add, *with him*, didn't he? Because his attention was dead set on Griffin when he'd spoken. He was jealous too.

"I'm afraid you don't have a choice. I can't force Savanna to go with us, but this is my team, my op, and you're not coming." And with that, Carter started for the plane, letting them know the discussion was over.

Well, Griffin sure as hell would force Savanna to go with them. He had to keep her safe, and the best way to do that was with his team.

Savanna turned to the side and set her eyes on Griffin. "Give me a minute alone, okay? Be on the plane in a second."

He didn't want to walk away from her, but he lightly nodded. He remembered he'd left their duffel bag of clothes in the bathroom, so he started that way for it. And he told himself not to look back at her. He was worried he'd see Shep hugging her. Touching her. And irrational as it was, he'd lose his control again.

He cursed under his breath as he pushed the bathroom door open. *I'm so fucked.*

CHAPTER SEVENTEEN

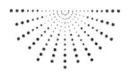

"I'm in good hands. I promise. But I have to save Nick, and—"

"Wait, what? This isn't about saving Nick. This is about saving you." Jesse lightly gripped Savanna's arm as if she'd lost her senses.

"I have to," she whispered around the tight knot in her throat. How could she explain this without crying? "Marcus died without ever forgiving his brother. And that hurts me to think about. If somehow, I can help Nick find redemption, I feel like . . ."

"Marcus is gone, Savanna. You can't repair that relationship by trying to change Nick's ways," Shep spoke up in a terse voice. Worry lines formed on his forehead at the idea she was more focused on helping Nick than protecting her own life.

"I don't expect you to get it. I barely understand it myself. But there has to be some good in him. He's been sending me money to help me every month since his brother died. He cares, maybe not enough to exchange his life for mine, though. He may be a criminal, but—"

"There are no buts. This is pretty black and white," Jesse said. "If Marcus refused to forgive him, he had a damn good reason. He would kill his own brother for what he's done by endangering you. Believe me when I say that." He hung his head as if hating his choice of words, and he released her.

"I'll be okay. Griffin won't let anything happen to me." She looked Griffin's way as he exited the bathroom holding their shared duffel bag, and her chest squeezed at the sight of him.

So much had happened today.

So. Damn. Much.

They started the day with a baking lesson and ended it by running for their lives, *again*, after being tracked down by a group of PMCs who thought she was a traitor. Throw in Jack accusing Griffin of cheating with his wife and the news about Nick hiding a key in Marcus's Mustang that possibly opened a mysterious safe-deposit box in Greece, and she was ready to call it a night.

That was the definition of a long day.

"Trust me when I say you want me going with you," Jesse said in a deep voice. "There are things you don't know about me. Skills I have and—"

"Yeah, so I've noticed. You going to tell me about what you've been keeping from us?" She crossed her arms and pointed her attention back on Jesse once Griffin was out of sight and inside the jet.

"Let's focus on one problem at a time," Jesse replied.

Problem? What kind of problem did Jesse have? That's what he'd implied, right? "I need you to stay with Ella." Savanna looked back and forth between Jesse and Shep, but she knew Shep wasn't going to join her side on this. "Think about this. These people are willing to go through me to get to Nick. It's only a matter of time before they decide to target someone *I* care about to get to *me* in order to get to Nick. I can't have anything happening to Ella or Beckett's daughter because of me."

Jesse frowned, but she could tell he was coming around to giving in to her request by the way his shoulders fell.

"Carter has some of his men keeping watch here, but I've seen you in action, Jesse. Who do you think I'd trust to protect our friends and family more than you?" She unfolded her arms and reached out for Jesse and Shep, placing a palm on each of their forearms. "Please."

"Fine. But I want updates. Like every hour," Jesse grumbled. He pulled her in for a quick hug and then strode up the steps into the plane. Probably to issue threats to the guys about guarding her with their lives.

"I don't like you alone with him," Shep said, gently placing his hands on her shoulders.

"I won't be completely alone," she reminded him, knowing full well what he was referring to. But where was this jealousy coming from? Savanna was pretty confident that's exactly what it was. But Shep had admitted their oops-moment was a big mistake. Said they could never be more than friends not only because of Marcus but because he was a self-proclaimed asshole. Playboy was more like it.

"Savanna, maybe I . . ." Shep's eyes thinned, and his words appeared to get stuck in his throat.

"Maybe what?" Thinking better of it, she held up a hand, having decided that right now wasn't the best time for proclamations of any kind. "Tell me when I'm home. Okay?"

He drew her into his muscular frame for a hug, and when she untangled herself from his embrace, she spotted Griffin standing by the steps of the jet waiting for her, his eyes on the ceiling instead of them.

"I'll see you soon." She patted Shep's chest before

turning away to follow that inexplicable magnetic pull guiding her to a man she barely knew. A man who, for reasons she'd yet to figure out, she wanted to know everything about.

"Hi," she breathed out. Now that they were face-to-face and about to board a private jet to an exotic Greek island, she could almost convince herself she was living out one of her romance novels with Griffin as her hero. He'd certainly played the part when he pinned her to the wall at the cabin and acted out the steamy scene she'd recited at his request. It was a moment she'd relive for the rest of her life.

She trusted that life would be a long one, and Marcus seemed determined to watch over her to ensure that.

"You ready to go?" Griffin asked.

Savanna followed his gaze to Shep, who'd given them space while he waited for Jesse to exit the plane. Shep was a kind, considerate man, a good friend, and she cared about him deeply, but that was as far as her feelings went. And she was pretty sure he felt the same toward her. His hasty *maybe I* was an impulsive reaction to Griffin.

Griffin, on the other hand, made her come alive in a way she hadn't known was still possible. And he'd be lying through his teeth if he denied the potent connection flowing between them. His responses to her were more telling than he wanted to admit. That baloney he'd handed her about not allowing himself to fall for her because he'd break her heart *before* she could break his made her wonder if he was more familiar with romance novels than he let on.

"Yeah, I guess I'm as ready as I'll ever be," she said softly. She exchanged one last look with Shep and another hug with Jesse, who'd just stomped down the stairs looking grouchy as hell, then boarded the jet.

The plane was spacious and, from the looks of it, even

had a bedroom in the back. She didn't know what kind it was or any specific details, but it had to have cost a fortune.

She settled into one of the leather reclining chairs and buckled in. Griffin sat across from her instead of next to her, leaving the window chair empty on her right. "I can't believe this is my first time leaving the country."

"Why haven't you traveled?"

Savanna looked over to where Gray and Jack were sitting closer to the cockpit. Oliver and Carter were talking, sitting not far away from them. She had no idea why she'd chosen to sit on the far end of the plane, near the doors leading to the bedroom, but based on Griffin's weird mood, she hadn't expected him to *want* to sit near her.

"Because I, um, got my passport in 2014. And then it just didn't feel right to use it after, um."

So many ums. So many uncomfortable pauses whenever she spoke of her late husband around Griffin, worried that any mention of Marcus would give him more ammo to avoid her, which she was pretty sure she didn't want to happen.

"Oh," was all he said, then remained quiet until they were coasting at cruising altitude. "I'm glad Marcus was able to be an open book with you. That's not easy to find, especially in a serviceman."

Savanna took a minute to absorb his unexpected words. "He used to tell me that every chapter of his life brought him one page closer to his epilogue." Her eyes welled with sudden tears at that memory, at how poetic Marcus was at times. "He said I was his epilogue. His happy ending." She sniffled and swiped a hand beneath her eye at the realization she was crying. "And then I . . . I used to say . . ." Her voice cracked as she spoke, and she hiccupped, emotion swelling in her chest from out of nowhere. "I used to tell him he was my prologue. He was only my beginning. That my life started once we met."

Griffin quickly unbuckled his seat belt and slid his large frame into the chair beside her.

With watery eyes, she looked over at him, knowing damn well she was most likely closing the door on anything more happening between them. The ring didn't need to be on her finger for this man because he still saw it as if it sparkled in the light.

Griffin looked to the front of the cabin as if checking the location of the rest of the team, then he set his hand on top of hers, which lay on the armrest between them, and gently squeezed. "If he was your prologue," he said, his voice still gritty, "then you still have a lot of story left." His brows tightened as he held her eyes. "Many more chapters. And I believe he'd want you to experience the best story possible."

More tears fell down her cheeks, faster this time. "I felt stuck on the same page for the longest time," she whispered, worried her voice would break again. And maybe her constant book references were a bit much, but for some reason, Griffin seemed to understand her and her connection with reading more than she'd anticipated most men would. "And then a stranger came into my life and called me Sugar." She closed her eyes. "And the page turned."

CHAPTER EIGHTEEN

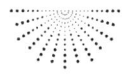

OIA, SANTORINI - GREECE

"When you said you had a safe house on a compound, well, I have to admit this is not what I was expecting," Savanna said as she and Carter strolled the property.

"This used to be a hotel. Fifteen bedrooms, so there's plenty of space." As they walked, Carter tucked his hands into the pockets of the black slacks he'd changed into on the flight over. Savanna had spent half of their twelve-hour-plus flight asleep and the other half alternating between looking up info about Santorini and reading a book she'd downloaded onto Griffin's secure phone. "I prefer not to stand out, so better to rent a place that blends in, you know?"

She considered asking Carter how he was able to afford this hotel-slash-"safe house" on a Greek island that, according to what she'd read, was considered one of the most beautiful and romantic destinations in the world, but she bit her tongue. He obviously didn't have a cash flow problem, which only reminded her of how much trouble she was in financially. But that wasn't her main priority right now, so she did her best to sweep that problem to the side for the time being.

Her hands went to the whitewashed stone wall of the veranda as she looked off to her left at the pristine white houses that looked like sugar cubes with blue accents and appeared to be carved right into the cliffs in the distance. "This place is like a dream," she murmured, wishing she was there for a romantic vacation and not because Nick had put a target on her head.

It was after five p.m. in Greece, so they were eight hours ahead of Alabama. The sky was clear, and the temperature was a mild mid-seventies. Basically, perfect.

"It's pretty nice," Carter casually said, standing alongside her now.

She wasn't sure where Griffin and the others had gone after exiting the SUV upon arrival, but Carter had offered her a personal tour of the property. She was almost surprised Griffin left her side, but then, he'd barely said a word to her since she'd poured her heart out to him on the jet. Of course, yesterday, on their way to the hangar, he'd told her that it would be best if someone else kept a close eye on her.

But when Jack offered to do it, Griffin shot down that idea. The man was confusing.

She couldn't help but wonder what happened in Griffin's past that had him so sure she'd break his heart.

"Why Greece?" She looked toward the endless blue water of the glistening Aegean Sea, then over to Carter.

He smiled and opened his palms. "I like being by the water. My place on the French Riviera was compromised, so I relocated."

"A helo pad with what I'm fairly certain has a Black Hawk parked on it. Several sports cars in the garage. Ten armed guards I counted on our tour of the property. Do you also have some type of aerial defense system overhead to intercept a rocket?" she asked with a smile, and Carter only shrugged. "And if men try to drop in from a helicopter like yesterday at Griffin's cabin, what will happen to them?"

Carter's dark eyes fixed on her as he lightly tipped his head, studying her. What was on his mind? What was this mysterious man thinking about?

The sea breeze suddenly whipped her hair across her face, and she shifted it behind her ears before turning away from him and toward the gasp-worthy views. *Paradise. I'm in paradise.*

"Will your men be able to get those two Greeks to talk?" she asked when he remained quiet.

"If I couldn't get them to open up, then most likely not. And Gray won't let me torture them," he said on a sigh as if it was a terrible inconvenience not to be able to inflict pain on the men.

"I guess Gray has a moral compass. Did you lose yours?" She hadn't meant to speak her thoughts aloud, especially to a man who was going through all of this trouble to save her, but she wasn't always great at keeping her mouth shut.

"I lost mine the day my wife was brutally butchered," he said in a solemn tone, and chills chased down her spine at his words.

"I'm so sorry," was all she could manage. "I didn't realize you were a widower. I'm sorry we have that in common."

Carter braced his hands on the stone wall, which looked to be made from the volcanic rock found on the island. His jaw was tight as he eyed the water, and she sensed he was reliving the horror of his past the same as she'd done countless times. The memory of her husband's execution streamed online for the world to see.

And as always, when that image came to mind, her stomach flipped, and she set a hand on her abdomen.

"We're ready to go," someone called out behind them, but she took a moment to collect herself before tracking the voice to Jack.

Hm. Another J. Heartbreaker too? Maybe she needed to forget that TikTok video once and for all.

Griffin was standing alongside Jack. Oliver as well. But Gray wasn't in sight.

"Where are we going?" She set her eyes on the man who'd made her feel so much in such a short period of time, but his gaze was concealed by aviator shades.

Griffin had also changed on the flight over. Jeans and a white polo. He'd washed his hair, and it was a little spiky and pushed to the side. *Handsome as hell.*

"You're not going anywhere," Jack said while striding closer, but Griffin remained standing a good ten feet away.

"You guys worked during most of the flight. But if you found out something, why haven't you told me?" Were they keeping her in the dark? Worried she couldn't handle it? *I own a café. I bake cookies and brew espressos. I'm not an operator,* she reminded herself. But still, after everything they'd been through together, she wanted to be kept in the loop, especially since it involved Marcus's brother.

"We're narrowing down possibilities as to what this Elysium might be. Although, we've eliminated that it references a person," Oliver spoke up. Of the three men outside on the veranda with her, he appeared less guarded than the others. Not quite laid-back, just more easygoing. "But we did find the location that matched the symbol from the picture. You were right, the place is like a bank but not for money. Antiques, rare belongings, and personal valuables that people want to keep safe are kept within one part of their state-of-the-art vault. The other part of the vault is for individual safe-deposit boxes. We made an appointment to have a look since they have no website or public records online in order to maintain discretion."

"Oh, okay." Savanna folded her arms when another bluster of air hit her. She'd changed into a pair of jeans and a pink button-down blouse after using the shower on the plane. But the sleeves were rolled to her elbows, goose bumps evident on her forearms.

"Gray is staying behind to work on some more leads. We're doing our best to figure out who Nick worked for by trying to track some of these Greeks' past movements, but my guess is their boss is damn good at covering his tracks for us to still not find anything," Carter added, then looked to Griffin. "I assume you're staying with Savanna? My men are here, but—"

"I'm staying," Griffin announced in a deep voice that brooked no argument. Savanna was struck with relief. She didn't want to be without that man. She felt safe with him, and even if he believed he'd failed her at the cabin yesterday, she disagreed.

"Thought so." Carter tipped his head as if to signal to Jack and Oliver to head out. "We shouldn't be more than a few hours."

Once they were alone, Griffin said, "I can show you to your room. It has a patio with the same view if you feel like sitting outside and reading to pass the time?"

"You know how to make a girl smile," she lightly teased. "Is it safe to sit outside?"

"I wouldn't let you do it if I thought there was a sniper on that sailboat waiting for the perfect shot," he said while pointing toward the water.

She glanced at the sailboat bobbing in the water off in the

distance as he approached her. "Thanks for putting that thought in my head. Maybe I'll just read on the bed."

"This is your first time abroad. Sit in the sun." His voice was softer now. And when he lifted a hand and gently swept back her hair, which had blown across her face again, she went still.

She slowly pivoted her attention to his face, wishing she could see his eyes to get a read on him. Why was she so desperate to kiss him again? To have his tongue tangle with hers in a seductive slow dance? He was one hell of a kisser.

For some crazy reason, when she'd thought Griffin had slept with Jack's ex, her stomach had done a sickening somersault. She hadn't experienced jealousy since she was in her early twenties when the "frog hogs"—women whose goal was to get their hooks into a SEAL—used to flirt shamelessly with Marcus when they went out to the bars in Virginia Beach. Marcus never gave them the time of day, and her gut told her Griffin would be the same.

But I'll never find out. "Okay, take me to my room." *And then fuck me senseless up against the wall. On the bed. Balcony. In the shower. Screw my brains out until I can't walk.*

She scolded herself as they walked along in silence and did her best to keep her mouth shut and not voice *those* thoughts.

"Not how I imagined my first trip out of the States, but I can't complain about the location." *Small talk, Savanna. Just make small talk,* she told herself as they entered the whitewashed stone building that sat on the cliffside.

But her thoughts swung back around to dirty the moment she chanced a look at the chiseled jaw of the man walking alongside her wearing his *Top Gun* aviators, not a hint he'd been badly beaten yesterday. God, he was so sexy.

"You're blushing."

Savanna abruptly stopped and palmed her cheeks to discover they were on fire. She was too young to be having hot flashes, right? Her eyes went from the aviators now hooked to the neck of his shirt on up to his dark, hooded eyes.

She didn't have to tell him that within seconds she'd skipped straight to a fantasy playing out in her mind. He knew. *She* was an open book, unlike him.

His lips remained in a tight line as he pointed to the door a few paces away. "Your room." Two distinct lines cut across his forehead as he studied her while she slowly lowered her hands from her face that had to be redder than red, a contrast to her normally olive skin.

Griffin's eyes held hers as he drew in a deep breath, exhaled slowly, and swallowed hard. Then, reaching into his back pocket, he pulled out a key card as if they really were in a hotel and opened the door. From the looks of it, he was having his own dirty thoughts, but he was doing a better job of keeping them in check.

"Carter arranged for someone to shop for you. The dresser should be full. Knowing Carter, he instructed the personal shopper to include everything you could possibly need, including underwear bound to be more exciting than what I packed for you."

Oh my. Exciting underwear? And now her cheeks were on fire again. "He really pulls out all of the stops." She forced a smile and brushed past him to check out her room.

It was simple but elegant. A king-size bed with an antique white headboard and a quilted bedspread the color of the Aegean Sea reminded her of the small whitewashed houses and their blue dome-shaped roofs that dotted the cliffs. Other than the lamp on a nightstand by the bed and the matching white antique dresser, there was no other furniture. "It's amazing. You'll be next door, I assume? Am I okay alone?"

Maybe you should sleep with me. In my bed.

"That door connects to my room," he said, pointing to what she'd assumed was a closet by the bed. "I'd prefer you to keep it unlocked so I can get in that way if needed, but yes, you'll be safe."

Connecting door, huh? Annnd she was two seconds away from whipping up a new fantasy.

Griffin crossed the room and drew the floor-to-ceiling curtains open to reveal the balcony and the gorgeous view he'd promised. After a long pause during which Savanna figured he was taking in the view, he slowly turned toward her, one hand gripping the back of his neck. His dark eyes pinned her with that intense, broody look she'd quickly grown familiar with. The man's mood seemed to change as often as the wind. Joking and sweet one minute, growly the next. There was a reason for this change in mood, and it wasn't good, was it?

"What else did you learn on the plane?" she challenged. "Look, I know I bake cookies and brew coffee for a living, but since this is my life on the line, I'd like to be kept in the know." Plus, Marcus had educated her over the years. She knew a thing or two about special operations.

When he remained quiet, she decided she could wait a few more minutes to find out what that dark look in his eyes was all about, so she went over to check out the new clothes in the dresser.

Griffin had been right about Carter being a full-service host. The top drawer was filled with red, black, and nude lace lingerie. She lifted one set from the drawer, forgetting she had an audience as she admired the matching red bra and panties, but startled when Griffin placed his hand on her forearm as though prompting her to put it away.

Savanna peered at him over the curve of her shoulder to find his head cocked, eyes on the bra as if picturing her in it.

"Nothing Carter didn't already say outside. Nick's boss most likely had him steal something from the Archer Group that was inside a vault, and that's why Joe's team is after him. And we're coming up empty on tracking Nick's past whereabouts aside from your place. And nothing on the Greeks, either, that is of any use."

"Don't you think it's a little weird Nick would risk his life by double-crossing his boss?" She'd voiced the thought that'd been brewing in the back of her mind all day.

"Money makes people do crazy things. I assume he decided to sell whatever his boss wanted him to steal and keep the money himself."

Her shoulders sank. "I don't know. I guess he didn't realize the shit storm he'd stir up when he betrayed his boss, but something tells me there's more to all this."

"I know you want to believe Nick is redeemable, but I don't want to see you get your heart broken."

"That seems to be the theme for you," she whispered, then finally turned back toward the dresser, which had him releasing his hold of her.

She put away the lingerie and closed the drawer. "Any other news?"

When she turned toward him, nearly colliding with his large, muscular frame, the slant inward of his brows was a yes.

But what was it he didn't want to share?

She leaned back against the dresser, and in an attempt to stare the answer out of him, folded her arms and steadied her gaze as she waited for her Jedi mind trick to draw out the information.

Griffin swiped a palm over his jaw and the shadow of what would quickly become a beard if he didn't shave soon.

His expression hardened the same way Marcus's used to right before he shared the news he'd lost someone in combat. And if the dresser hadn't been propping her up, she'd have stumbled backward at the grave look in Griffin's eyes.

"What is it?" she cried, tears welling in her eyes. She knew what Griffin was about to tell her was going to hurt. And she was tired of what she called "the hurt." The pain that sliced through her like a machete whenever the darkness of what happened to Marcus swarmed her thoughts.

"I asked Gray to look into something for me," he began in a steady voice.

"Joe," she said, awareness settling in. "You took a bullet for him when your team was sent in to assist Joe's squadron in Iraq. That means you operated with . . ." *Marcus.* Her hands slid down to her abdomen, where the pain always struck first.

"I couldn't remember him, which didn't make sense. So, I wanted to read the official report, find out what happened after I was shot that day. See how Marcus fits into, um, the story." He took a step closer and ran the pad of his thumb over her cheek as if once again wiping away flour. When her breath hitched at his touch, his hard expression softened ever so slightly. "After I lost consciousness, Marcus took out the sniper that shot me and then helped carry my ass over a mile to an exfil site and got me on a helo to safety."

"You're saying Marcus saved you after you saved Joe?" she whispered in disbelief at the news there was a connection between her husband and the man standing before her. And was that supposed to mean something? Or was it just a twist of fate? Nature of the job? Two special operators who'd crossed paths once upon a time ago.

"Marcus didn't want any credit. Based on his words in the report, he blamed himself for the fact someone from another unit took a bullet for one of his own teammates. He asked for his name not to be shared with me. He didn't believe he deserved to be thanked."

Sounds like Marcus. "I-I need to sit down."

Griffin lowered his arm and turned to the side as if to offer her passage to flee.

Her legs didn't seem to want to work, though.

She couldn't move.

Recognizing that she was clearly on the verge of an emotional breakdown, Griffin stepped forward, wrapped his arms around her, and pulled her against his body.

He hugged her tightly, one warm palm stroking up and down her back as the other cradled her head beneath his chin, giving her exactly what she needed at that moment. Comfort.

Savanna remained in his embrace as tears streamed down her cheeks and over her lips to drip off her chin. She lost herself in her sorrow but finally, with a shuddery breath, pulled back and looked up at him.

He framed his hands on her hips for a moment before sliding them up and over her arms, then to her face, and held her cheeks between his palms.

"I survived that day because of your husband. And I'll do everything in my power to keep his wife safe. I'd do it anyway, but knowing this . . ." His dark brown eyes vanished from view when he sealed his lids tight.

Wife. Griffin would never lose hold of that word. He'd never be able to see her as more than Marcus's wife, and she didn't blame him. She was certain this officially cemented the wall between them in Griffin's eyes.

And it broke her heart.

Because now she was convinced Marcus placed this man in her path for a reason. *He* sent Griffin to her.

"I'm going to go check on Gray," he said a moment later with eyes open. "And then work out to let off some steam," he added after releasing her face and stepping back.

"Aren't you in pain?" was all she managed to say, her heart and mind conflicted. The already tattered pieces of her heart felt as if they were about to be carried out to sea and lost forever if she let the only man who made her feel anything since Marcus slip away.

"I'm tough. Don't worry." A small smile formed on his lips. "But I might swim a few laps in the indoor pool I spotted earlier as my workout." He reached into his pocket and handed her his phone. "Here," he offered. "In case you feel like reading."

She accepted his phone and smiled. "Thanks for downloading the Kindle app for me on the plane. But maybe I'll join you for a swim in a bit? Not sure if I want to be alone here," she admitted.

"I would never leave you if I didn't believe you were safe here." He gently gripped her arms. "Trust me when I say that Carter's safe houses are really damn safe."

"No, I mean," she said around a shaky exhale, "I don't want to be alone."

He unhooked his sunglasses from his shirt before taking another step back as if he didn't trust himself to be so close to her. He was prepared to shield his eyes from her even indoors, too, wasn't he?

She doubted Delta operators were afraid of much, but this one seemed to be terrified of her.

CHAPTER NINETEEN

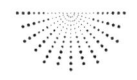

An hour had passed since Griffin revealed that her late husband had saved his life. With Griffin's permission, she'd phoned Jesse's new burner to let him know she was okay, then decided to sit on the balcony and try to read. The temperature had dropped a few degrees as evening settled in, and it really was too chilly to be wearing the bikini she had on.

Considering all the sexy lingerie and bikinis among the clothes purchased for her, she had a sneaking suspicion that a man had done the shopping. A woman would have gone with comfort, especially knowing Savanna wasn't actually there on vacation. But then again, maybe that was the cover story Carter put out there.

Savanna laid Griffin's phone on the dresser and peered at her reflection in the mirror above it. Her breasts were dangerously close to spilling out of the bright blue triangles of the bikini top, but the tiny black bottoms tied precariously at her hips were kind of sexy. She did a little spin and noticed her ass looked pretty damn good in the thing.

"I'm losing my mind," she mumbled under her breath.

"I'm not on vacation." But she needed to distract herself from the chaos. To not focus on the past for once or get lost in the fear of unknowns. So many unknowns. Particularly the possible ramifications of Nick's actions.

She considered reading again. Slipping into bed and back into a fictional world where she'd be safe. It was a smoking hot mafia world too. But while she was reading on the balcony, it'd been hard to focus on the fictional man living on the pages because she longed for the flesh-and-blood man who was literally somewhere in this fancy safe house, half-naked and dripping wet.

"Screw it." Maybe she couldn't have Griffin, but she could imagine it, right?

After slipping off her bikini bottoms, she pulled down the blue cover on the bed and slid between the cool sheets, then pulled the top sheet up to her hips. She closed her eyes and allowed her hand to slowly wander over her top, down the smooth skin of her stomach, and finally between her legs. It seemed she'd become some sex-crazed woman the moment Griffin had walked into her life not even two days ago.

A hell of a lot had happened in those two days, not the least of which was an indescribable connection with Griffin, one that went beyond desire. But the man seemed to be honor-bound by his history, brief though it was, with Marcus. And he was doing his best to deny that connection and keep himself from giving in to the desire she knew he felt. So for right now, her only recourse, short of throwing herself at him, was to get herself off like she'd done back at the cabin.

Only now she could call up the memory of his mouth devouring hers, his tongue slipping between her lips, and his fingers pinching her nipple. But best of all, the way he'd brought her to a shattering orgasm.

She strummed her fingers over her clit, finding her sex already soaked at the idea it was Griffin's hand instead.

Her nipples strained against the small triangles attempting to contain her breasts, and she bit into her lip to stifle a groan as she imagined Griffin taking her over his knee and spanking her for touching herself instead of waiting for him to do it.

She wasn't sure why that fantasy popped into her head because she wasn't even into that . . . or was she? Because the thought of Griffin spanking her ass, demanding that she take her punishment, made her even wetter.

His large palms rubbing soothing circles over her stinging bottom afterward, telling her how well she did, then tossing her onto the bed and bracing himself over her naked body.

Bringing his lips right against her ear and hissing, *You belong to me, and only me,* as he settled the crown of his cock between her thighs and pushed into her in one shockingly swift movement that'd have her back arching off the bed.

Damn, she was close to coming just thinking about Griffin dominating her like that. Pleasuring her. Owning what Savanna wanted to be his.

She rubbed harder and faster, her breathing accelerated but then . . .

She stopped on the cusp of her orgasm, one she was dying to have, and cursed under her breath. "I want you," she whispered. "I want it to be you touching me." She swallowed and opened her eyes. *Talking to myself. Great.* But she needed to feel a man's hands on her. A man's touch. *Griffin's* touch.

Savanna lifted her hand from her oversensitive sex and got out of bed, washed her hands, and put her bikini bottoms back on.

She cinched the tie of a short silk robe she found hanging in the bathroom closet—and wow, they really did think of everything—then opened her bedroom door to go search for Griffin.

One of Carter's men stood at attention across the hall. *Of course, Griffin wouldn't just leave me alone.*

Smiling, she asked, "Do you know where Griffin is?"

The man's gaze quickly skated from her face to her bare feet and then back up to her face. "I believe he's at the pool. I'll escort you there."

"Thank you. And how long have you been with Carter?" she asked as they walked, curious if he'd be tight-lipped or willing to shed some light on the mysterious Carter Dominick.

"Two years, ma'am."

"Military?" she asked, noting the polite but serious tone in his voice and his deference toward her.

"Air Force previously," he said while stealing a quick look at her before returning his attention to the frosted glass door on approach. The hours of operation were still printed on the door from when the place had been a hotel.

He stepped aside and held it open for her. "Thank you. And thank you for your service," she added, and he nodded before turning away to give her privacy with Griffin.

Did he suspect there was something going on between them? How?

And is there something between us? She let go of her thoughts as she spotted Griffin swimming in one of the lanes, alone inside the room with a decent-sized pool in it, and a hot tub off to the right.

She let go of a nervous breath while unfastening the robe, then tossed it onto a chair. When she looked back toward the pool, Griffin stood in the middle, swiping his wet hair back with both hands and staring as though surprised to see her there.

Water rolled down his bruised chest, and his broad shoulders arched back when he dropped his palms onto the surface of the water. She hadn't yet had a chance to really study the ink wrapped from shoulder to elbow on one side, but her fingers itched to touch him there.

"Mind if I join you?"

"Will that thing fall off in the water if you do?" He tipped his head, dark brows drawn together as he pinned his gaze to her breasts.

"Blame whoever went shopping for me. Carter clearly didn't know the size of my breasts."

Griffin scowled and opened his mouth as if he were about to say, *He sure as hell better not*, but then slammed his lips together into a hard line.

"Are you a peach or a cherry man? Which is your weakness?" she blurted as she watched his eyes laser-focused on her breasts. "My guess is cherries." She sent him a playful smile, hoping to cover up her what-the-hell-was-I-thinking moment.

He tipped his head to the side and dropped his focus lower as if trying to check out her ass. "From where I'm standing, both." The seductive way he spoke sent a flare of heat through her body and down into her toes. "Sorry," he said with a shake of the head. "I shouldn't have said that."

"I started it," Savanna reminded him in a soft tone.

"Easton see you in that?" He stalked toward her, revealing more of his magnificent body as he moved into the shallow water.

"Air Force guy?" She turned toward the door as if she expected to see him standing guard there, but it was closed, and when she shifted around, Griffin's palms were splayed on the concrete of the pool's edge.

"Did he?" Griffin repeated in his growly voice, the one he used whenever he mentioned Shep. *Jealousy?*

"Just in the robe." She took a step closer to the edge of the pool and looked down into his eyes, the dark lashes appearing thicker now that they were wet. She was two seconds away from becoming lost in those deep brown irises when he popped up from the water in one quick movement, taking her by surprise.

"I don't like that, either," he rasped before circling his arms around her body and falling backward into the pool, taking her with him. Another shock.

"You're going to hurt yourself," she scolded after whipping her wet hair back from her face. Her eyes landed on his bruised torso, but he didn't seem to be feeling any pain at the moment. His gaze was solely focused on her body. "Also, you're lucky the water isn't cold."

"Yeah, and why's that?" he teased, his voice laced with desire.

She peered at Griffin's large hands patting the top of the water at his sides, splashing a little water in her direction. But she was caught up in the view of the vein in his forearm that ran up his bicep. So damn sexy.

And now, she couldn't help but think about that hand spanking her. She just might come undone right there in the water with him inches away, all wet muscles and sexy hair.

She fingered her own wet locks and rolled her tongue over her bottom lip, doing her best not to reach out and run her hands over the hard wall of muscles gleaming before her.

"I heard you, you know. When you were touching yourself."

Well hell, this wasn't what she'd expected.

And also . . .

What?!

"How? You were already in the pool and—"

"Sugar, were you touching yourself before you came out here?" he asked in a low, sexy voice.

"I . . . I thought that's what you were talking about," she stammered. "Wait . . . you heard me at the cabin?" When he nodded slowly, the devilish look in his eyes bolstered her nerve. "What'd you do after?" she whispered.

Tell me that you stroked your cock while you pictured me touching myself, and I'll suck you off right now.

"You know what I did," he muttered, then turned his hand palm-up on the water, inviting her to take it.

And when she did, he clasped their hands together and yanked her closer. Her free hand landed on his chest while his slid around to the small of her back.

Griffin pulled their linked palms under the water as she silently counted his rapid heartbeats pounding beneath her fingers. But she wanted to feel her nipples pressed against him instead.

Apparently, he did, too, because his hand traveled up her spine and untied the knot at her back, then swept up to her neck and did the same, allowing the little triangles to drop free from her tits and fall into the water between them.

"Looks like I have only one weakness, Sugar," he said as he wrapped his fingers around her wrist and guided her hand away from his chest. "And that's you."

Griffin let her hand drift free from his under the water, then firmly cupped her ass with both palms. Dark eyes pinned to hers, he gave her a little boost and guided her legs to wrap around his hips, all the while never breaking eye contact. The way he was looking at her made her a little speechless. Like he was finally seeing her as a woman and not just Marcus's widow.

She linked her wrists behind his neck as he moved into

deeper water, keeping her back to the door, probably worried someone might walk in on them. The man didn't like to share—that much was obvious. And it was a hell of a turn on.

Once her breasts dipped below the surface of the water, he leaned in and skated his tongue along the seam of her lips, demanding she open for him. A demand she was more than willing to comply with. Butterflies took flight in Savanna's stomach when a deep moan vibrated from Griffin's chest as their tongues met, and he reached up to caress her breast.

She groaned against his mouth and wriggled her pelvis closer to him, feeling the bulge in his swim trunks fighting against the material.

"I need to fuck you," he rasped between kisses, which he was basically doing, just with his tongue. In and out. Rough with intensity, followed by a slow dance. If his kisses were any indication of the rest of his skills, well, heaven help her, she'd probably set off the security system with her moans. "I have to be inside of you," he added in a low, husky voice as if the world depended on it. As if the walls would crumble around them if he didn't take her right then and there.

He cupped the nape of her neck as he continued to hold their mouths close and tortured her now with slow, sweeping movements of his tongue. Licking her lips like he was separating the folds of her pussy instead.

"You have no idea how badly I want you," she confessed, then realized maybe he did have a clue based on the hardness of his cock she couldn't help but rock against.

"Not here," he hissed. "I can't have someone seeing you naked while I fuck you into—"

"No, don't stop. Keep going. Tell me what you want to do to me." Her nipple hurt as he pinched her, but the best kind of hurt that went straight to her clit.

Griffin nipped her lower lip and pulled her back with his

grip on her neck, then broke their mouths apart to peer into her eyes.

He released her breast and slipped his hand beneath the fabric of her bikini bottoms. They were in the water, but she knew he'd be able to tell the difference between that and the slickness between her legs. She was beyond ready for him.

"I'd splay you on your back and spread your legs wide before kissing my way down your body until my tongue found the tight walls of your pussy," he said while breathing hard, his chest rising and falling against her body. "I'd eat you like you were the sweetest dessert. Until you fluttered around me and begged me to fuck you. Only then would I slip my cock between your pussy lips, just the tip, just for a moment before ramming into you in one—"

"What the hell?"

Griffin had let go of his words at the voice booming from behind her, and Savanna wanted to cry. Not because they'd been caught.

But damn it, because now Griffin wouldn't finish what he'd started. And she needed to hear more. Needed for him to follow through on his words and give her what she desperately wanted. Him.

Savanna unlocked her legs from his hips and found the pool floor, but Griffin kept her body pinned to his to protect her near nakedness.

She couldn't believe Natasha's brother had caught them wrapped in each other's arms in the pool. Would Griffin get fired?

"I have news," Gray said a moment later when neither she nor Griffin managed to formulate any type of explanation as to why they were in the pool together, and she was topless. Oh yeah, and she had been on the brink of riding his hand to get herself off. "Meet me in the lobby in five."

She waited for the door to click shut before her shoulders dropped, and she searched for her floating bikini top in the water.

"Are we . . . is he going to . . .?"

"Fire me?" Griffin finished for her while securing her top, but he didn't give it back to her yet. "No, I'll be fine."

She reached for her top, but he shook his head. "It'll take only seconds to dry off. A minute to walk there." He threw the top toward the steps of the pool. "But I like to be on time, so that leaves us with a little more than three minutes to make you come. And guessing by how wet you are, I'll need less than two."

Holy hell. Not what she expected. But damn, it was what she wanted.

He pulled her back into his arms and hoisted her up, his strong arms holding her as he strode through the water. He set her on the ledge of the pool, hopped out for a second, grabbed a towel, then set it on the floor before directing her to lie down.

"What if someone else walks in?"

"They won't." And the man seemed confident because like hell would he let someone else see him going down on her.

She wordlessly watched as he followed through on his promise, taking control of her the way she wanted him to do.

He peeled her bikini bottoms down, pausing for a moment to stare at her smooth, aching pussy, then he tossed the bottoms over his shoulder. She sat up on her elbows, needing to watch this man's face dip between her legs, a visual she'd never forget for as long as she lived.

His scruff teased her inner thighs as he set his mouth on her sex, eyes lifting for a moment to catch her staring at him before resetting his gaze to her center. And when he flicked his tongue against her clit, she couldn't help but moan his name.

She desperately wanted to slip her hand through his hair and guide his movements, but she couldn't stop watching this man devour her. Because wow. *Wow, wow, wow.*

His tongue stroked up and down in soft, fluid movements. It was slow and sweet and painfully teasing. And just when she was about to beg for more, he thrust two fingers inside her and curled them up, stroking against that bundle of nerves while sucking on her swollen nub.

Two minutes with his mouth on her? She wanted a lifetime. But today, she'd be lucky to last one minute.

She captured her bottom lip between her teeth to resist crying out his name—or calling out to God—and her head tipped back and her arms went lax as the orgasm started to crest. She landed on her back, careful not to bang her head on the cement as she let the ecstasy take control.

Her body trembled, and she squeezed her thighs together, unable to handle him between her legs anymore. The pleasure was almost too much to handle. She'd never . . . this was . . . unbelievable. And new. And she wasn't sure how to untangle what that meant, so she chose not to.

"You okay?" Griffin asked while rising to his knees a moment later, and she sat back up on her elbows, her focus falling to his shorts, and she realized he'd be the one suffering now.

"I'd be better if you could slide inside of me and screw me like you wanted to."

He leaned down and set his lips to her belly button before kissing up to her mouth. "Tonight, sweetheart," he said after pulling back slightly and pinning her with a look filled with desire.

"You promise?" She was scared he'd remember those

lines he insisted were there, and he'd change his mind. Now that he'd had his mouth on her and knew he was capable of obliterating every thought, worry, or problem with only a kiss, how could she not want more?

He shot her a devilish grin. "The only one capable of stopping me from taking you tonight," he began while bringing his mouth against the shell of her ear, "would be you."

CHAPTER TWENTY

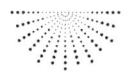

When Griffin and Savanna had arrived in what was once the lobby of the former hotel, Gray promptly sent them back to their rooms. Treating them like misbehaving kids, Gray ordered them to change from their swimwear. But Griffin was fine with that. He'd steal as much alone time with Savanna as possible.

After he dressed in jeans and a black tee, he rapped at the door connecting his and Savanna's rooms. "You decent?" he called out. Not that it mattered much since he'd just seen her completely naked. *While I sucked on her clit and licked her to orgasm.*

"Come in," she called back.

He wasn't prepared for his heart to beat double time when he opened the door to the sight of her gorgeous smile aimed right at him as she slowly walked his way wearing high-waisted jeans with a white blouse tucked into them. Her honey-colored hair, which looked darker since it was wet, hung over her shoulders and dampened her shirt.

He let the door swing shut behind him and strode to meet

her, immediately reaching for her hair and shifting it around to her back. Savanna's hazel eyes fluttered when he cupped her tit to discover the bra lacked any padding. "Bad girl," Griffin scolded under his breath, his erection still painful and begging for release inside his jeans. "This white blouse and thin bra are tempting enough, but the wet hair means the guys are going to get a peek at what's mine." He released his hold of her, knowing he was a second away from unbuttoning her top and forgetting about Gray.

"Mm. And are you going to punish me later?" Her sultry voice went straight to his cock, and the sudden blush on her cheeks was adorable as hell.

She spun so that her back was to him. "I can't believe I said that," she groaned.

Oh, game on. She couldn't backpedal from that spicy comment. No damn way.

Griffin let out a low laugh and swatted her ass. She jumped and squeaked before tossing him a saucy look over her shoulder. Her teeth skated over her bottom lip before she smiled.

"We should go out there before he gets grumpy." Griffin adjusted himself in his jeans, but when she started walking toward the door, the sight of her ass in her own jeans had him running a hand down the ridge of his cock over the stiff fabric.

He'd never wanted a woman so much in all of his life. He'd also never been willing to forgo his own rules for a woman, either.

Once in the lobby, Griffin did his best to tuck away his thoughts and kill his erection. Her safety was the priority, not how many ways he could make her come.

The lobby was an open and airy space decorated in a

casual style, similar to their rooms. Carter and the others had returned, and they were gathered around the three leather sofas that surrounded a large white coffee table at the center of the room.

Griffin sat next to Savanna on the couch that had a view of the front door, which would offer a great look at the sea if the sun hadn't recently set.

"Who wants to share first?" Griffin asked, and from the looks on his team leaders' faces, both Gray and Carter had news.

Gray shifted his laptop to the table as Jack sat alongside him, and Carter and Oliver took the third sofa. "What'd you find out about the vault?" he asked Carter.

"We got there just before closing, but they've made quite a few upgrades in the twenty-plus years since Nick's dad designed the main vault," Carter began. "I mentioned to them I had some valuables I'd like to store in one of their safe-deposit boxes. And they proclaimed their vault is completely secure and has never been breached."

"Once inside the vault, you need more than just the key to access your safe-deposit box," Jack added. "Retinal scan. ID. And a passcode."

"So, we were right. If Nick does get captured, there's no way he can be forced to break into the vault since it's the one vault he can't breach. And even if he's strong-armed inside during business hours, they'll be missing the final piece to access the safe-deposit box—the key," Jack remarked.

"We're working on hacking into the security camera feeds inside the place, as well as obtaining all CCTV footage in and around the area, but I doubt we'll get Nick on camera," Carter said, although he didn't seem too disappointed. From the sounds of it, they didn't need any more confirmation that

Nick had obtained a safe-deposit box in Santorini. The key matched up to those used at the vault, and the photo linking him there years ago proved he knew all about the place.

Griffin fought the urge to reach out and set his hand on Savanna's thigh or take hold of her hand, knowing this whole damn mess couldn't be easy for her. Gray now knew Griffin had crossed a line with her, but hopefully, he hadn't shared that mistake with the others.

Mistake?

Shit. He didn't want to believe it was a mistake. Being with her at the pool hadn't felt like one at all, and what was that supposed to mean?

"Well, if our theory is right and Nick stole something from the Archer Group that was of national security significance, my guess is that it was from one of their locations not far from Santorini," Gray spoke up, drawing Griffin's attention. "I did some digging, and the closest office for the Archer Group is in Sicily."

"Which makes sense seeing that the Naval Air Station Sigonella is also there." Jack shifted back on the couch and crossed his ankle over his knee. His eyes landed on Griffin for a second, and the animosity that he'd shown Griffin for the past two weeks appeared to finally be gone. "But what would Nick have stolen from Archer's Sicily site? Isn't everything done electronically these days? Wouldn't someone hire a hacker, not a safecracker?"

"Then Nick stole something tangible. Maybe blueprints for one or more of their projects stored there?" Savanna suggested, and Griffin once again wanted to hold her delicate hand.

Instead, he set his palm on the small space of leather between them, and when Savanna placed hers there too, pushing her pinkie against his, Griffin bit down on his back teeth to keep himself from slipping his hand over hers.

"Most companies have physical copies stored in a secure location as backup in case of a cyberattack," Carter noted, and having been CIA at one time, he probably had the most knowledge among them on the subject of the top-secret inner workings of the government. "Maybe Nick's job was to infiltrate Archer's Sicily office, take photos, and then get out before anyone noticed. Not to actually remove anything from the site."

"But clearly, someone noticed. And now, it seems a lot of *someones* know about it," Griffin stated the obvious. Every time he thought about multiple people or groups coming after Savanna, his blood pressure spiked. "It appears the Archer Group doesn't want Uncle Sam to get wind they've been compromised, which makes me curious as hell about what Nick has his hands on."

"Our original theory may still be on point, that the Archer Group is trying to handle this on their own because they don't want the media to find out they had a breach. Or risk losing future government contracts," Oliver pointed out.

"Maybe. But from my experience, companies like Archer who have government contracts are required by the Department of Defense to store everything related to those projects in specific government-approved storage vaults," Carter explained. "And no surprise, those locations don't show up in a Google search. So that means—"

"There could be an inside man at the Archer Group, and that's how Nick was able to access the location in the first place." Griffin stood, feeling anxious at the news and still not trusting himself to keep his hands off Savanna. The magnetic pull between them was beyond anything he'd ever felt before.

He circled the couch to stand behind her and set his palms on the leather. "That could be the real reason the Department of Defense wasn't notified of a breach. The inside man was expecting Nick's boss to send someone. But then Nick double-crossed everyone by taking off with the goods. And now they're not only hunting him down, but someone at Archer is trying to cover their own ass before word gets out about the breach and before whatever was stolen falls into unintended hands."

"Stands to reason that only the uppermost echelon in the Archer Group would be privy to these vaults," Carter continued, "so coupled with the fact that a site almost as secure as the Pentagon was infiltrated—"

"It won't be hard to identify the traitor," Savanna interjected in a soft voice, swiveling back to catch his eyes, her long, dark lashes fluttering for a moment, and his stomach dropped at the idea of something happening to her.

"The inside man is trying to control the damage and using Joe and his men for that purpose." Carter paused as if to mull over another thought. Was he wondering if Joe was also a traitor? "And the others chasing Nick are dying to get their hands on whatever Nick now has." Carter shook his head and turned to Gray. "Where are we at on Elysium?"

Griffin did his best to keep his attention on Gray rather than the woman who had his heart beating double the norm.

"I haven't found any Elysium-related chatter," Gray started, "but since the word means heaven in Greek, what if it was the name of a project the Archer Group worked on relating to something like aerial defense? Satellites, maybe?"

"I hate to say this, but Joe provided that name. What if he was trying to throw us off?" Jack raised the point that Griffin didn't want to hear.

"*Or* it confirms Elysium is something only someone at Archer would know about," Griffin tossed out his own hopeful idea, needing to cling to the belief he hadn't taken a bullet for a man who was now a traitor.

"We need to head to the Archer office in Sicily to poke around." Carter rose from the couch. "See what we can find out. We discussed it on the plane, but I think it's time we go to your father, Gray."

"He may be your dad, but as the Secretary of Defense, will he really help us?" Griffin asked, looking at Gray. "Or will he want to take control of the mission once he discovers why we need to gain access to the Archer Group?"

Gray stood and moved around the table as if needing to be on his feet to work through his thoughts. "With the Archer Group's connection to the Department of Defense, my father might be one of the few people we can trust to help us figure out what the hell was stolen. Once we do that, we can narrow down a list of possible suspects to identify the inside man. There can't be that many people privy to where top-secret intelligence is stored."

Good point.

"He may want to assign a different team to look into this, but I'll do my best to convince him we're in the best position to handle it," Gray added.

"I'm going to have another go at these guys we picked up from Jesse's house while you call your father," Carter said, his voice gruff, exasperation crawling through his tone. "We were able to track the last location for the eight guys to Rome before Alabama, which was a bit of a surprise since the first three came from Athens. But we confirmed they're Greek citizens."

"So, it's possible their boss is in Rome right now?" Savanna asked as she stood.

"Anything is possible at this point, but my gut is telling me that Nick's boss may be a middleman, and he planned to fence the intelligence when Nick handed it over," Carter answered. "There are only a handful of people in Europe I can think of capable of unloading that kind of intelligence without the CIA getting wind of the transaction."

"I think I know who might be able to help us narrow down that list and fast, especially if this person is Italian or Greek," Griffin noted, and Carter nodded as if on the same page.

"Who?" Jack and Savanna asked at the same time.

"Emilia Calibrisi," Carter answered before Griffin had the chance. "She's an Italian billionaire. Lives in Ireland now, but she'll have a pulse on any criminal activity in this region, as well as who'd be capable of selling something that valuable without being noticed."

"Emilia's actually how we met A.J. and his team." Griffin wasn't sure why he'd just offered up that information. Or why he added, "When we kidnapped Jesse's sister." But Jesse wasn't there, so.

"You mean when we *rescued* Rory." Carter swung his focus to Savanna, whose mouth was wide open, a look of surprise on her face. "There were pirates involved and well . . ." He was stumbling through his words, which was unusual for the man.

"I take it Jesse doesn't know about this," Savanna said, the hint of a smile on her lips. At least she didn't look mad at Griffin for keeping that not-so-small detail from her.

"We rescued Jesse's sister essentially by kidnapping her." Griffin had just begun working with Carter at the time, and it was quite the *Welcome to the team.* They'd saved Rory and a few others on A.J.'s team from honest-to-God pirates only to discover Rory had been on the hunt for a wildlife trafficking operation. Griffin had been worried his return to civilian life was going to be a boring adjustment, but that first op with Carter's team proved otherwise.

"Maybe you should have mentioned this to me. You know, like before we went to Jesse's house in the first place," Gray said with a grunt at the end of his words.

"It was need to know." Carter peered at Griffin with a sharp look.

"I can see why you didn't bring it up to Jesse, though," Savanna surprised Griffin by saying. "He'd probably—"

"Go John Wick on my ass?" he asked with a smile. *Why am I grinning like a fucking schoolboy right now, especially over this conversation?*

Savanna nodded, then gave him a little wink to let him know she happened to be on the same page. Same paragraph. And even the same word on the line as him.

It didn't matter what they happened to be talking about, the connection they shared seemed to only get stronger. That was a little . . . scary, wasn't it? *But hell, I don't get scared, do I?*

"Okay," Savanna said a moment later, blinking a few times as if trying to focus her thoughts. "So, are you talking about asking Emilia to find someone who sells items on an online black market? Like an auction?"

Griffin rounded the couch to face her, putting his head back in the game, where it needed to be. On the job. "I would say yes, normally. But in this case, there'd be a digital footprint for that sale. And I'm betting whoever is after such intel wouldn't want to take that risk. The seller will most likely go old school. Meet in person."

"What should I do while you're working? How can I help?" she softly asked, nervously wringing her hands. "Are you hungry? Do you have a chef here? Let me do something."

"Yes, we have a guy who does the cooking, but he's running leads for me at the moment. So, if you don't mind, that'd be great. Thank you. Kitchen is down that hall," Carter said while pointing. "Hang a left, and it's the second door. There are a lot of us. You sure you don't mind?"

She smiled, her dimple appearing. "Not at all. I need to keep my hands, and well, thoughts busy." Her gaze swept to Griffin once everyone but Gray left the lobby to chase down leads. "What will you do?"

"Actually, I need to have a word with Griffin," Gray interjected, and Griffin had a pretty damn good idea what that "word" might be.

"I'll check on you soon." Griffin lightly squeezed her shoulder and tipped his head toward the hall leading to the kitchen as his way of saying everything would be okay.

"What's up?" he asked Gray once they were alone.

"Don't sleep with her. That's an order."

Blunt. To the point. Expected even, and yet, it pissed him off.

"Is this you talking as my new team leader, an officer, or just an asshole?" He hadn't meant to voice his thoughts, but Savanna's nervous habit of blurting her thoughts had rubbed off on him, so it seemed. Not that he was nervous. But he was tense with so many unconfirmed theories bouncing around and Savanna in the mix.

He was used to hard facts and a plan of action, not so much being part of the intelligence-gathering process. Tell him who to save or where to point his rifle, and he was solid. But throw in a gorgeous woman who was also a widow . . . one he'd had his tongue sliding across her pussy twenty minutes ago, and well, fuck. New territory.

Gray grumbled out, "All of the above. And yeah, if that makes me an asshole, so be it. Better have me pissed at you than A.J. Believe me when I say that. Or hell, Jesse, for that matter." He shook his head. "Besides, do you really want to break that woman's heart? I know your reputation. She's been through enough."

And he knew that. Understood that. But whenever she was within kissing distance, he seemed to lose his mind and his control.

"I need confirmation from you that you understand me before I can get back to work." Gray pinned him with a hard look. "She's an assignment. Not a woman you met at the bar."

"Says the guy nicknamed Romeo." And there went his mouth again. "I have no intention of hurting her." That's the last thing he'd ever want to do.

"Then I need you to give me your word."

"So, my word is good enough for you, then?" Griffin asked, still trying to get a feel for his new boss. The guy had bigger balls than Griffin had initially thought when Carter introduced them.

"It sure as hell better be." Which was as good as Gray saying, *Since I may have to take a bullet for you one day, you'd better not be a lying son-of-a-bitch.*

Griffin thought back to the pool and Savanna's arms over his shoulders. To her sweet kisses. The way she moved against him in the water, and gave her body to him completely, without any shyness, as he went down on her. And the promise of tonight . . .

"Roger that," he finally hissed, hating himself for his response.

Gray demanded he tell the truth, so that meant his words to Savanna by the pool were now a lie. He'd told her she would be the only one able to stop him from taking her into his arms tonight.

Truth be told, he was somewhat relieved Savanna had been declared off-limits.

Because he knew he'd choose her. He seemed incapable of *not* choosing her.

And then, somehow or in some way, most likely the both of them would get hurt.

CHAPTER TWENTY-ONE

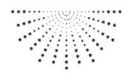

Griffin paused when he spotted Savanna through the open door that led into the industrial kitchen, which was probably a quarter the size of one you'd find in a Marriott. She had on a black chef's apron, and her hair was now in a messy bun with a few strands framing her face. She was absolutely breathtaking, even while doing something as mundane as chopping an onion.

He replayed Gray's warning in his head and wished it weren't true. He'd only known Savanna for a handful of days, and yet, who was he kidding, he'd end up hurting her just as Gray predicted. And Gray hadn't needed to work alongside him for long to recognize genuine trouble when he'd walked in on them in the pool area.

Griffin doubted he was capable of changing his ways, and he wouldn't risk Savanna becoming collateral damage because of his own demons.

Savanna set down the knife and reached into her back pocket, still unaware of his presence. Producing his phone a moment later, she put on music but startled when she looked up to see him standing there.

"Hope you don't mind. I love music, and obviously, I still have your phone." She held up his work phone, then swapped it for a glass of wine that sat nearby on the counter.

"I don't mind at all," he returned, finally walking through the door and circling the counter where she worked. There was already a huge pot of water on the stove, but it hadn't started boiling yet. "I see you found the wine."

She faced him and lifted the glass. "I couldn't help myself. I assume you can't have any? Is there a handbook of rules you have to follow while on a job?" Gold and green flecks shined in her hazel eyes as she smiled and offered him the glass.

"Rules." He accepted the glass anyway. "I've been breaking those lately." *But I have to behave now. Some damn way.*

"A sip won't hurt." She shrugged, her gaze falling to his mouth as if she were planning to watch him have that taste.

He'd much rather have another taste of the sweetest woman he'd ever encountered, and he wanted a lot more, but . . .

Letting go of a deep breath, he brought the rim of the glass to his mouth.

"Chianti," she told him as he tried it. "Tuscan blend."

"It's good." He handed it back after a small sip, knowing there was no way in hell he could drink and keep his hands to himself around her. It was hard enough to manage when he was sober. "What's that smile about?" he couldn't help asking when she took a healthy swallow of the Chianti, then swiped away a drop that'd dribbled down her chin.

She set the glass down, picked up the knife, and resumed chopping onions. He ought to offer her some help, but as he studied her from where he'd positioned himself, leaning back against the counter next to her, he had a feeling he'd lose his focus and cut off a finger. That'd be really smooth for a Delta guy too.

"Every time I drink Chianti, it reminds me of one of my favorite movies. I doubt you've heard of it. *Under the Tuscan Sun* with Diane Lane. It's based on the book of the same name. Also, one of my favorites." She tilted her head to the side, like she was offering her neck, and slid her gaze his way. Damn, he wanted to trail his lips up that smooth column of skin.

He shifted around to face the counter, worried she'd notice the bulge forming in his jeans before he could put a lid on that growing problem.

Placing his palms on the counter and peering at the pile of onions rather than the sexy woman standing beside him, Griffin said, "Tell me about it." Why did his simple question sound like he'd just asked her to describe in detail how she'd touched herself earlier when he'd been swimming.

And shit, now he couldn't help but remember that Easton had been parked outside of her room. Had he heard her?

"In the movie, Diane Lane plays an American novelist who runs away to Italy for a fresh start after learning her husband cheated on her. She was crushed by his betrayal but losing the man she loved absolutely devastated her. And in Italy she brings a crumbling villa back to life while also finding love again." She paused. "You know my obsession with books, so naturally, when one of my favorite books is made into a wonderful movie . . . I've watched it many times, and it never fails to pull at my heartstrings."

He wasn't sure how to respond to that, so he remained quiet, perfectly happy with listening to her talk.

"The idea of a writer in Tuscany sitting behind some old-school typewriter just makes me smile too," she went on, beaming.

"Very Hemingway."

"Exactly." She shot him a quick, adorable smile, then blinked rapidly and wiped away a few tears with her knuckles. "Onions," she said, leaving Griffin to guess whether it was the onions or the plot of the movie bringing on the tears.

"Why don't you write? Sounds like you have what it takes."

She shook her head before setting down the knife and facing him, so he lifted his palms from the counter to give her his attention, hoping his jeans were no longer tented. "No, I suck at writing. Totally happy with reading." She shrugged. "Besides, I think I've suffered enough in my life. I doubt I'd be able to handle book reviewers throwing one-stars at me like I'm the target in an old-time carny knife-throwing act," she added while simulating throwing a knife. "I'm rambling."

"And it's adorable," he said, letting the words slip free and watching her cheeks flush pink. "So, I take it we're eating Italian tonight?"

"I don't know any Greek recipes by heart, and with such a big group, I figured pasta would be best. Rigatoni with vodka sauce and a caprese salad." She pointed to the mozzarella on another cutting board nearby. "It'll be good, I promise."

"I have no doubt." He opened his palms. "How can I help?"

"I don't think I need anything but the music playing and some good company." She peeked at him and added, "So if you want to go grab Oliver or one of the guys to come hang out, that'd be great."

The smartass winked at him, and he was on the verge of slapping that cute butt again.

"But really," she said while using her knife to slide the onions into a big frying pan sizzling with butter. "This is an easy recipe. Need to let the garlic, basil, and onions simmer for a bit. No big deal."

He folded his arms across his chest and leaned against the counter again while watching her profile as she sipped the wine and pushed the onions around with a spatula.

For a woman who'd been through the wringer the last few days, she was handling it remarkably well. She was resilient. And he knew that'd make Marcus proud. He also knew because of that, she'd most likely fall in love again one day, and she deserved it.

Just not with me.

But he also knew they could never be friends, and the thought of not spending more time with her after the op had a pit developing in his stomach, and it was a feeling worse than getting punched repeatedly yesterday.

He'd take a million more punches to protect Savanna, though. And honestly, his body could handle the beating. Not that he wanted it, but he'd been trained to deal with a lot over the years.

"You know," she began in a soft voice while setting down the wineglass to fully face him. "I really don't know much about you aside from your dad being in the Army, and you were born in Kentucky. Did you grow up there?"

Talking about his past was typically a hard limit for him, but he also didn't want to be an ass again, especially after she'd proclaimed Marcus was an open book. Of course, he didn't want to lead her on, so he'd have to walk a tightrope here. Be considerate without giving too much of himself. *I can do this. Maybe.*

"I spent maybe eight years there before we were relocated to Georgia, then to North Carolina. But we were also overseas in Germany for two years when I was twelve."

"Your accent seems to come and go. Not nearly as

Southern as Jesse's. More like how it is with A.J. I guess because you both served abroad for so long."

"Probably. I tend to go more Southern mode when I'm around people saying y'all," he teased, referring to her. "But your Southern isn't exactly Bama. Or Tampa. Or . . ." He thought back to her profile he'd read. "Or Georgia."

She chuckled. "Yeah, I love being a mystery," she joked. "But it might have to do with my Cuban grandmother's influence. She played a big role in raising me."

Right. She'd told him that she and Marcus had wanted to raise their kids bilingual. Damn, he just wanted to hold her and take away all the sad memories.

"I miss her a lot." She reached for her glass as if needing to drink away whatever sad thought had popped into her mind. "But you know everything about me since you read the report. What about your mom? What's she like? Did she work or?"

He dropped his focus to the unfinished concrete floor at the mention of his mother. He loved her, sure. But he didn't know if he could ever forgive her. He'd even considered going by his first name again once he turned eighteen and was on his own, just to piss her off since she was the one who'd called him Griffin all of his life. But by that point, the name James was reserved for his father.

"Yesterday in the truck, you said your mom liked Greek mythology," Savanna went on when he remained quiet, as he struggled to find a response that wouldn't put him in a foul mood.

"I'd rather not talk about my parents." It was the only answer he was comfortable with, but the drop in her shoulders and the disappointed look in her eyes when their gazes met made his chest hurt. "They're divorced," he said under his breath, then pinched the bridge of his nose. "It was messy. They tried to make it work, but when I was eighteen, they divorced, and I joined the Army."

"Oh."

He dropped his hand to the counter. "Divorce is common. Don't apologize. I can feel that coming. And it's not necessary."

"Yeah, sadly, it's more common these days, but that doesn't make the pain any less." She set her glass down again and took one small step his way. Oh hell, was she going to try and comfort him because of something that'd happened over twenty years ago?

"Anyways." He needed to move this conversation in a different direction. "I became a Ranger, and then I was pushed into selection for the Unit. You know, Delta Force. Twenty years after being in the Army, Carter offered me this gig."

As she quietly studied him, he wondered if she'd press for more about his past or let him move on. "And you've been with Carter for about a year?"

Thank God. Moving on. His chest fell with relief. "Yup."

"And have you ever been in a serious relationship?"

And back to serious. *Shit.*

"Sorry, not my business." She started to turn, but he surprised himself by reaching for her arm, gently pulling her to face him. He knew he needed to release his hold of her, but he wasn't in the mood to let go.

"I don't . . ." was all he managed to say. But she should recognize he'd be dangerous to her beautiful book-loving heart.

"Um." She chewed on her lip, and when she noticed she was doing it, she stopped and looked toward the stove. "I can add the sauce now. Unfortunately, it's from a jar but better than nothing."

He let go of her so she could pour two jars of sauce into the pan. She moved it around a bit, then when the water began boiling, she dumped a few boxes of rigatoni into the water.

The few minutes of quiet had him uncomfortable but also curious what she was thinking. "So, what do you like to do for fun?" she asked after covering the sauce and skipping to another song on his phone.

"Small talk? Are we doing that?" He didn't mean to say that, but was she going to ask him his favorite color next? He doubted she liked small talk, just like him. And the last thing he wanted was a forced conversation.

She shrugged. "Just want to know you."

"Still?" He eased one step closer. "After what I said?"

Savanna's brows drew together. "Yes, even after what you really *didn't* say." But there was doubt in her voice, and he read it in her hazel eyes, too, so he backed that one step up again. "What's your favorite NFL team?"

She didn't give a damn about that, and he knew it. "I have another fatal flaw," he admitted. "I hate football, which is a Southern sin."

But his words had her smiling and her dimple popping. *And* his heart aching at the sight.

"Probably spent too much time overseas and learned to like the European version of football instead."

"Soccer, huh?" She worked the knot, which was at the front of her apron, loose but kept the apron on.

"Well, can you do me a favor? When you're in Alabama, pretend to like football and maybe root for Bama? They're pretty protective of that college team, and things might get dicey if you root for Auburn or Tennessee."

"Roger that. I wouldn't want to be in any kind of danger."

She grinned. "They really do take college football seriously there."

"Sounds like it." And that one extra step he'd placed between them like caution tape was gone again.

"Do you like music?" She abruptly grimaced. "Sorry, that's small talk, right?"

"That's okay," he decided. As long as she didn't push about his personal life and his lack of any real relationships, he could handle this, he supposed. "All kinds."

"Dancing?" One brown brow arched as if this was an important question.

"Rarely."

"And if I asked you to dance with me?"

He pointed to the ground. "Like now? Here?"

She ran her hand down the column of her throat before setting it over the top of her blouse and apron. "Maybe."

He took a moment to listen to the unfamiliar song playing now. A sad one, from the sounds of it. "Not really dancing music."

She peered at the phone. "That's Kygo. My favorite, actually. And this song, 'Love Me Now,' is—"

"Fucking heartbreaking," he finished for her. Because the lyrics had him wanting to completely close the last bit of space between them and hug her. Hold her forever.

But before he could either abort mission and withdraw *or* pull her into his arms, Carter strode into the kitchen.

Griffin turned away from the woman who muddled his thoughts and made him want to ignore Gray's order, as well as his own fears. "What's up? Did Gray talk to his old man?"

Carter circled the large counter space to join them and sniffed the garlic-infused air. "Yeah, and we have the greenlight. The Sicilian Archer Group site doesn't know why we're actually paying them a visit, though. Secretary

Chandler told them we'll be conducting a random security check given that they house records for DOD projects."

"Wow. So, Secretary Chandler is really letting us handle this?" He was shocked, to be honest.

"Only because A.J. and his entire team are overseas handling another assignment, and I assume they'd be his go-to for a situation like this otherwise," Carter explained, speaking candidly, probably because Savanna was most likely aware that her husband had once worked off-the-books ops for the President.

Griffin and Carter hadn't been directly informed of this information, but after working on two missions with A.J. and the others, it wasn't exactly rocket science to put two and two together. Plus, Carter had told Griffin that before he left the CIA, he'd heard there were ten guys close to the President who handled the "unhandleable" for him.

Judging by the lack of expression on Savanna's face, this wasn't news to her, so Griffin's assumption about A.J. and the others was probably spot on. And now Savanna knew *they* knew.

Savanna took a tentative step forward, placing her closer to Griffin's side.

"Secretary Chandler is putting together a list of everyone at the Archer Group who'd be aware records connected to DOD contracts are stored in their vault in Sicily," Carter said.

"What about the Elysium Project, if that's what it's called?" Savanna asked.

"Chandler said the Archer Group uses a naming system for their in-house designs, so it's possible they referred to a project as Elysium until it was completed and handed over to the DOD, who then renamed it," he delivered the news in a somber tone. "He's seeing what he can find out, but the name Elysium didn't register in the DOD's database."

"So, we can't confirm or rule out something called Elysium is or was stored there." Griffin set his palms on the counter and bowed his head.

"Right. But once you and Gray show up at the Archer location tomorrow, I guarantee word will get back to whoever provided Nick's boss intel to allow Nick to get inside that facility in Sicily." Carter had casually tossed out the fact it'd be Griffin to roll out for the job.

"*Griffin* is leaving tomorrow for Italy?" Savanna asked, and Griffin lifted his head to glance at her.

"Gray and Griffin are the only two on the team who still have top-level government security clearance since they're also technically private military contractors. They just don't usually do gigs for Uncle Sam these days. But with that status, it enables them to walk onto a property connected to the Department of Defense," Carter said. "And I can't exactly show my face, anyway. The CIA is, uh, still looking for me."

Griffin bit back a smile at the uncharacteristically sheepish look on Carter's face at his admission to Savanna about his "rogue" status with the Agency.

"But if Griffin goes poking around, won't the person who sent Joe and his men for me in the first place . . . won't they use Griffin to try and get to me once he's away from you all and more out in the open?"

"We won't let that happen, Savanna. But I'm certain Joe's team is working for the inside man," Carter answered.

"It's still possible Joe isn't aware that whoever sent him after Savanna is a traitor. He may only have need-to-know information, and he's been told to keep a lid on the situation," Griffin found himself defending Joe.

Carter remained quiet, and Griffin got the message loud and clear. Carter believed Joe was capable of betraying his country. Griffin may have taken a bullet for Joe, but Carter wasn't going to make excuses for the man, though Griffin held out hope Joe had somehow been duped. "Maybe," he finally said.

"But once this inside man knows you're onto them, what will they do?" Savanna reached for Griffin's arm, but when Carter's gaze fell to her hand, she immediately let go. "If you don't think they'll go after Griffin or Gray, then what?"

"We'll smoke the inside man out, don't worry," was all Carter said, his attention moving to Savanna's eyes. "And Griffin will be back before dark tomorrow," he added as if sensing Savanna's worry about him leaving her. "I'll go round up the boys for dinner. Pretty sure they're starving. We should have that list of suspects from Secretary Chandler later tonight."

"Oh-okay." Savanna kept her eyes on Carter until he was gone, then peered at Griffin.

He hated leaving her. More than hated it. But he didn't have a choice in the matter. "Carter will keep you safe while I'm gone, I promise."

"But safe from who? We're still unsure how many people are trying to get to me to get to Nick." She faltered a little as she headed toward the stove. Griffin reached out and set a hand on her hip, hating that she was scared now.

"You know I'd stay with you if I could," he told her, not ready to remove his hand, to let her go. When she laid the spoon down and shifted closer, he framed her hips with both hands as he studied her worried eyes. "You'll be here tonight, though."

He closed his eyes, hating what he was about to say next.

"Gray gave you orders, didn't he?" she whispered, and his shoulders fell. "He told you to stay away from me." He slowly opened his eyes as she added, "But the question is, will you?"

CHAPTER TWENTY-TWO

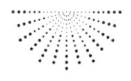

"You think we'll hear from Gray's dad tonight?" Savanna asked once they'd closed themselves inside her bedroom. She yanked at the hair tie, her locks tumbling in waves over her shoulders. "We're lucky you have such a high-level government contact," she added when Griffin had yet to speak. She tossed the hair tie on the dresser and spun around to see why he was still silent.

After they'd had dinner with the rest of the team, everyone scattered from the dining area and got back to work, leaving her and Griffin alone. Each time she stole looks at Gray throughout the meal, his eyes darted between her and Griffin. Judging by how tightly the man's jaw was locked whenever their eyes met, he was clearly concerned that Griffin wouldn't follow through with his order.

God, she hoped Griffin disobeyed.

"Where's your head at?" she softly asked, making her way to where he stood at the window.

He had a palm on the glass, his eyes set on the view of the water, not that it was all that visible in the darkness. Carter had minimized the lighting around the former hotel—and for good reason.

When she set a hand on the middle of his back, Griffin hung his head and sighed, prompting guilt to rear its ugly head within Savanna. "It's okay. I would never want you to do anything you'd regret."

A low, grumbly sound left his mouth. Were those words? "I wouldn't regret . . . it's not that."

"You're afraid of hurting me?" She ran her hand up and down his hard, taut back, hoping to ease his tension some. "Or getting hurt?" she whispered at the memory of his words just the other day in the truck in Bama.

His other hand went to the French door now, and she peeked over his shoulder at his tense hands. "I have two condoms in my wallet right now. I always have two. Because I do pick up women in bars. I have meaningless and casual sex." His harsh, low tone—and well, his words—had her lowering her hand and stumbling backward. "And then I disappear once they fall asleep." His voice became even deeper, which she hadn't thought possible. "I'm an asshole. But I never wanted to give anyone the wrong idea. To let them think I was the kind of guy who'd still be there when the sun came up."

She swore her heart skipped a few beats just then. He was sending her a message. Letting her know if they were to have sex, he'd peace-out immediately afterward. He wouldn't be like Marcus, who'd brought her breakfast in bed. Who'd sent her adorable messages after their first time together. No *good morning, beautiful* texts.

Even if Savanna insisted that she didn't care, that what he was able to offer was enough, he'd know she was lying. Because it was very much a big fat lie. No matter how much she tried to convince herself otherwise. It wasn't just Griffin's touch she craved. Timewise, they barely knew each other, but she truly believed there was a connection that ran deep between them. *Maybe it's all in my head? I imagined it. Wanted to believe there's hope for me. That I won't die alone.*

Griffin remained unmoving aside from the flex of his biceps as his hands clenched into fists against the glass. "The idea of leaving you alone in that bed after I've had you . . . doesn't seem possible," he rasped. "So, to answer your earlier questions," he began while slowly dropping his fists and turning to face her, a dark, predatory look in his gaze, "it's obvious I've never been in a serious relationship, and it's not the divorce that messed me up—it was my mom's cheating."

Savanna's heart squeezed at the sad look in his eyes competing with the one of desire.

"And also," he said as he erased the space between them, set his hand on the curve of her hip, and pulled her close. "No, I won't listen to Gray. Because I want you." He tipped her chin up and fixed his eyes on hers. "I'd break orders for you. It seems I'd do just about anything for you. Probably burn the entire fucking world down just to have you in my arms." His lips seized hers in the next moment, taking control.

That kiss surpassed the ones she'd read about in romance novels and made her feel weak. Made her forget how to use actual words the moment his lips crashed against hers and took possession of her mouth as if he truly owned her. Had he not been holding her to his powerful frame, she'd have collapsed to the floor.

She was intoxicated with emotion. Dizzy and overwhelmed by so many feelings that her chest felt like it was about to burst. And as the kisses continued, goose bumps scattered across her skin each time Griffin gently bit her lower lip before teasing her mouth apart to slip his tongue inside.

His hands worked up the silhouette of her body before he framed her cheeks with his palms and eased back to look into her eyes. He wanted to say something. To warn her, maybe? To tell her he still might break her heart after this, but she didn't want to hear it. And when he bit down on his back teeth, his jaw clenching, she was pretty sure he didn't want to say it, either.

She reached between them and fisted the fabric of his black tee in an attempt to beg him to back away from his dark thoughts and stay with her. To lose the sudden haunted look in his eyes.

"James Griffin," she whispered softly, not sure why she'd used his given name, but it'd just slipped free from her mouth, "please make love to me." *Love.* Not the naughty fantasies she'd been having since he'd walked into her life a few days ago. No, she wanted love. Needed it. The naughty could come later. *Please let there be a later.*

"Say that again," he said in a husky tone as one hand went from her cheek to the nape of her neck. Between his commanding gaze and gripping hold, she was literally weak in the knees.

"Which part?"

Griffin closed his eyes for one second. "No one has ever said either to me before."

He'd never made love before. One-night stands were about sex, not love. She'd be his first, wouldn't she? The thought of sharing such an intimate experience with him made her heart race as if she were sprinting a 5k. This man deserved to know what it felt like to make love, how much different sex could be when it was more than just a physical release.

"James Griffin," she said in a hushed tone, barely able to get her voice to work, "make love to me."

Those hooded eyes fixed back on her, and the intensity of his stare had her clutching his muscular arms, worried she'd lose her balance.

Griffin trailed his hand from her cheek to her ass and squeezed it in her jeans. He kept his hand at the back of her neck and guided her face to his. He sucked on her lip before something seemed to snap.

His control.

A low growl rumbled deep in his chest, and he stepped away from her, peeling his shirt over his head and tossing it to the floor, revealing his golden tan chest still marred with bruises from last night.

And then he came at her with quick movements, like a jungle cat pouncing on its prey, which had her walking backward and bumping into the dresser. His fingers worked in a hurry at the buttons of her blouse and clasp of her bra, ridding them from her body in record time.

"Now, take off the rest," he commanded, his tone sending shivers down her body. She was more than happy to comply, watching greedily as he did the same. And when her gaze slipped to his cock, she realized that no amount of foreplay would get her entirely ready for him, but damn, if the thought of that bite of pain mixed with pleasure didn't do something to her.

He palmed himself while his gaze journeyed from her breasts down to her toes. "Fucking perfect," he said under his breath, stroking his hard length from root to tip. Seeing the effect she had on him had her stepping forward and kneeling down where he stood, then sliding her hands up his thighs.

"You don't need to—"

"I want to," she whispered, their eyes locked as she moved his hand away so she could feel him for herself.

When she wrapped a hand around him and licked his crown, he hissed, "Fuck," while fisting her hair.

She drew as much of him as she could into her mouth, swallowing when he hit the back of her throat. He let out a string of unintelligible words as he worked himself in and out of her, sinking deeper with each thrust. The sensation of him filling her like this was so erotic that she couldn't help but slide a hand down to her clit to try and ease her desire for him.

"Hands off. No touching yourself," he bit out, which only turned her on even more, so she brought her hand to the base of his cock and sucked him harder. "I can't . . . your mouth is too good. You have to stop," he growled out a minute later, then hooked his hands beneath her arms to command her to stand. "Another time. But right now, I have to be inside of you, Sugar."

She felt the muscle of his thigh twitch beneath her other hand, and yeah, he was definitely on the verge of losing himself and pouring into her mouth.

"Please," he rasped while setting a hand on her head again, messing up her hair as if she was torturing him. A *good* torture, she hoped.

Savanna forced her mouth away to find him staring down at her with his dark eyes, and there was something primal in the way he studied her.

He guided her to her feet only to scoop her into his arms and carry her over to the unmade bed. He set her head on the pillow, grabbed a condom from the end of the bed—which he must have thrown there while she was staring at his dick and wondering how she'd walk straight tomorrow—rolled it down his erection still wet from her mouth, and climbed on top of her.

He tipped his head as he eyed her soaking wet center. The lamp by the dresser was the only light in the room. Not too bright, but just enough to see every expression. Every look of longing in his eyes. And every carved detail of this man's muscular and powerful frame.

He had one rock-hard thigh on each side of her legs as he thumbed her clit in soft strokes, his eyes not leaving her swollen flesh as if he were resisting the urge to taste her like he'd done earlier at the pool.

"Another time," she promised, repeating what he'd said to her. "If I don't feel you inside of me soon—" He cut her off when he pushed three fingers into her tight walls as if trying to prepare her for what was to come. Three fingers wouldn't ready her for the girth of his cock.

"Please, Griffin," she cried as he increased his speed, only to cry out again when she felt him slip free of her.

He shifted onto his forearms, lying on top of her so that her breasts touched his chest, and kissed her with feverish intensity. She reached between their bodies and secured a hand around him. She couldn't wait any longer.

"It's going to hurt, Sugar," he said when lifting his head to look into her eyes.

"But only for a moment." She positioned the head at her sex, rolling her hips up just enough for the tip to slip inside her.

His eyes narrowed, but his breathing was a little labored as if the very idea of finally having her had left him breathless. Same for her.

She leaned up and placed a kiss on his lips, and that was all it took for him to thrust into her completely, filling her deep, and as she'd predicted, the bite of pain came with the most amazing pleasure.

"Griffin," she moaned, doing her best not to lose eye contact with him.

"You okay?" He shifted one hand to the side of her face and caressed her cheek, but based on the intense look in his eyes, they were on the same page.

The way their bodies felt together like this . . .

Her eyes began to water from the intrusion, and her lids fluttered closed, but when he started to slowly move again, his cock slick with her arousal, her body began to relax.

She felt the unmistakable heat of his tongue against her cheek, licking her tears before bringing his lips to hers, the saltiness spreading throughout her mouth as he continued to move at a steady pace.

"Harder," she begged, opening her eyes and bringing her legs around his to urge him faster.

Griffin lifted his mouth from hers. "If I go harder, it'll turn to fucking. And then we'll both come too soon."

Right. She did her best to keep her eyes from rolling to the back of her freaking head as he kept up with the same pace, and she could tell by the tenseness of his jaw and the strain in his neck that he was fighting against the desire to fuck her senseless.

But she knew he was loving this, too, the slow, rhythmic dance of making love. Something maybe he'd truly never done before.

She savored every moment. Every heartbeat. Every look in his eyes.

She ran her palms along the hard ridges of his triceps, and her fingertips bit into the muscle as he began to pick up the pace some. Supporting his weight with one arm, he reached between her thighs and brushed his knuckles across her clit.

Her vision blurred, and she neared climax as he began rubbing her sex with the pad of his thumb in small, circular motions.

Caged beneath this strong man, she never felt safer.

"Come for me, Sugar. Because I'm fighting like hell to wait until you do," he gritted out in a dark voice.

His request sent her over the edge, and she clenched around him as she came with the most intense orgasm of her life. She moaned and cried out his name, doing her best not to be too loud in case anyone was outside their room, but this was . . . incredible.

At the feel of her coming undone, he finally let go, his hips stuttering with a few more thrusts as he chased his own release.

When he stopped moving on top of her, he pushed up onto his palms and stared down into her soul. "That was . . ." He closed his eyes, and she watched the movement of his throat as he swallowed.

"That's okay," she returned in a soft voice and reached for his cheek, and his lids parted. "I have no words, either."

CHAPTER TWENTY-THREE

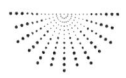

GRIFFIN LAY ON HIS BACK AMIDST THE TANGLE OF SHEETS IN Savanna's bed, unable to take his eyes off the vision of her naked body straddling him, her full lips poised in a sexy pout as she slowly trailed her short nails up his chest. They'd made love not even thirty minutes ago, but she was ready for round two.

"I want the naughty version now," she said, her throaty voice making his cock twitch, especially with her bare ass so close to his erection. "Slow and sweet was amazing, but I want . . ." That cute blush slid up her throat and to her cheeks. "Don't hold back with me, Griffin. I want you to lose total control and just . . ."

"Just what, Savanna?" He wanted to hear the dirty words come from her sweet mouth.

Cupping the back of her head, he drew her in for a fiery kiss until she pulled away and sat upright, her perfect tits on full display, just begging for his touch. He reached up to palm them both, teasing his thumbs across her nipples, the same dark rosy color as her lips. He wanted to taste both. For-fucking-ever.

What does that mean?

He shook away thoughts of tomorrow, preferring to leave the future out of this moment.

Right now, his teammates were working on her case, like he should have been, but nothing and no one could steal him away from this incredible woman shimmying on his cock and staring at him as if he were her entire world.

Him. Someone's world. He'd never thought that possible.

She pushed his hands down and parked them on her hips, then slowly slid her palms up her torso to cup her tits and pinch her nipples. He was going to lose his damn mind watching her touch herself.

"I want you to-to . . ." Her adorableness knew no bounds.

His quads flexed as he fought the urge to flip her over, wrap an arm under her belly, and yank her to her hands and knees. Worship that beautiful ass before ramming his cock into her tight wet pussy, holding her down against the mattress with one hand and pulling back on her hair with the other. She wanted the naughty version? He'd damn well give it to her. He'd give her anything she wanted.

He dug his fingers into the soft skin at her hips when she finally freed the words, "Spank me."

Well. Fuck. Me.

He had to work the knot down in his throat before he could talk. Sweet and so, so dirty for him. Just how he wanted his woman.

My woman?

She set her hands on his chest and slowly gyrated her hips in circles. "I've never . . . and just wondered . . ."

"Is that right? You've never had that tight little ass spanked for being bad?" Just the thought of seeing his handprints bloom across her silky, untouched skin had his balls instantly tight and ready to explode. He'd come all over her any second.

"And then I want your mouth on my—"

"Cunt?" He cocked a brow as she worked her lip between her white teeth.

"I've never liked that word, but when you say it, I do." She reached for his hand and cupped it against her pussy.

"You're fucking drenched, Sugar." And damn, was she ever. He loved that her body responded to him like this, completely in tune with his.

"It's all because of you. You turn me on, and I've just nev—" Savanna stopped herself mid-sentence.

That "never" would remain unspoken. Griffin was certain she'd nearly revealed how sex with him made her have feelings she'd never experienced before. And that would have been tantamount to betraying Marcus.

Although this moment hadn't killed his erection, it now felt like there was a third wheel in the room. But was it all in his head, or was it Marcus?

"Griffin." A sharp knock at the door startled them both and had Savanna immediately shifting off him in search of the covers. "Your room is empty," Carter announced from the other side of the door.

At least it was Carter and not the sex police, Gray.

"One second," Griffin called out while standing, covering his erection with both hands, hoping to quickly calm his dick down. *Good luck with that, buddy.* His mind was still foggy with the image of a naked Savanna sitting on him seconds ago, saying she wanted him to spank her and then eat her pussy—so yeah, he'd need a hot minute.

He shook it off the best he could and pulled on only his jeans. He checked over his shoulder to see Savanna's cheeks red, but her body was covered by the comforter, at least.

Griffin cracked the door so as not to offer anyone a view of his woman in bed. "You have news?"

"We got the list of possible suspects from Gray's dad. We're going to discuss them in the lobby if you'd care to join." Carter motioned for Griffin to head into the hall, and Griffin slipped out of the room as carefully as possible but kept the door ajar so it didn't lock on him.

He didn't have the key, and he'd prefer Savanna not to have to open up for him and risk anyone getting a view of her.

"There's something else," Carter said. "Not sure if you want to share this with Savanna, but I managed to pull a little more intel from one of the guys."

Pull something out, huh? Like his teeth? "What is it?" And why wouldn't he want Savanna to know?

"Apparently, three other guys accompanied Nick on the job. He said Nick not only took off with what they were sent to acquire, his words, but Nick killed the other three before doing so."

"You sure he didn't lie to you?"

"You know me better than that. I wouldn't tell you this if I didn't believe it."

Griffin dropped his head and closed his eyes, knowing Savanna wouldn't be able to handle hearing that. Theft was bad enough. But murder, even if they were criminals, was a whole other level. "Don't tell her. Tell the team I don't want her to know."

Carter nodded once Griffin pulled his focus back up. "You good? Aside from what I just told you, I mean?"

After a quick look both ways in the hall to ensure they were alone, Griffin answered as though Carter hadn't literally caught him with his pants down. "Am I good? Why wouldn't I be?" A bullshit lie, sure.

"Because Gray didn't have to tell me what he said to you, I read the situation at the dinner table. He ordered you to stand down, am I right?"

Griffin bowed his head, trying to figure out which direction to go with this conversation that suddenly felt like an awkward game of truth or dare. Tell the truth or dare to lie to a man whose job with the CIA had been to interrogate the worst of the worst. Like he had earlier today.

Plus, Griffin was shirtless and wearing only jeans. Kind of hard to bluff his way out of this one.

"So, you disobeyed a command from your new team leader?" Carter asked when Griffin had yet to deliver an answer.

"Yes," he said under his breath.

"She's an assignment," Carter said in a hushed tone, probably so Savanna wouldn't overhear. "I'm not a fan of you screwing an assignment. Same page as Gray." The pause that followed gave Griffin hope that his boss, who could be a ruthless SOB when warranted, was about to toss out a *but*. "But, if your cock keeps her from panicking, then so be it." He stepped back and looked down the hall. "Meet us in five. Ten if you need more time."

Griffin was torn on how to respond. Even though Griffin held a higher rank upon leaving the Army than Carter, who hadn't been in as long, the man was now his superior. Part of him wanted to punch Carter for implying that Savanna was just a quick fuck for the sake of the job. The other part of him, though, wanted to thank him for not losing his shit, as well as the offer for more time with Savannah.

"Be there in ten," Griffin returned, his voice sounding clipped now that he was tense and wound up. If Savanna would let him, he'd like to . . . bang her? *She's not a one-nighter,* he reminded himself. That seemed to stop the beast inside him from demanding he grab hold of her hips and plow inside her while she screamed out his name.

As he entered the room and caught sight of her clutching the comforter to her chest, her hair a beautiful mess around her shoulders, he wondered if he was doing the right thing by withholding the info Carter had just revealed about Nick. Savanna was so determined to save the man. Shouldn't she know he was a cold-blooded killer? And if he didn't tell her and she found out he knew, would he survive the fallout?

"Everything okay?" she asked, a worried look on her face.

No, Nick is a killer.

But rather than speak the words, he chose to lose himself in thoughts of her instead, picturing what she'd look like as a brunette, which he assumed was her natural color. Although the different shades of blonde she had going for her were also hot as hell. What was he thinking? She'd look beautiful no matter what.

He rid himself of his jeans in one fast movement, his dick coming to life at the thought of fucking her hard and fast, nearly to the point of pain. And based on her confession, it seemed she wanted a little pain in the bedroom.

Sex. He was choosing sex over hurting her with the truth about Nick, telling himself she'd lose her mind if she knew. Plus, he'd do anything to have her in his arms again. He couldn't get enough of her.

"We have ten minutes." He stroked his cock as she let go of the comforter. "How do you want me?"

She smiled, a wicked gleam in her eyes as she released the comforter and flipped to her hands and knees, presenting him with that fucking bitable ass of hers.

"You're one of a kind, you know that, right?" He secured the other condom over his length and joined her on the bed.

He pressed down on her shoulders, the action tilting her

hips a fraction higher. *Perfect.* A shudder ran through her body, and he reveled in the knowledge that this was a first for her. *So many firsts tonight.*

Without wasting another second, he spread her cheeks apart and plunged his tongue into her pussy, then dragged it back up and over her tight little hole, which drew out a startled moan from her.

"Not tonight," he said as he glided his cock between her cheeks. "But I will own every part of you, I can promise you that."

She gazed at him from over her shoulder. "You know what I want, Griffin. Stop making me wait and ju—"

Smack.

Then he swatted her again.

Then one more time.

And she arched her back and sank into the sensations, her pussy glistening even more, which told him he was on the right path. He smoothed his palm over the light mark he'd put there, growing impossibly hard at the sight.

"Please," she cried out, begging for more.

"Sugar, if I do, you might have trouble sitting later," he murmured.

"Give it to me," she commanded in a low, almost husky tone that had his balls tightening even more.

He spanked her harder this time, her ass cheek sporting a bright red palm print. He needed to be back inside her, so he drove into her in one thrust, the fit just as tight as before, practically choking his dick, but fuck, did it feel fantastic.

Savanna moved with him and squeezed the walls of her pussy, which would absolutely be the death of him one day, but he'd die a happy man.

"You first. Always," he said, reaching around and sliding two fingers through her folds to circle her clit. Savanna's pleading whimpers only served to spur him on, bottoming out with each ragged thrust.

Not even a minute later, she bit into the comforter to stifle her moan as she came, and he found his release the second she did, collapsing against her back, their skin slick with sweat.

Realizing they didn't have much time left before Carter came back and broke down the door, Griffin pulled out and removed the condom, tying it off and tossing it in the en suite trash can.

He came back to find she had rolled over to her back, eyes closed and a look of serenity on her face, and he could feel himself losing a little bit more of his heart to this woman. He leaned down, brushed a chaste kiss to her lips, and sat at the edge of the bed as he smoothed a hand over her unruly hair, wishing like hell he could climb back in bed with her.

Her lids fluttered open, lips tipping up into a smile so genuine, so completely happy, that he couldn't help but return it in kind.

"As much as I would love to stay here and keep exploring your body, we need to get dressed and head downstairs."

"What, are you telling me I'm not presentable the way I am?" she teased. "I guess I should find something a bit less revealing this time, wouldn't want to give Easton a heart attack."

"I know you're joking, but I'm an only child and never learned to share. I'm already thinking about how quickly we can get back up here so I can have you again, maybe for the rest of the night before I have to go," he admitted, hating that it was wheels up in the morning, and he'd be leaving her behind.

That was out of his control, but keeping the truth about

Nick from her was his choice, and with that thought, Griffin's good mood tanked.

"So, you'll be staying the whole night in my room?"

He didn't have any more condoms, and he'd need to find a way to rectify that problem soon, but there were plenty of other things they could do. He'd love to see her back on her knees again, and this time, let that beautiful mouth finish what she'd started earlier.

He replayed her words in his head, though, realizing there was still a hint of worry there that he'd leave her before the sun came up.

"Absolutely," he whispered before leaning in to kiss the only woman he'd ever shared the truth about his mother with, and . . . at some point, he ought to tell her the rest of that story. But for now, he just wanted to leave his demons in the past and live in the moment.

And maybe never tell her Nick was a killer.

CHAPTER TWENTY-FOUR

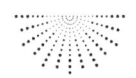

THE MEN WERE ALL SITUATED AROUND THE LOBBY FOCUSED on their laptops and iPads, but it was Gray who looked up first when Griffin and Savanna joined them.

Gray's eyes met Griffin's for a moment before his attention turned to Savanna and scrutinized her like he was Sherlock-fucking-Holmes looking for clues. What happened was none of Gray's business, and Savanna deserved some happiness, which was why he'd chosen not to tell her the new intel about Nick.

But damn the guilt he felt for keeping the truth from her, especially after still choosing to have ridiculously hot sex.

"You good?" Gray asked Savanna.

"I'm okay," she answered with a smile.

Carter tipped his head, eyes on Griffin as if letting him know the "Nick secret" would remain just that, and Griffin lightly nodded before asking, "What do we know?"

Gray returned his focus to Griffin for a moment as they sat on the only empty couch opposite him. "My father said that aside from a handful of government officials, himself included, there are only five people at Archer who would have knowledge of the records housed at that office, as well as access to the vault where the records are stored."

"Does he vouch for all the government officials?" Griffin asked. "Or are we including everyone, aside from your old man, on our suspect list?"

"He doesn't want to rule anyone out, but he said we should handle the list of Archer names, and he'll take point on the names on his side," Gray answered, seeming calmer than Griffin had expected him to be.

Maybe Carter hadn't mentioned that he'd discovered Griffin in Savanna's room? Another secret he opted to keep.

But then Gray skewered him with a steely gaze while cracking his neck like an MMA fighter . . . shoving his palm under his chin and twisting his head until his neck popped. Griffin shook his head. *No, he knows, and he's pissed I disregarded his order.*

Officers. Sometimes they could be such a pain in the ass. But there was a reason Carter insisted they work with Gray, Jack, and his guys. They were the yin to Carter's yang, providing a more subdued vibe to the wilder side that was Carter and his team. Plus, Gray's contacts were currently an obvious perk.

"We have to make this fast because my father needs us to fly out tonight instead of tomorrow morning. The site's security director requested we arrive at zero seven hundred hours before the employees arrive at eight. We'll be meeting with the security team," Gray dropped the unexpected news.

Now he wouldn't be spending the night in bed with Savanna as he'd hoped.

"My program is almost finished decrypting the email that contains the names we need to target at Archer," Gray said a few seconds later. "While that wraps up downloading, I have a few more details my father shared with me." He perched the laptop on his thigh and looked around the lobby at everyone gathered there, his eyes landing on Griffin last.

He really hoped Gray wasn't going to hold a grudge. It wasn't the best way to start their working relationship. Neither was nearly coming to blows with Jack. It'd been a rocky beginning so far, that was for sure.

"Archer Group has pitched at least ten different projects to the U.S. government in the last three years, all of them held at the secure facility in Sicily," Gray began, his eyes moving to the laptop. "The DOD awarded seven of the projects to Archer, but the other three went to rival companies who'd presented similar proposals but for lower bids."

"Similar, huh?" Griffin sat taller when a theory struck him, and based on the hard line of Gray's lips, he was on the same wavelength. "How similar? Is it possible this isn't the first time that vault was breached? What if our inside man is selling secrets to a competitor? For personal gain, or maybe he's being blackmailed."

Griffin glanced at Savanna as she asked, "But if all the plans kept at that location have already been pitched, then doesn't that rule out a rival company being after the blueprints for, let's assume, this Elysium Project?"

"Most likely. Unless they have a new project in the works that my father is unaware of," Gray noted. "Or I'm totally off base about there being an inside man, and hell, all of it. And Joe's team is really just trying to locate the thief and prevent media fallout."

"Your hunches have never been wrong before," Jack spoke up.

"What if we're looking at this the wrong way?" Griffin stood and folded his arms, needing to think through his thoughts while moving. "What if the Elysium Project is already a done deal and is currently in operation by our government? What if it's a *country* and not a company that's after the Elysium Project? Possibly to learn a defense system to duplicate it for themselves, or attempt to sabotage . . ."

"That's the one possibility I'm really hoping isn't the case," Gray said in a grim tone as if he'd already considered the idea and wanted to nix it, but could they? Not yet. "All right. I've got our list of suspects." Gray tapped a few keys. "The owner and CEO of Archer. The CFO. The chief engineer. President. And lastly, their liaison with the DOD." He read off the corresponding names, then leaned in closer to the screen with a shake of the head.

"What's wrong?" Griffin parked himself alongside Gray to see what gave him pause.

A photo of a blonde woman dressed in business attire was displayed next to her biography. "Sydney Archer? She's the liaison?"

"And the owner's daughter," Gray added, but Griffin sensed there was something else bothering Gray aside from the fact their inside man might be a woman. It was doubtful that the owner or his daughter would betray their own company but also not impossible. "I know her." Gray shoved his laptop toward Griffin and stood, clearly shaken.

Well, okay. Griffin rose and offered the laptop to Carter's now outstretched hand. "Care to elaborate?" he prompted.

Gray looked to the floor as he ran both hands through his hair, then faced the room. "We went to West Point together," he said, suddenly smiling as if a memory struck him. "I knew her as Sydney Bowman, though. That's the name she told me, at least. It's not like I hacked the college records to verify her story. She probably asked the professors not to use her real last name, preferring not to be known as the daughter of a multi-billionaire." From the purposefully blank expression on Gray's face, there was more to the story than the two of them being just classmates at West Point. "She was a freshman while I was a senior."

"What do we know about her?" Griffin asked.

"Four years in the Army after West Point. She's thirty-seven now. Married at twenty-seven but divorced at thirty-three and went back to her maiden name. Her son is thirteen, and it looks like she and her ex have joint custody, but the son attends school where his dad lives, most likely because she's always traveling for her job," Carter read from the screen as if he were reading off a grocery list, and Griffin had to assume the information wasn't in the company bio. "And her ex-husband works at the Department of Defense. He's headquartered at the Pentagon. The dad and son have a place in Arlington. Looks like she has a condo in D.C. He's not the biological father, but he legally adopted him when they married when her son was young. So, he raised him."

"He's not yours, right?" Jack joked, probably the only one who could get away with that since he'd been friends with Gray since they were kids in Texas from what Griffin had learned. "You two do the tango at some point?"

"Funny. Real fucking funny," Gray grumbled. "No, I have no kids out in the world that I'm aware of, and before you ask if it's still possible . . . I haven't seen her in fifteen years."

"Hm. You happen to know that specific number off the top of your head, huh?" Oliver arched a brow in surprise.

"Well, from what Gray's dad sent, Sydney's currently at the Sicilian office in Catania. So, it looks like you'll have a reunion tomorrow morning," Carter announced. "But, interesting fact, Joe's team would report to her as she's liaison *and* head of security operations."

Not exactly a nail in her coffin, but it sure as hell didn't help. "Yeah, that's . . . well." What could Griffin say?

"She's not the enemy. I don't believe that," Gray abruptly

announced in a gritty voice as if everyone was ready to declare her the traitor.

"People change. Fifteen years, remember?" Jack issued the reminder as if drawing from his own experience. Had his divorce messed him up? Griffin wouldn't blame him, considering he himself still felt disillusioned about love because of his mom's infidelity.

"She stays on the suspect list," Carter announced, declaring the subject closed for discussion, as was appropriate. Gray needed to remain objective and not let his feelings, positive or negative, for Sydney cloud his judgment.

Annnd the main reason Gray didn't want Griffin getting involved with Savanna—she was the assignment. But he knew for damn sure he'd already placed her above their mission to retrieve whatever was inside that safe-deposit box. How could he not?

He shook free his wayward thoughts to focus. "Where are we at on Nick's boss? You hear from Emilia?" He looked to Savanna to get a quick read on her, but she was standing now, back to the room, eyes out the window that overlooked the Aegean.

Thinking about Greece and the Aegean Sea reminded him of his childhood when his mother would read Homer's greatest works to him before bed. The story of the Trojan horse and Troy had always been his favorite. Probably because it was basically an early war tactic, and he'd already been groomed by his father to join the Army before he'd learned to ride a bike.

His mom loved the military, but she had other aspirations for Griffin. She wanted him to be a scholar or something. Yeah, that wasn't his idea of a good time.

Savanna shifted her wavy hair to her back only to gather it up, twist it around her fingers, and hold the messy bun at the top of her head, sighing as if she were tired. Then she let it go. Only to do it again.

She was definitely nervous, and he wished he could wrap her in his arms and console her.

"Emilia will have a list by tomorrow. I also sent her photos of the two men we're holding in case she might have better luck tying them to their boss as well," Carter said before checking his watch. "You two should head to the jet," he added, looking at Griffin and then Gray.

Griffin had absolutely no clue what time it was. The last few days had been a blur ever since he first stepped foot into Jesse's house and came face-to-face with Savanna.

"Grab an overnight bag," Gray said to him as if recognizing his thoughts were elsewhere, but from the sounds of it, his new boss's thoughts were now also circling around one particular woman. And they'd be facing her tomorrow.

"Right." When Griffin turned, he found Savanna's eyes on him, and he tipped his head to the side to motion for her to follow him to his bedroom.

She was smart and waited a minute or two before joining him, not that Gray wouldn't know she was on her way to say goodbye.

Griffin was in the middle of stuffing a quick change of clothes in a bag when he looked up and saw her enter his room through the adjoining door. "Hey."

"Hi," she whispered as the door shut behind her.

"You'll be okay, I promise." He zipped the bag and slung the strap over his shoulder before meeting her halfway. He placed his hands on her hips and drew her into his arms, setting his chin on top of her head.

"Please don't die on me," she murmured into his chest.

He stiffened at her words. God, one more reason for him not to consider a future with her. Hell, they hadn't even gone on a date yet. His job was risky, and well, he *could* die. What would that do to her? How would she cope with losing someone else?

He didn't want to think about that right now, though. He couldn't make any promises about anything. So, he leaned back and did his best to silence her worries in the only way he really knew how.

With a kiss.

CHAPTER TWENTY-FIVE

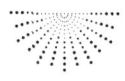

"Good morning." Savanna offered a cup of coffee to Oliver when he joined her in the lobby. The next mug of java went to Jack. The two guys crowded around the table of food she'd set up, acting as though they hadn't eaten in days despite the two servings of pasta they'd each inhaled last night. Both men scooped heaps of her scrambled eggs onto their plates alongside her homemade biscuits. "The coffee isn't exactly specialty, but it should work."

Jack looked up mid-bite. "Coffee is coffee to me," he said around a mouthful of buttery biscuit while catching the falling crumbs with his plate. Savanna chuckled. He wasn't even done loading up his plate before he started to devour the food.

Boys. Well, men. But really, often the same thing.

She slapped a hand to her heart. "I feel deeply offended by that comment." And her thoughts immediately slid back to her money problems and the fear she'd lose her café. *Not important right now*, she told herself.

"Did either of you sleep last night?" She spied the clock on the wall. It was barely six in the morning, and only three hours ago, she'd hung up with Griffin, ordering him to get some sleep.

As soon as he'd checked into his hotel room last night, he'd called her on the burner he'd given her prior to leaving. Was it three or four hours they'd been on the phone?

She was pretty sure she'd done most of the talking. Well, rambling. But he seemed to enjoy just listening. Every so often, she managed to pull out a tidbit from him about his life. But she hadn't wanted to push the subject of his mom, and whether or not that was why he'd avoided serious relationships over the years. But it had to be part of the cause, right?

Somehow, their conversation felt almost as intimate as when they'd made love yesterday. And then, of course, Griffin started talking dirty to her at some point, and they had hot, hot phone sex.

Chills chased over her arms as she remembered the seductive way he'd spoken to her. The erotic things he'd said. Her cheeks heated at the memory of the naughty lines that'd fallen from her lips too. So unlike her. But this man made her feel bad in a good kind of way.

She closed her eyes for a moment, waiting for the familiar pang of melancholy to appear in the pit of her stomach. Over the years, whenever she considered the possibility of falling in love again, she sank into a chasm of despair.

But so far, she'd had neither of those reactions. Savanna opened her eyes and looked up, almost expecting to see Marcus. *Is this okay?* His presence was so real that she felt the need to seek his permission. Maybe if she opened one of the French doors, a *yes* would be carried in by the wind.

I'm crazy. Savanna reached for her phone in the pocket of her cardigan, which she'd paired with a white tank top since it was a breezy morning, the sun not quite as awake as everyone else in the room.

"Where's Carter?" she asked as Oliver and Jack sat on the couch.

"He'll be here in a few," Oliver said. "On the phone with Emilia."

Right. The billionaire. Out of curiosity, Savanna had Googled Emilia while waiting for Griffin's call last night. Not only was the woman stunning, but she was married to another billionaire. A handsome Irishman who, it appeared, came from a family of hotties too.

She'd also called Ella, Jesse, and even Rory last night. Jesse was still simmering over the fact he wasn't there to help out. Ella and Rory, on the other hand, were more focused on extracting details about Griffin from her. Savanna had been reluctant to kiss and tell, worried she'd jinx things, but she had to tell someone. Also, maybe get their blessing and approval that it really was "okay" to feel something for another man.

Savanna's stomach did a little flip when a text came through from Griffin, and she couldn't help but smile as she read his simple but perfect message.

Griff: *Good morning, beautiful.*

God, she never thought she'd be on the receiving end of those kinds of messages again in her life.

A photo popped up next. A seaside view with cliffs in the distance, similar looking to where she was now.

Savanna: *Good morning, handsome. It looks amazing there.*

Griff: *Be better if you were in my arms enjoying the view.*

His sweet and unbridled honesty felt almost too good to be true after his warnings the last few days, but she didn't want to self-sabotage, so she shut off her thoughts the best she could.

Savanna: *I wish. :) How is Gray? Still grumpy?*

Griff: *We're in the car on the way to the site now. He hasn't brought "us" up. I think we have Sydney Archer to thank for that. He's been distracted since her name was tossed into the mix.*

Savanna: *They have history?*

Griff: *I'm thinking so. Not about to ask.*

Savanna looked over to see Jack setting his laptop aside and going for second helpings. She may not be an operator like the guys, but at least she was able to provide them with delicious food.

Savanna: *You know, Rory remembers you from last year.*

Griffin: *Talking about me, huh? ;)*

Savanna: *Maybe a little.*

Griffin: *Well, I am unforgettable. So.*

Savanna: *I'd say so. And why don't they have a lip-biting emoji?*

Griffin sent her a cute emoji with its tongue out and then *just* the tongue emoji.

Griffin: *We're here. We'll call right after.*

Savanna: *Be careful.*

She contemplated an emoji. The right or wrong one could be total make or break, right?

Just go with a kiss, she told herself, then quickly sent it, and he hearted it.

It'd been so long since she'd dated, she didn't know how to untangle all of the emotions flooding her system right now. She was on overdrive. She was also pretty sure if she ever tried to swim in the "single pool," she'd never stay afloat.

"You okay?" Jack was on approach, another biscuit in hand.

Savanna tucked her phone back into her pocket. "I'm okay. Nervous."

"Understandable." He was quiet for a few seconds, focusing his attention on the floor, then looked up and somberly said, "I've been wanting to apologize about, well, what happened at the hangar in Alabama."

"Oh. Um. You don't owe me an apology." It was Griffin who deserved Jack's apology, and he'd already done that.

"Well, I was out of line. I shouldn't have snapped. It was unprofessional."

"You were also looking out for me," she said, recalling the scene that had unfolded in the restroom. "And I appreciate that." But in her mind, it also served to remind her of Griffin's self-imposed policy of no friendships with married women. And despite everything that'd happened between them the past few days, did he still see her as married? Would friendship or "more" ultimately be out of the question once they were back in the real world and no longer in the throes of danger?

"Yeah, but I was also just pissed and acted like a jackass." Jack grinned.

"Well," she said, dragging out the word a touch, trying to regroup and focus, "we all make mistakes, and you were misinformed." Savanna stepped forward and patted him on the shoulder. "It's okay, really," she added, sensing his guilt still lingering between them.

A moment later, she spotted Carter pouring himself a coffee but bypassing the spread of food.

Jack followed her gaze. "Yeah, don't expect him to eat. The guy is a hard-ass, but he cares, and I know he's nervous about not being in Italy with the others."

"Yikes. What does it mean if *Carter* is nervous?" Her heart sped up. "Should I be freaking terrified?"

Jack was the one reaching for her shoulder this time. "Shit, that's not what I meant. We just hate being on the sidelines. Makes us edgy. Tense."

She peered up into Jack's eyes to see if he was telling the truth or trying to downplay it just to calm her down. It was possible it was a little bit of both. "I'm going to go talk to him," she said, turning away from Jack but still within range to hear him curse under his breath, most likely because he'd worried her.

"Good morning," she greeted Carter as he thumbed through something on his phone, holding the cup near his mouth without actually taking a sip, his eyes laser-focused on the screen.

He finally brought his dark gaze her way and drank his coffee while lowering his phone. "Thank you for the breakfast." He smiled, and yet, it felt forced.

"You're welcome. Not going to eat?"

"I don't usually eat breakfast."

She contemplated lecturing him, but her gut told her she'd be wasting her breath with the man. "Hear from Emilia yet?" she asked instead.

"She promised me news this morning, so I should hear from her soon." He pocketed his phone in his dress slacks. She could tell he was wearing the same clothes from yesterday based on the untucked and wrinkled white dress shirt. He probably hadn't gone to bed. And why did he dress like a businessman when every other guy had on jeans, tees, and often backward ball caps?

Carter had been in the CIA at one time and now had to remain under the radar, and she'd love to know the details surrounding the reason. Carter was also obviously wealthy if he could afford a safe house as luxurious as this and all the toys that went with it. But Jeff Bezos was a gazillionaire, and you didn't see him walking around dressed in James Bond attire. Now that she thought about it, Carter would make a damn hot James Bond, minus the British accent.

"Well, that's good. Hopefully she can help us narrow down who's hunting Nick." But what terrified her the most were the others—the "everyone" Joe warned them were coming for Savanna. Were they people who desperately wanted what Nick stole? "And what if it's a terrorist?" she spoke her next thought aloud.

"Nick's boss?" He tipped his head to the side as if surprised she'd suggest Nick, even though a criminal, would align with a terrorist? *Especially* after his brother was killed by terrorists.

"No." She shook her head, needing to quickly squash that possibility. "I meant, what if Nick's boss was supposed to steal the Elysium Project for a terrorist? You said you believe the boss is a middleman, so what if the *buyer* is that kind of bad guy?"

The kind who killed my husband. And she did her best not to think back to the horror of watching her husband die.

"Right now, we're swimming in a sea of assumptions. I would say it's possible Nick's boss wanted the plans himself, but since both the Greeks and Joe alluded to many *someones* coming after you, it's hard to believe Nick's boss wanted the Elysium Project for himself." Carter pointed his gaze to the floor, and there was something he wasn't telling her, wasn't there? Why was he leaving her in the dark?

Right. I'm me. Not them. "Tell me. Am I right to be worried that the people who are trying to hijack these designs want them for more sinister reasons than personal profit? They might want them to—"

"Hurt the U.S.," he cut her off, confirming her fears. He

let out a sigh as if about to share something he wasn't in the mood to disclose.

His brows became slashes as his lips drew in a tight line, staring at her as if he were trying to resist a Greek siren from luring the truth from him.

When his expression relaxed somewhat as if giving in, he said, "The CIA has off-the-grid locations around the world used for interrogating terrorists. For years, there have been concerns that the sites have vulnerabilities." His one hand disappeared into his pocket. "Back when I was with the Agency, they were floating the idea of creating some type of aerial defense system to intercept and destroy immediate threats. Rockets. Artillery shells."

"Like Israel's Iron Dome?" she asked, trying to draw up a visual in her head of what he was saying.

And there went that pang in the pit of her stomach, but this time it had nothing to do with her love life.

"Yes, like that. I don't know if the government implemented the program for those locations, though, but if they did . . ."

"You think the Elysium Project could be it?" She clutched her stomach, almost spilling her coffee.

"Another assumption. And I haven't brought this up to anyone other than Gray because I'd prefer to be wrong on this."

One more reason Carter didn't sleep last night and why Gray was most likely grumpy.

"How do we find out?"

"I spoke with Gray in the middle of the night and asked him to approach his father about it. See if he could confirm whether the DOD does have such a system operational for the CIA black sites. He should hopefully hear back from his dad, despite the time difference, once he leaves the Archer Group location this morning."

"You're telling me this, but you haven't told the others?"

"I don't want to throw their focus. It already feels like we're chasing our tails, bouncing from lead to lead. Why add more until I know for sure?"

Well, from where she stood, she didn't see it that way. She was impressed at how quickly they were figuring everything out. Lucky A.J. had brought them in.

"They're only blueprints for the Elysium Project, though, right? It's not like whoever has the sketches could use them to locate those sites, right?"

"Not necessarily. A few high-level people at Archer would need to know locational details, especially the head engineer, in order to design the plans. So yeah, it's possible that whoever wanted those sketches wanted them for the purpose of attacking those secure sites."

"But if only a few people even know about these projects—"

"My guess is someone at Archer most likely contacted Nick's boss, not the other way around."

"And wanted Nick's boss to sell the plans on his, or her, behalf?"

He nodded. "Right."

"Shouldn't we be sounding some major alarms right now if there is even a chance this defense system you told me about is in jeopardy?"

A quick smile brushed across his lips. "Of course. If Gray's father believes there is a threat to those sites, he'll activate whatever contingency plans or security measures the DOD has in place. Trust me when I say that there are always many layers of complexity within any government operation."

"If they follow that protocol to safeguard those sites, will Archer know?"

"No, that'd be several levels above Archer's security clearance."

"So, if those sites can be kept safe even if those plans get into the wrong hands, then why do you look like your dog died?"

"I do have a dog, by the way, and I'm kind of missing him right now. He always travels with me, but I decided to have him sit this op out." So, he did have another side to him. Good to know. "But," he said as if realizing he'd lost his focus. Probably lack of sleep. "That means even if Joe is unintentionally working with this insider, he's aware of the security breach, and he's choosing loyalty to his company over the country, knowing full well the risk if the DOD isn't made aware of a breach."

"Oh." Had Griffin thought about that, too, but was blinded by his friendship with the man? He only seemed to go rage mode toward Joe back at the cabin when *she* was at risk.

"So, if someone does want those plans to carry out an attack on our black sites, we're most likely dealing with a terrorist as the main threat to your safety."

She hadn't wanted to be right on that one. *A terrorist cell is coming after me because of Nick?*

Carter rested his mug against his abdomen. "Like I said, this is why I feel like we're spinning in circles. Too many possibilities and too many hypotheses to test. We just don't have the time to chase after so many guesses."

"This is all over my head," she confessed. "But I appreciate your honesty. I won't say anything to anyone."

His brows lifted as if he didn't believe she wouldn't tell Griffin. "It's not a secret. I'd rather have more facts, though. And it'd be nice to simply rule out one possibility if Gray's dad says there is no Iron Dome-like defense for those black sites."

She slowly brought her mug to her mouth, her hand shaking a little because, for some reason, everything inside of her screamed Carter's concerns were spot on. "Is there something else you want to tell me?" she asked when sensing Carter was still holding back.

He quietly studied her but then shook his head.

"All right. I think I'll go clean the kitchen," she sputtered, her nerves becoming like a stranglehold around her throat. "I left it a mess."

Savanna started to turn, but Carter caught her by the arm. "Yes, there is something." He let go of a deep breath. "I just wanted to tell you that, um." He looked around the lobby for a second. "At dinner last night, um."

Okay, what had a man like Carter tongue-tied enough to drop two "ums"? What could be harder for him to talk about than the possibility of terrorists coming after her to get to Nick?

"What?" she whispered.

"I've known Griffin for twelve years," Carter began while removing his hand from her arm.

Oh. He was going to bring *that* up? He knew she and Griffin had slept together. This conversation was clearly harder for him to talk about than what he'd just told her regarding his Elysium Project worries, huh?

"He's not the type to fall in love. At all."

I know. God, did she know. Griffin had pretty much made that clear.

"He's also never looked at anyone the way I saw him looking at you last night during dinner." He bowed his head and squeezed his temples between a thumb and forefinger.

Wow, he really was uncomfortable with this conversation.

"Are you about to warn me not to hurt him?" Savanna asked when he let go of his temples to meet her eyes.

"If you're anything like me, you have no plans to remarry after having your spouse murdered," he finally admitted, catching her by surprise, "so yeah, I don't want to see my best friend finally meet someone who makes him want to change his ways only to get hurt."

She blinked in surprise, but she also kind of appreciated the raw honesty. "You're not worried he'll break *my* heart?" *Because I am. That's exactly what he told me in Alabama.*

His eyes thinned as he replied, "No guarantees there, either," and then he turned and walked away.

Well, hell. She was glad he'd left because she honestly didn't know what to say. Her thoughts were now all over the place.

She discarded her mug as soon as she could get her feet to move, then went to clean up the kitchen. With the music on, she tried to lose herself in the mundane task of cleaning and not to think about Griffin. Or terrorists. Or the Elysium Project. Or the men who killed her husband. Nothing. She just wanted blank space in her head.

It was maybe thirty minutes later when Oliver joined her in the kitchen with an abrupt announcement. "Gray and Griffin just left the site. They're about to call."

She dropped the dish into the sink and peeled off the yellow gloves in a hurry, practically jogging to keep up with Oliver to get back to the lobby.

Carter had his phone out when she joined them. One ring later, he answered on speakerphone. "What do we know?" he prompted.

"From the looks of it," Griffin began, and she was a little surprised he was speaking instead of Gray but also relieved to hear his voice, "we have an inside *woman*, not man."

CHAPTER TWENTY-SIX

"YOU'RE SKEPTICAL, THOUGH, AREN'T YOU?" SAVANNA raised her voice slightly since they were all on speakerphone. As soon as Gray and Griffin had boarded the jet, Gray called them back to continue filling them in on their visit to Archer Group.

"I'm struggling to believe the owner's daughter would not only sabotage the company but jeopardize the safety of the nation. A country she risked her neck for in battle," Gray answered without deliberation.

Sydney Archer had served, same as Griffin and Gray, but . . .

"There is one other possibility," Griffin suggested as if trying to ease the hell that Gray seemed to be in at the idea of an old friend being a traitor. "Sydney was taken."

Savanna abruptly stood from the couch in the lobby. "You think Nick kidnapped her? Theft is one thing, but kidnapping?"

The sound of a deep exhale came over the line. "You're not really that quick to defend a man you met for all of five minutes, are you? A murderer?" Griffin seethed, his tone raspy and . . .

Wait, what?

"I can't wrap my head around the fact you still believe a man that your . . ." Griffin added in a low, gritty voice. "That your husband wouldn't even forgive, can be redeemed."

Husband.

There it was.

Was he placing Marcus between them once again? Did something happen to make Griffin believe she was off-limits again?

"Murderer," she whispered, just now realizing what he'd said. She turned toward Carter and saw a look of surprise on his face. Not because he hadn't heard this news. No, he was surprised that Griffin shared it with Savanna. "Do you all know?" She looked around the room, one by one at everyone as she waited for Griffin to speak again. To explain.

"I'm sorry," Jack was the only one to speak up.

"Nick killed the three men who were on the job with him before he took off with what he stole," Carter finally explained what Griffin hadn't wanted to tell her. He'd let the truth slip out of anger, and now he was most likely regretting it.

"When did you find out?" *And what if it's not true?* But she knew they'd argue with her, so why bother? She'd find out the truth herself somehow. Thieves were redeemable, weren't they? But a murderer? Unforgivable.

"Yesterday right after dinner," Jack told her. So that's what Carter had wanted to tell Griffin when they'd gone out in the hall. And Griffin had come back into the room and made love to her . . . with that secret between them.

"I'm sorry." Griffin's apology meant she was right. She was hurt by his lack of admission, and yet, she understood he was only trying to protect her. He knew how she'd react to the news.

In Griffin's eyes, defending a criminal was insane, and maybe it was. After all, her only tie to Nick was Marcus, but some part of her felt that if she severed that tie, she truly lost Marcus forever.

"We can talk about that later," Carter began, and she nodded in understanding. "Start over from the beginning," he directed Griffin and Gray.

There was a lot of background noise, and she assumed the pilot was preparing for takeoff. It'd be less than a two-hour flight and most likely quicker since they weren't flying commercial.

"We were taken on a tour of the site by the head security guard, but the man said he didn't have authorization or the security clearance himself to access their main vault where the hard copies of their projects are stored," Gray repeated what he'd explained on their first call, but he was walking them through the details a bit slower this time. "The vault can only be opened by certain DOD personnel or one of our five suspects at Archer."

"And that's when you asked him about Sydney?" Oliver spoke up, scratching his jawline, standing near Carter, eyes on the phone.

Savanna exhaled, trying to find a way to get through this and not run crying from the room.

"Right," Gray answered. "He said Sydney had only been at their Catania location in Sicily for three weeks, but then last week, she'd sent out an email that she was taking a vacation. No location provided. The man said it'd been unexpected, especially since she hadn't been there long, but she's the owner's daughter, so no one pressed. Her out-of-office email provided no return date."

"We requested security footage to be pulled from the day her out-of-office email went into effect," Griffin spoke up, his tone still low. Angry at her for worrying about Nick? Or worried *she* was angry because he didn't tell her the truth? She had no clue.

Savanna turned away from the room and smoothed her hands up and down her arms, her nerves getting to her, and the uncomfortable knot in her stomach intensified.

"There was some type of glitch in the security feed between zero seven hundred and zero eight hundred last Friday," Gray went on. "When we asked why this wasn't reported or didn't raise any red flags, the security guard said it *was* reported. Well, more like emailed to Sydney."

"Sydney was also at the Sicily office two other times this year. Shortly after each of those visits, Archer lost two major contracts to their rivals," Griffin quickly dropped the bombshell. "Unfortunately, we can't confirm if those projects were stored in Sicily. Same goes for the Elysium Project."

"But I did speak with my father, who said Archer Group was awarded a project for an aerial defense system designed for the CIA black sites. That was a few years ago, so it's currently operational. Chances are it was the Elysium Project."

"Shit," she whispered under her breath, knowing what that meant.

"My dad's activating the security measures to protect those black sites just in case. That's one major problem we can check off as being handled now," Gray added while Jack and Oliver focused on Carter with puzzled looks on their faces.

"So, the black sites will be safe? The military and CIA officers working there won't be at risk now?" Savanna double-checked, and that was something.

Murderer or not, would Nick do anything that'd put the lives of the military in danger after what happened to his brother? That would be even harder for her to wrap her head around.

"Yeah, the breach has initiated backup protocols. And any information the Archer Group possesses about the satellite orbital positions that would reveal the black site locations will be altered. Naturally, Archer Group won't be notified given the potential leak," Gray followed up with more details, and it was all good news so far. That was something.

Carter looked at Jack and then Oliver, but there was no apology in his eyes or in his tone as he explained his hypothesis about the Elysium Project he'd previously only shared with Savanna and Gray.

"You told her but not us?" Jack's forehead creased. More surprise than anger.

"It just came out," Carter said, shaking his head as if dismayed about sharing that intelligence with her.

Unlike the "Nick being a murderer" secret.

"So, whatever Nick's boss had him steal can still be used to recreate our defense systems, which isn't ideal," Griffin noted, "but at least our people and sites will be safe."

"I still don't think Sydney is behind this," Gray said a moment later. "I know her. She wouldn't do this. She's either really on vacation, and our insider took advantage of that opportunity, or she's in danger."

Carter was quiet for a moment, contemplative. "We can't rule out any possibilities. Sydney could be the threat, or she could be the hunted one."

"Wait, you think . . ." Savanna blinked in surprise at his words.

But if Nick was capable of murder, kidnapping wasn't a stretch.

"It's possible it's not just Nick everyone might be after, but *who* Nick might have. The daughter of a billionaire with knowledge of a whole collection of top-secret government projects sounds like motivation to come after Savanna for the purpose of getting to Nick. And by way of Nick, to Sydney," Gray explained whatever she assumed Carter had been suggesting.

"Maybe," was all Carter would say.

Chills crept over her skin, and she did her best not to lose herself to dangerous *what-ifs*.

"What about Joe and his team?" she found herself asking, her thoughts quickly switching directions like the weather during a Southern summer. "The only way Joe could possibly know the Sicilian site had been breached, and *which* records were compromised, is if the insider told him. Because the insider knew Nick double-crossed them all, and he sent Joe's team to hunt Nick down," Savanna said, more so trying to work through her own thoughts to understand how Joe fit into it all.

"And Joe may also be searching for Sydney," Gray responded.

"Or taking his orders from her," Griffin tossed out.

"Which is why we can't rule out any names on our suspect list. And it could still even be someone at the DOD," Carter replied. "Gray, when you're en route, ask your dad if Sydney's ex at the DOD happens to have access to any of the projects with Archer. See if he's on your dad's list of suspects."

Oh, God.

The puzzle.

The pieces.

Too freaking many.

"We'll talk more when we arrive," Gray said. "Our jet is taking off. We have to end the transmission now."

She hated the quick goodbye, and she was still upset with Griffin that he withheld information from her.

"See you in a few hours," Gray spoke up, and Griffin remained quiet before the line disconnected.

Her stomach was full-on somersaulting, and not in the lovey-dovey way.

"You okay?" Jack asked her, and she realized they were alone in the lobby now. Oliver must have followed Carter to wherever he went to phone the Italian billionaire.

"Why, do I look not okay?" She semi-smiled.

"You're pale." Jack's brows pinched together. "But everything will be okay."

"Everything-everything?" *Even with Griffin?* she couldn't help but wonder, which she felt selfish for still worrying about at a time like this.

Jack smiled and nodded. "Everything-everything."

CHAPTER TWENTY-SEVEN

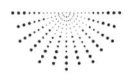

Griffin found the door to Savanna's room propped open, so he walked in without a warning knock. She was standing in front of the French door, looking out at the sea.

"Hi," she said as if sensing he was there despite his quiet steps, but she didn't turn toward him. And that was nearly as gutting as what he knew would play out next. He'd gone over the conversation in his head during the flight, and every outcome sucked.

And sadly, he wasn't even throwing into the mix the other problem—that after finding out Nick had killed three men, Griffin had walked back into Savanna's bedroom and had sex with her.

He'd surely pay for that too.

"Hi." Griffin let the door shut behind him, and when she finally turned, he was struck once again by how beautiful she was. She had on fitted jeans, her short ankle boots, and a white tank top with a cardigan. Her hair was a little wavy and hung over her shoulders. But her eyes were downcast.

He set his back to the door and propped a booted foot to it, resting his head against the wood as he studied her. They both knew why they weren't going in for a welcome-back hug or kiss. And it wasn't just because of Nick.

He was certain Savanna had felt the change in his mood over the phone, and the air crackled with . . .

Crackled? What is wrong with me?

But it was there. The tension. And not the sexual kind. Filling every space of the room, suffocating him.

He was about to lay news on her she didn't want to hear but most likely had seen coming. But which would they discuss first? Nick or the other thing weighing on his heart?

"What changed?" She took a few steps his way, hesitancy in every small stride.

Door two, then. The Nick conversation would have to wait.

"How'd we go from you wishing I was there in Italy with you enjoying the view to you looking as though you'd rather go do flutter kicks on the beach with a bunch of Teamguys at BUD/S?"

God, this woman and the visual she'd just painted almost steered him off course and back to where he shouldn't be. But he had to do right by her, and it was better to piss her off now than down the road.

"You said Gray didn't lecture you, but you reverted to Mister Moody before the flight back here. Even if Gray did say something during the flight, it still doesn't jive. I'm going to take a wild guess and say it's not just because you're mad at yourself for learning about Nick and choosing to fuck me instead of telling me the truth."

Ouch, that hurt.

He deserved it.

But it was still a painful blow.

"I'm sorry about that. Truly. I thought it'd be best if you didn't know. You had hope for him." He was quiet for a moment, letting her process his apology and decide if she'd accept it. "And as for the other part, I struggle to keep my hands to myself around you. I buried the truth about Nick to be with you. And I'm an asshole for that."

"I'm not sure that's an accurate description," she snapped. "But I can forgive you for it," she added softly. "What I can't understand is what I think you're about to say next."

Standing a good pace or two away, she crossed her arms. And her hazel eyes lit up brighter with the anger she was prepared to throw his way like a World Series pitch in the ninth inning with everything riding on the need for a home run.

He considered pushing off the door and closing the gap between them, but he didn't trust himself. She had power over him he didn't understand, and he needed to maintain some distance. Funny thing was it wasn't even his dick doing the thinking when it came to this woman—it was his heart. And Griffin was terrified of that. "Gray didn't lay into me," he said, "I did it to myself."

"You lectured yourself about sleeping with me? About whatever it is you're feeling for me that you're now trying to deny?" she whispered, her words faltering a little as that mama bear tenacity he admired so much waned with the hurt building inside her now. He could see it written all over her face. Those expressive eyes spoke volumes. Her full lips, untouched by makeup, could provide an entire soundtrack. The hollowing of her cheeks as her lips pouted in preparation for an angry lecture were . . .

Griffin shook those thoughts free, feeling as though his mother had somehow snuck into his brain and sprinkled some literary jargon in there. His mom spent enough time in his head as it was, and he did *not* want her there now. It was a constant reminder as to why he doubted he'd be able to give Savanna what she both wanted and needed.

"We barely know each other," he started, eyes moving to the floor because she'd bewitch him if he kept looking at her. "I know that was true yesterday too." He lifted one palm, asking for more time to work through his thoughts, assuming she'd be throwing back a line or two of her own at some point, and he doubted he'd be able to resist her standing there being mouthy at him without taking her into his arms. "But while I was at the site this morning, a thought hit me hard—a thought that I've been pushing out of my mind for selfish reasons, which is that my job could put you in danger at some point. And then there's the obvious fact you brought up yesterday that I tried to dodge . . . this work is dangerous, and I could die because of it."

Her shuddering intake of breath had him peeling his attention up to find her heart on display in the dejected look on her face.

"I want so badly to be who you need, so much so I let myself believe it was possible yesterday."

"But you realized this morning I'm not worth it?"

His boot hit the ground as he readied himself to go to her, but fuck, he had to hold back. For her. He had to hold back for her.

"It's not like that."

"We barely know each other. I get that. But don't you feel there's something there between us?" She gestured between them with that gutted, forlorn look in her eyes.

"You know I do. I can't explain it, either. It's happened so fast, though, that I'm a bit blindsided, and I just—"

"What?" she cried, taking a step toward him.

"I can't compete with Marcus," Griffin finally confessed. "I can't compete with his memory."

Savanna looked to the ceiling and shook her head. "No one is asking you to compete with him."

"But *I* feel as if I would be. I didn't know the man, and I wouldn't assume to know what you had together. But I know you believed him to be your 'forever.' That's a hard act to follow, Savanna. Maybe someday another man will walk into your life—I just . . . well, it can't be me."

"That's not—" She dropped her words and shook her head again, eyes returning to his face. "Over twenty years in the service, and I'm what frightens you the most?"

"Yeah, you do." Hadn't he said as much in the last few days? Hell, maybe not. He could barely add two and two to get four since he met her, his thoughts and feelings going every which way since they'd begun breathing the same air.

"I'll admit, this has moved really fast. A week ago, we hadn't even met. I'm just as confused and scared as you are, but it's a good kind of scared. An anxious, excited kind of scared that has me hopeful for the first time in years that it's possible to—"

"Please, Savanna," he cut her off. "Don't. I warned you I'd hurt you. I broke my own rules and crossed the line. I messed up by letting you believe there's hope for something between us."

She pinned him with an angry look. "What really happened in Sicily that has you doing a Jekyll and Hyde on me?" she rasped.

He deserved everything she was throwing at him for his bullshit lies and excuses. He knew that and hated it. But it had to happen. A quick, and what he'd hoped clean break. Rip off the Band-Aid and move on.

"Your trigger was Nick. Why?"

And damn did she just read him. Like. A. Fucking. Book.

Well, it wasn't so much Nick himself as it was her belief the man was still redeemable.

He released his thoughts, knowing he had to get through this and fast. The longer it took, the harder it'd be for the both of them.

"What is it?"

"While I was walking through the Archer site this morning, I realized I was thinking about you the entire time, and not as part of the assignment. And then every conceivable problem that could arise if you and I were to try to be a couple assaulted me like I was being riddled with bullets."

For some reason, his body was more fatigued and achier today than it had been yesterday, despite the time lapse since he'd had his ass whooped. Or maybe his stomach hurt because of what he was doing to this woman?

"The other thing I realized is that I'm like my father in many ways," he mumbled. "I didn't know that until I met you, though." Because no one had ever made him feel this way. "I would sacrifice the world to save the one I . . ."

His dad would have done anything for his mom. Griffin now knew he was capable of the same. The rage he'd felt just thinking about a future with Savanna and, down the road, some man making a move on her . . . like what happened with his mom, was tenfold now with Savanna's gaze on him.

"And that was before I realized I could ever fall . . ." God, he couldn't get through this in complete sentences. "The way Shep touched you at that hangar was enough to make me want to throttle him," Griffin confessed the dark, ugly truth. He'd never experienced jealousy before because no woman had drawn that feeling out of him. But deep in his gut, he'd known that if he were to ever let himself fall for a woman, he'd struggle.

Savanna stumbled back a step. "So, you wouldn't trust me

around other men, especially if one tried to cross the line with me?"

"I-I don't know," he admitted. "I'd want to." His voice cracked this time. Everything hurt on the inside. "I, uh, clearly have trust issues. Really, *really* bad trust issues."

"Shep. Jesse. Any guy in my life, even a friend . . . that'd be hard on you?" Tears welled in her eyes as if she were now fully comprehending how truly messed up he was and why he shouldn't have ever touched her in the first place. "Your mom slept with her friend?"

Jack-Fucking-Pot. "Not just any friend. The man who encouraged her to become a writer. He was her best friend before she met my dad." He closed his eyes, realizing he'd yet to reveal that bit of news to her before now.

"Oh." The sadness in that one word was heartbreaking, and her voice cracked when she continued. "Your mom is the author. The books on the shelves at the cabin were written by her? That's your mom. Her pen name. It's why you didn't want me touching the books."

He lightly nodded, his words stuck in his throat.

"Why does your dad still have them? I mean, I don't understand." She winced. "Sorry, not the point," she said, her hazel eyes shimmering with tears.

Griffin took a minute to calm down and collect his thoughts. She didn't deserve his anger. She deserved sunshine and puppies and a man who could love her without question. Not a man who'd be consumed by worries that she would ultimately cheat, like his mom. "He's proud of her still. Even after everything they went through, after every new release, he still asks her to send him a signed copy he can collect."

She tipped her head, swiping away the tears.

"They tried to work things out following her affair, but she ultimately went back to her friend. She chose him, not my dad. She married him once she and my father divorced," he laid the news on her. "And she broke the strongest man I've ever met. She's why his place is fortified like a military installation, not because of what happened to him in Vietnam. He fucking snapped after losing her. Always level-headed before then." Pages of memories from his childhood of his parents so happy together between his dad's deployments pushed into his mind and had his hands shaking. "He would have taken every bullet or every beating if it meant keeping my mom safe. He'd trade every sunset for the rest of his life to see her smile." Griffin dragged a hand along his jawline. "He'll never be happy again. Never get over her."

Savanna closed the space between them and set her palms on his cheeks, and it was only then, when she touched him, did he realize there were tears on his face too.

That wasn't . . . no.

"So, you see, I'd never ask you to stop being friends with Shep and the others, but I also know I wouldn't be able to keep the fear from creeping in that at some point, one of them would make a move on you. And then I'd have to kill him," he told her as bluntly as possible. *Be like Nick. A killer.*

He'd never killed an innocent and never thought he would.

But he barely knew Savanna as it was, and yet the enormity of his feelings was inexplicable, so what would happen a month from now? A year? Ten?

"Griffin, you wouldn't do that. I don't believe you." Her tender voice and her hands on him were knives to his heart because he wanted to say he could change, that he'd learn to let go of his issues and figure out a way to trust again. Anything to have a shot with her. How could he not take that shot when he'd never felt this way in his life and in such a short period of time?

But the risk.

The risk was so great.

Not for him, as he'd originally thought. His heart no longer mattered.

It was hers. And there wasn't a chance in the world he'd jeopardize her heart, especially not after everything she'd survived.

He set his hands on top of hers. "I'm sorry. I shouldn't have ever touched you. Kissed you. And I'm sorry about not telling you the truth about Nick." *And for opening up to you.* "I need to do my job, though. And that's to keep you safe." He chanced a look into her eyes, hoping he'd find the strength necessary to officially wave the white flag and retreat.

"If I'm not worth fighting for, then you're right," she whispered while backing away from him, a haunted look on her face as tears spilled freely down her cheeks. "You can't compete with Marcus. Because he'd have the guts to never surrender. To never back down. He'd have the guts to fight for me."

Griffin's hands tensed at his sides, and he bowed his head. "I know. Like Joe said," he recalled, "Marcus was the best of us."

CHAPTER TWENTY-EIGHT

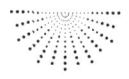

Griffin pounded the heavyweight bag in the gym, ignoring his achy ribs, hoping it'd crush the pain in his heart. Forget helping the team chase the new leads, he'd be useless in his current state.

After thirty minutes of pummeling the bag as if it were the man his mother had married, whom he'd never consider a stepdad no matter how much his mom pleaded, he was sweaty and exhausted. And the pain in his chest hadn't subsided. Not at all.

Panting and barely able to breathe, he dropped to a knee, one gloved hand to the ground, and let out a deep roar. And, just as he'd seen Savanna do, Griffin tilted his chin up in search of Marcus's ghost. His spirit, or whatever, seemed to follow Savanna around to protect her.

"I know," he seethed. The only person he was angry at was himself. "I know, all right." He lowered his gaze to the concrete floor beneath his knee. "Fuck."

Talking to the air. And air didn't talk back.

Besides, Marcus wouldn't hover over him. He'd be with

the woman he loved, the woman that had Griffin officially losing his mind and talking to the ceiling.

"Bro, you okay?" Jack called out from behind.

"We bros now?" Griffin retorted around a groan of agony as he pushed himself off the ground to face Jack.

"I was hoping we'd established a truce."

Eyeing his teammate, Griffin slowly began removing the boxing gloves. "Did you ever meet Marcus?" he asked instead. Jack cocked his head and narrowed his eyes as if trying to decipher the nature of Griffin's foul mood, though Griffin's question made it pretty clear.

"No, but not too long after Marcus died, the man who replaced him helped save Gray's sister and me," he answered, brows pulled together.

And now Griffin couldn't help but wonder if Jack would ever trust again, either? His wife cheated, but he hadn't known until after the fact, so he supposed it probably stung less.

Savanna would never cheat, damn it. I don't need a year of dating to know that. But would that annoying, gut-wrenching feeling let him truly accept that? Or would she become collateral damage to his baggage? His parents had been married for sixteen years, though. Sixteen years of love between them, and his dad would never have believed the love of his life would cheat with her best friend, either.

Your mother made a mistake, his mom's brother defended her years after the affair when Griffin had still been unable to forgive her. *She's still a good person*, his uncle had continued over beers one night when they'd been camping. *But they say if you're capable of falling in love with someone else, then maybe your heart never truly belonged to the first.*

Well, she married that mistake. And now Dad is trying to

drink her memory away, and it's not helping. Griffin had ordered him to drop the conversation after that.

Was Savanna truly capable of falling in love for a second time? Was there room in her heart for another man without diminishing her feelings for Marcus?

"You like her, huh? That was fast," Jack said, stating the obvious.

Griffin almost laughed. That was like announcing the sky was blue and the grass was green—well, when it wasn't dead, like he was feeling on the inside right now at the thought of walking away from the only woman who ever made him feel anything. Even jealousy because yeah, he felt that too. And that's what scared him. Because he knew how toxic it could be.

Griffin pulled on his tee and cracked his neck, his breathing beginning to return to a normal pace.

"Between you and Gray both having your boxers in a bunch about women, I guess it's a good thing the rest of us are here to work," Jack said when Griffin never answered him.

"Smartass," Griffin responded under his breath, but he knew Jack was trying to ease the tension, which he supposed he appreciated.

"Weird that Gray seems so compelled to believe Sydney's innocence when he hasn't seen her in fifteen years. She must have left one hell of an impression on him."

"Yeah, about as crazy as Savanna's insistence that a man she doesn't know can't be all that bad." Shit, was he talking about Nick or himself?

Griffin had the odd urge to look skyward again, to see if the man who watched over Savanna would send him some guidance as they left the gym, which made him feel downright certifiable. But according to the after-action review, Marcus had never left Griffin's side until he'd gotten him to safety that day years ago. *Am I alive for a reason?*

"Hey, we've got news," Oliver said as he trotted down the hall toward them, adding the "hurry up" gesture. Carter must have received word from Emilia.

Griffin stopped just short of a heartbeat at the sight of Savanna standing alongside Carter in the lobby. When her gaze swept to his face to see he'd joined the rest of the team, she immediately looked away.

He felt the dagger right where he deserved it after what he'd said to her. In his heart.

"What do we know?" Griffin asked, finally getting himself to move again and round the couches to where Carter stood, balancing a laptop in hand.

"Emilia identified Nick's boss," Carter said, but why didn't he look happy about that? "She's a hundred percent certain."

"Who?" Savanna asked tentatively as if preparing herself for upsetting news.

"Stefanos Loukanis. He's basically an Italian Sotheby's. Runs a legitimate auction house in Athens and Rome. He also sells items off-the-books that can't be sold legally, many of which his own team steals. From Van Goghs to Fabergé eggs. Whatever a client might want, he finds a way to get it," Carter explained. "He's been on Emilia's radar for a while, but he'd been off-limits because of some deal. I don't know. She couldn't explain. But she said that deal has expired, and he's all ours if we want him."

"Nick helped steal for him," Savanna murmured as though finally accepting what Marcus had known long before he'd died. His brother was irredeemable.

"Emilia tapped into her contacts at AISE, basically Italy's CIA, and she was able to find footage that didn't show up for us." Carter looked at Savanna. "You may not want to see what Emilia sent me."

"I need to know. No more secrets," she said with a slight nod, and Griffin's shoulders collapsed at witnessing this beautiful woman doing everything in her power to remain strong.

"This was taken last night." Carter showed his screen to everyone gathered around him.

Griffin stood behind Carter and Savanna, and he did his best not to inhale her sweet scent. Or peer at the curve of her tan shoulder that was no longer covered by her cardigan.

"They have Nick," she cried. Savanna may have been closer to accepting that Nick wasn't one of the good guys, but that didn't mean she wanted to see him hurt.

She turned away from the screen, which had her bumping straight into Griffin, her hands meeting his chest like the first time they met in Jesse's kitchen.

He reflexively grabbed hold of her shoulders, and she slowly lifted her eyes to his face. More tears. More worry about a man she didn't know, a killer. Her heart was nearly too big for her chest. He'd never met such a caring and *forgiving* person in all of his life.

Why couldn't he be as forgiving, and then maybe, just fucking maybe, he could move on? Be happy.

"Sorry," he said under his breath at the same time she did, and they both removed their hands from each other.

She sidestepped him, and he clenched his teeth in an effort not to say or do something dumb. Like tell her in front of everyone he was an idiot to push her away. That he wanted to fight for her. That he'd light the world on fire if he had to if it meant being with her even one more time.

"The footage is outside a private hangar at the New Orleans International Airport. Emilia was able to track

Stefanos's jet back to the U.S. Luckily, Italian Intelligence has been monitoring his movements for a few months, preparing to take him down soon. But my guess is Nick never left the States after he dropped the key off at Savanna's."

Carter handed the laptop off to Gray, and he replayed the footage of Nick with his hands bound and body clearly banged up as Stefanos's men shoved him toward a limo.

"Looks like they flew round trip between Rome and New Orleans," Carter added.

"Just Nick? Not Sydney?" Gray asked, playing the footage once again as if trying to locate the blonde that had him shook since yesterday.

"Just him, and I have to assume if Nick had taken Sydney, Stefanos's people would have located her too," Carter told Gray. "That doesn't make her the bad guy, though." He held up a hand, trying to squash an impending objection. "Not yet."

"I assume we can easily get an address for Stefanos, then," Savanna said. "We can find Nick. Save him."

Save Nick? Was that the mission objective?

"We have a location, but according to Emilia, his property is being monitored by Italian Intelligence. We can't just fast-rope in without the bad *and* good guys knowing about it," Carter said.

"Can these AISE agents save Nick for us? If we tell them he's there?" Savanna asked, and Carter shook his head.

"In their eyes, Nick works for Stefanos. I assume they won't ruin whatever surveillance operation they have going on to save a criminal," Carter told her, his tone gentle, which Griffin was surprised the man knew how to do.

"So, what do we do? How do we get to Nick?" Savanna folded her arms across her chest, scanning the group of men, her eyes falling to Griffin last. She ripped her attention away just as fast and pinned her eyes on Carter. "You still need what's in that safe-deposit box. I'm sure the DOD would prefer to recover what Nick took, regardless."

"There's a way to infiltrate Stefanos's property without anyone knowing," Carter told them. "He's hosting an event tomorrow night. An auction for charity."

"A cover for his illegal operation?" Jack asked.

"That's what Emilia thinks." Carter turned from the room and looked out the double doors, sunlight pouring into the lobby.

Griffin hid his hands in the pockets of his black gym shorts, doing his best to focus on Carter and not check on Savanna.

"The good news is that it's a Renaissance-themed masquerade party. Masks are ideal for concealing the criminals that will be there to bid on the items not publicly displayed, I assume. But also helpful in getting us in too. Emilia is working on securing tickets for us." Carter faced the room again.

"Do you think Joe's team knows Stefanos has Nick and will be there too?" Griffin asked.

"I assume the Archer insider knows, but the question is whether or not they drop their pursuit of Nick and Savanna. Joe may have initially believed national security was at stake, but whoever sent him on the chase did so with the intention of Stefanos ultimately acquiring the Elysium Project. Now that Stefanos has Nick, the Archer insider may consider his *or* her ass covered once again," Griffin offered his thoughts on the matter.

"And what, lie to Joe?" Savanna replied, but she wouldn't look at him. "Say the threat has been neutralized?"

"Possibly," Carter answered before Griffin could.

"Does that mean we're back to assuming Sydney Archer

is at the top of the suspect list and wasn't abducted?" Oliver tossed out what Griffin knew Gray wouldn't want to hear.

"Or whoever at Archer is working with Stefanos encouraged Sydney to take a vacation, not wanting her at the office when Stefanos's people showed up," Gray pitched a new idea, grasping at straws.

"Let's handle one problem at a time. We'll deal with Stefanos and Nick now. Then find out who wanted the Elysium Project in the first place. Archer after that," Carter said, then looked to Gray to see if he was in agreement, and Gray gave a hesitant nod.

"I would say now that Stefanos has Nick, Savanna's safe, but if Nick admits he hid the key at her place, we're back to square one. Let's hope he can hold out until tomorrow night," Jack said.

"Hold out?" Savanna sputtered. "He's being tortured." She was in panic mode now, her eyes wild as she looked between Griffin and Jack.

The woman couldn't handle any more loss, and she was worried Marcus's only living family was on the verge of being tortured to death by Stefanos. And as much as Griffin hated the guy, he didn't want Savanna to endure that pain. Hell, he was guilty of causing her pain too.

He hadn't realized he was so desperate to feel everything she'd unleashed in him, and he'd all but marked her like a wild animal, locked her in a room, and shouted *Mine!* for all to hear. Until he'd come to his senses, knowing he'd never be able to overcome his trust issues, never be enough for her. He was ashamed of the whiplash he'd subjected her to.

"Like hell are you going to offer yourself to Stefanos tomorrow if that's what you're about to suggest. You want to trade yourself for a thief and a killer? I know you care about this man because he's Marcus's brother, but the answer is still no. Let us handle this." Griffin reached for her arm, urging her to face him so she could see the "hell no" in his eyes.

"You won't be able to get into the party armed, and you know it," she said, raising a valid point, but that was also *beside* the point. "I can be the bait. During the party, I'll reveal myself to the men, and they can take me to their boss."

"What if they have facial recognition software set up at the entrance to verify the identities of their guests before they mask up?" Griffin asked.

Savanna peered at his hand on her arm, and he forced himself to let go. "Will Emilia know about that?" she asked Carter. "Can she find out from his past parties what security is like?"

Griffin peered at Carter and shook his head, but Carter let out a gruff sigh and said, "I'll ask."

"No." Griffin was about to grab his boss's arm next. "You can't be serious."

"Emilia says his estate is massive. A sprawling maze of tunnels. I'm sure she can find a way to help us get weapons into the party, just not through the front door. But we won't be able to find Nick's location without drawing attention from Stefanos's men. We can follow Savanna, though, when they take her to Stefanos." Carter faced Griffin, head angled, eyes narrowed in challenge or apology, Griffin wasn't sure.

Griffin didn't care which, though. He wouldn't let Savanna offer herself to Stefanos.

"Over my dead body does she go to that party," Griffin hissed, stepping forward to confront his boss, doing his best to keep his hands at his sides because they were locked and loaded.

Punch his boss and fight anyone standing in his way? He would if he had to.

Which also meant, in his gut, he knew he was the burn-the-world-down-to-save-the-woman kind of man. And it made him a horrible operator and a shit human being who'd sacrifice the world for the benefit of one. But this woman made him . . .

"Outside." Carter jerked his head to the doors. "Now."

CHAPTER TWENTY-NINE

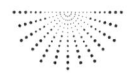

ROME, ITALY – TWENTY-FOUR HOURS LATER

THE CITY LAY BEFORE HER IN SUCH PICTURE-PERFECT DETAIL it almost felt like a dream. She had a clear view of Vatican City, and her thoughts wandered to the *Davinci Code*, Dan Brown's novel she'd loved reading years ago. The adventure and excitement. The legends and secrecy. She'd fallen in love with Rome in the pages of that book, and now here she was, and her world was as dangerous as one of fiction.

Savanna focused on the dome of St. Peter's Basilica, hoping her mascara didn't smudge as tears filled her eyes. She was in a beautiful city, and she'd never felt so alone. Not even Marcus's spirit, which she almost always felt surrounding her like a protective shield, seemed to be there. "Where are you?" she whispered, looking out the window at the view of the holy city. If there were ever a place to feel Marcus, wouldn't this be it? They were both Catholic, and he'd even mentioned bringing her here one day. Exploring every inch of the city together hand in hand.

Her shoulders fell even more when her thoughts drifted to

Griffin and how he'd broken her heart yesterday. He'd rejected her plain and simple. He'd let his fears and his mother's betrayal consume him and refused to see that they had something worth fighting for. And then he'd done his best to prevent her from trying to save Marcus's brother.

When Griffin and Carter had stepped outside the doors of the hotel in Santorini and begun arguing, Savanna thought Griffin was going to attack his friend. At one point, he'd even shoved Carter, who'd just stood there and allowed him to release his anger. Probably hoping to break him down to the point he'd be able to convince Griffin that Savanna was necessary for their operation.

Operation? I'm part of an op, one that feels like something Marcus would have done.

Once Carter and Gray received word from Emilia that she could get them into the party without exposing their real identities, they overrode Griffin's objections, and the two team leaders promised they'd keep her safe. The key, and the fact that she wouldn't have it on her person, was added insurance for that. Griffin hadn't been convinced if the scowl on his face had been anything to go by.

He also hadn't spoken a word to her since then. No doubt punishment for insisting they use her to save Nick.

For a man who wouldn't fight for her heart, he was ready to kill anyone who put her in harm's way. Wasn't that a contradiction?

The knock at her hotel door had her smoothing her shaking hands down the shimmery silver gown they'd managed to find at the last minute with a little help from Emilia. Despite being petrified, Savanna wanted to do this. For Nick, but more so for Marcus.

"Can I come in?" That familiar deep voice was everything she needed right now.

"Jesse?" she rasped in shock and turned in a hurry to get to the door.

Jesse was standing in the hall, hands in the pockets of his tuxedo pants, looking like her knight in shining armor. She was so happy to see him she nearly stumbled into his arms as he went for a hug once inside the room.

"What are you doing here?" she asked, swiping away a tear.

"Carter filled me in last night. I gave him all the reasons why I needed to be here for this party, and I didn't give him a choice about letting me come."

"I should be mad at you for leaving Ella, but God, I just . . ." She was going to cry and ruin her mascara. "I really need you."

"Shit, Savanna. What's wrong?" Jesse pulled her back into his arms and held her, setting his chin on her head. "Aside from the obvious."

How would she tell him that as crazy as it sounded, she'd fallen for someone in a matter of days when no one had stirred any interest inside her since Marcus? "I, um."

"Growly Griffin?" Jesse surprised her by reading her thoughts.

She eased free from his embrace and leaned back, her hands on his biceps as she looked into his eyes. It really wasn't the time for this conversation because she needed her head on straight for the op, but she had no one to talk to, and she felt as though she were losing her mind. "How'd you know?"

He lifted a brow and pointed to the door connecting her room to the one where the team was prepping for the night's mission. "Did you not hear him through the wall, demanding I knock some sense into you and keep you here?" Jesse's lips twitched into a smile. "Griffin was the only one in the room whose veins were in danger of popping at the idea of you going on the op. He had the kind of look I'd have if—"

"Ella were placed in a similar situation?"

His shoulders collapsed at her words, and he looked toward the window that displayed a stunning view of Rome.

"Are you going to try and talk me out of this?"

His light blue eyes returned to hers. "I know you better than to ask you to change your mind once it's been made up. A stubborn Southern woman."

"Mm-hm. Guilty as charged." But also, she still refused to believe someone who shared Marcus's blood could be a killer. And if he were only a thief, then she'd do what Marcus hadn't been able to, forgive Nick.

The idea of a soul unable to pass on because of unfinished business in this world was most likely only a false notion, but why did she feel like Nick was Marcus's unfinished business?

"I won't let anything happen to you tonight. I promise." He reached for her shoulder and squeezed. "And growly Griff won't either, I take it."

"And, um, what does this mean for you that you're working with the guys tonight? A one-time thing?"

He removed his hand and swiped it through his styled blond hair. "I don't know."

"You said it made you feel good to do something again that had purpose. Are you considering working with them *after* tonight?" *Running from Ella again?*

"Let's take it one night at a time." He cleared his throat, then added, "So, what happened with Griffin? Why do you look so upset if he's clearly got some insta-love thing going on for you? That's what your books call it, right?" He twirled a finger before tucking one hand in his slacks pocket.

"Insta-love? Griffin doesn't love me. And wow, you actually listen to me when I talk about my books?"

He smiled and shrugged. "Maybe."

"Then you remember I hate insta-love stories. Totally unbelievable. No one falls in love that fast."

"Didn't you with Marcus? Why not with Griffin?"

Not *that* fast with Marcus. Her gaze crashed to the floor and that lonely feeling she knew so well bloomed in the pit of her stomach at the mention of Marcus. "I've always felt Marcus's presence with me. Always. But he's not here right now." She searched the view outside as if he might be there and had only taken a quick holy break.

"Maybe that in itself means something, Savanna," Jesse softly said.

"What?" she whispered, turning his way.

"Maybe Marcus isn't hanging around now because he was only here until he knew you were taken care of, and now you are. What if he guided Griffin to you?"

"By putting me in danger?" She was on the verge of tears, mascara be damned. This was all too much to take in.

"Maybe he wanted to save his brother too?" Jesse suggested.

"Since when do you believe in anything spiritual or otherworldly?" Savanna laughed out a sob.

"Sweetheart, you believe, and that's all that matters. You don't need me to tell you. I can see it in your eyes."

"My very own Hemingway standing before me. Who would have thought that you had a soft side?"

"Don't you dare tell anyone." Jesse drew her back in for a hug as the door clicked and opened.

Savanna freed herself from Jesse's arms and erased her tears with the backs of her hands at the sight of a broody-looking Griffin in the doorway, his key to her room in hand. Had he seen Jesse's arms around her? Was he having flashbacks to his mother?

"We have news." Griffin's dark eyes raked over her. It was the first time he'd seen her dolled up, and actually, the first time she'd had on makeup since they'd met. The dark look in his eyes didn't appear to be anger directed at Jesse, but rather lust directed her way, and it had her stepping back. "Can I have a word with her first?" he asked Jesse, and Jesse patted her on the back as if to say "everything will be okay" before leaving the room.

Griffin placed the key card into his pocket and kept quietly studying her once they were alone. Like Jesse, he was in a black tuxedo, and his hair was styled and glossy, combed off to the side. Handsome as the devil and able to seduce any woman.

But he hadn't been the one to seduce her. She was fairly certain she'd seduced him.

His eyes journeyed over her once again. She was wearing her hair in loose curls that framed her face, and her eyes were made up to match the dress with glittery silver and gray shadow. The floor-length gown hid her pretty silver shoes and was constructed of layers of satin and silk, with a shimmery skirt, a deep V down the front, and nearly no back. She felt like Cinderella, but she wasn't going to meet her prince at this ball.

"You look . . ." His jaw tightened as he found her eyes again. "I don't have words."

"Well, you've barely said any words to me since yesterday, so I guess that's not surprising." She turned but gasped when he reached for her wrist and spun her around in one fast movement.

He was breathing hard, staring down into her eyes as if he were on the verge of crushing his mouth over hers and saying to hell with everything.

She swallowed, the lonely feeling gone with him holding

on to her and his heated gaze warming every inch of her exposed skin.

"If anything happens to you tonight," was all he said, dark eyes cutting straight through her with a tortured look. He was worried about tonight, but she recognized the familiar achy desire they shared for each other there too.

Marcus sent you to me. She'd somehow known almost since the moment they'd met.

"I have you to watch over me," she whispered, lifting her chin a little, worried her legs were going to buckle, and she'd lose eye contact with him soon. "You," she repeated, letting him understand she was leaving her trust and faith in him now.

As much as she loved Marcus, and she always would, it was time to start a new chapter. And she needed this frustrating man to believe it could be with him.

He bowed his head and set his forehead against hers, and in a gritty tone, said, "I won't let anything happen to you. I promise." He abruptly pulled away as if he didn't trust himself to be that close without claiming her mouth. "Come on." He reached out as if to take her hand but immediately pulled back. After blinking a few times, seemingly conflicted, he turned. "We discovered another of the *someones* looking for Nick. Very unexpected and a potential problem tonight."

Savanna stopped in her tracks at his words. "What? Who?"

"We'll fill you in next door," he said, already on the move, which forced her to do the same.

Upon entering the other room, Savanna momentarily forgot there was news when she witnessed Carter and every one of his men dressed in tuxedos, looking every bit the part of 007. So, when Carter announced, "MI6 is after Nick," her heart nearly stopped.

"Wait, what?" Savanna's back went to the wall by the door as she tried to absorb the shocking news. That was one possibility that had never come up in all their back-and-forth theorizing.

"Emilia got wind that MI6 operatives will be at the party tonight, looking to get to Nick as well," Gray said, spelling it out for her.

"They can't possibly want Nick for the same reason? The Elysium Project," Jack added.

"We have no clue why they're gunning for him, but it could be a hiccup," Carter said. "We don't want to accidentally take out an MI6 operative."

"What does this mean?" Savanna's gaze skated around the room, bouncing from guy to guy.

"It means we're going to have to reach out to them. We'll get word to my father to give a heads-up to both Italian Intelligence and MI6 that the U.S. has people on the inside as well. Friendlies."

Jack peered at Savanna and smiled. "What he's saying is that Carter doesn't seem to be so great at playing well with others. And he's going to have to tonight."

"I'm still the bait, though, right?" she asked and immediately felt Griffin's gaze on her at the use of such an offensive word to him.

"Unless MI6 or the Italians object, then yes, you'll be the one to lead us to where they're keeping Nick," Carter said in a low voice, his focus sweeping between Griffin and Savanna. "We stick to the plan. You take off your mask and identify yourself when we give you the go-ahead."

Jesse picked up a beautiful silver mask, which would cover half her face, its sides decorated with white feathers that looked almost like angel wings. "Here. You'll be needing this."

Letting go of a deep breath, in anticipation of what was to come, she took the mask.

Savanna cut through the room and passed Griffin, who pushed his hands in his pockets as though preventing himself from reaching for her on her way to the window.

She clutched the mask and stared out at the city, now bathed in shades of orange and gold as the sun began its descent, making the buildings glow. Closing her eyes, she whispered, "Just breathe."

CHAPTER THIRTY

Griffin eyed Savanna as she stood at the bar, her back to him and her hair swept over one shoulder, offering a view of all that flawless olive skin exposed by her almost backless dress.

During their brief moment together back at the hotel, he'd contemplated handcuffing her to the bed, not just to keep her safe and away from the auction, but to cut that dress clean off her body and claim her as his.

He'd reined it in and controlled himself. Somehow.

But his restraint was slipping the longer he watched the asshole at the bar chat her up. The guy had no idea how close he was to losing the hand he was using to touch Savanna's forearm.

Griffin pulled his focus away from the bar to get a grip, feigning interest in the band playing outside on a raised platform for the extravagant party at Stefanos's estate.

It was cool outside, so heaters were set up around the open area where people wandered around viewing items in glass cases for the silent auction while a few masked couples danced here and there.

The sprawling estate was over two hundred years old, and although the team had accessed the floor plan, they assumed Stefanos had made updates when he acquired the property two years ago that probably hadn't been carried out through the proper channels. Which meant they'd be in the dark tonight. Who knew how many secret tunnels or passageways there were? The damn gardens surrounding the party were a maze in themselves.

Italian Intelligence was on standby outside, but they didn't have the legal authority to enter. They were still on "sit and wait" orders from their government until they had concrete proof Stefanos was more than an auctioneer.

Stefanos had yet to make an appearance, but they had to assume he was busy conducting his illegal affairs somewhere else on the property—and Nick somewhere there as well.

No sign of Joe and his team, which wasn't surprising. If his boss was the insider, Joe was no longer needed now that Stefanos had Nick. Griffin still believed Joe was under the impression national security was really at stake, though.

As for MI6, they were similar to the CIA in that they didn't always concern themselves with legalities. There were currently two operatives inside the party, ready for the go-ahead from Carter over comms to move in. Working with MI6 had been unexpected, but they'd take whatever help they could get since they had fewer men than ideal for such a massive property with an unknown number of tangos.

MI6 had only agreed to collaborate with Carter's team if they promised to hand over Stefanos as well as let them speak with Nick.

Carter had met the two MI6 operatives there with them tonight on a previous occasion, and he said they were about as "James Bond" as they got in real life. So, the best of the best had been sent. Griffin wished that was more comforting, but bottom line, Savanna was at a criminal's party, and it made his trigger finger itchy to draw down like he was in one of the old-fashioned Westerns his father loved.

Griffin worked his fist loose, doing his best to remain steady like a Unit operator.

The guy Savanna had been talking to offered her his hand and motioned with the other to the dance floor. She peeked toward Griffin as if seeking permission, and he clamped his teeth together, ready to shake his head in a resounding no when he witnessed her quickly seek Gray's "okay" instead as if realizing asking Griffin was a mistake.

She must have gotten the go-ahead because she was now moving toward the dance area hand-in-fucking-hand with the stranger.

What really did Griffin in wasn't the man's hands on her hips. Nor was it her arms draped over the guy's shoulders.

It was every turn they took that had Savanna's attention pivoting straight to Griffin with a slightly frightened, nervous look in her eyes. A plea to be saved.

Maybe he was hallucinating. Maybe he just wanted a reason to go cut the guy's dick off because his pelvis was dangerously close to brushing up against Savanna.

Griffin shifted uncomfortably, his jaw locking tight as he watched them. As he told himself not to draw the 9mm tucked beneath his tux jacket provided by Emilia's plant on the catering staff and shoot the guy in the hand that was now brushing up along the smooth, bare skin of Savanna's back.

But he couldn't shoot a stranger for dancing with her when they had a mission to complete. A fireworks display was scheduled to begin at twenty-two hundred hours and would last for fifteen minutes. That was their window to handle everything without anyone outside knowing what was going down inside the mansion, which is where the team assumed Stefanos and Nick were.

And while he wouldn't be able to kill every man who hit on her, not after he, himself, had given her up, that didn't mean he had to let the dance continue.

Griffin took one step forward, surrendering to his impulses to separate the man from Savanna.

Gray was in his ear immediately, issuing the command to stand down, but Griffin mumbled, "I think the fuck not," even though his comm was muted.

His quick, angry strides had him at her side in two seconds.

He fisted a hand by his thigh and placed the other on the man's shoulder, almost hoping he'd ignore the order, "This dance is over."

The coward backed off—*smart man*—then tipped his head goodbye to Savanna and retreated.

Didn't I retreat just yesterday? But when he secured his hands on Savanna's hips, and she draped her arms over his shoulders to dance, he pushed away all thoughts but that moment.

"I thought you were going to kill the guy," she murmured.

"You weren't comfortable," he replied.

"No," she returned softly. "But what makes you think I'm more comfortable now?" she rasped, her hazel eyes so big and bold with the silvery-gray mask framing them.

"Because you belong with me," he answered without hesitation.

Her eyes narrowed in confusion. But she remained quietly moving from side to side, letting him take the lead, opting not to go for another round of arguing on the night of the operation. She had better control than him, so it would seem.

Her body felt perfect in his arms, and they moved

together as if they'd been dance partners for years. At times, just being near her was a mind trip. Like they'd been brought together by an otherworldly force, and Savanna was his guardian angel sent from heaven to bring him back to life. So why did he continue fighting it?

Let. Her. Go. Griffin thought back to the voice he'd heard in his head at his father's cabin. Could he have misinterpreted the meaning of those words? He had no doubt it was Marcus, but had Marcus been ordering himself, and not Griffin, to let go of Savanna?

"Savanna," he whispered, with no clue what his next words might be, but Carter's voice in his ear grabbed his attention.

"It's time," Carter announced.

When Griffin slowly released his hold of Savanna, she drew in a small, shaky breath that had him leaning in and saying, "It's going to be okay."

She nodded.

"Come on." Griffin unmuted his comm, then reached for her hand. Her palm felt warm and delicate inside his rough one as they walked with fast steps toward the mansion, cutting through the partygoers. "Restrooms?" he asked one of the guards standing outside the entrance.

The man eyed Savanna up and down before answering, "First door on the right." Griffin knew there were more guards inside the foyer area, given that the guests had access to the bathrooms inside. And he was counting on that.

"What are we doing?" Savanna whispered as he guided her around the corner, thankful they were alone by the bathroom door for the time being. "This isn't the plan."

In one quick movement, Griffin had her pinned to the gold-hued wall and his knee between her thighs. He was desperate to tear the fabric of her dress and slide his hand up between her thighs to find her pussy. Even now, at a time like this, he was out of his mind for her.

He cupped her chin and pulled her mouth to his. With the masks on, he had to slant his head to align their mouths, and when his lips touched hers, she stiffened in surprise. But as he deepened the kiss, sliding his tongue inside her mouth, she relaxed against him, clutching his biceps before grabbing at the lapels of his tux jacket, both of them lost in the moment.

This actually *was* part of the plan, she just hadn't been made aware of it until now. But like hell was he going to allow anyone else on the team to make out with Savanna.

Moving his hands up the sides of her torso, he caressed her ribs over the silky fabric of her dress before slipping one hand into the V and cupping her breast. She moaned into his mouth, a feverish whimper he ate up with a kiss, devouring her to the point he nearly lost sight of why they were there. He wanted to take her against the wall. Make her his again. Show her just how much she belonged to him in every possible way.

Not here, though. He had to remind himself they were on an op, as well as in public, and he'd be damned if he let anyone see another inch of her skin or hear the way she screamed out his name.

"What are we doing?" she whispered frantically between kisses. Her chest heaved against his as thoughts of all the erotic things he wanted to do to her played out in his head, knowing full well it couldn't happen there. But until Carter gave the signal, they had to stay put.

Kissing her again, tasting her sweet mouth, and touching her soft skin was the slap to the back of the head he needed to remind himself that he *wasn't* a coward. He *didn't* retreat. He *would* fight for her. How could he not?

"You've got company," Carter abruptly announced in his ear.

Griffin slammed his palm against the wall over her head and removed his other hand from her breast to reach beneath his tux jacket in preparation for what was to come next.

The order from a guard, spoken in Italian, one he assumed meant *move on*, didn't break their kiss. He needed to draw the guard as close as possible.

Savanna stiffened, which let him know the man was drawing closer. The guard continued speaking in Italian as he approached them, and the moment the man's hand met Griffin's shoulder, he quickly turned, grabbed him by the arm, and twisted it behind the man's back while shoving the barrel of his gun there as well.

"You're clear. We have the foyer covered," Gray alerted over comms as Griffin looked left and right down the hall, confirming they were alone as the guard cursed when Griffin twisted his arm harder.

With a puzzled look on her face, Savanna stared at Griffin with wide eyes. Her instructions had been to reveal her identity to one of the guards when the fireworks started and switch on the camera hidden in her necklace. She wasn't aware they'd changed the plans after talking with the MI6 operatives. He'd been worried she'd protest, so they'd left her in the dark. Another secret, but this one was meant to keep her safe.

"You speak English?" Griffin hissed. When the guard quickly nodded, Griffin continued, "I have what your boss wants. I *will* shoot you if you don't take me to Stefanos." Griffin met Savanna's startled eyes before he added, "The guards in the foyer are occupied at the moment. They won't be coming down the hall to help you."

With the fireworks about to go off, the team hoped the

guests would remain safely outside as well, though they had a backup plan if needed.

"Your boss has been searching for someone. A woman," Griffin said, testing the waters to see how much the man knew. "Are you aware of this?" When the man didn't respond, Griffin gave his arm another twist. "Yes or no?"

"Yes," the man hissed through a bite of pain.

"Do you know what your boss is looking for? What he wants?" Another twist and the man nodded. "Good. Your boss has Nick Vasquez now, so he doesn't need the woman anymore."

The guard slowly pivoted his attention to Savanna as if making the connection.

"He still wants to talk to her. She may know something. Nick won't talk," the man spat out a moment later, then cursed in Italian.

"Yeah, that's what I figured. Which is why *I'm* here with her. But she doesn't have access to what your boss wants, I do."

The motion of Savanna turning and peering down the hall had Griffin following her gaze to see the only man he was supposed to see approaching them.

"Get her the hell out of this place," Griffin told Oliver on approach, which prompted Savanna to lift her hand as if she were about to argue. "I've got this," he said to her, hoping she knew that also included doing his best to save Nick. And then she could decide after all of this if Nick was ever truly worth saving.

Savanna's eyes remained locked on his as Oliver held on to her, pulling her away from the scene. The knot in his stomach eased up as he watched Oliver escort her to safety. And now, he could focus on the task ahead.

"No alerting anyone over your comm," he told the guard,

noticing the coiled wire that went to his ear, less sophisticated than the wireless ones Griffin and his team used. "Take me. Now."

The guard slowly moved, taking a right down the hall, the opposite direction Savanna had disappeared with Oliver. There was no way in hell he'd be able to let Savanna get caught in the crossfire he knew would go down.

After walking down a few halls, they came across three guards, which Griffin had anticipated was bound to happen. Griffin released the guard and shoved him forward and over to the other three men in the hall.

"We're out. She's safe," Oliver said in Griffin's ear a moment later, and Griffin's body relaxed at the news. He slowly knelt and set his weapon on the floor, assuming he'd be patted down and his weapon confiscated before being led to their boss.

"Who are you?" One man stepped forward, and the Italian guard Griffin had strong-armed spoke to the man in Italian, most likely explaining what Griffin had said.

"This is true?" the man asked, and Griffin assumed him to be in charge of the others.

When Griffin nodded, the guy directed two of his men to pat him down and check for additional weapons.

"Fine. I'll take you to him. Take off your mask and come with us."

Griffin tossed his mask, and the man motioned for Griffin to walk ahead of them.

The tracker he was wearing had already been activated, so between that and his comm, Gray and the others could keep tabs on him as well as have a heads-up as to how many tangos they might encounter to get to him.

They navigated down a series of passageways before going below level. Downstairs, the walls were made of stone and the air was damp and musty like that of a basement.

"In there," the man said a few turns later, nudging Griffin into a room off to his left with the butt of his gun. "Wait here."

Griffin looked around the space lined with wooden crates, probably filled with stolen goods. But there were no entry points aside from the one door, from what he could tell. Not ideal.

"I won't talk unless Nick comes too," Griffin spoke for the first time since he'd handed himself off to the guards. "I need to see he's alive."

The door pulled closed before they offered a response, though. Once alone, he checked his watch. It was one minute to twenty-two hundred hours. "I'm in a room below ground. Only one way in," Griffin announced over his comm.

"Roger that. Waiting for the HVT to show himself with Nick before we advance," Gray responded.

"We've counted over twenty guards on the property so far, aside from the ones you've come across," Jack spoke up.

"If he doesn't bring Nick, we switch plans," Carter announced.

Contingencies for their contingencies.

But damn, did Griffin hate being unarmed.

"Roger that," Griffin answered, then positioned his back on the far wall in the storage space, so he had eyes on the door.

He barely heard the fireworks outside, which was good news in case this dragged out longer than they hoped. No one at the party outside should hear the gunfire from their suppressed weapons.

Fortunately, Griffin didn't have to wait long for Nick to show up. The door opened, and a guard brought him inside, then shoved him onto his hands and knees. Nick lifted his head to peer at Griffin, one eye swollen almost completely shut.

And for the first time, Griffin felt bad for the man. In addition to the swollen eye, blood originating from a wound at his scalp rolled down one side of his bruised face. "Who are you?" Nick croaked out to Griffin as Stefanos entered the room with six more guards.

Before Griffin could think of an answer, Stefanos motioned for his men to flank Griffin's sides.

"How many more men are here? How'd you get a weapon onto the property?" Stefanos stroked his black beard. He looked younger than his age of fifty, and he appeared to be fit as well. "My men are checking everyone at the party now. You should tell me. Save me the trouble."

"Just a couple eggs short of a dozen," Griffin said, a seemingly random comment but intended to alert his guys as to the number of guards present. The plan was to buy himself time to get his men down there, and he'd do his best to throw off the assholes however he could. Humor often worked as a mind fuck. "I was the only one armed. Snuck it in with the biscotti. They were excellent, by the way."

Nick attempted to stand, but one of the guards kicked him back down as Stefanos sidestepped him.

"Comedian," Stefanos said. "I don't have time for jokes. My man tells me you have what I want." He drew a Glock from behind his tuxedo jacket and pointed it at Nick's head. "So should I go ahead and kill him?"

Nick dragged his one semi-good eye up to peer at Griffin. The fact Nick had kept quiet without giving up either the safe-deposit box location or Savanna meant there was some decency in him, or he was trying to buy himself time before an imminent execution.

Jury was still out.

Griffin reset his focus on the boss and casually folded his arms over his chest. He wasn't used to being so up close and personal with the enemy, nor the one to do the talking. For most ops, whether with Carter or the Army, he'd been behind the scope of his long gun and on the flat of his belly, taking down targets before they knew what hit them. This was new.

"You presold or promised the Elysium Project to someone who's a hell of a lot more dangerous than you, am I right?" He noticed the beads of sweat on Stefanos's brow. He really was terrified. And most likely off his game, which Griffin and his team would use to their advantage. "Then you didn't deliver, so you've sent your men everywhere trying to hunt this man down." He tipped his head in Nick's direction. "Well, you need us both alive to save your own ass."

Stefanos lifted his gun and aimed it at Griffin. "Really, you think so?" He arched a thick, black brow, but when he drew his free hand across his hairline, wiping at the sweat, he gave himself away. The fear was prominent. Even his hand was shaking. "How is it you know of the Elysium Project? Who told you?"

"En route," Carter said into his ear. "Preparing to handle the threats. Give us sixty to ninety seconds."

Griffin just needed to keep this prick talking for that long. "Savanna had no idea where Nick went, she hadn't seen him in years, but Nick did hide the key to a safe-deposit box at her house. Inside that box are the plans to the Elysium Project." Well, he was assuming that was true. "And I have both the location of the safe and the key. But you need Nick's retinal scan and passcode to access it as well." Griffin let his arms relax at his sides as Nick started to sputter blood as if worried Griffin might sacrifice Savanna. Or try and make a shady deal.

Stefanos's shoulders visibly collapsed. "Where?"

"A two-hour plane ride from here. Your home country."

Thirty to sixty more seconds.

"Boss." The guards must have been alerted of Griffin's team over their comms. "We have reports coming in. Shots fired inside the house. We should move you to a safe location."

"The others upstairs will handle them. We need to get to the plane," Stefanos said, already on the move for the door. "Call the pilot. We'll take the chopper to my jet. They come with us. We'll use the back tunnels."

The farther away from civilians, the better. His men were tracking Griffin, and they'd collapse onto their position at the right moment.

"Copy," Gray said into Griffin's ear, letting him know he heard Stefanos.

One guard reached for Nick's arm and lifted him off the ground, and two men held on to Griffin's arms, and he didn't put up a fight. No, he'd save that for the right moment.

The other three surrounded Stefanos in a circle with guns drawn as they left the room and slowly advanced down the hall toward an open archway leading to a tunnel.

A few more turns later, they moved up a set of stairs, which led to the main level.

Griffin barely heard the blades of the helo outside, hidden by the sound of fireworks popping into the air, but the helo had to be nearby.

"Moving to your position now. Handling the pilot out here," Carter announced.

"Seven," Griffin told Carter a moment later, letting him know the total number of tangoes accompanying him.

"Roger that," Carter answered. "Prepare to take cover."

"Seven what?" Stefanos turned to eye Griffin, then he

cursed. "You didn't check him for comms?" he hissed toward his guards at the realization Griffin had someone in his ear. "Fuck. We need to move."

"Now," Carter announced, and Griffin shifted his weight to the left in one fluid movement, then jerked his right arm free at the same time.

Griffin freed himself of both men before knocking the guard's gun loose at his three o'clock. Stefanos and the others were distracted by the gunfire just outside.

Griffin shot the man he'd disarmed and quickly snapped out a shot to eliminate the threat on his right before he could unload on him.

And in one fast movement, he grabbed hold of Nick and blocked his body with his own to . . . heaven help him, protect him.

Griffin crouched in the hall, keeping Nick behind him, weapon aimed in case anyone came through the door that wasn't on his team. He'd lost sight of Stefanos and the other men who'd been protecting their boss. But they'd gone straight into the belly of the beast—finding themselves facing his teammates.

"All clear. Let's exfil," Carter said. "We've secured the package," he said, letting Griffin know he had Stefanos alive. "Do you have yours?"

Griffin looked back at Nick to see him on the ground. He offered Marcus's brother a hand, wondering if Savanna's instincts were right about him. "Yes, I have the package."

CHAPTER THIRTY-ONE

Griffin and Jack helped Nick into the safe house that the two MI6 operatives had set up, and at the sight of Savanna jumping up from the couch, he faltered, nearly losing hold of Nick.

"Griffin," Savanna cried out, and he'd been expecting her to call out Nick's name first. "You're okay. I mean, they said you were, but I just needed to see . . ." She was visibly shaking and on the verge of tears. He wanted to drop Nick and throw his arms around her, just as relieved to see her without a scratch, even though he knew Oliver had kept her safe.

"Savanna?" Nick slowly said her name, his tone one of disbelief, before he went down like a sack of potatoes, nearly taking Griffin and Jack down with him. With him on his knees, both Griffin and Jack were forced to release their hold of him. Unable to stop himself, Griffin moved around Nick and pulled Savanna to his side.

She remained quiet while leaning into him, and he wrapped an arm around her back, setting his palm on her hip as he held her pinned to his side, her focus planted steadily on Nick.

Carter and Gray entered the house next with Stefanos bound and gagged, then shoved him to the ground not too far away from Nick.

The two MI6 operatives, who'd said everyone could call them Jane and John Doe for all they cared, followed Jesse into the room a few seconds later.

They'd sent the AISE agents an anonymous tip that there'd been an exchange of gunfire in Stefanos's home just after they'd left, which gave them probable cause to enter and handle any other armed men who may have tried to rescue Stefanos.

Thankfully, the mission went down perfectly. *Too perfectly, though?* he couldn't help but wonder, but Savanna was safe, and Nick was alive.

"You good?" Jesse asked, eyes on Savanna, but she didn't budge from Griffin's iron grip.

She also didn't fall to her knees and throw her arms around Nick, which was what Griffin had expected her to do. After all, he was Marcus's brother, and even though she didn't exactly know him, she'd gone to bat for him.

"I don't understand why Savanna's here," Nick said around a cough, then turned his attention to the two MI6 operatives. John Doe tossed his jacket on the couch and began rolling up his sleeves as if preparing for an interrogation.

"You involved her," Griffin told Nick. "They either discovered you were at her house recently, or they tried to use her to draw you out," he said while peering over at Stefanos on the ground. "Either way, you put a target on her head." His tone was rough and cutting, but ultimately, Savanna had been in danger because of him, and he should have felt guilty for that.

"I'm sorry. I shouldn't have done that," Nick apologized, his shoulders sagging.

"Get Stefanos into the other room," Jane instructed her teammate. Once John had taken Stefanos away, Jane turned and angrily said, "Did you double-cross us? What happened?"

Double-cross MI6? Griffin almost lost his hold of Savanna at the accusation.

"What do you mean?" Savanna spoke up, freeing herself from Griffin's hold and taking a step closer to Nick and the operative.

"It's okay. You can talk in front of them," Nick rasped. "I assume you all worked with Marcus when he was alive?"

"No, but we're friends of Marcus's, um, team," Gray responded, sounding a bit uneasy sharing that information when they still didn't have a handle on what was going on.

Jane stood and shifted her dress back in place, turning her attention on Carter. "Sorry we didn't tell you before, but Nick was undercover for us. We've been trying to infiltrate Stefanos's operation in order to take down some of his clients. Mostly terrorists."

"What?" Savanna gasped. "I don't understand." And yet, Griffin heard that familiar hope cut through her tone.

Nick crossed one arm over his abdomen and sat back on his heels. "I didn't double-cross you," he told Jane. "I had no choice but to run after this last job."

"What were we supposed to think?" She folded her arms across her chest. "You didn't reach out. Why not? We have protocols."

"It was complicated. Sydney Archer is involved, and we don't have much time. She's in danger. If they got to me, then it won't take them long to find where she's hiding," Nick said, nearly choking on his words.

"Sydney?" Gray prompted, stepping forward, his arms falling to his sides. "Tell us what happened."

Nick grimaced as he held his ribs, which were most likely broken. "I was sent to break into a vault at the Archer Group. Third time this year. Like the previous times, once inside, the others on my team would take photos, and then we'd leave without anyone knowing we were there."

"You allowed Nick to steal for Stefanos?" Jack spoke up, directing his comment to Jane.

Griffin assumed John was already interrogating Stefanos in the other room, and Griffin noticed Oliver was MIA, so he was probably assisting.

"The last two sets of blueprints Stefanos sent Nick to copy from the Archer Group were sold to the company's rivals. Projects that were never put into operation. It's shitty, yes. But ultimately, there's a greater-good thing at play. Nick has been feeding us names of terrorists that have hired Stefanos for other jobs. He's been helping us take down those threats this year," she explained, her tone casual, as if this was all par for the course.

Carter didn't seem surprised, and Griffin had to assume the CIA employed similar tactics.

"But this time was different," Nick rasped. "This time, I was tasked to steal the blueprints for the Elysium Project, one I recognized as being fully operational. Allowing Stefanos to hand over the blueprints to the terrorist who bought them would breach our national security and risk a lot of lives . . ." His voice trailed off. "Marcus was murdered by terrorists. I couldn't just hand over the plans for the greater-fucking-good this time and let more people die the way he died."

Griffin lost his hold of Savanna as he tried to wrap his head around the overflow of information.

"What about Sydney?" Gray pressed.

Griffin pushed both hands through his hair as Nick continued, "The other reason I ran was that I didn't know until the last minute the three men working with me had been tasked to kill Sydney Archer. Stefanos timed it so we'd arrive at the same time she did that day. He seemed to know her patterns, and that she always went to the office an hour or so before it opened." Nick shook his head. "We were to kidnap her and make it look like an accident."

"And that's when you killed the men?" Gray quietly asked.

"Sydney helped me, actually. She's more of a badass than I am, to be honest," Nick responded, eyes shifting over to Savanna once again.

"Why not alert us?" More like "Jane Bond" than Jane Doe in Griffin's eyes.

"After we took out my team, Sydney explained that she'd gone to Sicily because she suspected there was an insider leaking intelligence. She believed she was close to discovering the truth, and the insider found out. That it's either someone at the DOD or in her office who ordered the hit on her. Once I confessed that I was working undercover for MI6, Sydney asked me to help her," Nick quickly explained.

"Why hide the plans you stole that day in the safe-deposit box, though?" Carter asked. "Why not destroy them to avoid the risk of them falling into the wrong hands?"

Nick looked his way. "We did destroy those copies. I never went to Greece after Sicily. That safe-deposit box was for MI6," he said while angling his head to Jane. "Inside it is intel I've been collecting on a different terror suspect working with Stefanos. Everything was stored on a USB and hidden in that box in Santorini." He pivoted his one good eye to Jane. "When I ran off with Sydney I couldn't drop the key at our designated place, so I took it with me Stateside. I hid the key where I thought it'd be safe, planning to let you know about it once Sydney was taken care of." He shook his head. "I thought I was careful. I'm so sorry, Savanna."

"A Ring doorbell camera and fender bender," Jack told him. "That's how you were caught."

"But they would have come after Savanna to get to you anyway, from the looks of it," Jesse noted.

Savanna crouched before Nick, mindful of the dress she was still wearing. "Everything happens for a reason. I-I forgive you."

Of course, she would. She was a saint. A living saint.

But maybe everything did happen for a reason.

"Do you know who the Elysium Project was sold to?" Carter asked.

Nick shook his head. "A terrorist group, that's all I know. A different terrorist than the one you've been chasing," he tossed out toward Jane.

"Do you have the key?" Jane turned to Carter, but Carter's eyes thinned as if not ready to shove aside their mission for the sake of hers.

"First, you need to save Sydney," Nick responded, opening his one eye to see Savanna there. "She's outside New Orleans, and whoever asked Stefanos to kill her won't stop until they find her."

Griffin peered at Gray, who'd tossed his tux jacket and was in the process of yanking off his bow tie at the mention that Sydney was still in danger. "Why'd you go there?"

"Because the man she believes might be the traitor lives outside the city, and we've been monitoring his movements. I was captured when I was heading back from his estate to where Sydney and I had been working," Nick slowly explained.

Griffin was still struggling to wrap his head around how Nick, the thief, was now Nick, the undercover agent and hero.

"Who does she think is the mole?" Gray asked in a rush.

"The chief engineer, the main architect of all the plans. She said he had a beef with her father last year and wanted to quit but couldn't because of a non-compete clause in his contract," Nick shared. "She thinks he's the one after her."

"Then we better make sure we get to her before he does." Carter twirled a finger in the air. "Let's get to the jet." He looked at the female MI6 operative. "I'll give you the key after we handle our business."

The woman stared at him for a moment, contemplative. "Fine. We'll handle Stefanos. But if you don't deliver, I'll track you down, and you know it."

Carter simply winked, and it was one of the first times it didn't look out of place for him.

"I'm coming with you," Nick said, struggling to stand. "I put you all in this mess, and I have to see this through. Plus, you won't be able to find this place without me. It's not on the map."

"You did the right thing. Marcus . . . he'd be proud," Savanna added in a strangled voice, and Griffin's heart squeezed.

"I'll always be a criminal in Marcus's eyes," Nick whispered. "He died before he knew I changed, that I changed for him."

CHAPTER THIRTY-TWO

"Are you okay?" Griffin softly asked, the sound of the bedroom door of Carter's jet closing behind him. Savanna had excused herself to the bedroom to change her clothes and catch her breath for a second or two. To process everything that had happened tonight. And the fact that Nick wasn't a bad guy. Not anymore, at least.

She slowly turned, still clutching her shirt to her chest that she'd been about to pull on when Griffin slipped inside. He was still wearing his white dress shirt and black pants, but he'd lost a few buttons, the bow tie, and the jacket. Still devilishly handsome.

"The door wasn't locked. What if it'd been someone else who'd walked in here?" His voice had taken on that deep tone she craved.

"Then I guess they would have seen me in my bra. I don't see what the big deal is," she casually tossed out, not sure why she was playing with fire.

The growly man standing before her was the same alpha male she'd encountered on the dance floor earlier. The one who'd lost his mind at the sight of another man dancing with her. His possessiveness had been a contradiction to what he'd said before they left Santorini, but the way he'd kissed her for their "cover story" had been anything but fake. He'd delivered something different in that heated kiss in the hall . . . *acceptance*.

Acceptance that he could no more fight the pull between them than he could fight gravity.

Savanna set the shirt on the bed, allowing him to take in the sight of her wearing only jeans and the pink lace bra. Her nipples strained against the lace, begging for Griffin's touch.

"You love to sass me, don't you?" He pushed away from the door and closed the small bit of space between them. Dipping his gaze to her chest, he reached up and pulled one bra cup down to palm her breast. The touch of his strong warm hand on her breast stoked that fire he'd started and had her releasing a shaky exhale.

"It's not my fault you bring it out of me," she whispered, lifting her chin.

"Is that right? So I'm the only one who gets to see this side of you?" He slid his free hand around her hip and smacked her ass just hard enough to draw out a gasp. She pushed back against his palm, craving that mix of pain and pleasure that only he could give her. Had that desire always been inside her, just lying dormant until Griffin came along and woke it up? Whatever the reason, she didn't want to go back to the old Savanna.

"Well, you were, but I was under the impression you were done with me."

He stilled his hand caressing her ass as if remembering what he'd said to her back in Greece. "I don't think I can quit you, Sugar."

She closed her eyes, and when his hand slid around to the zipper of her jeans, she set her forehead against his chest.

"You can't?" she asked, wanting to make sure she hadn't heard him wrong.

Instead of answering her question, he quickly used both hands to yank her panties and jeans down to her ankles, and she squealed in surprise.

Now on his knees, he buried his fingers into the flesh of her thighs and looked up at her with those deep brown eyes. "A DEVGRU team has been dispatched to go after the terrorist Stefanos presold the Elysium Project to," he casually shared the news before sliding his tongue along her clit.

"Oh?" she breathed out.

"Mm-hm." He added more pressure with his tongue, and were they really doing this?

Of course, for a minute back at Stefanos's estate, she'd thought Griffin might take her against that wall. The heat between them had been off the charts.

"I guess we're lucky Stefanos is so afraid of that terrorist he sold the project to that he easily squawked and gave up his name in an effort to save himself," he added between gentle licks.

The man was torturing her. Job talk followed by long sweeps of his gifted tongue. Why did it arouse her even more? He was a devil playing a game of cat-and-mouse with her.

"Tell me more," she demanded, gripping his shoulders as he plunged two fingers inside her tight walls, and she stifled a loud, breathy moan.

"There's a team of FBI agents watching the engineer, so if he tries to make a run for it before we save Sydney, they'll stop him."

In. Out. He moved his fingers in a slow rhythm as his tongue danced over her sensitive skin as if he hadn't just shared something important.

"And we can't send people to get to Sydney ahead of time?" she asked before biting her bottom lip so she didn't cry out.

As crazy as it seemed, she needed this moment with him possibly more than the promise of a tomorrow. Because she knew in her heart that he'd give her that, too, when he was ready. When he'd worked through whatever baggage he'd been carrying around for years. And she knew a thing or two about baggage. So, she'd give this man time to figure things out if he needed it.

"Nick says they won't be able to find the location without him, and he trusts Sydney to protect herself until we're there," he said, mumbling against her abdomen and punctuating it with a nip of his teeth.

"Griffin," she hissed.

"Don't move," he commanded, which was downright impossible, but the deep, authoritative order had her body scorching hot. "Good girl," he said a few intense seconds later, followed by, "You can come now."

And she released so flipping hard that her toes curled and her mind officially powered off.

What just happened?

Griffin slowly kissed his way up to her breasts, rising to his feet as he did so, and placed a final, chaste kiss on her forehead. "What are you doing to me?" He grinned and shook his head.

"To you, huh?" Her legs were so wobbly she nearly collapsed into his arms as she found her breath again.

"You've cast some type of spell on me, I swear."

"Oh yeah?" She lifted a brow. "I've bewitched you?"

"That's an understatement."

She swallowed and lifted her chin. "But the real answer is that I belong to you, remember?"

He cupped her chin and drew her in for a kiss but stopped when someone knocked.

At least the knock came *post*-orgasm.

"You ready? Nick's hoping to talk to you," Jesse called out through the door.

"Be right out," she told Jesse as Griffin eased his face away from hers. "We'll talk after."

"After Nick?"

He picked up her shirt as she fixed her jeans back in place. "After Sydney is safe."

Once her shirt was on, he opened the door, and they went out to where Nick sat.

There was a gauze bandage wrapped around his head, and his eye was still swollen shut, but he was sitting upright and looked a little better. Painkillers and plenty of water seemed to have helped.

Savanna sat opposite Nick, and Griffin assumed the seat alongside her. She wanted to hold his hand, to seek comfort from his touch, but she set her palms on her jeaned thighs instead to try and get through the conversation with a man her late husband had never been able to forgive. Looking at him was like looking at Marcus, though, and it wasn't easy.

The rest of Griffin's team, as well as Jesse, sat near the cockpit, most likely to give Savanna some space.

"How'd you start working with MI6?" Griffin spoke up when it was clear her words were still stuck somewhere between *Is this really happening* and *What the hell is going on?*

"It's not like that." Nick set the water bottle on the empty seat beside him. "Interpol arrested me in 2014 while I was breaking into the vault of a private home to steal a rare artifact. They cut me a deal, help them out, and no prison time."

"Help them how?" she whispered, leaning forward a bit, her knees nearly touching Nick's.

"Go undercover?" Griffin asked him, and Nick nodded.

"They wanted me to use my skills to infiltrate various criminal enterprises and feed them information. But one of the agents also said something to me that struck me. And they clearly did their homework on me before making me the deal."

"What?" Savanna's voice cracked that time.

"He said this could be my chance to earn back my brother's trust. To do the right thing. In 2014, Marcus was still alive. The agent knew my brother had been in the military, and they somehow also knew we'd lost contact over the years. I wasn't sure if I could do the right thing, to be honest. I didn't trust myself, but I decided to try. Better than doing time, I decided. And if I could do it, maybe I could prove to Marcus that I wasn't such a bad guy. I really wanted to try for him." And now it was his voice breaking.

Nick's one good eye closed, and Savanna was doing her best not to cup her mouth and cry.

"He died before I had a chance to let him know I was doing good." Nick slowly opened his eye again, and an unexpected tear escaped. "I've been on loan to various agencies around the world since. And this past year, with MI6."

Tears rolled down Savanna's cheeks, and she was unable to stop them from falling. She noticed Griffin watching her from the corner of his eye.

"My cover's blown now, so I don't know if they'll throw me in jail since I can't be of use to them anymore. Not that it matters, I guess."

"I won't let that happen," Savanna spoke up as if she could ever truly do anything about that, but she'd try. A.J. had pull with the President, and Gray's dad was Secretary of Defense. Surely, she could get him some sort of immunity, get-out-of-jail card. "But where'd the money you've been sending me come from? It was from you, right?" she asked when Nick remained quiet. "Was that from your old, um, work?"

"No, I knew you'd never want dirty money. And my brother would roll over in his grave if I did that," he remarked. "They seized everything I had when I started working for the agencies. After Marcus died, though, I renegotiated the deal. I requested ten thousand to be set aside every month for you, or I wouldn't help anymore."

Wow.

"From Interpol to MI6 and so on." Nick nodded. "It's clean. Don't feel guilty you spent it."

"She didn't," Griffin told him.

"What? Why not?" Nick leaned back in his seat. "Oh, because you assumed . . ." He didn't need to finish that line of thought. Looking at her now, he had to know she was like Marcus, and she'd never spend money she believed had come from an illegal source.

"Thank you for trying to take care of me." She reached for Nick's hand and lightly squeezed it.

"I wish Marcus could have seen that I'd changed." Nick kept hold of her hand as he looked up at her.

Savanna turned to look out the window of the jet, and a fluttery sensation filled her chest. "Oh, I think he knows."

CHAPTER THIRTY-THREE

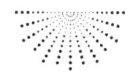

JUST OUTSIDE NEW ORLEANS, LOUISIANA

"Getting to her won't be easy, not when she's expecting an attack. But a few days with that woman is all I need to know she won't go down without a fight." Nick pointed to the screen with the aerial display from one of the drones Carter's men had set up over Sydney's location, offering a view of the swamp and wetlands down below.

Gray accidentally bumped into Savanna as he leaned in closer to the screen inside the 18-wheeler moving truck they'd rented and turned into a command center, where the men were prepping to infiltrate the property for what would now be a rescue mission. "That's a lot of heat signatures scattered all over the place."

"They're searching for her," Savanna whispered, taking a step back to look at Griffin, who was dressed in camouflage gear and face paint. Carter had everything they'd needed on the jet for any type of situation from the looks of it, thank God. And Griffin looked every bit a Delta operator at that moment. Intimidating. Deadly.

"Sydney chose this location on purpose. The Cajun cottage is practically invisible until you're right in front of it. Mother Earth has pretty much reclaimed the outside of it. And the houseboat on the water with a light on inside is the diversion. Only way to get to the cottage is by water, and then through acres of forest," Nick continued to explain.

"But they found her somehow. Well, they found her location," Jack said while strapping on his vest, catching Savanna's eyes for a brief moment. "I assume they used Archer technology to do it like they did to find Griffin's father's cabin."

"Does that mean this mole sent Joe and his team, or even another Archer team, to assassinate the owner's daughter?" It was a hard pill for Savanna to swallow. That veterans would commit murder for the right price.

"My guess is he hired a group of mercenaries to go after her. Criminals," Carter answered, slipping on a chest plate beneath his vest of ammo.

"No way is Joe one of those men out there gunning for Sydney," Griffin said without hesitation. "He let us walk away, and he gave us the Elysium clue." Griffin was as protective of Marcus's teammate as she had been of Nick. Hopefully, they'd come out two for two in the end.

"Our insider won't risk assigning a team of men from his own company to kill Sydney. I have to believe that," Gray added in agreement with Griffin.

"Does that mean you shoot to kill tonight?" Savanna placed a hand to her throat, the idea making her uncomfortable.

"Would you rather we shoot them with rubber bullets?" Carter asked, his focus on loading his weapon with a full magazine, but she saw a hint of a grin on the man.

"These men are hunting Sydney to finish the job

Stefanos's men failed to do. They have a kill order," Gray said solemnly. "We cut down anyone standing in our way of getting to her."

"If we can even find her," Nick said.

"Wait . . . you're going?" Savanna asked. "You're not in the best condition, even though your eye does look a little better."

"He has to. He knows the best route to get to the cottage and where she might be hiding," Carter was quick to respond.

"I've had some time to recover. I'll be okay." Nick's voice was still hoarse, so Savanna wasn't quite sure he was telling the truth, but he seemed determined to not only save Sydney but to keep proving himself worthy to Marcus, even though he wasn't there to see it.

And that had her heart swelling.

Carter's team had managed to acquire a flat-bottomed swamp boat for moving across the water to reach their location, which wasn't ideal with ten tangos on the ground moving about in search of Sydney. There *had* been twelve. Two tangos stopped moving not too long ago, and Nick had suggested it was Sydney's doing. Nick mentioned she was handy with a bow, and she'd been practicing during their days together.

"What about the alligators and snakes out there?" Savanna hated to raise that point, but it had to be another reason why Sydney chose that location. The more obstacles to get to her, the better.

"That's why we're not swimming in," Oliver said as he walked up the ramp they had positioned to get in and out of the back end of the truck. And Jesse and Beckett followed him in.

Jesse had asked Beckett to meet them when Carter's plane landed in Louisiana. They'd be keeping Savanna company while the rest of the team went looking for Sydney. Beckett also had a direct line ready to call the FBI when the time came to take down the man who'd sent these thugs after her.

"I'm surprised Sydney stayed here after you didn't return," Jack pointed out once Jesse and Beckett had joined them in the moving truck.

"Nowhere else to go, and she's stubborn," Nick commented while accepting a plated vest from Griffin. Bulletproof vests didn't always save lives. Marcus had been wearing one. "Sydney wanted to complete her mission. Confirm her suspicions as to the identity of the traitor."

When her attention swept back to Griffin, her stomach dropped. The man was about to put himself in danger again, just as he'd been doing since he was eighteen. He'd survived for over twenty years, but . . .

No. No what-ifs, damn it.

"I need some air." Savanna bypassed everyone inside and made a quick escape out the back end of the truck and down the ramp. It wasn't quite dark yet, but the gloomy evening sky held an ominous feel to it that had her rubbing chills from her arms.

"We'll have cameras on our chests, similar to police body cams." Savanna turned at Griffin's words to see he'd snuck up behind her. "You'll have a view of what's happening. Not the best view because of the hour, but we'll be using them so Jesse and Beckett can keep tabs on us and provide intel if needed over the radio."

He was barely recognizable in his military-type getup. And her *what-if* brain started working double time again. "Marcus didn't bring you into my life just to have you join him," she sputtered, then blinked a few times at the realization Griffin had heard those thoughts because she'd spoken them.

"You really think he sent me to you?" Griffin stepped forward and reached for her arm, holding her in place as if she might be carried off in the soft October breeze coasting through the air.

"I do." She reached for his face, paint meeting her palm. "So," she whispered, doing her best to fight through the fear, "go be the hero you are. Go rescue the girl."

* * *

JESSE WALKED SAVANNA THROUGH EVERY STEP OF THE mission as soon as Griffin and his teammates rolled out forty minutes ago. It had taken longer than she'd liked for them to glide across the water in the swamp boat, but they hadn't been detected. And by the time they reached their designated landing spot, there were only nine tangos. Which meant Sydney had taken out another man on her own.

"Sydney really is a badass," she said while collapsing into the folding chair next to Jesse. He and Beckett had three laptop screens showing various camera views of Griffin and the others. She could see everything in real time, but it was growing more difficult to see their movements now that the sun had set.

They were also being monitored by tracking devices so Jesse and Beckett could also feed the men each other's coordinates when they split up, which was happening now.

It was hard for her to sit on this side of the cameras. It reminded her of watching from inside the panic room at the cabin when Joe and his teammates were pummeling Griffin.

"Which one is Griffin? And Nick?" she nervously asked Jesse. He reached for her hand and gave a squeeze before pointing to the one screen where their tracker beacons lit up with little green dots.

"That dot is Griffin. He's number three. And that's Nick. Number six." Jesse looked behind him to where Beckett stood. "You handling this okay?"

Savanna followed Jesse's gaze to peer at the sheriff. A.J. had said this was out of Beckett's wheelhouse, but he'd once been part of the LAPD, so it was possible that he'd participated in operations of this kind back then.

"Just—"

"Nervous?" Jesse finished for Beckett before setting his eyes on the screen.

"Just surprised you seem to be so good at all of this. You were a Ranger. I wasn't aware you did this kind of stuff in the Army," Beckett said instead, but yeah, the man had to be nervous. There was more than one life hanging in the balance. It wasn't just Sydney out there but Griffin, Nick, and the others.

"Man of many skills." Jesse winked at Beckett before returning his focus to the screens, inching closer to the table against the one wall.

"It still amazes me Carter did all of this so fast." Savanna spied Beckett open his palms to the air before switching her attention back to the one laptop with the little green dots moving.

She spotted who she was fairly certain was Griffin from the camera mounted to Gray's chest on the second laptop. And Nick appeared to be close to the two of them. Carter, Jack, and Oliver had gone the opposite way. Three and three.

"Maybe you'd care to enlighten us sometime about that odd gap in time between when you left the Army and came home," Beckett said as if needing to fill the silence as they tracked the team's movements.

"No idea what you're talking about," Jesse said before reaching for the radio. "Midas, you have a possible tango on approach at your ten o'clock. Hundred paces out. Could be Archer or an enemy. Be careful."

Savanna was more concerned Sydney would accidentally shoot them, but that was another reason they'd suggested bringing Nick with them. He hadn't worn face paint, so he'd be more recognizable to her as a friendly.

"Midas is . . .?" she asked him.

"Griffin's call sign," Jesse answered before sending another message when Carter and his men closed in on another possible target, and he issued the team the warning.

"This is Midas. Tango down. Not Archer," Griffin came over the line.

Down to eight.

"This is Ace," someone that sounded like Jack said. "Target down."

Seven.

"I think I have Archer's position. Digitally sending the coordinates to you now," Jesse said a moment later, noting that another tango had been taken out, but not by anyone on their team, which meant it was Sydney's handiwork.

"Roger that," a few of the guys answered at the same time.

"This is Midas. I'll move to that location," Griffin said, and she assumed he'd handle Sydney since he had Nick with him.

"This is going well, right?" Savanna asked a moment later, then closed her eyes, worried she might have jinxed the operation. After everything had gone so smoothly in Rome, would they be so lucky again tonight?

"It's okay. Everything will be fine." Beckett lightly gripped her shoulder from behind, and she reached back and patted his hand in thanks while opening her eyes.

"Be advised," Jesse began in a rush a moment later, which

had Savanna's heart racing. "If she's still in that general area, you should be closing in on her soon, but you have company. Two tangos collapsing on your position from your three and nine o'clock."

Despite the cypress trees cutting in and out of the picture, the camera on Gray's chest gave her a view of Griffin and Nick stealthily advancing ahead of him. Griffin appeared to have night-vision goggles on as well as he moved with his rifle positioned in front of him.

"Roger that," Gray responded a moment later, just as the sound of gunfire popped over the radio.

"It's Nick, don't shoot," he called out, but then more shots were fired, and Savanna couldn't see exactly what was going on.

It was a blur and rush of movements.

The two "enemy" dots on the screen were still active, and they were heading toward the three green lights—the good guys.

Shit. Savanna jumped from her seat, her heart battling to break free as adrenaline surged through her.

No one was talking. No one was telling them what was going on, and she could barely see.

"Fuck. Get down," someone yelled . . . and that someone was Griffin.

Jesse stood when more gunshots burst over the radio, and then two enemy lights stopped moving.

But . . . number three stopped too.

"What's going on? What happened?" She bent forward and leaned closer to the screen to try and see through Gray's camera lens.

"I think . . . I think Griffin just took a fucking bullet for Nick," Jesse exclaimed, and that's when Savanna saw Gray standing over Griffin as he lay still on the ground. "Not the throat, damn it," he added, destroying her hope the vest had stopped the bullet.

"No, no," she cried, reliving the moment Marcus was killed right before her eyes, and now . . .

Disbelief became like a vise around her throat, strangling her breath. And tears streamed down her face as she clutched her chest and stumbled back, but Beckett caught her before she fell and blacked out.

CHAPTER THIRTY-FOUR

Savanna slammed her fists against Griffin's vest-covered chest when she reached him on the road near the truck. "You, damn it. You!" she cried, still hitting him like a crazy person.

"I'm okay," he reminded her, his tone soothing, but he snatched her wrists and stopped her from pounding him. "But my chest still hurts, so maybe stop hitting me," he said around a laugh, which also sounded like him making light of it to hide the pain.

"Oh shit, I'm sorry." She stepped back and cupped her mouth, forgetting he'd not only had a bullet graze his neck, where a small white gauze was now taped, but he'd taken one in the vest too, which was definitely going to leave a painful bruise.

"It's okay, Sugar." He pulled her in for a big bear hug, wrapping his arms tightly around her.

"You have to stop jumping in front of bullets for people," she whispered before he brought one hand between them and cupped her chin.

"It was Nick. What'd you want me to do?" It was too dark

outside to see his face clearly, but she heard the weight of his emotions in his tone. She didn't need to see his eyes to know they'd be expressive too.

"You almost died. That bullet could have pierced your throat."

"Ah, it was like a fresh shave." The smile in his voice nearly had her smacking him again.

"It's not funny." She tried to ease out of his arms, angry at him for getting hurt, damn it. For putting someone else ahead of himself like always. But that was the kind of man he was, and she both loved and hated that. It meant he'd constantly be at risk, and now she might have a panic attack. "I watched you get shot on screen. I thought . . . I thought I lost you."

"You saw?" His voice dropped an octave that time as understanding dawned—he was remembering that she'd told him she'd watched as Marcus was killed. And now, the only man she'd ever felt anything for since had been shot before her eyes. "I'm so sorry." He held the back of her head and brought her cheek to his chest, and despite the loaded vest of mags between them, she heard his heart pumping overtime. "We're all okay. Everyone. Sydney. Nick. *Everyone.*"

"And next time?" Savanna stepped back, needing a minute to find her breath and slow her own heart rate down as it seemed to compete beat for beat with his.

Griffin released his embrace and moved off to her left, placing himself in the line of the small track of light catching the road from the open truck doors.

Savanna peered over at Sydney and Gray standing nearby, Sydney with a bow still in her hand, holding it against her thigh as they talked. The rest of the team was back inside the truck handling the "wrap-up shit," as Jesse had called it.

"You know what I do for work." Griffin's voice drew her gaze back his way.

"I know," she said softly. "And I love that about you."

"But can you *handle* that about me?"

Before she had a chance to summon a response, Sydney and Gray joined them. "I just spoke with my father," Sydney said after quickly introducing herself to Savanna. "The FBI are moving in now."

"And Joe and his team?" Griffin asked, folding his arms across his chest only to wince and let them fall again, obviously forgetting he'd taken a bullet.

"I know Joe," Sydney said in a low voice. "There's no way he'd intentionally help a criminal. But he placed the company's interests over that of the nation, which is still problematic. I'll talk to him soon and handle the situation."

"They weren't vets out there tonight, right?" Savanna asked.

"No, definitely not. Just your basic bad guys," Sydney said with a shrug.

Basic bad guys, huh?

"Come on, let's move out. The police will be here soon to clean up the mess we left out in the swamp," Gray said.

"What happens next?" Savanna couldn't help but ask.

Gray looked to Sydney. "She'll handle the situation at Archer. And Nick needs to go help MI6 with the safe-deposit box in Greece." He paused. "As for us, we roll out tonight before the police catch wind we were ever here."

Right. Carter, the rogue one. "Griffin too?"

Griffin and Gray exchanged a quick look. "He can escort you back to Birmingham, but you have Jesse and Beckett, so our work is pretty much done."

Work. Gray had to know she wasn't just Griffin's "work." Just like Sydney wasn't "just" someone from West Point.

"Come on." Gray motioned for Sydney to head up the

ramp into the back end of the truck just as Nick joined Savanna and Griffin on the street.

"You shouldn't have put yourself in danger for me," was the first thing Nick said once he was with them.

"It's what he does," Savanna softly said and positioned her gaze on Marcus's brother, shock still coursing through her. "Will you come back after Greece? Visit me? There's something I'd like to give you."

"If, uh, they let me. But if you really want me to," Nick began, "then yes, I'll find a way."

She smiled and stepped forward to wrap her arms around him. Nick was slow to return the hug, and she wasn't quite sure how to interpret that. Was it merely because of the alpha male standing off to his left? Or did Nick believe that if Marcus were alive today, he'd still consider him unworthy?

Once she let go of Nick, she waited until he was back inside the truck to face Griffin. "Are you going to take me home?"

Griffin stepped closer. "I think Jesse and Beckett have that covered." *No*. Was he pulling back because she'd hesitated when he'd asked if she could handle that his work was often dangerous?

And *did* she hesitate?

Shit.

"I need to head back to Pennsylvania with the others for now," he responded in a somber tone, a match to his overall body language now.

"But you still owe me that talk," Savanna reminded him, hating the tears springing from her eyes. It'd been an emotional night. An emotional week, actually.

He stepped forward and gently gripped her arm while dipping his head to try and capture her gaze in the dim lighting. "We'll have that talk." Griffin's focus moved to the truck, and she spotted Jesse and Beckett looking their way, waiting for them. "You'll be in good hands, but yes, I promise. Cross my heart and . . ."

"Don't finish that sentence." *Don't say hope to die.*

But the ache in her chest told her that maybe some time apart would be good for the both of them.

Just not too much time. Or she might lose that "bewitching" hold over her Delta operator.

CHAPTER THIRTY-FIVE

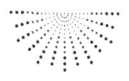

BIRMINGHAM, ALABAMA - ONE WEEK LATER

SAVANNA STORED THE LAST OF THE BINS ON A SHELF IN THE garage and paused at the sight of the lone car that sat inside. The red Mustang wasn't in as bad of shape as the guys had led her to believe after Oliver had ripped things apart during his search. But it'd need work, that was for sure.

"Hey, you okay?"

Savanna turned her attention to where Ella stood in the doorway of the garage. "Yeah, that's the last of it, right?"

Ella dusted her hands together a few times as if to say, *All done*.

She'd helped Savanna clear out all of the Halloween decorations from her café earlier that evening since Halloween was now behind them. Savanna had also needed something to do to keep herself busy.

Still no calls from Griffin. No word from Nick, either. And she was going stir crazy.

Ella's brother, A.J., and his teammates were Stateside now and safe after whatever clandestine op they'd been on, which was a relief, but A.J. had to wrap up some things in D.C. before he could come to visit. He was still in shock at everything that'd gone down after he left Jesse's. Hell, so was she, for that matter, and she'd lived it.

"You thinking about Griffin or Nick?" Ella motioned for her to join her in the house, and Savanna finally got herself to move. "Or Marcus?"

It was the anniversary month of his death, and though it'd been years since she'd lost him, right now, it felt like yesterday when the guys had shown up wearing their dress blues to give her the bad news in 2015.

After his death, she'd heard their team leader, Luke Scott, apparently had a breakdown of sorts from the guilt and had demanded no one on the team allow themselves to fall in love, and had declared from that day forward, there would be no more widow-making.

"They're all married now. Most with kids," Savanna said, forgetting Ella wasn't inside her head to know what she'd been thinking. "They all fell in love, anyway. Including your stubborn brother, A.J."

Ella hit the button to shut the garage door once they were both inside the house, and Savanna paused in the hallway to peer toward the foyer where Jesse had killed a man.

I should move.

Marcus's spirit seemed to be done following her around, and frankly, he was the only one she'd ever want haunting her, so she didn't need some stranger who tried to kidnap her doing it.

"Yeah, I guess they're all married," Ella said, maybe catching on, as they went into the kitchen, and Ella uncorked the bottle of wine she'd brought with her tonight.

"Chianti," Savanna said, reaching for the bottle,

remembering her time in Greece with Griffin and the first night they'd made love.

"You okay, sweetie?"

"What if what we had wasn't real?" Savanna blinked away her tears and handed the Chianti back to Ella so she could pour the wine. "I never believed insta-love was possible. Maybe what we had was only insta-lust, and we were both just caught up in the moment. The adrenaline rush. And Marcus didn't really send him to me because Marcus," she said, choking on an unexpected sob, "is dead. Dead people don't really . . ." She let go of her words and collapsed to the floor, not sure what had suddenly come over her, but Ella dropped right along with her.

"It was real," Ella said in a confident tone. "You know it was, and you're both taking time to prove that. Because time won't extinguish whatever flame that man lit inside you, and I can for damn sure see it shines brighter every day, even while you're apart."

Savanna swallowed down the lump in her throat.

"You've always said you believed Marcus's spirit was with you, but now you don't feel him anymore. I think he's finally moved on, or whatever you want to call it, because he knows you're taken care of," Ella added, and now she was getting choked up. "He may have been angry and disappointed in Nick, but I'm sure he'd want his brother to be okay, and you helped him with that."

"That's all my crazy talk," Savanna sputtered, swiping the tears from her face, but they just kept coming.

She missed Griffin.

So much.

She'd spent so many years mourning Marcus that it was strange to find herself missing another man. But *this* man now had a grip on her heart and her mind.

"You know better than to lie to me," Ella challenged. "It's not crazy. It's real. You love Griffin, and there's nothing wrong with that. I don't care if it took one day or two years for you to fall for him." She tipped her chin so Savanna would look into her eyes and see the truth there as she added, "The heart has no concept of time. Believe me, I know."

"Oh, Ella, I'm sorry. I know you're still . . ."

"No, this isn't about me or Rory's dipshit brother," Ella quickly said, her Southern twang growing stronger along with her anger toward Jesse. "You are a strong-ass woman, Savanna. And—" Ella stopped talking at the sound of a knock at the back kitchen door.

"Am I Interrupting?"

"Jesse?" Ella rolled her eyes at the sight of her nemesis.

"I found someone outside I thought you might want to talk to," Jesse added while opening the door, not waiting for an invite.

Savanna pushed up to her feet and wiped the tears from her face at the sight of her brother-in-law. "Nick."

Nick's bruises had faded quite a lot, and overall, he looked much better—healthy and even happy. And now that he was healing, his resemblance to Marcus was even more striking. "Hi." He shot her a small, nervous smile.

"I'll just take Jesse to help me with something outside." Ella grabbed hold of Jesse's bicep, needing both hands for the task, and dragged him out the door.

"Hi," Savanna finally returned in an equally quiet voice. "Are you free now? From your obligation to MI6? I mean," she said, feeling her cheeks heat with embarrassment. "Is it okay for you to be here?"

Nick rested his back to the counter, his eyes going to the wine she'd yet to drink. "They cut me loose. After I handed over the USB drive, MI6 wiped my records clean. They said I deserve a fresh start."

"A fresh start? That's nice." For some reason, Savanna was nervous. She sidestepped Nick and offered him one of the glasses of Chianti Ella had just poured, needing a sip of hers to take the edge off. "What will you do?"

"You know, I was thinking about following Dad's footsteps and maybe making sure assholes like me can't break into shit." Nick smirked before taking a sip of his wine.

"You're not an asshole."

"I was. There was a reason Marcus never forgave me."

"But he did," Savanna said. Letting go of a shaky breath, she set her wine on the counter. "Come with me." She led the way to her living room, where she'd stored the box of Marcus's things she'd made sure to grab from Carter's jet before returning home last week.

"What's that?" Nick asked as she knelt and opened the box.

This wasn't going to be easy, but she promised herself she could get through this moment when or if Nick showed up. She grabbed the pile of unsent letters, then stood and faced Nick, once again struck by how similar he was to her late husband. "Here."

Nick accepted them with brows drawn tight. "He wrote to me?" A rattle of emotion came out with his question.

"Well, he obviously didn't send them, but yes. Such a stubborn man. But Marcus told me that in each letter he wrote, he forgave you. I thought you might want them." She sniffled and brushed away fresh tears.

When Nick looked up at her, his eyes were watery too. "Thank you," was all he seemed capable of managing to get out.

She went back to the box and pulled out the photo

Griffin's team had used to track down that safe-deposit box in Greece. "You might want this as well."

"This is how you found the safe-deposit box, huh?" He smiled as if impressed while peering at the picture from his teenage years. "How'd you know to search the Mustang?"

"I remembered the one and only time we met." She smiled. "Another time Marcus was stubborn."

He returned her smile this time. "Yeah, well, that man was protective of you, and for good reason. His stubbornness came from a good place."

"I also want you to have the Mustang. The guys tore through it searching for that key, but I know Marcus would want you to have it. It needs work now, but please take it."

He was quiet for a moment. "I will if you promise not to be stubborn about that money I sent you. I want you to use it."

"No, you should take it," she said while vehemently shaking her head. "For your fresh start. It'll help."

"I have plenty saved for a rainy day. Don't you worry about me." He looked up at the water stain on the kitchen ceiling. "Maybe buy a house? Pay off your café? It'd make me feel better to know you're okay."

She blinked in surprise, trying to grasp the reality of what he was saying. He was offering to erase her money problems. She could breathe again.

He held up his free hand. "I promise the money isn't dirty."

"I don't know what to say."

He held up the letters. "I'm the one who owes you a million *thank yous.* You don't owe me anything."

"Will you come back from time to time and visit? Call, at least?" she asked when he turned, looking as though he was about to jet.

But he didn't leave, and he pivoted to face her. "If you think that's okay, I'd like that."

"I would too." She smiled, feeling a little piece of her heart sliding back in place at the feeling Marcus and Nick had truly made amends somehow.

"Oh, and, Savanna?"

"Yeah?" she whispered, smoothing her hands up and down her arms as chills crisscrossed up her spine.

"It's okay to be happy again. You know that's what Marcus would want, right?"

Savanna's stomach knotted at his words, and she lightly nodded. "I know." She swallowed. "I think I want that too."

CHAPTER THIRTY-SIX

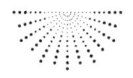

OFF-THE-GRID LOCATION IN PENNSYLVANIA - ONE WEEK LATER

"Falcon Falls," Griffin said with a shrug. "How about that? It's not like we're going to be listed in the White Pages, but—"

"Are phone books still a thing?" Oliver cut him off, petting Dallas sitting next to him on the couch at headquarters.

"I think so." Griffin honestly didn't know.

"Falcon Falls Security." Gray turned away from the screen at his desk to look at everyone. "I vote yes."

"Why that name?" Carter asked after calling his dog over to him. Dallas obediently leaped off the couch and rushed through the room to get to his master.

"All the waterfalls outside. And I saw a falcon on the way in this morning. I don't know. It popped into my head."

"Falcons represent freedom and success, right?" Oliver spoke up.

"Like I would know." Jack laughed and peered at Griffin. "But mythology boy over here might."

"Mythology boy, huh?" Griffin tipped his head and positioned his arms across his chest, wondering if Jack wanted to go hit the gym for a little hand-to-hand combat training. The "beef" was gone between them, but they'd kept up with the friendly jabs here and there. And he may have preferred it like that. Kept things interesting.

Jack had also seemed to be trying hard to distract Griffin since they'd left Savanna in New Orleans. They'd been training together and even had drinks at the bar a couple of times.

"I say yes," their new teammate piped up. "Falcon Falls." Jesse set his palms on the table in front of him. He'd been cleaning their rifles—new guy grunt work.

After only four days with the team, Griffin wasn't all that surprised Carter had brought Jesse in. Though he felt bad Savanna would be down one friend back in Alabama, especially one who'd always kept an eye on her.

At some point, we probably should tell Jesse we know his sister.

"All in favor?" Gray called out and was immediately answered with a chorus of ayes. "Then it's settled."

"Go make the business cards, then," Jack teased while joining Jesse. He hooked an arm over his shoulder. "You sure you want to be with us instead of Ella? From what I hear—"

"There's nothing between us," Jesse hissed a bit more defiantly than Griffin would have expected, and Jack felt the heat and pulled his arm free.

"Ah. You're a runner. Well, if shooting people helps you sleep better at night while abandoning a woman as beautiful as her, then so be it." Jack shifted out of the way as if expecting a punch to the chin any minute, but Jesse didn't react.

Aside from the clenched jaw muscles, he'd barely flinched at Jack's poor attempt at humor this time. Griffin was certain he'd read Jesse right, though. The man was running from Ella, but he couldn't figure out why.

Griffin was well aware of the reason he'd not yet returned for the "talk" he owed Savanna, but he had no plans on running from her. It was only a matter of when he'd hunt her down and take her into his arms. He just needed to get his head on straight and make sure he could truly be the man she deserved, and for that to happen, there was something he had to do first. But it'd take a lot for him to suck it up and actually do it.

She's worth it. God, she's more than worth it.

He'd been away from Savanna longer than they'd been together, and yet, somehow, his feelings for her had grown stronger in their time apart.

"Anyone else find it cathartic to check shit off a list?" Jack asked as he walked over to the whiteboard on the wall, obviously looking to change the foul mood he'd caused New Guy at the mention of Ella.

"What are you doing?" Oliver asked with a shake of his head. "Are you really listing all the bad guys we took down on that last case just so you can cross them off?"

"Abso-fucking-lutely," Jack shot back in a good-humored tone. "Everyone from the engineer insider to the terrorist buyer."

"Basic bad guys?" Oliver read one of the lines as Jack wrote it and laughed.

"That's what Sydney called the assholes who hunted her down in the swamp," Jack casually tossed out. Griffin was relieved that Joe's name didn't need to be on that list. Nick's either, for that matter. "Not bad for our first mission together."

"Yeah, but don't you think you could've used a woman's touch?"

Gray went dead still at the soft voice floating into the large space, and Griffin turned to find Sydney Archer at the entranceway of the tunnel. "How in the hell did you find us?"

Sydney had on black jeans with a rip in one knee, paired with a gray Army sweatshirt and black kicks. Her hair was in a high ponytail that swung side to side as she strutted into the room like she owned the place.

Dallas began barking, but Carter ordered him to stand down.

"Not a bad setup you've got here," Sydney commented, ignoring their "how'd she find them" question while looking around the space. "Batman vibes, but it'll work."

Jesse set down the rifle he'd been holding, and Griffin strode up alongside him to witness whatever was about to take place with Gray cutting across the room to get to her first.

"I quit my job," she said to Griffin's surprise. "My heart was never in it anyway, so I'm looking for work. I happen to be one of the best trackers on the planet, and my skills have been underutilized for years." She was so calm and casual. Confident and headstrong.

"Yup, she'll fit right in," Griffin said with a firm nod.

"Toss in her billions, with Carter's endless supply of cash, and we can actually get ourselves one of those Batman symbols installed to shoot into the air when we're needed, except ours will be a falcon," Jack joked.

"You seriously want to give up your job and work in private security?" Gray now faced her, hands on his hips. *This should be interesting.*

"I saw what you all did. I want to be part of it. And come on, it's more than security work," she returned in a bit gentler tone this time.

"What happened to Joe and his men?" Oliver asked when Gray and Sydney seemed to be playing a game of chicken to see who'd blink first.

"They weren't arrested because, from what we can tell, they really did believe they were going after a threat. And after the incident with Griffin, Joe began asking questions about the mission. I'm pretty sure he would've been targeted next because of that and for what he knew had we not handled this when we did." Sydney paused for a second. "But he still lost his job and security clearance for putting the company over national security." Sydney pointed her attention to Oliver now. "I think Gray's dad was happy to sweep this whole thing under the rug since the crisis was averted, and Elysium didn't end up in the wrong hands."

"Thanks to you," Gray quickly replied, clearly impressed with this woman.

"Word is you and Carter are in charge over here, so, what do you say?" she asked, looking back and forth between Gray and Carter.

Gray peered at Carter, who nodded his yes. "Okay, then," Gray said on an exhale. "You're in. You still using the same call sign?"

Sydney smiled. "Damn right I am."

"What is it?" Griffin asked.

"Juliet."

Jack busted out laughing as he resumed writing shit on the whiteboard. "Well, this should be fun. Romeo and Juliet," he said with a chuckle.

"Welcome to the team," Griffin said.

The Romeo and Juliet reference had him realizing it was

about time he man up and go after Savanna. No more waiting until his head was on straight or the stars aligned or whatever other bullshit he kept telling himself. If he wanted a happily-ever-after, then he'd better get to it. He looked over at Carter and announced, "I'm taking a vacation."

* * *

LEXINGTON, KENTUCKY - ONE DAY LATER

Griffin's pulse climbed with every step up the front porch of the big Southern home that sat regally on the several acres of property. There were horses in the pasture and green rolling hills in the distance. His mother's home was like the setting for a movie. *Picture perfect*, she'd told him over the phone after moving there with her new husband years ago.

Now that he was there for the first time, he'd have to agree. And Savanna would love it.

Griffin wiped his sweaty palms on his jeaned thighs as he stood before the double doors of her home, trying to find the courage to face her after all the missed holidays and family events she'd begged him to come to over the years.

He drew up an image of Savanna in his mind, finding the strength to go through with this conversation for her. For them. And then he rang the bell.

The door opened a minute later, and his mom took a step back in surprise.

"You didn't check your security cameras first, I take it?" He lightly shook his head. "Didn't I teach you anything?"

His mom erased the gap between them and threw her arms over his shoulders, startling him with a hug. One he hadn't known he'd missed so much.

"What are you doing here?" she asked after finally releasing him with one more squeeze.

He tipped his head toward the porch swing. "Can we talk outside?"

She looked behind her as if searching for her husband, then nodded and shut the door, stepping out onto the big, wraparound porch with him.

His mom motioned for him to have a seat on the porch swing, then sat next to him. Buying himself some time to summon the strength to speak, Griffin pushed the swing into motion using his booted feet. "I met someone," he finally confessed. "She's stubborn, smart, and sassy. So damn beautiful it hurts to look at her sometimes. But she's a little like—"

"Me," she finished for him, her voice tight with what he could only interpret as pain.

He side-eyed her and nodded. "Loves your books too."

"Clearly smart, then." She lifted a hand, and it was then he spied her wedding ring. It was a punch to the stomach, but it'd been years now, and he needed to get a grip. Focus on the . . . well, the mission. To find a way forward so he could be with Savanna and not weigh her down with his own fucking shit that she didn't deserve. If she'd still have him, that was. "Sorry, bad joke." She looked to the rolling hills in the distance. "You're scared she'll be like me in the way I hurt your father," she said softly.

He took a moment to truly look at his mom while her focus was elsewhere. Her black hair was in a loose bun at the top of her head, and he'd just noticed the pencil sticking out of it. Typical of her. Her skin wasn't quite weathered as one would expect for a woman in her sixties who loved the outdoors, but she had laugh lines around her mouth and eyes. His mom was happy, and that was something.

When she looked back at him, her dark eyes mirrors of his own, he swallowed hard. The expression on her face was soft and understanding rather than one of regret like he'd expected. "I will always love your father. Always," she said while reaching for his hand, and he surprisingly gave it to her. "But my heart somehow split into two, and I think I always loved Tony even before I met your father, but the timing had never been right for us. And then your father and I were together so long, and we had you . . ." She shook her head. "There's no excuse for cheating. I should have left your father before anything happened with Tony."

"You don't wish you never—"

"I can't explain the ways of the heart," she interrupted as if knowing where he was going with his question. "But I knew I couldn't stay married to your father if half my heart belonged to someone else. And I know that's not fair or the answer you're looking for, but I don't want you spending your life single because of me. Because you're worried that one day your woman's heart will split for someone else too."

"It's already split for someone else," he found himself mumbling. "But that other someone died."

His mom squeezed his hand tighter, and why did he feel sixteen again back in that garage punching the walls as pain flooded his system? Why did he feel so out of control of his emotions right now?

"Savanna's the most forgiving woman I've ever met," he added around that lump in his throat. "She deserves someone who can trust her. Someone who can, um, forgive others too." He nearly choked on his words this time, emotion constricting his chest. "The only way I can be worthy of her is to be able to . . . forgive you."

"Can you do that?" his mom cried, tears gliding down her face as she held tightly on to his hand.

He closed his eyes and was struck by the ridiculous notion that here he was, a thirty-nine-year-old man, a war veteran, someone who put himself in danger to save others even now as a special operator . . . and he was crying on his mom's front porch. "I want to. I really do."

"You must really care about this woman to be here, then," she whispered while sniffling.

Griffin forced his eyes open to peer at his mom. "I do."

She brushed away tears with her free hand, then lifted their clasped palms into the air. "Then how about we start with dinner and go from there?"

CHAPTER THIRTY-SEVEN

BIRMINGHAM, ALABAMA - THREE DAYS LATER

Griffin stared at the black Jeep in Savanna's driveway. Was that Shep's?

Am I too late? His body tensed as he stood stuck to the pavement, staring at her front door. He should have called. He shouldn't have waited eighteen damn days to show up.

Griffin's focus snapped to the door opening, and Shep appeared, holding a see-through bin of what appeared to be food. Baked goods, maybe.

"Griffin," Shep called out, stepping aside as Savanna made an appearance.

Savanna stood alongside Shep on the front stoop of her townhouse, unmoving as she stared at him, and it took all his restraint not to run to her.

Shep turned to her, and they exchanged a quick word. Griffin wasn't sure what he'd said, but she slowly stepped back into her house and shut the door.

His heart might have shriveled and died in his chest to see her turning away at Shep's directive. Griffin told himself to take a breath and collect his thoughts. To not assume anything or immediately throw down with Shep and fight him for Savanna.

Had she made her choice?

"Wait," Shep said as if worried Griffin was going to leave.

Griffin wasn't going anywhere, but he couldn't face the firefighter just yet. He needed to get a handle on his emotions first.

"It's not what you think. I told her I wanted a word with you before you two talk."

At that, Griffin looked over at Shep as he placed the bin in the passenger seat of his Jeep before walking to where Griffin was standing at the end of the driveway.

"Those cupcakes are for the station. She's been baking a lot while waiting for your ass to finally show the fuck up," Shep said in a low tone, either so Savanna wouldn't overhear or to let Griffin know he was a dick for waiting so long.

Waiting for me? So, she waited. He tore a hand through his hair as Shep closed the space between them.

"I'm not gonna lie. If I were in your shoes, I wouldn't want *me* being friends with her."

Yeah, that's not what he wanted to hear when he was trying to work through his issues and be a stronger, more trusting man for Savanna.

"I know she told you what happened when we were drunk a while back. Or, well, you guessed, I should say." Shep folded his arms across his broad chest, standing at the same height as Griffin. "So, I get why you wouldn't want us to be friends. I'd feel the same. And for a second, when I saw her with you back at that hangar weeks ago, I got a little jealous. Not gonna lie about it."

"Where are you going with this?" Griffin asked, doing his best to keep from snarling at the man.

"I'll never be good enough for that woman. I'm not the type to settle down and have kids." Shep held his palms open, his keys still in one hand. "I don't even want kids, and she wants a lot. I'd hurt her, and then A.J. and Jesse would go to jail for murder, and well, none of us want that, do we?"

"I'd kill you too," he found himself admitting, trying to forget the fact this man had had Savanna in his arms—and more.

"I reckon you would." Shep lowered his palms. "But also, I've never seen her look at anyone the way she does you. I do kind of want to hit you for making her wait so long, but if your reasons were honorable for that wait, then I'll withhold. You know, for Savanna's sake. She hates using her frozen peas for black eyes."

Griffin replayed Shep's words, hoping he heard him right.

"You can trust her, though. I promise. She'd never . . ." He offered his free hand. "You have my word I'd never cross the line. I want her happy, and if that's with you, then that's with you."

Griffin eyed the peace offering, and he finally accepted his palm.

"But if you hurt her, I'll kill you." Then he added, "And if you die on her, then I'll drag your ass back to earth and kill ya again."

Griffin had been a nervous wreck at the idea of facing Savanna, but somehow this encounter with Shep surprisingly relaxed him. Maybe it was what he needed to help him lose his baggage. If he could trust Shep to be honorable, then there was hope for him moving forward.

"Roger that," Griffin responded with a nod, his stomach

flipping again when he set his sights back on the front door, finding it open with Savanna there.

"See you around," Shep said before tossing a goodbye wave to Savanna and heading for his Jeep.

Griffin slowly walked to the front steps, his heart pounding furiously.

"You came," she whispered, tears in her eyes.

He stopped at the top step, keeping some space between them. "I'm sorry it took me so long. I wanted to make sure I was . . . well, that I could be the man you deserve before I did."

She sniffled. "And are you?"

"I hope so. I might need a little more fixing. You know, my head has been in my ass for quite a long time, but for you, Savanna, I'll do anything." He thought back to her words about Marcus in Greece. "I'll fight. I'll fight to be with you until my last breath."

Savanna stepped forward, and unable to stop himself, he pulled her into his arms, setting his chin on top of her head.

"Do you still want me?" he asked, his voice a bit raw with emotion. There was still the potential problem of his job. "My work," he reminded her.

"Without a doubt," she answered, easing back to find his eyes. "I know this thing between us happened fast, but maybe we could date or—"

"I would love to bake with you." He grinned.

"Come inside." She stepped back and held out her hand, and he followed her into the house, hating she still lived in a place where a man had been killed.

"I want to tell you something," he said once they were in the foyer.

"What is it?" She pointed her beautiful hazel eyes up at

him and palmed his cheek, and he did his best not to scoop her into his arms and kiss her.

"You see, I met this woman, and she's got the biggest heart in the world. She's the most forgiving person I've ever met." His voice gave out a little. "And I thought maybe I could be like her." He closed his eyes. "So, I visited my mom, and I took the first step to being the man she needs. And I forgave my mom."

Savanna's other palm found his cheek, and she held his face, which had him opening his eyes. "Griffin," she softly whispered. "I'm proud of you."

"I have something for you," he said after swallowing.

He stepped back and reached into his pocket.

"My passport?" She eyed it in surprise.

"You forgot it, and I . . ."

She arched a curious brow before peering up at him.

"I thought maybe we could fill it together?"

Her lips stretched into the most beautiful smile he'd ever seen in his life before she said, "I love you." Her eyes became watery, and she added, "I know that makes me crazy."

"Then I'm crazy, too," he admitted in a hoarse voice before pulling her into his arms and finally kissing her.

When he lifted her off the ground, she wrapped her legs around his waist, and he walked her to the wall for support. One hand on her ass, the other on the wall over her shoulder, she kept herself in his arms as he broke their kiss to say those "crazy words" for the first time in his life to anyone other than his parents. "I love you."

Savanna's short nails bit into his back as she kissed him again with even more intensity, and then he dragged his lips to her ear.

"Tell me, Sugar, did you touch yourself every day I was gone?" he rasped, and she bucked her pelvis into him.

"There's only so much baking a girl can do," she replied as he pressed his cock against her. "What about you?"

He gently nipped her earlobe. "No, I wanted to wait for it to be with you." Griffin brought his lips back to her mouth, brushing them over hers.

"Oh really? Well then. I guess I've been a bad girl for not waiting."

"Very bad," he murmured darkly.

"Mmm." She leaned back to catch his eyes. "Guess you'd better punish me."

EPILOGUE

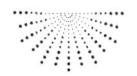

TUSCANY, ITALY - ONE MONTH LATER

"I still can't believe you set this up." Savanna accepted the glass of Chianti from Griffin, her eyes on the vineyards off in the distance from their villa. She was naked beneath her short red silk robe, after hours of lovemaking that'd begun the moment they'd walked into the place.

Technically, the sizzling heat began before then while Griffin drove the little black sports car up the winding roads to their villa. He'd slipped his palm beneath her dress and gently thumbed her sex over her satin panties.

"This place is everything and more." She stretched her back, her body sore from their lovemaking. A good kind of sore. But after two weeks of missing this man while he'd been working on another job, they had time to make up for, and the trip had been an unexpected surprise.

A.J. and his wife, Ana, had been over for dinner when Griffin showed up earlier than she'd expected after his assignment in Costa Rica, and he'd greeted her with a kiss and two plane tickets.

She was relieved that A.J. and Griffin got along so well and that A.J. hadn't felt the need to deck him the way he had Shep.

And now, we're in Italy. A new stamp in her passport on a trip with the man she loved.

Griffin wrapped his arms around her from behind as they stood on the veranda and took in the view of the setting sun.

"All that's missing is a typewriter," he said into her ear, his warm breath coaxing chills to form on her arms beneath the robe.

"I have you. I don't need more." She leaned forward to set her wineglass down, and he didn't lose his hold of her when she turned in his arms and set hers over his shoulders.

"No?" He lifted a brow. "You sure?" He brought one hand between their bodies and freed the knot of the robe, allowing the fabric to drape open. It was only sixty outside, so her nipples stood at attention in the brisk air, but the heated way he stared into her eyes even though they'd just made love began to warm her again.

"What if someone sees us?" She playfully lifted her brows up and down to tease him. Although not a lot of time had passed since they began dating, Griffin had held to his promise to focus on his trust issues, though he still growled when other men looked at her. And she didn't want him to change in that department. She liked her rugged, alpha male being all growly like that.

"True. Someone might be wandering through that vineyard," he said as if dead serious, then pulled her back inside in one fast movement and shut the door.

"Forgot my wine out there," she teased.

"Why, you want me to pour it down your body and lick it off you?" But he had her flat on her back on the rug on the wood floors a heartbeat later, all thoughts of wine forgotten.

His strong, muscular arms held his weight over her as he stared into her eyes. She hooked a finger in the waistband of his black briefs, the only thing he was wearing, while biting her lip. Then her attention skated to the ink on his shoulder. The feathers shielded a man in armor holding a sword, and Griffin had told her a few weeks ago the armored man represented all his brothers in arms.

"Make love to me," she whispered, ready for him again.

The robe was open to her naked body, and he shifted his body to reposition his mouth over her breast. He ran his tongue over her nipple, and she buried her fingers into his defined back muscles as he moved his weight to his forearm on one side to work his other hand between her legs to her soaking wet center.

"I'll never get tired of this," she panted out when he fingered her hard and deep.

All of the erotic and naughty things they'd already done in the bedroom since they'd met somehow felt like the tip of the iceberg with this man, and they had so much more to explore. And they had time to do it, too. Thank God.

Her body heated, and her nipples pebbled hard once he buried his cock deep inside her in one hard thrust, and her back went off the floor.

She loved all the ways they made love, but him on top, peering into her eyes, always made her heart squeeze. The connection was so deep. So real.

Am I really this lucky? This blessed to find love again?

Savanna gave herself over to the orgasm, not able to fight it, not even but a few minutes later. And then Griffin came, pouring himself inside her. He collapsed alongside her and linked their hands together, and they stared at the ceiling for a few quiet minutes before he broke the silence.

"I may have gotten you something . . . that missing something."

"What do you mean?" She rolled her head to the side to look at him.

"I, uh, had something shipped here before we arrived." He cleaned her up, using her robe, then slowly stood. "Be right back," he said with a smile before striding from the room naked.

She grabbed her robe, but it was sticky now, so she couldn't wear it.

Naked it is. He won't mind.

But she nearly fell back onto her ass when Griffin came into the room with an old-fashioned typewriter in his hands. There was a piece of paper already inserted.

"Where'd you get that? And why?"

He wordlessly set it on the desk by the doors leading to the veranda, and when he faced her, his nerves appeared to return. "It's my mom's. She wrote her first book on it thirty years ago," he told her. "She wanted you to have it in case you felt like . . . having your own, um, Hemingway moment."

She cupped her mouth as tears filled her eyes. "You inherited your mother's romanticism whether you care to admit it or not," she rasped once she'd managed to unglue her hand from her mouth and work the words free.

"There's something on the paper if you want to take a look."

Savanna eyed him a little suspiciously, then walked up alongside him and bent over to retrieve the paper. Typed on the page was, "Will you be my prologue?"

"Griffin?" She held the paper to her body as she faced him, trying to wrap her head around the meaning of the words.

"*Te casarías conmigo?* Will you marry me, Sugar?" he

asked, his voice rough with emotion.

"You . . . you learned that in Spanish to ask me?"

He smiled. "I'm already fluent. I've been waiting for the right time to tell you."

The paper slipped from her hands as she stared at him with lips parted until she finally put two and two together at what he was trying to tell her. "Our babies can be . . ."

He nodded, and his handsome smile stretched. Eyes filled with tears. Hers, too.

"*Sí.*" She briefly lifted her eyes to the ceiling as if feeling her abuela there. "Yes. Yes, I want to marry you," she cried and tossed herself at him.

"*Te quiero,*" he said into her ear. "I love you," he added before kissing her, sliding his tongue inside her mouth.

"I can't believe you held out on me," she added once their mouths were free, but the shock had yet to wear off.

"Life's better with surprises." He winked and drew her back against him. "And, Sugar, you were life's best surprise for me."

* * *

WALKINS GLEN, ALABAMA - CHRISTMAS EVE

"Did you ask him to sing that?" Savanna peered at Ella's brother, A.J., performing the Maroon 5 song, *Sugar,* with two of his brothers. They were set up on the deck of their parents' home on their sprawling ranch.

"Of course," Ella responded with a chuckle.

A.J.'s voice had to be a gift from God, like his father's. And his brothers weren't half bad themselves. Of course, moody Beckett didn't join them, but his daughter was on the mock-stage dancing her heart out.

The Hawkins family knew how to throw a party, that was for sure. Savanna was pretty certain the entire town had been invited. A.J. and his nine teammates were there with their families, as well as Savanna's parents and Griffin's. The place was bustling with activity and a lot of mistletoe kissing and dancing going down.

Before the party had started, A.J. and his teammates, along with Griffin and his colleagues, had made a toast . . . one to the past—to Marcus . . . and one to the future—to her and Griffin. And although Griffin had known Marcus's teammates prior to tonight, it'd felt like they really welcomed and accepted him into the family, one they'd never dropped Savanna from in all those years.

It'd been one hell of an emotional toast for them all, too, especially when A.J. played Coffey Anderson's "Mr Red White and Blue" as they stood around a bonfire and raised their glasses.

Savanna had been choked up, but Griffin held her hand and got her through it. He was her rock now. The reason Marcus felt it was okay to say goodbye. To move on.

"He knows that I told you he calls me Sugar now." Savanna tucked her hair behind her ears as she caught sight of her fiancé maybe twenty feet away while talking to Jesse and Jack.

Griffin lifted his beer her way and shot her a knowing smile, and she did her best to shoot him a saucy look back.

"Yup, he knows," Ella said. "But who cares, a guy has to know there are no secrets between best friends."

"There might be a few secrets left between *some* friends." Savanna turned her attention toward Jesse as he seemed to be pounding back the drinks a bit more than normal after his slightly awkward hello with Ella not too long ago after he'd arrived. It'd been the first time they'd seen each other since he left behind his business there to work with Griffin's team, barely giving Ella warning he was taking off. "I think Jesse's hiding something from us." She peered back at Ella, who was dressed in a gorgeous red wrap dress, similar to the one she'd designed for Savanna.

"Well, after what we learned about Rory, I guess secrets run in the family," Ella commented. "Rory stopped running when she met the right person, though." She tipped her chin toward Rory's husband, who worked on A.J.'s team. "It's safe to say I'm not that someone for Jesse."

Savanna shook her head. "The problem isn't you. It's him."

"I don't know." She took a sip of her red-and-green-colored vodka-something cocktail. "I should really start dating for real."

"I knew those other dates you were going on back in October were bullshit." And Ella had stopped going on them once Jesse was out of town.

"Trying to make him jealous so he'd remove his head from his ass didn't work."

"You really going to be *done, done, done* this time?" Savanna followed her gaze, eyes set on Nick, who'd surprised Savanna by accepting the invite to join her and Griffin for Christmas. He was talking to Gray and his sister by one of the food tables.

"Nick asked me on a date," Ella blurted, and Savanna choked on the sip she'd taken of her own drink.

"Oh." What was she going to say to that?

"I said no," Ella told her straight away. "He's a man of the world. Not someone who wants to stick local, and it's time I get serious and find someone who loves not just my home but me."

"Shit, I'm sorry." Savanna could barely believe that she

was no longer a side character in someone else's love story. She'd been watching couples fall in love for years, assuming it'd be impossible for her to ever do the same, and now she was planning a spring wedding. She pinched herself just about every other day. "But it will happen." *Just maybe not with Jesse.* And that broke her romantic heart.

"I don't know." Ella sighed.

"I mean, I suppose Jesse isn't really permanently gone from here. Or he doesn't have to be. I'm making it work with Griffin even though his job isn't here."

She and Griffin were having a house built in Walkins Glen, but she'd commute to Birmingham for the café. And now that she could afford to hire help when Griffin needed to be in Pennsylvania between his jobs, she could stay there with him too.

Before Ella had a chance to reject Savanna's comment, which she'd assumed was coming, Griffin began waving them over.

They cut through the party to get to where the guys stood, then Ella surprised Savanna by stepping in front of Jack and offering her hand.

How much had Ella drank? Because damn.

Not just a J name, but Jesse's new co-worker.

Well, this should go well.

"Dance?" Ella asked Jack, and Jack pivoted his attention to Jesse for permission, and the glaring look Jesse sent back had Jack shaking his head.

"Sorry, I have to, uh, take a piss." Jack shrugged, then hightailed it out of there.

Smart man.

"I'll dance with you," Jesse blurted, and his expressive blue eyes became hooded as his brows dipped like someone else had hijacked his voice. "Come on." He snatched Ella's drink and handed it off to Griffin without waiting for her response.

"Well, that was—"

"Confusing," Savanna cut off Griffin after Ella hesitantly took Jesse's hand and walked toward where her brother and the others were still singing. A new song this time.

Griffin discarded Ella's drink and his own in the trash can set up nearby, then tossed Savanna's next. "I'd like to dance with my future wife."

"Oh, would you?" She smiled as he took her into his arms, looking incredibly handsome in his dark denim jeans, cowboy boots, and button-down black shirt. *And he's all mine.*

"I would." He pulled her into his arms where they stood, not bothering to leave that spot. "And then I'd like to unwrap you later for an early Christmas gift," he said into her ear, and her body tightened with anticipation for "later."

She set her head on his shoulder as he held her, and they simply moved side to side. She was so freaking happy, but then her heart leaped from her chest at the sight before her. "Babe," she said, pulling back to excitedly swat his chest a few times.

"What?" Griffin twisted to the side to see what she was looking at.

"Your dad. He's . . . totally enamored by Liz." Savanna watched Griffin's dad take a small red napkin and pat Liz's cheek as if helping to remove sauce or something. "I think he's flirting. Look at him."

"Is Liz single? And how young is she? She looks young." Griffin wrapped an arm around Savanna as they watched his dad smile at whatever Liz had said.

"She's sixty, and she's the one who owns the bakery in town. The reason I didn't want to open one here and have us be competitors." Savanna beamed at the sight. Maybe after all these years, his father just might find his second love too, and Liz, a widow like Savanna, could use that second chance as well.

"I haven't seen Dad smile like that in a long time," Griffin said while coughing into a closed fist as if his emotions were choking him up. Such a strong man, but he hated showing his sensitive side. He was getting better at it, though, which she appreciated. Still a total alpha in the bedroom, though, and she preferred that. Damn, did she ever.

"You know what I think?" She repositioned herself in front of him and draped her arms over his shoulders, linking her wrists behind his neck.

"What is that, Sugar?"

"This is going to be the best Christmas ever."

"And why is that?" he asked. Oh, he knew damn well what she was going to say, but he wanted to hear it.

"Because I have you," she said while bringing her mouth close to his.

"Part of me thinks next Christmas will be better," he said before gently kissing her, then drawing her lip between his teeth.

"Why is that?" She repeated his line as he released her lip, and her body ached with the need for him to touch her, but there were *way* too many people there.

He angled his head and brought his hand to her abdomen. "Because if I have my way, you'll be pregnant by then. And you being pregnant at Christmas can only be topped by—"

"Having our child with us the following year," she finished for him.

And God did she love this man and how often they were always on the same page.

FALCON FALLS CROSSOVER INFO

Crossover Information

The Falcon Falls Series is a spin-off from the Stealth Ops Series (Echo Team, books 6-10). There is also mention of Emilia, a character from my Dublin Nights Series.

I love having worlds crossover. Below is information on where you'll find some of these other characters - as well as where else you may have first met the characters from Falcon Falls.

Gray Chandler was in *Chasing the Knight* and the epilogue of Chasing the Storm. Jack London was also in Chasing the Knight. **Chasing the Knight* stars Gray's sister, Natasha.

In *Chasing Daylight*, we first meet the Alabama crew (Jesse, Beckett, etc). This is A.J.'s book. We also discover the tension between Ella & Jesse in this book, and that tension continues in *Chasing Fortune*, which is Jesse's sister's book (Rory).

A.J. is "visited" by Marcus in his book, *Chasing Daylight*. Marcus is mentioned in multiple books in the Stealth Ops series.

Carter Dominick was in *Chasing Fortune* and *Chasing the Storm*.

Oliver and Griffin are briefly in *Chasing the Storm* as well. But in *Chasing the Storm* - Griffin is only referred to as "Southern sniper guy."

Emilia - Italian billionaire vigilante - she stars in the book, *The Final Hour*. But you can find her in 3 of the Dublin Nights books: *The Real Deal, The Inside Man,* and *The Final Hour*.

What is Next?

Jesse & Ella's book releases early 2022.

Be sure to join my newsletter, Facebook groups, or follow me on Insta, TikTok, or Facebook to learn more about the upcoming releases. Plus, get access to teasers, giveaways, and more.

The Falcon Falls Pinterest muse/inspiration board.

Continue for a *music playlist*, reading guide, and Stealth Ops/Falcon Falls Family Tree!

PLAYLIST

Stay - The Kid LAROI, Justin Bieber

Die A Happy Man - Thomas Rhett

Arise - The Siege

Hips Don't Lie - Shakira, Wyclef Jean

If I Die Young - The Band Perry

What I Like About You - Jonas Blue, Theresa Rex

Leave Before You Love Me - Marshmello, Jonas Brothers

Good Life - G-Eazy, Kehlani

Love Me Now feat. Zoe Wees - Kygo

Unforgettable - French Montana

PLAYLIST

Wildest Dreams - Taylor Swift

Stay With Me - Sam Smith

Mr Red White and Blue - Coffey Anderson

Spotify Playlist

*Note: Spotify adds "suggested" songs to the end of my list, so you may see other songs there.

ALSO BY BRITTNEY SAHIN

Find the latest news from my newsletter/website and/or Facebook: Brittney's Book Babes / the Stealth Ops Spoiler Room /Dublin Nights Spoiler Room.

A Stealth Ops World Guide is available on my website, which features more information about the team, character muses, and SEAL lingo.

Stealth Ops Timeline
Reading Guide
Pinterest Muse/Inspiration Board

* * *

Falcon Falls Security
The Hunted One - book 1 - Griffin & Savanna
Book 2 - Jesse & Ella (2022)

Stealth Ops Series: Bravo Team

ALSO BY BRITTNEY SAHIN

Finding His Mark - Book 1 - Luke & Eva
Finding Justice - Book 2 - Owen & Samantha
Finding the Fight - Book 3 - Asher & Jessica
Finding Her Chance - Book 4 - Liam & Emily
Finding the Way Back - Book 5 - Knox & Adriana

Stealth Ops Series: Echo Team

Chasing the Knight - Book 6 - Wyatt & Natasha
Chasing Daylight - Book 7 - A.J. & Ana
Chasing Fortune - Book 8 - Chris & Rory
Chasing Shadows - Book 9 - Harper & Roman
Chasing the Storm - Book 10 - Finn & Julia

Becoming Us: *connection to the Stealth Ops Series (books take place between the prologue and chapter 1 of Finding His Mark)*

Someone Like You - A former Navy SEAL. A father. And off-limits. (Noah Dalton)

My Every Breath - A sizzling and suspenseful romance. Businessman Cade King has fallen for the wrong woman. She's the daughter of a hitman - and he's the target.

Dublin Nights

On the Edge - Travel to Dublin and get swept up in this romantic suspense starring an Irish businessman by day…and fighter by night.
On the Line - novella
The Real Deal - This mysterious billionaire businessman has finally met his match.

ALSO BY BRITTNEY SAHIN

The Inside Man - Cole McGregor & Alessia Romano
The Final Hour - Sean and Emilia

Stand-alone (with a connection to *On the Edge*):

The Story of Us – Sports columnist Maggie Lane has 1 rule: never fall for a player. One mistaken kiss with Italian soccer star Marco Valenti changes everything…

Hidden Truths
The Safe Bet – Begin the series with the Man-of-Steel lookalike Michael Maddox.
Beyond the Chase - Fall for the sexy Irishman, Aiden O'Connor, in this romantic suspense.
The Hard Truth – Read Connor Matthews' story in this second-chance romantic suspense novel.
Surviving the Fall – Jake Summers loses the last 12 years of his life in this action-packed romantic thriller.
The Final Goodbye - Friends-to-lovers romantic mystery

FALCON FALLS & STEALTH OPS FAMILY TREE

Falcon Falls Team members:

Team leader: **Carter Dominick - Army Delta/CIA**

- Dog: Dallas

Team leader: **Gray Chandler - Army SF (Green Beret)**

Family:

- Admiral Chandler (father)
- Natasha (sister)
- Wyatt (brother-in-law)

Jesse - Army Ranger
  Family / Friends -

- Rory (sister)
- Chris (brother-in-law)

- Friends: AJ, Beckett, Caleb, Ella, Shep Hawkins
- Beckett's daughter: McKenna

Griffin Andrews - Delta

Jack London - Army SF (Green Beret)

- Divorced (Jill London)

Oliver Lucas - Army Airborne

- Tucker Lucas - brother (deceased)

Sydney Archer - Army

- Divorced/Has a son

***

Stealth Ops Team Members

Team leaders: Luke & Jessica Scott / Intelligence team member (joined in 2019): Harper Brooks

Bravo Team:
    Bravo One - Luke
    Bravo Two - Owen
    Bravo Three - Asher
    Bravo Four - Liam
    Bravo Five - Knox (Charlie "Knox" Bennett)

Echo Team:

Echo One - Wyatt
Echo Two - A.J. (Alexander James)
Echo Three - Chris
Echo Four - Roman
Echo Five - Finn (Dalton "Finn" Finnegan

WHERE ELSE CAN YOU FIND ME?

I love, love, love interacting with readers in my Facebook groups as well as on my Instagram page. Join me over there as we talk characters, books, and more! ;)

FB Reader Groups:
Brittney's Book Babes
Stealth Ops Spoiler Room

Facebook
Instagram
TikTok

www.brittneysahin.com
brittneysahin@emkomedia.net

Pinterest Muse/Inspiration Board

Printed in Great Britain
by Amazon